A.J. SCUDIERE

NIGHTSHADE

FORENSIC FBI FILES ✦ BOOK 10

VANISHING POINT

NightShade Forensic FBI Files: Vanishing Point

FIRST EDITION

"There are really just 2 types of readers—those who are fans of AJ Scudiere, and those who will be."

-Bill Salina, Reviewer, Amazon

For *The Shadow Constant*:

"The Shadow Constant by A.J. Scudiere was one of those novels I got wrapped up in quickly and had a hard time putting down."

-Thomas Duff, Reviewer, Amazon

For *Phoenix*:

"It's not a book you read and forget; this is a book you read and think about, again and again . . . everything that has happened in this book could be true. That's why it sticks in your mind and keeps coming back for rethought."

-Jo Ann Hakola, The Book Faerie

For *God's Eye*:

"I highly recommend it to anyone who enjoys reading - it's well-written and brilliantly characterized. I've read all of A.J.'s books and they just keep getting better."

-Katy Sozaeva, Reviewer, Amazon

For *Vengeance*:

"Vengeance is an attention-grabbing story that lovers of action-driven novels will fall hard for. I highly recommend it."

-Melissa Levine, Professional Reviewer

For *Resonance*:

"Resonance is an action-packed thriller, highly recommended. 5 stars."

-Midwest Book Review

1

Donovan inhaled the scents of the woods. Underneath the rich, green flora, the sharp tang of blood was no longer fresh and was starting to decay. He took a hard sniff, trying to subtly open his nasal passages. With all the other investigators around, could he do it without anyone noticing?

Eleri saw. Turning her head slightly, she raised shoulder at him, her expression asking, *Did you get anything?*

He shook his head. He couldn't smell anything beyond what he could easily tell with his eyes. There was a body, and it had been brutally tortured and murdered.

"Hey boy! Over here!"

Once again, one of the cadaver dogs had turned the wrong way, deciding to make friends with Donovan rather than do his job. Donovan shrugged it off. "Dogs love me."

The handler made the usual excuses, though Donovan suspected it was the truth. As the man tugged the leash and turned the dog back to the task, he called back over his shoulder, "Sorry! He's not normally like that."

Then I guess you and your dog haven't encountered anyone like me before, Donovan thought as he tilted his head. Maybe the dog's confusion was understandable. Donovan hadn't known anyone like himself for decades—not other than his father. And if there was anyone Donovan didn't want to be like, it was Aidan Heath.

Ahead of him, Eleri carefully paced the edge of the crime scene. She might not smell it like he did, but she saw things he didn't. Tipping her head one way then another, she pulled out a flashlight, but he wondered if maybe that part was just for show.

She would want to touch the body, he knew. But doing anything without gloves—in front of the other investigators—would only be considered contaminating the evidence.

The victim, a man in his late thirties or mid-forties, was laid out naked, twisted, cut, and shot. Eleri knelt down, motioning Donovan over before pointing to the hands. "Several fingernails have been pulled."

Donovan pushed his face close. The body smelled of terror rather than pain. The lost nails weren't the natural consequence of a fight. Their Special Agent in Charge was right: They'd needed to be here yesterday, *before* this had happened.

"How long was he missing?" Eleri looked up at the local sheriff as he perused the border of the scene.

Donovan wondered the same thing. The way things looked now, the man had been missing for several days, maybe tortured, and no one had reported him. The Everglades seemed to be trying to reclaim him.

"I don't know yet," the sheriff said. "His wife didn't file a missing person's report. Said they fought a few days ago and he ran off. She figured he was with friends, and she was glad when he didn't come back that night."

Donovan wondered what kind of tangle that might lead to. The spouse was usually the primary suspect, and he didn't tend to fall into the trap of assuming that the wife was some meek, untrained creature who wouldn't have been capable of this.

So many things weren't what they appeared. *Including me.*

The sheriff grabbed at a belt loop and hitched his pants up, his mouth pressing together in what appeared to be an age-old habit he was probably unaware of. Between that and the good-old-boy talk, it had taken a while to catch on that he was sharp. Maybe it was his natural accent and affect, or maybe he was playing it up for the outsiders, but beneath the combover hair were eyes that didn't miss much.

"We're getting ready to take the body in, but we waited for you. Actually, we called for ViCAP..." He let it hang, as though to let them know he was wondering why, when he had specifically called for the Violent Criminals Apprehension Program, he had been sent two seemingly random agents.

"ViCAP gave it to us," Donovan answered calmly. Though he guessed that wasn't true. Chances were that his SAC had wrestled or outright stolen the case from the other division.

The sheriff nodded, though he clearly wasn't quite placated. "Y'all work in serial killers?"

Then why weren't they in ViCAP? The unspoken question hung in the air.

"Often," Eleri answered for the both of them. She said it with a smile. Though it was true, it wasn't the real answer, and this man would never get the real answer.

Eleri must have decided to declare that portion of the conversation over. She looked up into the sun, shielding her eyes. The day was already three-quarters through.

They'd been plucked from their break and sent here. Not that their break had been any kind of rest. Eleri had been helping Donovan track his brother and, for a brief moment, he thought about how jarring that information had been.

It was good now, to be able to focus on something else.

Eleri managed to pull his focus back with her next statement. "I'd like to come back tonight with my own dog."

Her own dog?

The sheriff hitched his pants again, and asked roughly the same thing, though he couldn't know what Donovan knew. He did know they'd just flown in. "You brought a dog?"

"I have a friend down here. I've worked with the dog before. He's excellent."

Yes, Donovan thought shrewdly, *he is.*

"There's three dogs here already." The sheriff waved a hand, indicating the two German Shepherds and a bloodhound.

Donovan, too, was ready to turn to Eleri and ask, "You have your own dog?"

But she was already talking her way into getting what she wanted. "I want to come back at night and do my own recon, since we're pretty certain that's when the victim arrived here."

Arrived was the right word, Donovan thought. He'd scented the trails on the way in. The body had not arrived alive. That, in and of itself, was an interesting undertaking.

"You see new things in the dark," Eleri told the sheriff, but she looked over shoulder with a frown as though she were looking for something that wasn't there.

That probably wasn't news to anyone here, and the man seemed to shrug her off, as if to say, *If that's what you want.*

He's good with it, Donovan thought. Some places actively wanted the FBI to come in and take the case, and others would do everything they could to thwart the Bureau.

Right now, though, Donovan was trying to figure out how Eleri was going to get both of them back out at night under the guise of making a pass at the scene with her dog. But then the wind shifted, and he caught a scent—a decidedly live human scent.

He held a finger up to Eleri, the best he could do in the middle of this crowd, to let her know that he was leaving.

2

The light blinked and flickered overhead, and Eleri felt her eyes roll upward. She huffed into the air at no one in particular, the man's liver clasped firmly in her gloved hands. "They cannot be serious!"

"Oh, I think they can," Donovan answered.

The DeSoto County's Medical Examiner's office wasn't the most up-to-date that they'd seen. It had the usual drain in the middle of the floor and a pulley system with spray nozzles, but it wouldn't surprise her if the computers booted up a green DOS prompt.

Being here could have been creepy; the parking lot had certainly given her the sensation she was being watched. But inside, it was just the two of them alone at night with the dead bodies. Eleri wasn't bothered by that. She felt competent sensing what was around her, and the only things around her right now were corpses and Donovan and an unfortunate flickering fluorescent overhead.

"Everything looks normal on my end," she offered up, the liver still in her gloved hands. She slid it into a flat-bottomed silver bowl, then marked the weight of the liver on the paper form.

They'd pushed their way in, insisting that Donovan act as medical examiner on this case. Though Eleri had expected an argument, the locals had once again accepted it. She set the liver aside and announced, "I don't see any evidence of disease."

"Same," Donovan said without looking up. His answer meant that he'd checked it already and didn't smell disease.

So she asked, "Toxicology?"

"He was drugged, but I can't place it. It's faded, too. Very faded." Donovan looked up at her as he said that and Eleri understood why.

Interesting.

If Donovan didn't smell anything fresh in the man's system, then it was either some unknown, new substance or he'd fully metabolized anything he'd been given well before he was killed.

"Am I ordering the tox screen?" she asked, peeling one glove. The local medical examiner had talked them through the setup before leaving them alone for the night.

Maybe Dr. Cara Mara was glad to not have to deal with this mess of a case—or to not work late. Then she wouldn't be held responsible if it all went to shit. She seemed smart and capable, despite the rhyming name. When she'd greeted them, her warm, friendly attitude had made them feel welcome, if not at home.

She'd also easily recognized the expression Eleri couldn't quite hide at the rhyming name. "I married into it, and I'm divorcing my way out. At the time, Mara seemed a much better last name than Brzezinski. But I'm coming to appreciate Brzezinski better these days."

She shook hands with a firm grip and made it clear that, while the facility might not be completely up-to-date, Dr. Mara/Brzezinski entirely was.

Eleri now found the forms with ease and requested a basic toxicology panel. They already knew it would come back negative, but it would be necessary as proof later. It wasn't as if she could just tell everyone, "Donovan didn't smell anything." Despite all the ways their SAC, Derek Westerfield, sent them out into the unknown, they were supposed to keep their talents hidden.

Eleri lined up her samples and labeled them before heading back to Donovan's side. He asked, "Cause of death?"

"GSW." She was confident in her diagnosis, despite all the different wounds he could have died from. "The gunshot wounds were definitively the final, fatal blow. The cuts and the bash he took to the head were first. Though I don't know the order there, and I don't know if they were intended to kill him. But he clearly survived all of that. The edges of the wounds show an immune response, meaning he was still alive for a while after he got them. He bled out enough from the slices and slashes, that the gunshots hadn't quite accomplished what they would on anyone else."

Though it clearly hadn't worked well, there had been an attempt by his blood to clot. Not that the body could close a gash of that size.

"Very good," Donovan replied.

Eleri continued. "Looks like a knife wound."

She couldn't say for certain—they could almost never say for certain. "Whatever it was, it was very sharp. And I think he would have bled out from these wounds if left alone." She pointed to the slices across the torso and the caved in portion they'd found on his skull after moving him.

"Which begs the question, why shoot him?" Donovan's hands stopped moving as he looked up at her. His eyes were questioning from behind the mask and plexi face shield. She couldn't see his nose or mouth, and Eleri wondered if he'd shifted them out—just a little—to smell better and maybe to taste the air.

"Maybe the killer didn't know he was already mortally wounded. They seemed to have tried everything in the book. Or maybe they were just impatient."

Eleri glanced around the room, her eyes giving a physical backup to what she already understood. The two of them were alone. So she asked, "When you followed the scent trail today, what happened?"

Donovan had walked off, clearly having smelled something. At the time, they weren't really in any position for him to explain. He'd simply disappeared and she'd covered for him. He shrugged. "It's hard to say."

Donovan leaned back over the body, reaching into the open cavity, and checking everything he could. "The scent headed into an area where there were too many different smells to distinguish it. I lost it."

"What smells?" she wanted to know. Eleri picked up the brain and started to put it back into place.

"Food, fire, animals."

"How far away?" She was frowning, trying to make his description fit. This body had been found in the middle of Hardee Lakes County Park.

"I don't know, maybe a mile or two? Eventually, I ran into a parking lot, smelled like a campsite."

She hadn't thought the Everglades would have much camping. Then again, what did she know?

Even being in the middle of Florida was still far too close to where they'd started last time. She was about ready for snow, or cold breezes and mountain tops. She was probably still traumatized by the events in Nassau. The air here felt similar. The humidity pushed in on her, and everything had a hint of algae.

She stood back, acting as Donovan's assistant and trying to figure out a way this series of wounds and injuries could have happened. Looking at the slashes and the angle of the wounds, she figured whoever had killed this man might have been shorter than him. Still, that kind of assessment could be deceiving.

At last, Donovan put the man's organs back into the body cavity. Together, they stitched the Y-shaped incision closed. When she finally peeled her gloves, the snapping sound was satisfying.

"Are you ready to go back out?"

3

Donovan stepped slowly, one padded paw sinking into the soft earth. He had to admit, Florida felt better this way.

He was normally just over six feet tall but now stood just over three. With his head down, his gaze came in barely twelve inches off the ground. The dirt bloomed with fragrances. He could tell the algae that grew in the park was different than what grew closer to their hotel.

Eleri had rented a large SUV with tinted windows for the duration of their stay here. As she'd driven them down the freeway, she'd told him, "Climb into the back. Get moving."

Then, at the parking lot, she'd opened the wide back door and watched as the "dog" hopped down. Together, they'd headed in, Eleri wielding a flashlight he would have preferred to do without. He'd loped ahead and she'd kept the light politely at her own feet.

About a mile up the trail, he smelled the sudden wash of fear as he approached the guard who was stationed to keep wayward night hikers and curiosity seekers away from the crime scene. "Hold it!"

"Yes?" Eleri had come quickly up behind him, and Donovan was grateful the officer hadn't pulled his gun.

"You need a leash on your dog, lady, and you can't go back here."

Though Donovan's innate reaction was to bare his teeth, he'd learned to let Eleri handle it. He was hidden far better as her "dog" than any other way he'd tried.

"No, sir," she politely rebuffed the poor officer, probably a rookie, with the command in her tone and a practiced flip of her badge. "FBI. This is my search dog. We're coming back at night to see if anything revealed itself."

Donovan fought a laugh. Actually, they were back at night specifically so they didn't reveal *themselves*.

"He works off leash?" The man had worked with search dogs before, clearly, his tone disbelieving.

But Eleri only replied, "Yes, sir. He's that good."

It shouldn't have felt so good to hear that, but it did.

Donovan had padded on past before the man could ask her dog's name. To this day, he was afraid she would say, "His name's Donovan." At some point, someone would say, "Isn't that your partner's name?"

The last thing they could afford was somebody checking up on them.

"He's huge."

"Yes, he is." Eleri's too-sunny tone said she wasn't going to stand here and discuss breeds or search techniques, even though this officer was likely bored out of his skull, left alone here at night. She walked past, following Donovan and pushing deeper into the Glades.

Donovan lowered his head to the path again. Even if anyone saw him, this should appear normal. As they approached the scene, she turned to him. "You got anything?"

One head nod up and down followed by a swing to his right.

She let him lead. It was difficult to have a conversation this way—the communication felt unidirectional. But he would tell her everything, later, after he'd gone into the tailgate of the SUV as the dog and crawled into the front seat as the man.

Now, he circumnavigated the scene, easily ducking in and out under the crime scene tape, which was more difficult for Eleri. She watched where she stepped, not only for the sake of not putting one of her nice boots into something too squishy, but for not messing up the evidence. A dog paw print was always forgiven. Donovan sauntered through.

He smelled the victim—one JP Talley. After being in the morgue and near the body, he could readily pick up the same scent. The cold, dead body contained the same signature, but it was the difference between sauce on the stove and sauce from the fridge.

JP Talley had not arrived here alive—something they'd been relatively certain of before, but now Donovan could check that box. The other scent here was decidedly female. He wondered, *Was that coincidental?* Was the woman the murderer? Or maybe she was the one who had found the body.

They'd been told that a hiker had called it in. They'd not had time to absorb more than that on their mad dash to get here while the scene was still fresh.

Right now, it didn't matter. He hadn't been allowed to scent the caller or something of theirs, so this was just Scent #3 right now. Scent #2, a male, mid-thirties, had stopped about ten feet back from the crime scene tape. Donovan could sort it later.

Westerfield had them in motion almost the moment the body had been found. The combination of slashes, gunshot wounds, and pulled fingernails had this one filed as a bizarre slaying. The locals had matched the odd execution method to a body they'd found a year ago.

Normally, three bodies were needed to determine a serial killer. But in special cases—with clear ID markers like this—it was understood that the first body found had not been the first kill. The work was too planned, too well performed—which meant it was at least the second body. That, in turn, meant this second find was at least the third kill and met the requirement to call in the FBI, or ViCAP, to investigate it as a serial killing.

Donovan was in the center of the crime scene before he even realized it. The earth squished between the pads of his paws and the scent filled his face and his lungs. He could almost taste it. But where was the killer?

Sniffing at the ground, he worked for anything he could pick up. But the only additional scent was the woman.

It was worth a shot to follow the trail of Scent #3. It was the same scent he'd picked up during the daylight. Only now, he wasn't stuck waiting for it to hit him. With his face altered and his nasal cavity wide open, he could intake more, sort better, and follow more easily.

This time, Eleri was close on his heels as he tracked it. They left the site at ninety degrees from where they'd entered and eventually wound up approaching a campsite. He heard the noises of people in the distance just as he lost the scent.

His head popped up, even though Eleri probably couldn't hear anything yet. The earth vibrated under his sensitive paws—just enough to tell him someone was coming. Before Eleri probably realized what he was doing, he was back at her side.

He hated leaving the odd, vanishing end of the scent trail. He hated heeling, but it was necessary. Sure enough, in just a few more moments, a woman and a small child, flashlights in hand, came around the corner. With his head held up, Donovan towered over the child.

The woman screamed. Though louder and more afraid, she had much the same response as the officer had on the way in. "Oh my God! He's huge!"

Eleri once again smiled and only replied. "Yes, ma'am."

"You should keep him—"

Beside him, he could feel the motions as Eleri simply flipped open her badge and added, "He's very safe, I assure you."

The woman quickly gathered up the child and headed back the way they'd come. There was nothing at this end of the trail that Donovan could use anyway. The scents of the woman and child, other hikers, and even hot dogs were now all twisted together. The last thing he needed was to scare anyone else.

Besides, the trail he'd needed had strangely vanished.

"Looks like we're going back the other way," Eleri commented with an almost cheeky tone as she turned to catch up.

Back at the site, they searched again, Donovan re-sniffing everything and not liking that he didn't get any more information than he had the first time. Giving up for the night, they once again passed the officer who, this time, readily waved them by.

Sometimes Eleri thought she was funny, and she would open the trunk and say, "In you go, boy," or something ridiculous like that. This time, she was quiet. She closed the door behind him and climbed up into the front seat, quickly starting the engine and shifting the SUV into reverse.

Donovan hadn't been expecting that. She didn't turn around or look over her shoulder but spoke into the empty space. "Someone's pulling in. I'm going to get us out of here before they see you."

4

Eleri stood over the skeleton back in the DeSoto County Medical Examiner's Office, grateful the parking lot hadn't made her check over her shoulder this time. Her first job now was to locate the original victim.

Luckily—though if it was lucky for anyone but her, she didn't know—the first body hadn't been claimed. Dr. Brzezinski had decided to keep it. Given the heinous nature of the death, she had preserved the woman's organs and boiled the remainder down to the bones.

She'd shown Eleri where the remains were before she'd left them alone the first time that evening. Now, Eleri and Donovan let themselves back in after searching the crime scene again. It would be better to finish the job tonight rather than wait until tomorrow and have to do their odd work with the staff all around them.

Dr. Brzezinski had given them the key and Eleri was taking full advantage. This time, Donovan acted as her assistant. He laid out the scapulae next to the humerus, the pelvis in line with the femurs, and let her sort through all the tiny wrist and ankle bones.

Though Eleri was the lead now, and it was tempting to just read the autopsy notes from a year ago, Donovan had insisted there was more he could do. It had taken Eleri a moment to understand that he could sense more, despite the fact that the samples had been preserved in jars.

With the skeleton finally laid out on the metal table, ready to be Eleri's patient, Donovan went after what remained of the organs. She ignored him as he pulled specimens from the shelf where they'd been neatly lined up, as if waiting for him.

He popped the tops and swirled the liquid, watching for ... something. Eleri didn't know. Then he would sniff and swirl and sniff again. She couldn't ignore it. After a few moments of watching him push his face down into the sample, inhale, and turn away, acting almost like a wine connoisseur, Eleri had to ask, "Does it have an oaky finish? Does it hint of acidic soil with elderberry and pine?"

He'd given her a dirty look and it took a shake of her head to knock that image loose as she turned back to the body. She had laid it out but mostly ignored what she was touching. Now she could see there were a few clear places where a knife had nicked the bone. Another spot on a rib looked like a bullet had pulled a chunk as it went by, and a clear circle was evident in the skull.

The size of the circle—no matter how neatly seared into the bone —didn't betray the caliber of bullet, only the maximum possible width. This skull matched the damage they saw on JP Talley, though the remaining evidence was scant when the victim was in skeletal form.

When Eleri decided she'd gotten most of what she could from looking at the bones, she moved to the other side of the room and pulled the slides from the case. Once again, Dr. Brzezinski had laid them out for easy access.

Eleri turned on the microscope and slid the first glass plate into place, then the second, then the third. All the organ tissues looked normal. The liver was fully functioning, the lungs those of a smoker, but smoking wasn't the cause of death.

Donovan stopped periodically and offered observations of his own. "Adrenaline, but not other drugs. I don't think even alcohol."

Adrenaline wasn't a drug they tested for. And it didn't offer them anything new.

Again, disappointed that she wasn't finding anything brilliant, Eleri pulled the autopsy report and began reading and sifting through the pictures. She hated pictures, but at least the family hadn't reclaimed the body.

The photos yielded more clues than the bones alone. Once again, several fingernails were absent, leaving ripped and rough nail beds behind. Again, these weren't nails lost in a fight, but purposefully pulled. Torture. She would need the police report to figure out how long the woman had been missing and if that matched the time frame for JP Talley.

Leaving the autopsy report open, she headed back to the table and the skeleton. This was why they had come in the middle of the night. She couldn't imagine the looks on the faces of the staff if they'd watched Donovan nearly taste test each of the organs.

He'd declared them all normal, except for the smoker's lungs, though he'd been able to say he thought she'd quit before she died. The preservative fluid was masking a lot of what he was used to scenting.

With a deep breath, Eleri placed her bare hand on the bones of the victim's forearm. She'd done the same with Talley's corpse. Though he'd offered flesh in resistance to her touch, cold or not, it was better than just bone.

This was maybe the easiest thing for her to check. Still, Talley had not offered the goldmine she'd hoped. Everything had been fresh and hazy. The images she'd gotten were flashes of his fingernails getting pulled. *Pliers.* The hand that wrapped around his, holding his finger steady, was covered in a glove. It had long, slim fingers, but everything beyond that was just fuzz from Talley's memory.

Whatever had happened to him, it scared him enough to blur all the memories Eleri could pull from him. She'd felt his terror, heard his screams, and fought the fear as he tried to beg for mercy.

Eleri had seen the tips of combat boots coming into his field of vision, but he'd managed to yield nothing else. So now, she placed her hand on what was left of this victim's arm. She hoped for more—that this woman was somehow astute enough to realize that she was going to die. Eleri hoped Earlene Beaman had gotten a good, solid stare into the face of her tormenter.

But though the images assailed her, this time they came from an entirely different source.

"Jesus, Donovan." Eleri flinched as several of the images popped into her head. "She had kids, young kids."

"Are they still young?"

"I can't tell. It's not like they're in clothing from the seventies or the eighteen hundreds." These weren't flashes of pain and terror, but happy memories seeping through her own skin.

Donovan snorted at her answer. "She's not old enough to have kids from the seventies."

"*Right*, which is why I can't tell whether her memories are new or old." Eleri bit off the sentence, sharply taking a breath, closing her eyes, and now curling her fingers around the victim's radius and ulna. The pieces moved and made the soft click of bones rattling.

Eleri saw a mirror in the morning. Earlene's face alive and staring back at her. Dark circles ringed the space under her eyes, regret smudging the shadows. But what did it mean?

Sucking in a harsh breath, Eleri pulled her hand back. *Fuck it.* Once again, nothing useful.

For all that she had done, and all that she could flare out when she was angry or scared—or worse, *both*—Eleri had yet to hone this skill to a point that it was truly useful. She needed to pull specific information, to pinpoint exact times and places. Instead, she was left operating with scraps of hazy memories.

Sure, the woman had young kids and played with them. One of her hands held a tiny toddler fist and the other a cigarette. Her dresses were a little stained and worn and the kids' clothes looked to be hand-me-downs. But what did that have to do with her murder?

She felt the flush of anger clenching her muscles at a talent that refused to respond. But she tamped it down and pulled out her tablet, calling up the police file on Earlene Beaman. The woman was in her fifties when she died; the kids were grown and moved out—so at least that was answered. Missing for three days. The same as Talley. Interesting. No one reported her ... *the same as Talley.*

Eleri printed it and the report on Talley. With both laid out on the counter next to each other, she got a better comparison. But nothing emerged. Her heart sank. "Did you smell anything the same on both of them?"

Donovan had put all the organ samples back in their neat line and came to look over her shoulder. "They were both afraid, but that's only logical. I mean, they were cut. They had fingernails pulled. So, no, nothing that connected me to a killer."

"What even links these two?" She pointed back and forth between the two files. "They both had kids, but in almost entirely different generations. Any two people over thirty are likely to have had kids! This woman lived in a trailer on the outskirts of town by herself and he lived in a McMansion in one of the new neighborhoods cropping up in between cities."

She took a breath and kept going. "He had a wife—she was never married—he had three young daughters and was the family breadwinner. He alone paid the bills on that house. But what links these two?"

She was getting frustrated, but Donovan had remained disengaged. His skills hadn't failed him. Or maybe he simply hadn't expected to get more than he did.

"Well, they called us down here to investigate a serial killing. And declaring a serial killer takes three bodies." He said it calmly. She didn't feel calm.

"We only have *two*," Eleri reminded him, not liking the fact that she'd almost snipped back about whether or not he could count. She was glad she'd held it back.

Because what Donovan said next was, "So let's go find the third."

5

"What are you looking for?"

Eleri snapped her gaze away from the window and tapped her fork on her plate. "I don't know. That's the problem."

The Pancake House between Astoria and Fort Myers seemed like just the thing. She'd wanted breakfast, despite waking up past noon. Donovan, always ready for food, had agreed. But now, the omelet wasn't sitting well.

She'd managed to make it through half of her order before he asked, "So, have you told Avery?"

Rolling her eyes seemed the only decent response. She didn't even have to ask what he was pestering her about. "You've been with me almost twenty-four/seven since we started this discussion. When would I have even called?"

"True." Donovan forked another sausage into his mouth. The food disappeared so quickly that Eleri didn't get a break. "I'm not expecting you to call the guy right in front of me. But you could have done it from your own room."

He added an emphasis, as though Donovan Heath was somehow the master of etiquette. She'd almost snarked that he had literally been raised by wolves, but she managed to hold it back.

"I need to do it when I have enough time."

"You're never going to have the time." He waved another sausage on the end of his fork. "The longer you wait, the harder it will be for him to handle."

Donovan was right, and she knew it—hence the dread knotted heavily in her chest. She really liked Avery. In fact, she might even be coming around to love him. But could she really love him if she couldn't tell him what she was?

Donovan might be the only one who fully understood her dilemma. The very act of telling meant that Avery would need to keep her secrets. She would have to trust him before he even knew about it. If it made him angry, it put her at risk.

But, worse yet, telling him put him in an awkward position. So did his not knowing. His very association with her was awkward and dangerous, and he didn't even know it yet. For almost a year, she hadn't told him. She sighed. "You're right, but we're neck-deep in an investigation."

"Are we, though?"

"I don't know what I'm doing at the edge of the Everglades if we're not!" *He was undermining her one excuse!*

"Here's the thing." Donovan leaned forward, and she couldn't help but wonder when Donovan Heath had become the distributor of social wisdom. *Oh, please do tell me the thing.* He did. "Westerfield said they wanted us here *before* the murder happened."

That wasn't the thing, she knew, but Eleri laughed, loud enough to gather attention from a few of the nearby tables. "That appears to be the one skill that is beyond our SAC."

Hell if Donovan wasn't right, though. SAC Derek Westerfield seemed to have a psychic knack for finding employees with special talents. He had another knack for talking people into joining his unit. He'd plucked Eleri from the psychiatric hospital and convinced her old SAC to sign her over to the NightShade Division. He'd convinced Donovan to leave a perfectly good career as a medical examiner to become an agent in a job he'd never considered, in a unit that technically didn't exist.

But he had yet to send them to a crime scene before the act was committed.

Donovan kept talking. "There's just over a year between the two murders. That means it's likely a year before the next one happens. So, we have plenty of time right now to take this slowly. The police are on top of the investigation."

"Sheriff," Eleri corrected softly. But he was right. The goals had shifted and ... "They may have a better hand at this than we do."

Despite being in the middle of Florida, which she'd always thought of as bustling city space, Astoria was a relatively small town, and it felt like it. "The sheriff might have a good idea which direction to start looking, but he might also be biased."

Donovan nodded and cleaned the last of the food from his plate. She found herself jealous of his ability to eat. "That's always the case, and that's why we're here. But we're not at breakneck speed. The body isn't decaying on the ground anymore while they wait for us to arrive. And we're not expecting any kind of major escalation by the killer in the next few weeks."

Eleri nodded again. They both knew they needed to get into the databases next. They needed to search for similar killings, though honestly, she would have expected one of the analysts would have found something by now if it involved pulled fingernails, knife cuts, *and* gunshot wounds. But nothing had come over the line.

"Are you done?" Donovan motioned with his fork, and she'd pushed the plate toward him. But he less seemed to want her food as to simply get going.

Donovan motioned for the check. Eleri was turning back to ask him where he thought they should start, when he clasped his hands on the table in front of him and said, "I'm giving you four days to tell him, but that's it."

6

So far, they had thirteen plausible cases.

She only nodded absently and flipped a file over as if discarding it.

An ominous number, Donovan thought. None of them directly matched the two cases DeSoto County had.

"I wish we had Noah. He knows Florida," Eleri lamented into the otherwise quiet air of the conference room. The Tampa field office had given them access to files and a quiet place to review them.

"He knows Miami. I get the feeling that's very different from 'general Florida.'"

Eleri had already contacted GJ Janson to see if she was available. If they could tap her for research, this might go faster. GJ's excellent pattern recognition skills and the extra pair of eyes wouldn't hurt. From Eleri's focused but not exactly pleased expression, Donovan figured there hadn't been an answer from the junior agent yet.

The cases they pulled were listed as violent, but none made them shout *Eureka*. Eleri pointed to three different files in turn. "If we do this one, then this one, then this one … we have a perfect progression. Death by knife wound. Death by gunshot with pulled fingernails. And this last one via gunshot puts us right at our time frame here."

Donovan's stood up and moved over to examine the cases she was discussing at closer range. "True."

It was expected that not all the murders would look exactly alike.

Old cases sometimes would show progression up to the current method. Serial killers didn't start out with their MO perfectly planned or executed the first time, at least not that anyone knew of.

This case? It was an odd duck, even among the odd ways the serial killers went about their business. It had no ritualistic tendencies and none of the signals of a mind that wasn't operating in reality. It also didn't have the passion of the killer who felt rage toward their victim —not like Edmund Kemper, who killed women as a way of repeatedly removing his abusive mother from the world.

This one was methodical, painful for the victim, and without any obvious posturing for the police to find. The bodies had served their purpose and simply been discarded.

"I think you're going back too far," he said.

"There's one year between these," Eleri said, pointing again to the new cases she'd sorted. "We don't know what the triggering event is. So we don't know if that builds up over time and one year is just the point where it's too big and he has to seek relief ... or if there's some event that starts it. If it's a triggering *event*, then the killings could happen at odd intervals."

"True. You do have a nice cluster for the area." Donovan knew that when they eventually figured it out, it would be almost easy to see the path. They would see where their killer had lived, how and why they had targeted their victims, and what the MO actually was. But right now, they held somewhere between two and ten pieces of a three-hundred-piece puzzle. They had no idea what the final picture would be. In fact, they didn't even know if all the pieces they held belonged to this particular puzzle.

It was always a mess early on. When he'd started with the FBI, Donovan had put his faith in Eleri. Now he had faith in his own investigative skills, too.

"Why did you give me four days?" she asked out of the blue.

He knew she was referencing his demand about talking to her boyfriend. "Four days seemed like a good number—not enough to put it off for too long."

"But you don't get to decide how I handle my relationship." She said it without ire, and she wasn't wrong.

"I know." He'd issued an ultimatum where truly he had no business. "But at the same time, how your relationship goes affects our work."

Hell, he'd never thought he'd hear those words coming out of his mouth. He'd never thought he'd be an FBI agent, and he'd never thought that of the two of them, he would be the one in a stable relationship. Not that Eleri and Avery weren't stable—they seemed perfectly stable. The problem was, Donovan knew something about their relationship that Avery didn't and that wasn't sitting well with him.

Donovan knew what Eleri could do, and she hadn't told her boyfriend, and then it had *gotten worse*. If she'd told him before Nassau, she might have been able to ease Avery into understanding her skills and accepting them. Instead, she'd had a flare of power, a rough fight, and then a bit of a mental breakdown.

It wasn't even her first breakdown. Eleri had been checked out of a mental hospital—Donovan found that out later—days before he'd met her. She'd checked herself in the first time after dealing with accusations that stemmed from the things she could do. Even she hadn't understood her powers at the time.

In fact, it was SAC Westerfield who'd managed to get Eleri released ahead of time. So right now, Donovan wasn't really keen on Eleri withholding secrets. She seemed just a little jumpy, often looking over her shoulder, probably watching for a threat that wasn't coming. Maybe she simply needed to be held accountable.

He could do that.

"What about this one?" He tossed another file at her.

"That's different ... on a military base."

"Pulled fingernails, though," he replied. He thought back to his old math classes: Two points defined a line. Three points could define an entire plane. In this case, their third point would provide an exponential amount of information.

Four points could define a space. That's what they were looking for. The problem was, when they didn't know what they were looking for, it became infinitely harder to find. These early stages of an investigation could be mind-numbing and he wished for Eleri's talent to aim them in the right direction.

Three hours later, hungry and nearly cross-eyed, Donovan tossed his pen down onto the yellow legal pad where he'd been taking notes. "I give up."

"Oh, thank god," Eleri gushed the words on a rush of breath. "I didn't want to be the first to tap out, but I gave up a while ago."

Glad for that, he laughed. "So we set this all aside, but you won't like what I have to say."

"Figures."

He laughed again. "I don't even have to say it. You know where we have to go."

7

Eleri placed one bare foot in front of the other on the leaf-lined path through the woods.

The air was still and calm ... too calm.

Maybe the air had recognized that sense of ominous foreboding, because at that moment, it changed. The wind suddenly kicked upward, grabbing her hair and tangling it. Though the dark night and the eerie sounds should have been terrifying, they were comforting.

It had been too long. Eleri had begun to think that this had disappeared, along with her sister. Emmaline had not died to Eleri when she had actually died. Only more recently, when Eleri put her bones in the ground, had Emmaline finally disappeared from her dreams.

Eleri had been petrified that Grandmere disappeared along with her. But now Eleri walked the path.

Picking up her pace, she ran now. In her conscious mind, she knew that speed in the woods was dangerous. She could step on a rock or trip on a root and get injured. But in her conscious mind she also knew *these woods*. These were Grandmere's woods, and no rock would dare puncture the tender soles of her feet here.

She pushed forward, the path widening as she went. *A new feature?* she thought.

Did she control this or did Grandmere? Maybe neither of them. For a moment, she stopped to consider the ramifications. But it was too late. She was already here, and there was no answer to a question that would now change her direction.

She ran until her lungs heaved, until she gasped for breath, but she wasn't frightened. Then she saw the glimpse of white sideboard peeking through the leaves and trunks—the little square house. She always came at it from this side. In fact, she didn't know if the woods even existed beyond the other sides of the house.

She stopped, breathing heavily, gathering her reserves. Then she picked up pace, running with renewed energy. *Grandmere!*

The front corner of the house came into view, offering a small, triangular porch with white railings. The corner was open, allowing a body to slip through onto the tiny platform and into the house.

The white panel door moved slightly, doorknob twisting. Eleri flung herself forward, only to discover that it wasn't Grandmere, but Alesse Dauphine.

Skidding to a stop, Eleri felt her heart pound.

Now, for the first time, she felt the cold twist of fear. The rising winds finally made sense.

With her recognition of her greatest living enemy in the house of her great grandmother, lightning suddenly cracked the sky, as though her very thought had brought it. It illuminated Alesse in her long, red dress.

"Welcome, Eleri," she said, her musical accent reflecting both modern New Orleans and centuries of voodoo and craft.

This was *Grandmere's* house. As far as Eleri knew, Alesse might have escaped from Blue Shoals, where the wolves lived, but she had been severely injured. The other Dauphine sisters were still at large. Were they here? Was this a sign?

Hell, Eleri didn't even know where *here* was, only that she'd always thought of this as Grandmere's house.

I am safe here, she lied to herself. Alesse Dauphine was certainly powerful enough to reach anywhere—anywhere that Eleri could reach, anywhere Grandmere could.

Eleri didn't respond. Pushing her way through the doorway, she shoved the woman aside.

Alesse felt solid and real enough, Eleri thought. But she darted into the house, running through the small living area and around the loop straight into the kitchen. She pulled up short again. Gisele Dauphine stood at the stove, stirring a large pot. Purple tendrils rose with the steam. It was all too showy, too classic witch cartoon.

It *couldn't* be real. It had to be a sign. And, if it was a sign, it was at least a message and at worst a *warning*.

The other Dauphine sister turned and smiled at her, but Eleri kept going, darting past. She slipped into the hallway and past the first bedroom and through the back of the house. In the back room, the rocking chair tipped back and forth, waiting for her. The band on her heart released and she could see the back of the old woman's head.

"Grandmere!" Though if she yelled it in warning or in relief, she couldn't quite tell.

But the figure kept rocking and didn't reply.

Eleri grabbed the chair as she darted around it, using the arm as a pivot point. She came around to the front, jumping as she almost got her toes crunched when the rail of the rocker came down.

"Grandmere!" she said again.

But as she met the woman's eyes, she saw that it wasn't Grandmere at all.

8

"Have you called Avery?" Donovan knew he was pushing his luck to open the day with that phrase.

Eleri merely glared. "I barely slept. And honestly, I think it's best that I do it in person."

"Why is that?" Donovan sipped at the strong coffee he didn't really want, thinking that an in-person meeting allowed for all kinds of terrible outcomes. At least on the phone, Avery could hang up on her. He could take time to think things over for a while—by himself—and initiate a conversation when he felt like it again. It was going to be a big conversation.

"Imagine someone told you what I could do, and didn't show you …"

She had a point. "Video call, then."

Eleri rolled her eyes. "It's not like I got any sleep anyway. I went to Grandmere's house."

"The shotgun in New Orleans?" Donovan found he was more concerned with exactly where she'd visited than with the idea that his roommate had somehow traveled in the eight hours since he'd seen her last. Eleri could do all kinds of things. He had learned it was best not to question the whys or hows.

"The house in the woods."

He'd heard of it. She'd described to him more than once, and more than once, she'd gone to this little house and brought back relevant information. "You haven't been there since we found Emmaline, have you?"

She shook her head, then dropped her little bomb. "Alesse Dauphine opened the door for me."

"Holy shit. Do you think she was really there?" It was a ridiculous question. Neither of them knew if the house really existed or if it ever had.

"And Gisele Dauphine was in the kitchen."

He would have spit the coffee he'd been about to sip. Thank God her timing was off. Two of the four Dauphine sisters in Grandmere's house in the woods? After having met Grandmere himself, Donovan's belief was that the house was real, but that it did not exist in this plane. It was somewhere only the most skilled practitioners could reach. So it made an odd sort of sense to him that the Dauphine sisters could show up there. Not that it was in any way good.

"What did Grandmere say?"

"She wasn't there. The person sitting in her chair was someone I didn't recognize." Eleri took a deep sigh, as if getting herself together, and Donovan didn't push. "I mean, I've seen her before, but I didn't know who it was. So, of course, when I crawled out of bed, I spent the next three hours looking. I've got to tell you, I think it was Aida Weddo."

The odd combination of syllables that came out of her mouth rang a bell but in reality meant nothing to him. "I don't even know what that is."

"She's a voodoo goddess, and she was in Grandmere's house … without Grandmere," Eleri added.

"What do you think it means?" Because he sure as hell didn't know. A stab of sharp jealousy punctured him. She was connected to women and creatures past. He didn't even know his own immediate family.

"I have nothing. Nothing!" Her hands were thrown into the air and starting to draw attention to their little conversation. They were sitting in a different diner today. They had decided to start with a decent breakfast this morning before getting their boots on the ground for the case.

"Do you think it's a callback to some centuries-old blood feud between the Remis and the Dauphines?" he asked.

He was still shoveling food into his face, as per his usual mode.

But Eleri had been disturbed lately and wasn't even getting halfway through her meals. She was looking out the window as though searching for something in the bushes or trees.

"You need to eat," he told her, pointing with his fork as though that would make it happen. At least she took a few bites before she looked up at him. She had successfully managed to brush conversations about Avery off the table, but he had to admit, this would do it.

She chewed as if she couldn't taste it, or it didn't mean anything. "This isn't a centuries-old blood feud, Donovan. It's *now*."

He was about to contradict her, and she maybe saw it or sensed it, but she rolled right through his thoughts.

"Donovan, they kidnapped my sister and killed her. That was *my* generation. This isn't some Romeo and Juliet, five hundred years ago, our grandfathers shot each other and our families have hated each other ever since, thing. This is *now*. Christina just pushed the Dauphine sisters out of the wolves' compound in the Ozarks. And I think my dream is a message that *now* might not just mean 'in my generation' but it may actually be *right now*."

He was sitting in a very public place and he had been worried about Eleri waving her hands around, drawing attention. But now he felt the old reaction—the sharp spike of fear, the intake of breath that preceded the bodily changes. He hadn't ever quite been able to quell the strike when it demanded change.

It was anxiety and sudden fear that pushed it. He'd seen what the Dauphine sisters could do. But now, he was the biggest danger to himself as his body fought to change and defend. Probably an innate reaction.

He was pretty sure that, in his adulthood, he'd learned to hide the way the bones in his face wanted to push and change. But the hair on his arms stood and appeared to be growing.

He dropped his fork with maybe too much of a clatter. They were in the middle of a case. They couldn't handle the Dauphines now.

9

"Excuse me, I have to take this." Donovan turned away for a moment, leaving Eleri to handle the interview. He wasn't upset to be able to step away. They'd learned nothing of value so far, but they had to check that box.

The message had popped up on his screen but he simply hadn't wanted to be rude, typing messages there in front of their witness.

GJ had already replied that she wasn't available to help sort files and find previous dead bodies. SAC Westerfield had sent her out on an assignment with new agent, Noah Campbell. They were following Miranda Industries, but only doing recon. Something about the assignment didn't seem right.

They should follow Miranda and get all the information they could, but… GJ and Noah? Was that the right pair to follow a company that was hiring and using wolves for drug trafficking? Donovan had frowned when he'd seen the initial message, and had even written back.

"Does that seem right?" he tapped out, though he could admit that he didn't know what *right* was.

GJ hadn't replied to that email. So the fact that she was replying to the new one first told him she was withholding something that she didn't want passing through these channels. That was disturbing.

But now, she told him, "No inkling from any Dauphines." She had been there for the last clash. She'd been in the Ozarks when Alesse Dauphine had had tried to kill them all.

He'd tried Walter, but Walter was still radio silent, off on some other assignment herself. Noah was with GJ, so Donovan had already gotten the answer about him, too. Christina—the other source he would readily go to—had simply replied with the shortest possible answer: "No Dauphines here."

Donovan didn't even know where *here* was and Christina didn't seem to feel the need to enlighten him. If something was stirring, it was deeper than anyone could see from the surface.

With no further information coming in, he returned to the room where Eleri sat on the faded brown and gold couch that had seen better decades, offering her calming half-smile that said she was listening and she was here for anything their witness wanted to tell them. Unfortunately, it didn't seem like anything valuable. The woman was still complaining.

"We understand that you've already told the police the same things and we really appreciate your time."

How many times had they had to say that?

"We're expanding the investigation," Eleri went on.

"Alright, then," the woman sighed, her cigarette drifting smoke all through the room. Not that they could complain; they'd come into her house, after all.

"My bedroom's right over there." She pointed with the tip of her lit cigarette and Donovan waited for the ash to fall. But, like a seasoned smoker, she didn't let it. "I watch out the window a lot. It's like TV."

He got the feeling that she had been rehearsing this, each time she'd been interviewed, and that he and Eleri were getting the polished version. Whether it was an apple or a turd remained to be seen.

The woman went through the usual, "nice family" "came and went a lot" and "didn't have a lot of visitors."

Donovan prodded. "How long have you lived here?"

"Eight years." She took another slow drag on the cigarette.

The woman droned on. It was information, sure, but Donovan didn't think it yielded anything other than the same thing all the other neighbors had said. "I barely knew the family's names. The Talleys didn't have friends in the neighborhood."

Donovan was about to be done here. This woman had been the last on their list. And, damn, she had been close to useless. He reminded himself that things that looked pointless early on often proved useful later.

They thanked the woman and headed back out through the immaculately painted white home and past the young woman and her own son who “hadn’t seen anything” and “didn’t pay attention to the neighbors.”

“Well, that was a big fat bust,” Eleri declared. At least she'd waited until she had the car door closed.

He agreed, but only started the engine.

She shook her head. “We’re at fucking spider maps, Donovan.”

He laughed. She referred to drawing a web of everyone the families had contacted and anyone those people had contacted, looking for some kind of connection between the two bodies they had.

“I think we're at financials first.”

“Surely, somebody already pulled that for us.” Her head had not left the headrest yet and she wasn't watching as he pulled out.

It had been a long day and he aimed for the hotel. They had separate rooms, but had gotten Eleri a suite, so there was a space where they could work without anyone looking over their shoulders and without having to drive all the way to Tampa. Being in Astoria had its advantages.

Eleri's phone rang then, prompting her to finally lift her head from the back of the seat. She pressed buttons, putting it on speaker before even saying hello.

Westerfield. Donovan didn’t even need to hear the voice.

Their SAC didn’t say hello. “I had an analyst running some things for you. And she got something.”

“A victim? Are you going to send us the files?” Eleri asked—the appropriate response.

Though her tone was purely lackluster, Donovan was more excited. A third victim would open a wealth of information to them.

“No,” Westerfield told them. “I'm sending you to him. He's still alive.”

10

At least Seattle's weather is slightly less humid than Florida, Eleri thought as she followed Donovan off the plane. The day was sunny and beautiful and hardly seemed like the time to be interviewing the live victim of a serial killer. But her odd, jumpy feeling, the prickling at the base of her skull, had faded with the trip.

Donovan shook his head. "It still smells like airplane."

Eleri hadn't known that "airplane" smelled like anything in particular, but she didn't doubt him.

Aside from the local police and sheriff, no one else was on the case they'd left behind. She prayed nothing broke while they were gone, but what she said was, "I hope this pans out."

"Why wouldn't it? I mean, Westerfield sent us here."

Even so, Eleri was reminded of their conversation the day before —that the one thing Westerfield hadn't been able to do so far was send them to a case *before* the crime was committed.

They'd been reading the files on the flight. Luckily, their row was only two seats across and there'd been enough space to keep anyone from staring over their shoulders at FBI paperwork. She trailed Donovan now, her wheeled luggage bouncing along behind her. "It's not even a criminal file. The analyst pulled it out of newspaper stories."

Donovan kept moving. "Why wouldn't it have been filed?"

"I guess that's the first question." She headed toward the waiting rental car still trying to figure out how to play this one. But they had called ahead and talked to Dexter Allen—who'd agreed to the interview, if not quite readily.

"First, food," Donovan declared.

She immediately shook her head. "There's not enough time for anything real." But she pointed to a few signs she could see cutting the air in the distance.

The goal was to do this as quickly as possible—in and out. The return flight was already booked for five hours from now. While that *should* give them plenty of time to sit down and have a nice meal at the front end, they couldn't risk the time loss. She didn't like that there were so many ways this could go off the rails.

They were eating flat burgers and fries that tasted more of salt than potato before she knew it. It was enough to keep her stomach from growling and nothing more. As Donovan pulled up to the small brick house, she mused, "Another small town near bigger cities. It's a little more out of the way. Is that a factor?"

"Who even knows?" Donovan asked. He was right, the two victims weren't enough to even know what was important and what wasn't.

"Do we still smell like airplane?" she asked out of curiosity as she unbuckled.

"Yes." His face scrunched up at the thought. So "airplane" wasn't a good smell. "And fast food."

Again, she had nothing to argue with. Eleri opened the door and climbed out, tugging her button-down shirt neatly into place. She glanced over at Donovan doing the same and thought, *Oh God, we do look like feds.*

At least the food in her stomach kept her steady and calm as the front door opened. She introduced them and they showed their badges, doing the usual polite shuffle getting into a comfortable space. In this case, it was Dexter Allen's living room.

She got out the recorder, explained the necessity and then apologized. "I'm sure there aren't any really good memories associated with this. But we need your help."

It took a few minutes to tiptoe their way around to "Where are your wounds? And what are they?"

Allen cautiously lifted the side of his shirt, and Eleri managed to retrieve her old training and not gasp. The skin revealed one long, angry red scar and pieces of two others that disappeared beneath the fabric and under the waistband of his jeans. All looked old to her.

"They slashed me up pretty good."

"I understand they also pulled your fingernails," she prompted softly, not surprised that Donovan was having her take the lead on this.

Allen held out his hand. Though all his nails were there, three were clearly malformed. Something about the way Donovan nodded briefly—and hopefully out of sight of the victim—made her think that her partner was agreeing that this was what a pulled nail would look like when it grew back in.

"Do you have any idea why these three fingers?"

"At the time? No. But it's a curious pattern, isn't it?"

Eleri nodded. The pattern was made curiouser by the fact that it matched the ones on JP Talley and Earlene Beaman.

Allen nodded solemnly, pulling Eleri's brain back to her task. She could compare victims later. "It took me a handful of years to start investigating. But everything they did was careful."

An odd choice of words. But she waited, since he seemed to want to talk.

"These nails are supposed to be the most painful to have pulled." He pointed on his hand to the misshapen ones as he barked a sharp and bitter laugh. "Not that I would know. They didn't pull the others for comparison. Truly, I suspect having any of your fingernails pulled with pliers is pretty damn painful, no matter which ones."

Eleri nodded, using her best sympathetic face. It wasn't conjured; she had real sympathy, but he had said *pliers.* She didn't move, didn't want to interrupt his flow of information, but she wondered if there was a way to find out what tool was used on the two victims they had.

"They messed me up good."

It was the third or fourth time he'd said it, and it occurred to Eleri from something in the way he spoke and gestured ... *They. Not singular.*

She'd been taking it to mean the man hadn't seen his attacker and didn't know which gender to use. But he was talking multiples.

"—the whole lot of them. They all knew exactly where to cut, which nails to pull. Three or four different ones every day."

That would dramatically change how they looked at this case.
"Where did this happen?" she asked.
"I was tortured in Marjah, outside of Kandahar, Ma'am."

11

"I am dead," Donovan declared as he parked the local rental car at the hotel. It wasn't quite true—he could go another three or four hours, but mentally, he was well past done. He needed to watch some really stupid TV and go for a run if he could.

How would he do that here? He didn't know his way around the Everglades, and neither did Eleri. But he did know that he wasn't capable of any needle-in-haystack searches right now.

"You don't have to tell me twice," Eleri agreed, the heavy sigh in her voice adding more weight to his decision to call the day done.

She lifted her carry-on bag out of the trunk. They hadn't even needed to touch it, but it did have an extra change of clothes for each of them. Because, as Eleri had pointed out, they might have cracked the whole case and needed to stay.

It hadn't happened.

Now, he followed her quietly down the hotel hallway, thinking of the whirlwind of new information. Westerfield's victim was a former POW. Donovan's brain couldn't even wrap around that as they reached the right floor and headed to their adjacent doors. He told Eleri, "Just give me my clothes back tomorrow."

He'd rolled the fistful into a grocery bag and handed them over. He'd never quite outgrown the rundown apartment buildings, rented trailers in parks, and all the roach-infested places he and his father had left in the middle of the night with nothing but a garbage bag of his things.

Here he was, "MD" after his name. He'd held a prestigious medical position, and though the district that he'd run wasn't LA or Maricopa or anything, he'd run it mostly by himself. He'd been the one others consulted, needing his opinion on hard-to-crack cases. He'd been at the front end of making a real name for himself. *Maybe that had been the problem.*

The last thing Donovan Heath needed was anyone knowing his name. It only occurred to him just now that that might have been half the appeal of Westerfield's offer to join the FBI, even though it meant heading to Quantico and learning to shoot guns.

Eleri offered him a small wave as she disappeared into her room.

His stomach was full—they'd stopped for a nice dinner and tucked themselves into a back corner, discussing the ramifications of their murder victims looking like torture victims from wars. It was interesting as hell—a brightly colored puzzle piece that had no edges or corner marks and wasn't anything he could place anywhere. But he knew that when he could snap it in, it would be big.

He flopped onto the small couch in his junior suite, unconcerned with having the smaller room. To his left, his bed was made, though he'd left it in a scramble. In front of him, a wide TV anchored itself to the wall. He didn't even bother to get out of his clothes and began flipping channels.

The second half of a very old Godzilla movie later, he gave up.

Beyond the bed, the open window showed the moon had risen and he felt the pull that he couldn't ignore. He yanked the heavy curtains closed, stripped naked, and hauled on sweatpants, a T shirt, and a pair of slip-on sneakers. He grabbed his mesh bag, his room card, and the car keys.

He should have told Eleri he was heading out, but he didn't.

Hopefully, she was already asleep, catching up on extra hours or talking with Avery. His four-day ultimatum would be up soon. Donovan decided he was going to drop it. It was her relationship and, though it would affect him no matter how it came out, it was hers to save or destroy.

He was in the car before he quite realized what he was doing, engine on, foot on the gas pedal. He couldn't go back to the crime scene, as there was plausibly still a guard there, watching them come and go.

He couldn't afford to be seen. So he looked up a new location, some park in the Everglades, and headed onto the nearest state road. When he stopped in the small gravel lot that felt just enough abandoned at night for his purposes, he slipped the hotel room key card into the little spot for sunglasses. He grabbed the keys and the mesh bag and headed into the woods.

Donovan went a mile on human feet before believing he was alone enough that he could risk it. He stripped his clothes, stuffed them into the bag, and tied it up into the tree. This alone was enough to warrant an arrest, but probably not enough to make anyone scream.

Then he did it.

He rolled his shoulders, flexed his hips, and leaned forward. He twisted his neck, feeling the welcome pain of the bones in his face rubbing against each other and popping into new places as they shifted.

Though he suspected the change would be wild from the outside, it was also wild from the inside. He could see the moment his orbitals slipped into place, because his vision altered with the slight differential in pressure. He always saw better than normal humans, though not quite with their full color gradient. But now it was like an almost fuzzy world coming into focus.

Sound pooled in his ears, as if the volume had been turned up and the static in the background filtered down to nothing. The scents around him bloomed and filled his face. He could only identify a handful of them and it fueled his curiosity.

On all fours now, he saw the night in a different way. Who knew what was out here?

He needed to run. He needed to stretch. He needed to feel the earth under the now-rough pads of four feet. And while he was out here, maybe he could play cadaver dog.

12

"You found *what?*" Eleri asked. She was still trying to get past "You did *what?*"

Donovan had apparently gone for a run the night before… all on his own. She'd seen him do the whole thing before, tying his clothes up into a tree. She'd heard him bitch about TV making everyone think there were werewolf fairies, and that wolves just jumped and transformed, and their clothes magically returned—folded—later. Donovan strictly informed her that no such thing happened, and he had to take care of his own crap.

"Conservation of mass," he'd muttered. It hadn't taken her long to figure out that was why wolf-Donovan was close to 200 pounds. Not a creature that could be confused for a coyote or an average house pet. These wolves drew attention when they were spotted. The black fur didn't help. Wade's was a sandy brown, but still unusual enough. She understood where the legends had come from and why.

"But now we have a real serial killer, El. I found *three* sites, two of which had bodies."

Ignoring why he went without her and *where* and all the rest of it, she asked, "What was the third site, if it didn't have a body?"

"It was where a body had once been." Donovan was once again scarfing down another huge meal. Eleri and GJ had come to the conclusion that changing burned a lot of calories.

She'd seen cadaver dogs alert on an empty site. She'd watched as a prisoner brought into the woods confessed that, yes, he had buried the body right there. Then, she'd spent hours sifting the soil, ultimately producing only one metacarpal and a small ankle bone. Everything else had been scavenged in the fifteen years since the crime. So she didn't question Donovan saying he had a site where a body was *not*.

Certainly not in a state park. *Were there jaguars here?* she wondered. They would certainly be big enough to haul off all the major parts before the body decayed enough to slip into smaller pieces. "So what did you find?"

"I don't know. That's why we need to go out today."

"You're just trying to get out of searching the financials," she accused with a bit of gratitude.

"I didn't really *mean* to find bodies." But she knew him, and he'd had his nose to the ground the whole time. He brushed off the suggestion and kept going. "You'll probably need to claim that you found them with your search dog."

The look on his face changed, indicating that he wasn't going to be happy about being the "search dog" again.

"Do either of these bodies pertain to this case?" As much as she was glad to leave tedious record searches for another day, they couldn't just abandon the work three days after they'd arrived.

"One might."

"How old was it?"

He shook his head. "I couldn't quite tell TOD. Too decomposed."

Time of death. Still the medical examiner.

But he was talking, and she had to pay attention. "I can't date it. I don't know how bodies decompose down here."

He held his hands out as if he were sorry. But he'd already done so much.

"I'm not sure it matches," he added between bites. "I really have no solid idea. There was just *something* about it..."

"Scent?" she asked.

"Yeah. But it was so faint that I can't be sure."

"Do you want to go out again?" It would suck for him, but that way, they could publicly and officially find the bodies he'd already found.

"I think you can just explain it. Then we hand the two unrelated cases over to the locals. Though I don't know if the third site will be any good. There's nothing there that I can see, nothing I can put my finger on."

It was rare that they operated on Donovan's hunches, but she wasn't against it. He'd caught something, and just because he couldn't file it into some specific evidence category didn't make it invalid. And they needed more evidence.

"Did you dig?"

"You know I did." A sly grin crossed his face, as though he had enjoyed it.

Eleri didn't understand any of it. Was digging such a pleasure? Then again, Donovan ate nearly-rare steaks and turned his nose up at beer. He was human, but not like her. And she was human, but not like others, either. She had no right to get upset that her partner liked to dig in the dirt.

She made the decision. "A search dog wouldn't dig. So we don't tell them about the empty site."

They would report the other two, but only after Eleri managed to make them look like professional work—as if she had been there with him and had dug enough to confirm a body before stopping. "We keep the one for ourselves."

Just as Donovan had declared it. It was either part of their case or not, but they could always hand it off later. Her brain was still mulling the information that she'd fallen asleep on last night. She'd tried to read a romance novel, but it was difficult to do when every time she closed her eyes, she saw JP Talley and the slices on his torso.

They were not exactly aligned to Dexter Allen's, but they were very close. The slices and then the gunshot on the bodies had looked as though the first attempt to kill had failed and the gunshots had been a second, more reliable, method.

Apparently, they'd read that wrong.

Everything before the gunshots was specifically calculated to *not* kill. It had all been about pain. The bullet was for when the killer was finished torturing them.

"Let me get my kit," she told Donovan as they left the table and headed back upstairs to the rooms. It had been easier to eat in the hotel restaurant that morning, especially once Donovan had confessed to what he'd done.

She reached into her huge suitcase and pushed aside pajamas, underwear, and her Book of Shadows and grabbed the handle of the old, black messenger bag. She'd carried everything in a medical bag until she realized that anyone who saw her carrying that into a national park would know something was definitely up. Even this one would make her look odd.

But she needed it. It had vials and spatulas for collecting samples. It had pop-open file boxes, in case she had bones to collect. It had crime scene tape, fingerprint magma powder, luminol, and even graph paper and dry erase markers.

Today, she wouldn't look like a fed. It was bad enough that she'd be hiking through the woods with a bag at all, but she changed her clothes and her shoes while Donovan waited. His choice of the loose casual wear he'd showed up to breakfast in made more sense now. And when he knocked on the door, she popped up, bag in hand. "I'm ready."

Letting Donovan drive, she saw the route he'd taken the night before. They walked deep into the Everglades. Donovan led the way, though Eleri was confident they were much slower now than when he was on his own. She had clocked him in the past. He could maintain twenty-five miles an hour speeds for several miles at a time.

At last, he said, "It's right here."

It was obvious to her that he'd covered up the clear signs of his digging from the night before. Being the forensic investigator she was, she knelt down and started to work slowly and methodically.

She pulled out her orange string and set up a grid line on a north-south axis. She took pictures and slowly brushed at the dirt. Though she knew Donovan had gone at the grave with big paws the night before, when they showed the locals, it had to look professional.

An hour and a half later, she looked up at Donovan. "You did it. This is number three."

13

"The DNA results aren't going to come back that fast," Donovan told Eleri as she checked her messages again. He was right, but she was frustrated anyway.

She tried to focus on ID-ing their vic. She told herself that she was in her own suite, that she was comfortable, that she could drink any of the overpriced beverages from the minibar. But what she wanted were results.

This body—the one they had brought back—had been carefully extracted from the ground. It had warranted every bit of effort to preserve all the evidence. TV shows didn't do justice to the kind of painstaking time it took. Not only were the bones themselves evidence, but so was the soil around them.

They'd sent all kinds of samples off to the labs last night when they'd finished. And Eleri had decided the bones had been in the ground for about five years. But—as Donovan had rightly pointed out—they weren't familiar with the Everglades.

The time of death might be off … way off.

She sighed and complained, "I could have done PCR and read the electropherogram myself before this."

Donovan held his hands wide, almost laughing at her. "In what lab?"

She sighed.

The bones were in a box in the corner now, as she wanted to have them handy if she thought of anything. So were Earlene Beaman's. Eleri was starting to feel a bit like a pirate, carting human skeletons everywhere she went.

Yesterday had been excruciatingly long. They'd informed the sheriff of one site and ported the skeleton and all their soil samples from the related site back to the DeSoto Medical Center. They'd cleaned the bones and processed all the samples for the labs. Around midnight, they'd managed to lay out the almost complete skeleton and examine it.

"Look at this...." Eleri pointed out a spot to Donovan. There was clear evidence of knife cuts along the rib cage.

"Looks like many of the same spots that JP Talley had wounds. And just like the scars on Dexter Allen," Donovan had murmured in the harsh glare from the overhead fluorescents. Again, they'd been alone in the county examiner's office at night. And again, the walk through the parking lot had made her look over her shoulder more than once.

Donovan then pointed to the sternum, which sported a neat hole from a gunshot, as did the skull. Eleri had recorded their findings. The front right temple showed a clean entry wound and the lower right occipital showed the exit.

She was thinking her way through it, but now she asked Donovan, "What made you think that this body was related to the case?"

He shrugged and shook his head. "A faint scent that matched to the Talley scene."

"Was that before or after you dug it up?"

He tipped his head as though he hadn't thought much about it. "Before."

She'd clearly tripped something. "Do you think the killer came back to check it out? See if the body had been discovered yet?"

"Maybe ..." was all he'd been able to come up with. At least it was something to think about.

Without evidence coming in from the labs—she'd checked again, *damnit*—Eleri once again tried touching the bones. She pulled the box up onto the sofa that sat under the wide window. There wasn't room to lay him out, so she sat next to the box and stuck her hand in. Wrapping her fingers around a femur, she waited.

But the result was relatively pointless. She saw bonfires and beer with friends. They looked like kids, high school maybe. That made sense, as this victim was relatively young. She saw a car—nearly antique, but shiny and low slung. Then she'd seen the image of a young woman lying naked under him, and Eleri yanked her hand back, stomach turning.

She hadn't needed to see that. Donovan caught the action as she walked casually to the sink, her stomach still upset as she washed her hands. "I think there's something about the age of the skeleton that changes what I see. The trauma of the death is fresh in the beginning. But it seems a lot of times, the longer it decays, the more the bigger memories come out."

Her partner frowned. "You don't think being tortured, slashed, and shot is a big memory?"

"It clearly wasn't big enough for Earlene Beaman." She'd gotten no memories of the crime from that skeleton, either. "It doesn't seem to be the highlight of this guy's life."

She wanted to name him, but they still hadn't quite figured out who he was. Having identified him as male helped immensely. Donovan was still sitting at the table, still sorting the missing persons reports from the area.

"I don't think he's there." She waved to the computer and the printed pages they'd laid out. Something told Eleri that they hadn't found his name among the missing, and that they wouldn't.

She hadn't seen his face in any of the images. Sadly, memories of looking into the mirror didn't seem to be the ones she could pick up. "If the people he knew simply thought he'd left without telling them, then he doesn't strike me as the most upstanding citizen, or the guy with the best friends."

Donovan was nodding along. He wasn't gathering up the reports to put them away, but he was close. "Do you think he was the kind that, if he didn't clock in at work one day, they would simply assume he was being irresponsible? Then, maybe five days later, they would assume he'd quit, rather than that something nefarious had happened?"

Eleri didn't know. Bonfires, old cars, and sex didn't tell her enough to distinguish him from any other early-twenties Florida dude.

She checked her messages again, hoping the botanist could identify the plant that had grown roots into the eye socket of the skull. She'd collected the entire thing, sending off pictures and saving the plant itself at the DeSoto lab, hoping someone could use it to determine how long the body had been in the ground. But honestly, the plant was probably seasonal.

"I want a better time of death, because he's not coming to us." She gestured to the reports. "We're going to have to go out and find this guy.

"You're assuming we *can* find him." Donovan looked up and leaned back, probably as happy as she was to not have his face down over the old files anymore.

"What do you mean?" They could find the missing vic, couldn't they?

"We're assuming he's from Astoria, or at least this area. This is the Everglades. If I lived in a five-hour radius of here, this is where I'd bring my bodies to decompose."

Crap. She had to agree with that.

Donovan did tend to run off-trail, not the kind of places the average hikers go. When they'd retraced his steps yesterday morning, she'd passed through more than one standing bog—though she was certain that's not what it was called in the Everglades. Anyone willing to put on a pair of tall boots could bury a body where most others wouldn't check. It might never be found. If not for Donovan's roving nature, this one might not have been.

But, while Donovan had been on his run, he'd found *three* sites, producing two almost fully intact skeletons.

How many more bodies were out in the Everglades?

14

Donovan threw his pencil down onto the yellow legal notepad. "The third body was supposed to give us *more* information, not *less*."

Eleri looked sympathetic. It was getting even harder to determine a plausible connection between Earlene Beaman, JP Talley, and this unidentified skeleton.

The evidence was certainly enough to tie them together, but they'd found nothing more. His brain was dead. He had the dumb. "I'm tapping out."

Eleri joined him, making the large office chair creak as she sighed and leaned back. "So let's ask a different question."

"Let's ask it over dinner," he countered, checking the time. The days were filled with information gathering but, as of yet, all he'd gotten were a handful of more puzzle pieces. He still had no idea what the picture would look like or where any individual piece went. He'd yet to click any two of them together.

Eleri stood, making the effort he couldn't quite bring himself to. She looked around the suite. The large table she'd requested the hotel bring up, held all the papers they'd spread out. The beauty of being here was that they could leave everything and walk away. Donovan was more than happy to change the conversation for a few minutes to finding an adequate restaurant.

"I want steak." He always wanted steak, but this time, Eleri didn't comment. She simply walked around the small space as if happy to be moving her legs.

He looked for local restaurants and wasn't finding anything. "The next time we're in Tampa with a few hours to kill, I want to go to that restaurant in Ybor City. The old one, over a hundred years old."

Eleri didn't reply, but her expression said both *of course* and acknowledged that it was unlikely they'd ever be in Tampa with enough extra time for a four-course meal. He could dream. Just apparently not about steak. Not tonight.

"I'm giving up on steaks. Let's do Mexican." He held up the address and then followed her out of the hotel, quiet until they were seated in the back corner of the bright but shadowy restaurant. Even so, it was a bit crowded for his taste.

Eleri let him put his back to the mirrored wall, knowing he felt safer that way. She leaned in. "The good news is, I don't think anyone can overhear us."

Donovan nodded as he tried the salsa, the heat happily blooming through his sinuses as he managed to put off the discussion for just a few more moments. Eleri wasn't having it, though.

"This body seemed more hidden."

He nodded along, still shoveling in chips, hungrier than he'd expected. But she was right. He'd gone deeper into an area less traveled by humans, and this body had been buried well enough that the scavengers hadn't pulled it up. It was only as he was nodding along that he caught her point.

"Beaman and Talley weren't, though. Talley was left on the surface, just abandoned as if waiting for someone to find him. And Beaman..." she trailed off as Donovan searched his memory, trying to think back to what he'd read.

"I don't recall how long they took to find Beaman after she was dead."

Eleri shook her head. "She was apparently readily identifiable. So she couldn't have gone through that much decomp."

"With the weather down here—" he lifted his hand as if holding up the humidity that weighted the air. "—it would happen even faster than usual."

"Dr. Brzezinski's report suggested that she was killed very shortly after the last time she was seen." Eleri leaned forward, another puzzle piece shaping her expression. "So what changed? Why get *worse* at hiding your bodies?"

15

"How much further out do we go?" *This sucked.* He hated spider maps to the depth of his soul.

Donovan remembered training at Quantico—searching buildings with a designated partner and getting shot. He remembered the adrenaline and the bright pink paint splatter on his vest, letting him know that he was dead and he had failed.

The academic work had been more to his liking. The research into interrogation techniques, serial killers, and the psychology behind crime and evasion was fascinating. The legal aspect was terrifying. At one point, he decided it was virtually impossible to put someone away for the crime they'd actually committed. One needed to simply find some bizarre clause the person had violated and put them on trial for that, much the way Capone had gone down for tax evasion.

But no one had warned him that he wouldn't always be running through pop-up scenarios and shooting criminals. He wouldn't always be interrogating witnesses. Sometimes witnesses couldn't be found and he would spend three days making spider maps.

He could feel his teeth grinding. He'd learned about contact tracing in med school. At the time, the epidemiological tracing had seemed wildly useful. Now, looking at a graphic that showed all of JP Talley's acquaintances, all of his wife's acquaintances, and all three daughters' immediate acquaintances—yes, he'd listed the known contacts of the two-year-old—he didn't feel the same.

In the end, he'd basically filled out an entire map of Astoria. Eleri had done a similar one for Earlene Beaman. Though Beaman, it seemed, had lived a less-connected life, so Eleri's job had been a little easier. But Beaman had two sons and Eleri had to contact trace them, too. One of the boys had the good sense to leave the state, cutting down Eleri's map.

In the end, they'd fed the results into the system and come up with exactly zero overlap. Just in case Donovan hadn't hated it enough when he was doing it.

They'd then gone back and tracked another generation of contacts. It was still coming up with virtually zero reasonable overlap. Beaman and Talley had lived separate lives, despite the fact they lived in a town of less than 9,000 people.

"I can't do any more of these." The maps involved calling people, tracing financial transactions, and getting warrants to get access to records. Donovan looked across the table. "It's time for you to steal one of those bones and sleep with it under your pillow."

She raised one eyebrow at him, but he shrugged it off. It wasn't as if she hadn't done something similar before.

Eleri quickly countered, "I'll happily sleep with a photograph, but putting this guy's bones under my pillow crosses a line."

Donovan heard her exact words. It wasn't bones per se, it was *these bones.* There had to be a spell somewhere in that book she'd found in the attic…

"If we had a photograph of this guy," he said, "we wouldn't need you to sleep with his damn bones under your pillow."

He shouldn't have sounded so angry. He wasn't upset with Eleri at all. "I'm sorry. Ignore me."

"We have the bones." At least she didn't sound mad. "I've already touched them. I didn't like what I saw. I'm not anxious to add that into my dreams."

He frowned. "What exactly did you see that you didn't like?"

She'd reported most of it to him, but then she'd yanked her hand back. He hadn't pushed at the time. He just let her walk it off.

"I don't know. Everything I *saw* was actually fine. It was just the feeling I got toward the end that I didn't want to be touching this guy."

"Was that during the sex scene?" He was referring to what she had commented on as though she were relaying images from a movie to him.

She nodded. "I wonder why that was."

"Maybe you're just too puritanical." He offered it with an overly charming smile. But Eleri shook her head. Unfortunately, it left them at a bit of an impasse.

They were more than twenty-four hours away from when he'd found the remains, but they didn't have twenty-four hours of answers to show for it. In fact, he was wondering if he'd wasted a day and a half of their time. Donovan did believe that the extra set of bones would eventually prove useful. Then again, he'd believed this one would give up much more information, much faster than it had. So maybe he was just wrong.

The one result they'd gotten back was from the botanist. She had confirmed that the plant that had grown through the skull was seasonal. That indicated the skeleton had been in the ground at least six months past being skeletonized. But since they were relatively confident it was at least five years old, the new information was no use whatsoever.

A few more missing persons cases had trickled in. But none was a good enough match to even proceed to the testing phase. Luckily, the man was relatively young, and age estimates on a skeleton had narrower windows the younger the victim was.

Someone like Beaman—if she'd gone unidentified—might have been aged as somewhere between forty and seventy. That span would dramatically widen the missing persons search. He could be grateful for that little bit of information, at least.

"We need to have a fourth body," Eleri said as though confident one did exist. "Or even a fifth or sixth."

"Obviously, but where do we find them?"

"You tell me." She was looking at him directly, as though realizing something he didn't.

He thought about his path through the woods and the desire to stretch his legs combined with thinking he would just "play cadaver dog" while he was out. He responded, "I was just running randomly."

But Eleri tipped her head further, her expression knowing. "But were you?"

16

Eleri felt her ankle twist. But since it was under seven inches of thick, muddy water, she had no idea what she'd stepped on. Log? Nutria? Alligator? She had no clue.

Donovan's head popped up as if to ask *Are you okay?*

"Doesn't hurt. I just feel stupid."

The whole episode felt awful. Rivulets of sweat ran down her back beneath her pack. It wasn't that the day was too hot, it was simply too humid. Eleri was convinced it might not even be her own sweat, it might just be the humidity in the air condensing on her. Either way, it felt gross and she plucked at her shirt, tugging where it stuck to her skin. It only helped for a moment.

This was the second day they'd come searching the Glades—FBI Agent Eames and her trusty cadaver dog. She'd told the locals that his name was Biren, Donovan's middle name. Not that she ever used it and not that she would remember to use it in an important situation. But she was damn well going to try.

It didn't matter. They hadn't come across a single other soul the entire time they'd been out here.

"We triangulated everything, but there's nothing here, Donovan," she said, realizing even as the words came out of her mouth that she was complete shit at using a different name for him.

She was ready to tap out but wasn't going to say it. The problem was, her partner seemed to have boundless energy and wasn't affected by the heat at all.

They'd noted the locations of the previous bodies—Earlene Beaman, JP Talley, and their unidentified victim. Then they'd found the nearest Everglades park and started searching. Donavan had a good feeling about the location and—since he'd found the third body—Eleri figured that was as good a confirmation as she would get that they were headed in the right direction.

When they'd made it to the hotel the previous night, after their first fruitless day of searching, she'd showered off the sweat and sticky air and managed to get into pajamas before Donovan wandered into her room. He told her he'd smelled it—the same thing he'd smelled when he found the third victim.

So she'd come back out this morning, convinced there was something here.

Now, she wasn't so sure.

This was definitely needle-in-a-haystack searching. Eleri wouldn't have minded it if she wasn't so damn sweaty and occasionally stepping into things that were so damn gross. Get her a dead body decomposing into black ooze or bloated with gas and ready to pop any day. It was better than this swamp.

The night before, Donovan had offered, "I can search tomorrow by myself…" But she'd shaken him off quickly. It had sounded ridiculous. She needed to be here. She needed to excavate any bodies they found so they wouldn't have to cover his digging. They wouldn't have to leave a body unattended and hope that no one else found it in the meantime. And they wouldn't have to deal with what would happen if Donovan ran into a human who was petrified of a nearly two-hundred-pound black wolf in the freaking Everglades.

But as she looked around now, she realized no one was going to stumble across a body here, even if they dug it up and taped bright yellow crime scene tape all around it. None of those worries was ever going to be a problem.

Eleri curled her toes to pull her foot out of the sucking soil, trying to make sure her boot stayed on. It was a painful process and only got her one step farther.

She huffed out a breath. Donovan could cover a lot more territory without her. Even now, she was walking a relatively straight line and he was literally running circles around her. Initially, he hadn't gotten too far away, but as the day pressed on, he wandered farther and farther out of her sight.

She couldn't even see him now, not since he'd last put his nose to the ground and took off happily loping through the boggy land as Eleri slowly picked her way along behind him. The muscles of her feet and calves clenched to keep her boots on her feet and she was about five minutes from a bad cramp. She generally considered herself to be in good shape, but swamp walking seemed to take an entirely different set of muscles than she was used to.

The night before, she'd been exhausted. Tonight, she was going to be in pain.

Reaching down, she grabbed the upper loop of the boot, thankful that someone had thought of this, and pulled upward as she lifted her foot. The frustration and the aching muscles didn't make it any easier to catch her balance. She was also confident that her irritation would lead to mistakes, and mistakes would lead to going face first into the bog water.

She could still hear Donovan correcting her last night, as she now reached down and pulled on the other boot, slowly getting one step forward. "It's not a bog. It's a swamp or a glade."

She'd thanked him wryly for the vocabulary lesson, and promptly fallen dead asleep.

For some reason now, it occurred to her that Donovan's allotted four days had passed, and she had not called Avery. She had messaged her boyfriend a handful of times, as they often did. His career in the NHL and hers in the FBI made their schedules wonky enough that texting was the easiest mode if they weren't both readily available.

Donovan hadn't pushed, not for a while. Maybe he'd figured out that it was easier for her to push back against him when he was actively trying to shove her in one direction. Without his constant haranguing, she was starting to see the wisdom of what he said.

Still, she agreed with her own assessment: She needed to see Avery in person. He would need a demonstration of at least a minimal amount of her skills. Otherwise, why believe any of it? It was truly unbelievable.

She was reaching down for the first boot again, when she heard it —three sharp barks in a row. They were farther away than she had expected. Donovan had gotten ahead.

But three sharp barks, meant that he'd found a body.

17

Donovan had barked, hating the sound of his own voice this way. He tended to only speak as a wolf when necessary. But now, hearing no reply from her, he'd given another call.

Most of his communication with Eleri had been head gestures. Yes and no, tipping his head side to side for *maybe* or *I don't know.* This time, the barks had been necessary. Eleri was nowhere in sight.

Pausing for a moment, he flicked his ears in a variety of directions hoping to pick up on the small sounds that would tell him where she was. Sure enough, he found her. It wasn't so much the sound of her sloshing noisily through the standing water and sticky ground, but the grumbling and cursing that caught his ears.

If he could have smiled, he would have. If she was bitching about it, she was okay.

He turned back to the scent. It had started in the middle of the trail, just appearing out of nowhere and startling him. That was strange, but he'd followed it backward to where it clung to a spot covered in a good six inches of water with slime and algae. Once again, it was the same scent that had led him to the last victim.

He was confident now he was trailing the killer. If it wasn't the killer, it was definitely someone who knew where the bodies were buried. And this was the second time the trail had ended abruptly. He filed that for later.

Though the scent didn't come directly on top of the body, it had made it to the edge of the small marshy area. That let Donovan's now- hypersensitive nose pick up the decaying flesh under all the other flavors coming through the air.

He scented the green of trees and plant life that hovered thickly above. Below was a knot of floral decay. At nose level, the rise of algae and occasional burst of a flower sent out signals, as did the latent path of an animal.

A turtle popped up near him, neither of them any threat to the other. It eyed Donovan in a way it would never do if he was in his human form. He watched it for a few moments, telling himself that he was waiting for Eleri to show up and not just playing with a turtle. But then, the turtle suddenly disappeared beneath the water with a richly textured plop to accompany the move.

Donovan turned back to his job. This was going to be a mess but —maybe luckily, given the standing water and the algae slime—there would be nothing for Eleri to have to cover up.

He began to dig one paw into the warm wetness, pushing downward until he hit a slightly heavier mud. Once he was under the surface, he pulled backward, but the stroke hit nothing. He did it again and again. And each time he did it, the smell of human, long since passed, wafted up into his nostrils.

Unlike the humans he saw out with their poking sticks, testing the ground for softness and digging in an area that might be a grave, Donovan had no doubt that there was a body down here. This wasn't just a site where the bones had been scavenged—the smell was too strong. This body was *still here*.

He swiped a little more to the right, the scent stronger this time. He did it again and again until his paw hit something hard. This was the downside: Paw pads were more sensitive than people expected, but still weren't like a fingertip. The thick, rough surfaces were designed to protect him from the ground in the absence of shoes, not test the surface of a human bone.

While his nail shouldn't leave any obvious, permanent marks on the bone, he might leave micro scratches, and he was hesitant to test it again. He sat back before realizing he'd just sunk his ass into the same swampy water he'd been digging in. Too late now.

Barking three times again, he was met with a grumbled, "I'm coming."

As he listened to Eleri crashing through the trees and the plants behind him, he waited, rather than digging again.

Eleri showed up carrying the large pack. She carried all of it herself, the downside of his being in this form. She even had his clothing with her, not making him tie it up in a tree and leave it behind, chancing that someone would find it. However, unless he could find a shower, this wasn't going to be the place to change.

She spotted him then, ankle deep in the muck. He would have thought she'd be more excited about a body, related to the case or not. Honestly, he couldn't quite be sure the killer had been here, only that someone had come by—someone who'd been at or near the other two scenes they knew about. He couldn't think of another scenario except that it was the killer, most likely checking to be sure that this body was still hidden.

It was possible that this body wasn't related to the case. It could be that the killer had simply stopped by, maybe thinking this would be a good future dump site. Clearly it was: There was already a body here. Or maybe the killer had passed by this spot on the way to another one. As Eleri had pointed out, surely the Everglades were full of lost hikers who tripped, starved, or drowned and had simply been consumed by the swamp as well as every corpse left by a killer, purposeful or accidental, who'd decided this was the place to hide the evidence.

She pulled the pack off and looked around. Finding no safe dry ground to set it on, she hung it on the branch of a nearby tree. The supple limbs bent under the weight. There were no sturdy oaks with low branches for climbing here in the Glades.

When she turned back, he saw her examine the area where he sat. He understood her expression asking him, "Are you sure?"

This wasn't the kind of place she would want to wade into unless they were certain a body was waiting for them.

He nodded in a very solid answer, and Eleri got to work.

18

"Oh, gross." Her words echoed back to her from the tile of the shower chamber, but the DeSoto County ME's office was a welcome relief.

She and Donovan were not new at this and they'd purchased a ten gallon drum of water beforehand. So Donovan had been rinsed when they got back to the car and he was cleaned long before she could do the same. She'd put him into the back of the vehicle and waited while he went through the painful shift back to his human self.

She'd knocked on the window and watched as he climbed, now dressed, into the driver's seat. Eleri went about the business of laying out a thick beach towel on the passenger seat for her own dirty ass to sit on and tried not to resent that she stank and was sweaty while he was clean. She'd made him drive them back here.

The bones were in bags, and everything stored as properly as it could be. Though she was a professional and had brought waders and veterinary style gloves that went up almost to her armpits, she'd still managed to get some of the swamp on her. It was simply unavoidable.

Luckily, the office was deserted in the middle of the night, though she was confident there were cameras in several key locations. Every morgue dealt with the disturbing issue of someone eventually trying to steal at least one body. But this way, they didn't have to explain how she brought a dog in and left with a man. She hoped the cameras weren't good enough that she would have to explain why one of them arrived clean and the other filthy.

She used an inordinate amount of soap and kept scrubbing long after she was clean. She understood what she was doing now was merely washing her psyche, but she did it anyway. There were clean towels waiting when she finally turned off the water, but they were just a shade off of white.

Had they been cream, she might have let herself believe they'd been born that way. But the hint of gray told her that these—like everything else at the MEs office—were not being upgraded on the regular. She'd added fistfuls of conditioner into her hair, letting it sit for a moment and not rinsing all of it out. Her thick, coarse curls wanted to spring into shape. Her freckles were about the only thing that showed through the haze on the mirror. Both harkened back to an ancestry she'd only recently learned was thick in her blood.

She knew what the rough towel was doing to her hair, but she wrapped her head anyway. Stepping out into the steamy room, she felt her lip curl. Normally, the cool hit of leaving the shower was a pleasure for a warm-blooded girl. But here, there was no cool hit. Even in the medical center with the air conditioner running and filtering the best it could, the air was still too sticky for her to get completely dry.

The thing that motivated her to try to dry off was knowing that Donovan was in the main room, laying out the bones, taking samples, and rinsing them. Documenting the scene had taken all afternoon and well into dark. She'd brought up as much of the skeleton as she could, but they were still missing most of the ankle and wrist bones. Aside from half of one scapula and two different ribs, they'd managed to reclaim everything major.

Her clothing clung and her stomach grumbled, despite the two energy bars and bottle of water she'd fed it in the car. They'd gone too long without eating, but the vending machines here oddly had only chips and crackers—nothing that could be eaten over a body without producing enough crumbs to ruin an autopsy.

She stepped into the main exam room to find Donovan over the metal table hosing off the last of the bones.

"You got pictures?" It was dumb. Of course he did.

But he cheerfully answered, "So many."

Then he motioned to a second table where he'd left the full

scapula and a femur for her to examine for herself. They were still covered in swamp slime, uncleaned and waiting for every bit of inspection.

This man knew her. No one, but no one, would set aside algae- and slime-covered bones as a gift, except a medical examiner who understood his partner—the forensic scientist with profiling training.

"Thank you." She offered her best smile of the day, hoping her words covered up yet another growl from her stomach. She entertained the idea that they could come back and do the bulk of this work tomorrow, but the medical center would be hopping then. And she was beginning to think it was better to go vampire mode and sleep through the heat of the day. After spending the last days in the Glades, she wasn't sure she even breathed the air so much as it pushed its way into her lungs.

Stepping up to the second table, she heard the spatter of water on metal behind her as Donovan finished cleaning the remaining bones with the overhead sprayer. He'd already had the skeleton laid out mostly in order before he started.

"What samples did you get?" she asked but didn't look back. As he recited what he'd scraped and plucked and swabbed and packed into vials, she reached up for the sprayer overhead and watched as the algae either slid away from the bone or clung firmly.

The bones themselves weren't green, but a very yellowish-brown. Having aged in the swamp, the body had fully skeletonized amid whatever strange plants and pH the place preserved. She carefully searched the surface as one color washed away, leaving the other, truer color behind.

Swinging around the magnifying glass, she checked for anything other than bone, then asked over her shoulder, "Any tissue?"

"Nothing that was distinguishable from the algae or the muck."

She was thinking the same thing; nothing organic clinging to these bones had belonged to the original user. With the force of the water—not wanting to rub the bone clean, not yet—Eleri worked her way down to mostly smooth surfaces. All traces of the Everglades were gone, aside from the discoloring.

She picked them up and turned them over, gloved hands not quite as sensitive as bare fingers, and she headed back to Donovan's table, placing them into their proper locations.

He waved one open palm toward the skeleton. He then pointed to the humerus. "I'm guessing the vic was about five-seven."

"Did you measure it?" The box to do so remained pushed against the wall, untouched.

Instead, he plucked the bone and held it next to his own bicep. "Shorter than mine. I'm pretty good at estimating it this way."

She rolled her eyes at him. He was probably right, and she'd done it, too, but … she wouldn't make them do the measurement conversion tonight. Instead, she glanced at the skull and the pelvis.

"Female," she murmured, figuring he hadn't missed that part. She also noted that a good number of teeth were still intact. Though many were missing, she hoped for enough to perform a dental match.

Then, Donovan pointed again. It was difficult to see with the discoloration. But there it was.

"Bingo," she said.

19

"I love you."

The words stared up at her from her phone screen as she blinked herself awake in the early afternoon. Another message from Avery ending with the same three words every time.

Eleri replied, telling him the case was going smoothly, if slowly. They'd been here for eleven days now and were making only the most plodding of progress. She legally couldn't tell him they'd found another victim or that they definitively had a serial killer. She did, however, send him a link to the local newspaper.

It seemed as though everyone they'd interviewed had decided to talk to the press. Though Eleri and Donovan hadn't confirmed the serial killer angle at all, a journalist for the local paper—a Jesse Nash—was speculating heavily and doing far too good a job at it.

So those few things were all that Avery could be told. He had no issue with sometimes not even knowing where she was. And she sometimes didn't know where he was, though usually his game schedule was readily available online.

Finishing up her message, she paused, then tapped back her own four words. "I love you, too."

But did she?

At one in the afternoon, in the sterile air conditioning of her hotel room, she questioned her own feelings. If nothing else was in the way, the answer would have been handy. *Easy*. Yes. She loved him.

But could he love her if he didn't know who and what she really was?

And how mad could he be when she told him the truth?

The answer was *very*. And righteously so.

Eleri began to formulate a plan.

Ten minutes later, her phone buzzed again and she picked it up with trepidation—her new feeling when she got messages from Avery. The sensation confirmed that Donovan was absolutely right. But this wasn't Avery. It was her partner.

"Who wants food?" The message made her smile. It was followed immediately by another buzz. "And who wants to do more spider maps?"

She laughed at that, coming fully awake with the knowledge that there might not be anything Donovan hated more than spider maps.

She wrote back, "Ooh. Also, financials!"

Though getting those would depend on them identifying the victim first. They'd done everything they could to examine the bones. They'd taken all their pictures, scrubbed them until the surface was a lighter shade, and examined everything again.

At five a.m. she had borrowed yet another bone box from the DeSoto County Medical Examiner's Office and placed this woman's bones in them. Eleri labeled it only "#4," but in her notes she estimated three years of time since death.

This woman could be a missing link.

Today their job would include further attempts to identify Number Three, and initial attempts to identify Number Four. Eleri stood up, stretching muscles that protested deep in their core. Though she'd hoped a good night's sleep would make everything feel better, she'd known it wouldn't actually happen. This morning—or this afternoon, as it were—her hopes were dashed.

She creaked her way into a fast, hot shower, fighting the urge to moan each time her leg or back protested. Not only did sloshing her way through the swamp require previously unused muscles, but she was also more than a little rusty at being down on her hands and knees, pulling up a skeleton. She got the feeling she'd been given a pass on Number Three, but with Number Four, her body was screaming "No more!"

She was in and out and drying herself before she could think about lingering in the heat. At least this time she felt she managed to get much closer to *dry*. She would never curse the Virginia humidity again.

Pulling on her clothing, she moved fluidly, refusing to give her sore muscles any attention. She ran a wide-tooth comb through her hair and thought again about the victims.

Chronologically, Number Three was the first victim that they knew of. Number Four was second. Probably about a year after that, Earlene Beaman would be third. Lastly, with another year gap, JP Talley would be the fourth.

Not being able to identify the earliest victim bothered her no end. It meant no contact tracing, no financials to check, no family members to interview, nothing except the confirmation that their killer had been working for some time.

Fifteen minutes later, they were back at what was now Donovan's favorite diner. On his first visit, he had discovered a breakfast plate called the Gator Chomp that was served all day. She couldn't say she was unhappy with turning two p.m. into breakfast time. She'd barely been up for an hour by the time the first bite of food went into her mouth.

The odd afternoon time left the diner relatively empty, and she finally didn't feel the need to check the trees beyond the parking lot. She hated the feeling of being watched and was glad it had finally left. However, with only the one server on shift, the next couple who entered was seated directly behind Eleri, which stymied any conversation they might have had about the case. She found she didn't care. She didn't have anything to add right now. Not until they figured out what was going on with Number Four.

So they talked about the weather and about Avery's latest win. She noticed she breathed easier, just chatting about normal things. For a moment, she fantasized a dinner party… but the image got filed under "never going to happen" because she couldn't imagine Walter passing the rolls and Donovan sitting at the table elbow-to-elbow with everyone else. But maybe, if she adjusted it …

Once again, Donovan didn't push her to tell Avery the truth, and Eleri began to admire the fact that she had been expertly played. She volunteered her plan to show her boyfriend in person not only what she could do, but why. Might as well admit that Donovan was right. He thoughtfully nodded as he shoveled food into his mouth.

"You're going to show him that book and everything?"

"Yeah. I need to dive in headfirst. Anything else is … pointless."

Donovan's seal of approval meant more than she had expected. Eleri finished the last sip of her coffee and paid the check—she had stopped eating minutes ago—as Donovan scraped up the last few bites from his plate.

They stopped by the Hardee County Sheriff's Office and shared the new information with the Sheriff. This time, as Tucker put one finger in the belt loop of his pants and hiked them, he looked thoughtful.

He carefully held the tablet Eleri handed him with the picture of the skull. He tapped on the image, his finger on the four top, front incisors—the only intact teeth that could be seen in the picture.

She added, "We think she was killed and buried about three years ago."

Sheriff Tucker looked like he had a thought. Sure enough, he silently handed the tablet back, disappeared into a storage room, and returned with a file.

20

"I found it," Donovan announced happily. "I found the one thing all four victims have in common."

Eleri looked up at him. She'd been hunched over her laptop, typing furiously, and occasionally tapping her mouse in between searching for something. Donovan didn't know what she might have been looking for, though he was confident she would tell him if she found anything of value.

"That's impressive, given that we still don't know who the earliest victim was."

"I'm just that good." He grinned, but then got serious. "The one thing they all had in common was nobody cared that they were missing."

That got Eleri's attention. He could tell that she mulled it over for a moment and eventually agreed.

"Earlene Beaman," he continued. "Nobody even knew she was missing until three or four days later. And no one filed an official report."

"I got the impression she was just kind of a lonely woman." Eleri's words opened the possibility that the woman wasn't disliked, simply unwatched.

"It's plausible," Donovan said, "but she did have a job—it was her boss who eventually reported her. By that point, they'd found the body and that made the match."

Moving as he talked, he set aside the paper folder on Beaman and tapped on the screen. "JP Talley. Remember, the wife said they'd had a fight and she thought he'd run off? There was no formal missing person's report filed for him, either. His body was found before she cared that good old JP wasn't just going to turn up later."

"And the earliest guy," Eleri started filling in. She was getting into it now, Donovan could tell. "We can't even match him to a missing person's report at all."

Donovan nodded. It was the new victim that had really solidified it for him. "And Josefina Wolkov—" he put his finger on the flyer that Tucker had brought out to them. It was something about the front teeth that had grabbed the sheriff, and the fact that it was female in the right age range.

Tucker had handed the envelope to Eleri, who had opened it and poured the contents onto a nearby desktop. She'd sorted through a necklace and a few IDs for the small x-ray films and offered up a preliminary dental match on the spot. It had taken three hours and a few skull x-rays, and she'd officially confirmed it.

The body they'd pulled up the day before was Josefina Wolkov—wife, hairstylist, and all-around flake. The clincher was her missing person's report. Her husband had filed it a *month* after she disappeared.

According to his interviews in the file, the two hadn't even been fighting. But Mark Wolkov made it clear the marriage had been slowly dissolving for several years. He was confident Josephina had several extra-marital lovers. And when she first disappeared, he was convinced she'd simply run off with one of them for a while.

When her work called, he'd said she'd left town. He paid the mortgage himself and so on. It was only a month later, when she hadn't replied to anyone and her mother had had a stroke, that he'd tried desperately to reach her. According to Mark, he was just trying to be a good citizen. He hadn't felt the loss of his wife and was considering filing for divorce.

He'd said when she didn't reply for a week about her mother, he realized she wasn't reachable. He'd filed an official report then, believing the police would have better luck tracking her down. But no one had had any luck finding Josefina. Mark had signed over open access to all their financial and phone records. He'd agreed to every search the police asked for. The notes said he remained a person of suspicion because he didn't seem upset that his wife was gone.

Only once he realized that she'd not touched their joint bank account, and that none of her cards had been used, and her ID hadn't been scanned for any travel since the last day he'd seen her, had Mark Wolkov begun to suspect foul play.

"These people went missing and no one told the police, Eleri. No one cared they were gone."

"Actually, I get the feeling sometimes the families were *glad* they were gone."

"Talley's wife seems upset."

Eleri motioned with one hand to make her point. "But not upset enough to report him. She did nothing at all until after the body was found. I think she wants us to think she's sad, but she isn't really." She paused. "I think you're right, but what do we do with this information? Does it help us identify victim Number One?"

Currently, that body was the one with the least information. Donovan thought about it for a moment. "It sounds like we need to interview Talley's wife, Rebecca, again. And then we need to interview Mark Wolkov. They have to know something they aren't telling."

21

"Go back upstairs, honey," Rebecca Talley pushed her oldest daughter out of the room as she twisted her fingers together, before looking up suddenly.

Eleri followed her line of sight. One of the younger daughters was at the top of the stairs.

Rebecca tried again, her voice firm but authoritative. "Kaylee, please go back and play in your room with Marissa."

It was the oldest, Marissa, who protested. "Can I ask a question?"

Mrs. Talley tossed Eleri and Donovan a quick, apologetic look, but Eleri waved her off.

"When will we be able to come out of my room?"

"When I'm done here."

That wasn't good enough for the eight-year-old. "But when will that *be?*"

Clearly the kids were getting cranky, and Eleri figured they had about all they could handle. She motioned to Rebecca and answered the child herself. "I think maybe just another ten minutes."

It was an experiment of sorts. The daughter happily took the answer and seemed to believe she had a good grasp on what ten minutes was. She was also in charge of her younger sisters, including the youngest, who was still just a toddler.

Eleri remembered those days—how long it seemed, trying to

entertain a very young child when she was just a child herself. But the most interesting reaction wasn't Marissa's, it was Rebecca's.

The woman had something holding up her spine. But, with Eleri's announcement, she practically oozed relief that this was about to be over. Though Rebecca had played the perfect wife, Eleri was quite confident that they weren't getting entirely straight answers.

"How are your girls holding up?" she asked the mother as she heard the door click shut behind the older daughter.

"As well as can be expected," Rebecca offered with a blank shrug and a blink. But that was the issue, Eleri thought. How well could a child be expected to hold up when their father had gone missing and turned up murdered?

These two weren't acting out. They weren't screaming and crying. Maybe it was simply because people were around—many kids did behave better in the presence of strangers. Or maybe it was because the girls didn't miss their father at all.

Rebecca had certainly offered up enough evasive answers and excuses. "I'm not sure how I feel." "I think I'm not really reacting because I'm numb." "We had a fight, and sometimes he would stay out all night. So it didn't concern me at first."

Eleri tried something else and asked a bizarre question, hoping it didn't read quite as odd as it was. "How does the house feel without him in it?"

"Quieter." The word fell out of Rebecca's mouth quickly and easily. The stark truth. She backpedaled rapidly. "He had a big personality."

But Eleri's initial impression was that quieter was better.

She looked to Donovan, and it was clear from the way he sat, hands folded in his lap, leaning slightly forward, that he didn't have anything to add. He had his best comforting but blank expression plastered on his face and he was probably trying to smell if Rebecca was lying through her teeth.

Eleri found she was more interested in what Donovan had learned than any repetitive "I don't know" answers from Rebecca.

"We won't take up any more of your time," Eleri told her, standing up and offering a hand to shake. Rebecca Talley followed social protocol and also stood, but though her handshake was warm, her grip was limp. She didn't turn for Donovan until his own hand was out to thank her.

Then Eleri watched as he did that weird thing that Eleri always hated. He clasped his other hand over Rebecca's as though he were trying to be warm but was actually creepy. Eleri watched as Rebecca's shoulders tensed and so did her lower spine. She went stock still, a scared smile plastered on her face as she waited for Donovan to let go before reclaiming her own hand.

Interesting, Eleri thought and tried something else. She reached down for the glass of lemonade the woman had served them. "Can I help out? Clean this? Put our dishes in the sink, at least?"

Rebecca's reaction was swift. Too swift. "Oh no, I've got it! Don't you worry about it at all!"

"Well." Eleri put her best, kind smile on her face. "Please tell your little girls they can come out now and let them know we really appreciate them cooperating."

Leading the way out the door, she didn't look back. Donovan was close behind. As she climbed into the driver's seat, she stuck the key in the ignition and started the AC. She craved the air, even though the temperature wasn't down yet. Just going from the front door to inside the car had pressed in on her a little too much.

"That was weird," she told Donovan after he closed the passenger door behind him. "I mean, the way you grabbed her hand at the end."

"I know." He had a bit of evil glee underpinning his voice. "I wanted to see if she had the wherewithal to take control of her own hand."

"And she didn't," Eleri replied. "She didn't even reach out to shake your hand."

"No, not until I put my hand out."

"The house is quieter with him gone." Eleri repeated the woman's words.

Donovan nodded. "She's not unhappy that he's dead, and I think I know why."

22

"I didn't kill her, if that's what you're asking." Mark Wolkov stated the words calmly but clearly, his eyes shifting between Donovan and Eleri.

Donovan sniffed the air around the man.

Where Rebecca Talley had been nervous, Wolkov was calm. He smelled of the kind of relief that came with a long-standing stress being lifted. Tendrils of anxiety and old fights still lingered in the corners of the room, but Wolkov now was borderline serene. That alone didn't mean he hadn't killed his wife, but Donovan could detect none of the usual scent of lying.

If Donovan hadn't believed the statement—and hadn't been able to smell the accuracy of it—he might have followed this man as a suspect.

He and Eleri remained silent for a moment at the end of Wolkov's declaration of innocence. Sure enough, like most people, Wolkov filled the space.

"Our marriage was not good at the end. Hell, it was never great. But we didn't even fight—well, not much." His eyes darted away, making Donovan wonder what was coming. But his next sentence cleared it up. "We hadn't had sex in almost a year. And for longer than that, it had been few and far between."

Another pause, which Wolkov filled again. "I'm confident she'd had at least two—if not more—boyfriends in the past year."

The sigh he uttered was heavy and deep. "I don't like that my marriage failed. That's a personal black mark on me, but I spent five years trying to save it. And I just couldn't do it … I'm sad that she's dead. I really am. But she's been gone for three years. And once the police investigated it, I understood that she was actually gone, even if no one had found her body."

He emphasized the last word and looked between Eleri and Donovan, and then clarified, even though they hadn't quite asked for it. "I didn't know if she was dead or if she'd simply tried to disappear into a new identity. But if it was the second, then she didn't want to be found. Given the way things were going, if that's what she wanted, I wasn't going to pursue it. I figured maybe one of her boyfriends had enough money to buy her a new ID, maybe give her plastic surgery…"

He'd thought this through.

"What about the rest of her family?" Eleri asked, even though they both already had an idea from the reports.

"She came over from Russia, immigrated when she was in her teens. But it was just her and her mother. My family's Polish, but we've been here for several generations. I suspect if you genetically test me, you'll find the only thing still Polish is the last name. But Phina seemed to like it, though."

He sighed again, the sound heavy and sad. "It's my fault. I just wanted to get married. I wanted to have kids and have the kind of life my parents did. Her mother wanted grandkids and she talked about it all the time. I was young and stupid and didn't think to ask Josephina if *she* actually wanted kids. She seemed to agree to everything I said but, when the time came, there was always a reason not to do it."

"When did things go south?" Eleri prompted him when he seemed to come to a stop. Hopefully, they could prod him a little, and he'd keep running his mouth. Then Donovan could sit here and sniff the bouquet of sadness coming off the guy.

He seemed far more upset about the failure than the woman, though.

"About two years before she disappeared, I confronted her. She finally confessed that she'd never wanted children and she thought she could just keep putting me off."

Despite the mild depression, everything the man said smelled like truth.

Donovan had leaned forward and done as much as he could to

open his nasal cavities without freaking the man out. Wolkov was spilling everything, probably trying to be helpful. Though Donovan wasn't sure yet how it would play out, he suspected something here would be gold.

"That's when the marriage really started to fall apart. So please understand that I'm not losing it now because you found her body. Because I've been getting over it for the past four years. First while she was still here, and then after she was gone." He splayed his hands in front of himself, palms up, as if asking them to understand.

Though Donovan had never been in a similar situation, he felt he could relate.

Eleri backpedaled a little bit, finally really inserting herself into the conversation. "When you tried to save the marriage, what did you do?"

"Personally?" he asked, but immediately answered, "I tried to get over the idea that I had of what a marriage should be. I tried to just let go of the idea that I was going to have a family. I had to not want all the things I'd wanted."

"Anything else?" Eleri asked.

"I saw a therapist for a while. She was really helpful, saw the both of us, but we didn't go to her that long. I got the feeling that the counselor thought we'd be better off divorced, too."

"But you didn't get divorced."

"It seemed like failing at the time. I don't fail." But then he quickly added, "I realized later we'd failed long before and that divorce would have been the easier way out. Maybe if we'd gotten divorced, she wouldn't have wound up involved with whatever got her killed."

That, at least, seemed to bother the man. His scent changed slightly; worry emanated from him, though Donovan couldn't tell what it meant. Was he concerned for his wife in the past tense? Or was he concerned that whatever might have come for her would come for him, too?

23

"I'm sorry, I don't think there's anything more I can tell you." Greg Beaman put his hand to his head, as though holding on the backward baseball cap firmly perched there.

Eleri tried to sit as still as possible for the video conference. Keeping herself squarely in frame, she let Donovan stay out of view, hoping not to overwhelm Earlene Beaman's son with FBI agents crowding his screen.

They'd finally managed to get a hold of one of the Beaman boys. Though Greg had initially been reluctant, and then ultimately agreed to do the interview, now he seemed to want to back out.

"So you didn't really know where your mother was living?"

"No, not really. I mean, I believed she was still in Astoria." He'd answered the same question before and his tone indicated that he didn't want to answer it again. "We weren't in contact. I send her a Christmas card with a picture of my boys each year, mostly just because society tells me to."

"What do you mean?" Eleri thought she knew, but she wanted it in his own words.

"I'm a terrible son for not speaking to my mother. If I leave her alone, it's on me. Nobody seems to care *why* I'm not speaking to her.... My brother doesn't talk to her, either." He turned and motioned to someone off screen, possibly his wife, who reached into the frame and settled an infant into the man's lap. His arms crept around the child protectively, as though something on the screen might jump out and injure his kid. "Honestly, we print out nice Christmas cards and I don't send those to her because they have a return address on it. The year she moved, I didn't even look for the new address."

He paused again. "It was a relief. So I don't know who she was speaking to when she went missing. And I don't know where she lived, or who she interacted with on a daily basis. And I'm sorry, but I'm not going to sit here and cry crocodile tears. I spent years in therapy over that woman."

It was interesting to hear someone refer to his own mother as *that woman*. But all the information that they dug up on Greg Beaman made it an unsurprising answer. His younger brother, Jeff, had basically written an email saying the same thing, except that he didn't have anything to add and wouldn't speak to the FBI at all unless forced to.

"Just a few more questions and I'll let you go." Eleri gestured to the infant he was holding. The baby wasn't fussy, just smiling and seeming to watch the video, given her interested expression.

Eleri hated that she was bringing up bad memories for this man. It almost hurt to be solving the case of someone whose own children didn't necessarily feel justice would be served by finding the killer. But she tried again. "Do you and your brother still speak occasionally?"

"We're not close. Maybe every third year we have Thanksgiving together. We're in touch." The phrasing was off-hand, almost a shrug. She wanted to ask if their shared bad memories kept them away from each other or if it was something else, but that would be getting too personal. Despite what she and Donovan could do, they were still FBI agents, and making this man drudge up a painful past wasn't in the protocol.

"Can I reach out to you again, if we have more questions?"

There was another long pause. His body language froze for a moment before he took a breath. This was clearly something hard to say, but Eleri hadn't expected that from a relatively routine question that wasn't even about his mother. When the words came out of his mouth, she finally understood.

"I'd really rather you didn't. Just getting the email from you took an entire therapy session to work out. I know this call will be the topic of my next therapy session." He waved one hand absently, his lips pressing tightly. Eleri knew how to read body language, and his matched his words. "I'd really rather it just went away."

"I understand." It was all she could offer. "How about I don't reach out unless lives are at stake. Would that be okay?" She was driving a hard bargain and she knew it. Most normal, sympathetic people could not say no to that.

Neither could Greg Beaman.

When he reluctantly agreed, she tried to offer something he might want. "Do you want an update when the case is solved? Or not?"

Another deep breath. Another long moment of contemplation. Jesus. Earlene Beaman had done a number on this guy. "Let's say no for now. But if I get curious, can I reach out?"

"That would be fine." Eleri tried to keep her voice soft and reassuring. She wanted to say something stupid, like, "Hug your baby" or "It looks like you're doing better on your own." But none of that would be appropriate.

She thanked Beaman again and finally hung up, all the while watching as Donovan was pacing off screen. He was irritated that they couldn't travel to do the interview in person. Video completely killed his ability to sniff at their subjects.

The house often gave him a wealth of information, too. He could smell if the person drank regularly and what they drank. He smelled anxiety. The Talley's and their average noses couldn't tell what Donovan could. All of that had been taken away.

Eleri had been more than willing to fly out and meet Greg Beaman. But he was having none of it. Understandably. It was obvious that just speaking about his mother was giving him anxiety.

"That—" Donovan said, "was an abused kid."

She couldn't agree more. "Sounds like he got out and got away, though."

"It makes the Talley house make more sense."

"What do you mean?" *How were the two related?*

Donovan sat down on the small sofa next to her. "I told you that Rebecca Talley was anxious and that it lingered in the house. I didn't put it together at the time, but that kind of anxiety—the kind I could still smell eight days after he'd gone—it's embedded into the carpets and the walls. It's soaked into the paint."

Where was he going with this?

"That means somebody lived in a constant state of anxiety. Fifty bucks says JP Talley was abusing Rebecca, and maybe even the girls."

Slowly, Eleri nodded. Donovan was right. She began to wonder if they were finding a real link.

24

Eleri woke up unrested and anxious.

In her dreams, she replayed Greg Beaman's interview over and over. She saw his arms sliding protectively around the infant. She watched that move he did, with his hand coming up and head tipping down, making a motion to hold onto a hat that was already firmly on his head. She saw his eyes dart away each time he was asked to reveal information about his mother.

She now wanted to rewatch the real video over and over—not just her dream. At one point, dream Greg just kept saying, "I spent years in therapy because of her. I spent years in therapy because of her."

That was a shitty night, Eleri thought, hands behind her on the soft bed not quite supporting her fully upright. Her hand bumped the herbs and sachet she'd been toying with before she'd fallen asleep. Now, she tried to open up her lungs and breathe and let go of all the things that pestered her.

She'd also dreamed of Rebecca Talley, wringing her hands, her eyes darting side to side. She dreamed of a woman opening a bottle of scotch and pouring a small amount into a crystal tumbler. She gulped it, and then quickly, carefully washed out the glass and put it back to dry in exactly the same position it had come from.

None of that had happened during the interview. But Rebecca's nervous gestures and the complete lack of concern over her husband's first day missing was telling. Add in the information gathered from the Greg Beaman interview, and it created an interesting link.

She quickly dressed and headed down the hall to Donovan's room, glad to be the one to knock on his door this time. Her phone told her it was eleven in the morning. Their sleep schedules were entirely off because of their late nights spent at the DeSoto County Medical Examiner's Office. She was beginning to wonder if she was suffering sleep deprivation.

Though she'd been proud to be the first one up this morning, Donovan answered the door dressed and with a smile on his face. "What's for breakfast?"

He was always thinking about food. Physiologically, he must burn thousands of calories just being the creature that he was. Changing probably burned even more.

"I think it needs to be a working meal. Here," she told him, pointing to the floor in the hallway, though she actually meant the room in her suite.

The door handle of the car gave her an odd zing as she opened it, so she turned and checked the surrounding area. Probably still just leftovers from being pulled back onto a case before she'd truly recovered. Ignoring the sensation, she drove them in a loop around town, checking out every drive-thru they passed. But each time, Donovan's lip curled and he suggested they could do better. Half an hour later, they returned to the room with takeout of stacks of waffles and perfectly round and flat sausage patties, ham slices and more.

Donovan had been thrilled to find a Waffle House, but Eleri believed they were more useful as part of the National Weather storm system—Waffle Houses were the last thing to close in a crisis. Since she'd decided to go along with him, she found herself back at the table working not to get sticky syrup all over the paperwork and her computer keys.

This would have been safer if they'd simply bought something cheap, like biscuit sandwiches. But she didn't say it. Donovan seemed happy.

Having finally arranged everything and being in a relatively secure location—she didn't think her neighbors at the hotel were listening in—Eleri started with her thoughts. "Mark Wolkov said that he and Josefina had been in therapy for their marriage."

Donovan nodded, his mouth full, plastic fork and knife firmly in his grip.

"Eric Beaman said he spent *years* in therapy. Do you want to check up on Rebecca Talley?"

"It is an interesting angle," Donovan mused, "But we don't know that Josefina Wolkov was abusive."

"True. But emotionally, it sounds like she put him through the wringer."

Again, Donovan nodded. "And mystery guy—Number One—still unknown?"

There was nothing there. Not even in what Eleri had seen.

They had already scoured financials and even found the counselor Mark Wolkov had gone to.

"It'll be easier if we can get him to sign off on us looking at the session notes from his therapy. I mean, he handed over everything else pretty easily." Donovan finished the last bites of his food and stood to clear the little table of their breakfast. It took forever to find new snippets of information, and Eleri was eager to chase the one thing they had.

"I don't know. I mean, we should ask. But it's one thing to hand over where your credit card was. It's another thing entirely to hand over the things you told your therapist in confidence." She thought about it for a minute. "We might be able to get the therapist to give us a general idea, though?"

"I don't know. Sounds like a HIPAA violation to me."

Eleri felt her lips twitch. "We need Christina or Noah!"

Donovan laughed. "It's *still* a massive HIPAA violation. Even if the therapist doesn't know that it is."

Christina or Noah could have made the therapist either want to break HIPAA, or else believe they were holding a signed document releasing the information. Either one would have made getting the things Eleri wanted much easier. But Christina and Noah weren't here. And Eleri was pretty certain that neither of them would agree to such a blatant violation of privacy. "Then, let's see if we can just get him to sign it."

"If he does, it will tip him off that we're looking into that information."

"Is there an alternative?"

They didn't come up with a good answer. The roadblocks were

making her want to chew nails. They weren't blocks that she and Donovan couldn't cross either, just blocks that were very sketchy—ones her own morals didn't allow.

"I want to call Greg Beaman back and ask him who he saw for therapy. But I pretty much agreed not to reach out unless it was life or death." She sighed right as her phone rang.

Her eyes lifted to Donovan as she answered. "Hello?"

"Sheriff Tucker. Hardee County office."

She'd known that from the screen but appreciated his formal introduction. "What can I do for you, Sheriff?"

"I think it's about what I can do for you. I've got something you guys are going to want to come see."

25

Donovan felt his head snap back as Dr. Brzezinski pulled back the tarp.

The smell had multiple layers, but it wasn't the rotting flesh that made him recoil—it was the salt.

"Oh my god," Eleri replied from right next to him. "They got preserved with the salt and… it preserved them together."

This was new to all of them. It was too difficult to tell where the flesh of one began and the other ended. Their clothing was stuck together, limbs entangled. Donovan estimated the mass was maybe half or a quarter of what they'd started at.

It was clear that no one wanted to take a deep breath. Some of the others in the room already had menthol rubbed under their noses. The staff would be used to the smell of rotting bodies, but this was unusual.

The sheriff once again hitched his pants up and turned his head away.

"Where were they found?" Eleri asked, referring to what was clearly two bodies that someone—probably the killer—had salted for some reason and wrapped in a tarp. "What's the story?"

Donovan was curious. Did it even match their case? There must be some connection, because the Sheriff decided to bring it to them… not even just to DeSoto Medical Examiners, but to the FBI specifically. Clearly, someone had started the preliminary work of pulling and prying the two dried corpses apart, but they had quit before the job was finished.

"They were found near the beach in Sarasota. The dunes must have shifted and a couple beach hikers found the tarp. They got curious."

Donovan bet the beach walkers regretted that now. They were probably scarred for life. One skull peeked out from decaying meat, facing upward, almost at him. If this had been the way the hikers had found the bodies, they'd probably run screaming.

"Civilians called it in, and we sent our team out to dig it up. They were wrapped in a tarp, not in the Glades. So it was nothing we thought we should alert you over," the sheriff said, still standing far back from the body and pointing as though anything indicated from that distance would be easy to discern. His face twisted periodically as if fighting a bad sensation.

"We did a pretty quick preliminary ID. The clothing helped with that." He pointed again. "So did the necklace on one of the vics. We're still waiting on the dental records for a match."

"I can do that," Eleri volunteered. She was training in forensic odontology and Donovan always wondered if she might be capable of doing his dental work, should he need it. But he still didn't understand why they had been handed this case.

"Anyway, we had them on the table down in Sarasota. Didn't get very far, before we decided it should be yours." Tucker pointed again, though Donovan couldn't tell at what. He gave the man a pass because he was obviously fighting with the sight or the odd smell. "Take a look at the shirts and the hands."

Donovan had been doing his assessment in broad, bold strokes, but now he looked where he was instructed. The obvious gunshot wound to one victim's head wasn't concerning. If he and Eleri investigated every person shot in the head in Florida, they'd solve every case except their own. But as he looked more closely now, he could see slashes in the clothing, stained dark from what had likely been fresh blood at the time of the cut. The victim had been alive when it happened.

Donovan next looked down at the hands. There was very little tissue preserved there, some of it dried tightly onto the bone, but one hand lay flush against a pale pair of slacks. Blood stained the fabric again where the fingertips touched.

Donovan felt his gaze drawn to Eleri's, clearly asking, *What do you think?*

"This is one of ours." She followed that quickly with, "What's your preliminary ID?"

"Bonnie and Evan Merkel."

"What do we know about them? What do we know about their disappearance?" Donovan pushed.

The sheriff was clearly fighting something. Though he must have sat in on autopsies before, this set of bodies was bothering him. Donovan motioned beyond the doors, knowing he could see the bodies later, but he might squeeze more out of Tucker if the man was more comfortable.

Certainly, the sheriff looked immensely relieved to be leaving the immediate vicinity. "Seven years ago, the couple ran a group home in Sarasota."

Donovan felt his ears perk up. Eleri pushed through the doorway into the hall to listen, too, probably having the same thoughts he'd had.

Tucker went on. "They just disappeared one night. Left all the kids alone… it was a good three days before anyone realized the foster kids had been unattended for some time. But the kids all stonewalled us. Not a one of them would say what had happened."

Tucker looked back and forth between Donovan and Eleri. "Honestly, no one expected to get much out of those kids. That home was for the kids who'd been kicked out of multiple foster families. It was pretty hardcore."

Eleri's expression didn't change, and Donovan inhaled the pique in her interest.

The sheriff took a deep breath. "Those two were pillars of the community. Doing God's work."

Donovan was beginning to have his doubts, but Tucker was still talking.

"I'd met them. Good people. Not my jurisdiction, not my time, but I remember that they suspected a few of the kids of the murders. They never found the bodies, despite a good search." He took a deep breath, and the explanation helped with why he'd been distraught in the room. "The original ME said, given all the salt, that they could have been put in the ground within days of going missing."

He visibly gathered himself up and resumed his professional

report. "Anyway, between the gunshot to the head and the evidence of damage to the fingertips and slash marks on the torsos, I told him to pack it back up and bring it to you guys."

"Absolutely the right thing to do," Eleri said at the same time that Donovan told him, "You were right to do that. Thank you."

There was no doubt that they had a serial killer on their hands, and that he had been operating in the area for almost a decade. Until now, he had managed to go completely unnoticed. He was also leaving one very unusual chain of victims in his wake.

Eleri was already turning back to the room and asking permission for the two of them to use scrubs from the closet. The autopsy would be his, and Donovan was looking forward to it.

Dr. Brzezinski waved her already-gloved hands in a welcoming offer of *carte blanche* of her facilities. "It's all yours. I'd love to be able to sit in, if that's okay."

"Of course," Donovan told her. He would happily use another set of trained hands.

Eleri offered him an odd smile, but Donovan had other ideas.

26

Though Donovan was glad to have Dr. Brzezinski standing in for most of the autopsy, it took him three tries to get Eleri to understand his signals to ask the woman to leave.

"Top-secret FBI tests?" the doctor asked laughingly as she peeled her gloves.

At least she wasn't offended, he thought.

"Something like that," he told her, chuckling to make it go down softer, even as Eleri said, "It's more that we need to be able to discuss the case freely while we're standing over the body."

Completely unperturbed, Brzezinski saluted at the door and said, "Thank you for letting me hang out."

"No, thank you!" Donovan told her. "You were very useful."

She smiled at the compliment and then she was gone down the hallway, probably to the locker room. The staff had all gone home some time ago. The autopsy was painstakingly slow—not surprising for two bodies melded together even without all the intricacies of this particular case.

Brzezinski had stayed and lent a spare set of hands for all the scalpel work and water and fabric softener solutions. She'd offered a few observations as well.

"Why did you let her stay?" Eleri asked for the first time, now that they were alone.

The other doctor might still be in the building, so he didn't start on any of the tests he'd been waiting on yet. "I haven't been around another doctor doing an autopsy in a long time. I just wanted to see ... what's new or any tips I could pick up."

Eleri tipped her head. "Like the tablespoon of meat tenderizer in the softening solution? I hadn't seen that before."

"See?" Donovan grinned. Brzezinski was good.

It had taken time, even with all three of them working, to carefully pry the hands away from the bodies. They'd then had to swab the tips of each remaining finger. They'd cut away blood-soaked fabric and luckily got to send that to a lab instead of soaking it, filtering the sample, isolating any DNA and running chemical analysis on it themselves. But a lot of the tests were their responsibility, start to finish.

Once everything had been collected, they looked for usable fingerprints. Any remaining skin was desiccated, so it was difficult to tell. Brzezinski had quickly set up four bowls of varying sizes—likely because the office wasn't all that well stocked—and mixed up the solution herself, before setting each hand into a bowl to soak.

A good portion of the fingertips were missing, but she found one on each victim that just might work. So they'd run four soaks while continuing with the autopsy.

In the end, they'd only gotten fingerprints from one victim. Brzezinski's solution of fabric softener, water, and her special additive of meat tenderizer, absorbed into the skin and loosened it. That allowed them to deglove the finger.

Eleri had put on fresh gloves and slipped the now loose skin over her own in a method that was morbid enough that Donovan wondered how the first person had thought of it. Then, acting as if it were her own finger, she inked the skin and rolled the dead woman's fingerprint onto a card.

They still hadn't gotten dental records, and both he and Eleri were wondering why they hadn't been collected earlier. For beloved community members who'd gone missing, he would have thought all of that would be readily available in the evidence room.

But it had been seven years. Maybe the evidence had simply gotten lost. Natural disasters stole decades of evidence regularly. But the fingerprint ID would be helpful and he kept working while Eleri uploaded it and requested an AFIS match.

Donovan was glad he'd let Dr. Brzezinski stay. She'd pointed out that one of the tables had a bad wheel. He'd watched her as she'd rolled the one they were using across the room into the x-ray machine at an angle, something he wouldn't have thought of. Probably a quirk of the equipment here, like the bad wheel, but he filed it all away.

Eleri hit several keys on the computer system that was maybe even older than the other equipment in the room and headed for the door. She stood on her tiptoes and peered out the window for a moment before offering a smile and small wave and then telling him, “She’s gone.”

“Do you think Brzezinski is right about them salting the body?” Donovan asked her. He hadn’t wanted to put her in an awkward position in front of the other doctor.

For a moment, he marveled at that. Eleri and the FBI had humanized him quite a bit. He never would have considered anyone’s feelings before. He just did the job. He’d understood he was known for being brusque and straightforward, but now he was pretty confident those had been the only words that had filtered back to him. He’d likely been known as an asshole and a complete pain to work with.

His “brilliance” had been the only reason to put up with him. The sad part, he realized now, was that he wasn’t even brilliant. He simply had the ability to sense things his fellow medical examiners didn’t. He’d just been an asshole.

He wouldn’t have said it then, but now he was grateful for the change. He didn’t say anything, only looked up at Eleri as she thought it through.

Brzezinski’s theory had been that the killer had possibly just dicked it up. That they either thought they had lye or thought salt would do the same thing as lye and dissolve the body enough to hide evidence. Nothing much completely destroyed bones though, including a good acid bath.

“I think the salt from the ocean preserved the bodies, too. I suspect these results aren’t entirely something the killer did.” Eleri waved her hand over the table.

With Brzezinski’s help, they’d completely separated the two bodies onto different tables. The one they’d give a preliminary ID as Bonnie Merkel was still draped across the tarp that had been rolled around them both. Though the wrapper itself was waterproof, the way they’d been rolled up had not been watertight. It had still done a lot to preserve the corpses.

He wondered if they could ask the killer when he—or she—was found, "Did you know what you were doing with the salt?" Oddly, it had both preserved evidence and destroyed it in equal measure.

But Donovan only agreed with Eleri's assessment before doing all the things he'd held back while waiting for Brzezinski to leave. He lifted one of the silver bowls where Cara and Eleri had placed the excised organs and held it up close to his face.

Where normally he would inhale deeply, this time he started shallow. The salt had permeated everything and the smell of it was strong. He started with the brain, and then went to the kidneys.

"What is it?" Eleri asked. She'd been watching him and caught his change in expression.

"I'm not sure," he said. But when he got to the liver, he turned back to his partner and held the organ up. "I think we might have something."

27

Eleri woke at noon again. Apparently, this was her new habit, at least for this case. She liked the occasional sunrise, and she figured she would have liked to see one here, too. Instead, she was waking up right in the middle of the heat. Right as the day pushed downward on everything, making the air heavier and wetter.

They'd started late at the DeSoto County ME's Office, then she and Donovan had kicked Brzezinski out and stayed later. Sleeping in had become the natural result of her altered schedule.

Eleri wondered if her hands would cramp from holding a scalpel for so long. They'd taken the time to tease every piece of flesh from bone that they could. One thing in the office that pleased Donovan to no end had been an old, but full-sized, body kettle.

Once they had the corpses dismembered—something that happened more frequently than laypeople liked to imagine—they'd put the bones in and added meat tenderizer and set the kettle to a slow cook. Some of the bone still held onto little bits of flesh and dry tissue that they hadn't been able to pull away. Eleri had left a note for Dr. Brzezinski, hoping that the woman didn't suddenly need her kettle in the next twelve hours. They would have to go back to the office later today and sort the pieces.

Picking up the phone rather than getting up, Eleri called Donovan. She wasn't dressed and no longer felt the need to be the first to knock on the door.

"Morning."

She must have sighed it more heavily than she intended, because he immediately asked, "Same dreams?"

"Same dreams."

"Then that's the path we follow. We need to look into the kids in the group home, too. See if they were abused," he told her, clearly more awake than her and forcing her brain into action.

"Those murders were seven years ago." She could almost feel the gears grind.

Donovan said, "The home isn't there anymore, and the kids might not even be in the area. People like that … they move around a lot."

Eleri didn't reply, but she knew he spoke from experience. "I'm eating breakfast today from my minibar."

She couldn't deal with another fried egg muffin or stack of waffles that would taste delicious but leave her blood sugar plummeting. "Be here at one?"

"Sounds good. I'll take the car."

He had his own keys, so she signed off and flopped back down into the bed. Her first option was sleeping for the bulk of the time until he got here. She hadn't needed to put bones under her pillows—the dreams had come anyway.

For a moment, she remembered how she'd hid her skill from Donovan on their first case. She'd snuck a picture and stuck it under her pillow then tried to explain to him that she had a hunch. Which was, of course, the way she'd done it for years—trying to tell her fellow agents that she dreamed something and everyone should follow it was as ridiculous as it sounded. But now, Donovan simply said, "Then that's the path we follow."

She threw off the covers. Even if she managed to get back to sleep, which she knew from past experience wasn't likely to happen, it wasn't going to be restful. In fact, probably the best way to get good solid sleep was to solve this case… and work things out with Avery.

Her plan for that had been slowly modeling in the back of her mind. What should she show him to prove her skills? She could now form a small fire in the pit of her palm. I would look almost as if she had a candle wick coming out of her hand. As much as Eleri thought it was a pretty cool trick, it was relatively useless and could probably be duplicated from any cheap magic shop.

She considered reading his mind, but it seemed so invasive.

Telling your boyfriend that you were a witch from plausibly seven or eight generations back was going to be a rude enough awakening without her reaching into his head. Violating any last boundaries he had—or didn't even know he needed—wasn't going to make him want to accept her as she was.

Maybe she could conjure his grandmother's face in the bowl. Hell, maybe she should ask Grandmere what to do... *if* she could find Grandmere! Aida Weddo had been in the rocking chair at Grandmere's little square house in the woods.

Were the dreams coming because Eleri had consciously laid down each night trying to get back to that house, trying to see if Grandmere would ever come?

She had no idea. There were no easy answers. So she showered and sat down to the table she pulled up close to the couch. With her yogurt and granola on one side and a bottle of water and the paperwork on the other, it disturbed her that the minibar breakfast was the healthiest she'd eaten in some time. She simply could not keep up with Donovan's diet.

Eleri crunched her way through as she flipped the pages in the old files. She started today with Earlene Beaman's pictures—not the kind of thing the average person would examine over breakfast. But when had she ever been average?

She thought the ribs had shown the nicks from the knife quite clearly. The slashes to the body were obvious in the crime scene photos and from the autopsy report. So were the pulled fingernails. The gunshots to the head and the chest were the next obvious thing. But there had also been so much damage on the bone—things that were visible in the X ray alone.

She pulled out a radiograph of Earlene's forearm. There was no damage there from the killer, at least not that she could tell, but there was evidence of more than one old break. Her ribs also supported multiple, tiny, white lines from the x-ray, the kind that were brighter in the center and faded quickly. Her skull had a dent that wasn't congenital—it indicated something that had happened to her and healed that way.

Had Earlene Beaman been abused as well?

Eleri dove into the research. By the time Donovan arrived, she simply swung the laptop toward him as he entered. He looked at her for a moment and she almost opened her mouth, but then wised up and waited for him to close the door so she wouldn't broadcast anything into the hallway behind him. Unlike him, she couldn't smell if anyone was out there.

"All the damage to Earlene Beaman's skeleton… What if she was abused, too?"

Donovan nodded. "Abusers were often abused kids who didn't get any treatment or help."

Eleri shrugged. "It's the only parenting they know."

It was the simplest and filthiest of explanations, but Donovan didn't need more.

"I called the sheriff's office and he just sent this over. The Beaman family has lived in the area for some time and both Earlene and her mother—also deceased—had multiple ER visits throughout her childhood. There are notes in her mother's documentation that staff had encouraged her to press charges."

28

Donovan slumped backward on the tiny sofa. It was small enough—and he was long enough—that his butt almost slid off the edge. He almost crumpled unceremoniously onto the floor.

Eleri politely hid her laugh as he scooted himself back up. Nothing like trying to tap out and making an ass out of yourself.

"Are you ready to give up?" she asked.

He wasn't, not yet, but… "We've been here for more than two weeks."

"We have more information now," she pointed out, but he wasn't fully satisfied.

"Is this going to be one of those cases where we gather all the evidence, put it in a neat folder, and then leave it for the next person?" He was having a bad day and it was showing. The case was getting to him.

"You think we won't get enough information until he strikes again?" she asked.

"It's beginning to look that way." The cases that dragged on sucked. Closing a case felt good. And he had to admit that he and Eleri had a very good success rate. Hell, all of Westerfield's teams did. It might be why they were allowed to operate under such a wide umbrella. Maybe that made *not* closing a case feel even worse.

"You might be right," she sighed. "We keep pulling, but nothing actually unravels. Still, we're not done yet."

"I know." He imagined they could be in town for a month or more, pulling tiny threads here and there. There was no easy evidence about the kids in the home. He'd been disappointed, but not surprised, that no one had filed charges. There had never been any public accusations against the couple. Even so, Donovan was growing more certain that if this killer had gotten both of the Merkels, something had been going down.

Besides, Eleri was right. There were still more threads to pull.

She once again swung her laptop around to face him. "The Children's Home part of their situation made me think. These kids are in a home—a therapy situation. Wolkov went to see a therapist. We've got the information for that at least. I'm sure we can find out who the kids were assigned to."

"But is there any real link there?" Donovan asked. "A quarter of America is in therapy, so does that mean anything?"

"I don't see anything obvious, but maybe. We're pretty confident that Rebecca Talley was abused by her husband, right? So what if she visited one of the local women's shelters?"

"Oh." He caught on then and began doing his own searches, fingers tapping on his keyboard. He quickly rotated it for her to see the screen. She always did that, sharing her information transparently, and he'd picked it up. "There are three within driving distance. These two are definitely closer to where Rebecca Talley would be."

"The thing about women's shelters is that they have to have something or someone directly in these women's paths. Lots of the husbands monitor GPS on the phones or more. But yes, this is a good place to start." Eleri leaned in, looking more closely at the map.

"So the question is, will she tell us?"

"We didn't promise her we wouldn't call back with more questions. Not like Greg Beaman." He watched the slight flinch that crossed Eleri's face. It had been an effort at kindness.

"Shall we drop in unannounced?" Eleri asked.

It sucked. Donovan thought the woman had been through enough, but they needed the information. "Yes."

Having agreed, he found himself already standing and pushing away from the too-small couch that he shouldn't have sat on in the first place. It was definitely more Eleri-sized. Even as he stood up, his phone rang.

With raised eyebrows and growing excitement, he flipped the screen toward Eleri. "Look who's calling."

He gave her just enough time to recognize the name before he turned the phone to speaker and motioned her to be quiet. "Thank you for calling me back. Yes, yes, I think we can help you."

"I have a lot to get off of my chest," the man said.

29

"Smith is my last name because my biological parents remain non-identified. I'm one of those babies people find in a dumpster."

Donovan wanted to ask if it really had been a dumpster or if that was just a phrase the kid was using. He was still so young. Derek Smith had been thirteen when Bonnie and Evan Merkel had disappeared from the foster home.

"What do you want to know?" he asked, his hands clenched in such a way that even Eleri would be able to see he was holding back.

He'd driven down from Tampa to meet them, though, and he was the only one of the four kids that Donovan had found who'd agreed to talk to them.

So why hold back? Why the smell of tight muscles and the faint hint of fear? Derek wasn't afraid of Eleri and Donovan. He wasn't afraid of the FBI. But *what*?

Eleri was opening her mouth to ask a question, but Donovan interrupted. He was taking a gamble. The kid seemed incredibly straightforward. He was thoughtful, taking his time to form his words—something Donovan appreciated—rather than blurting something out that didn't make sense, or backpedaling. "What are you afraid of?"

"I'm afraid I'll get accused of a crime I didn't commit. I've spent my entire life under suspicion or paying for things I didn't do. I was kicked out of foster families for things other kids did, because they were simply better at lying about it than I was." He paused, gathered himself and continued. "I was put into juvie for something another kid did. A guy that I thought was a friend. He stashed the stolen things in my locker. Then it happened again, and I got an extra year added to my sentence."

There was another pause and Donovan moved his leg, tapping his knee against Eleri's and hoping the kid was too caught up in his thoughts to notice. She stayed quiet and they both waited. It didn't take long.

"Then I was stupid. I got to the group home and the Merkels were so kind and so loving. I realized later it was something they did to draw us in." There was a sheen on his eyes that told Donovan that he wanted to tell the story, but the telling was hard.

What he'd said wasn't the whole answer, Donovan knew. Derrick Smith's tension hadn't released with his words.

"We're not here to arrest you," Donovan reiterated his words from earlier, but pushed just a little harder. His nose sensed what his intuition might not. Smith had a goal here. "What else?"

"The kids at the home all bound together and I'm not gonna break that trust."

That was it, Donovan thought. He was concerned about betraying the bond.

Eleri saw through it, too, and started throwing out an option. "Maybe one of the other kids killed the Merkels. Maybe someone older than you, maybe sixteen or seventeen?"

Donovan agreed, one of the older kids would be able to keep killing in the pattern they'd seen, creating new victims in the years soon after. For a moment, he wondered if the unidentified victim was another kid from the group home, but he couldn't pursue that now with the wealth of information Derek Smith offered sitting right in front of him. Even with his tight statements and holding back, he was giving them a lot to go off of.

"I'm not going to ask you to name names," Eleri said, leaning forward.

Donovan leaned back slowly, shifting the bones in his face ever so slightly. As his sinuses opened up, he smelled the soap Derek had used before meeting them. The blooms on the tree near them wafted across the path and the almost greasy scent of palm leaves drifted down. And he smelled someone he'd picked up before...

But as he looked around, he didn't see anything odd. So he focused on Derek and hoped the slight breeze didn't change direction, because he'd seated himself directly downwind of Derek. The scent changed a little, telling him that Smith did relax with Eleri questioning him.

"I don't want names," she said again, adding, "I'm not here to arrest anyone. Did one of the kids in the home kill or hurt the Merkels?"

But the bitter sound that emanated from Derek Smith's mouth made it clear this was not what had occurred. "I don't think any kid there ever hurt the Merkels."

He paused, sat back, and seemed to be contemplating his choices again. When the words began to come, it was clear this was the story he'd come to tell. "The Merkels were the worst kind of humans ever. They abused the kids—every last one of us."

Eleri's voice lowered calmly. "In what way?"

Another harsh, cynical sound came from Derek and his hands came up. Donovan could see genuine tears forming in the corner of the young man's eyes now. "How *didn't* they? It was sexual for some of the kids. It was physical for most of us, and emotional. There was one little girl, An—"

He paused, open-mouthed, as if realizing he'd almost given her name. Then he paused and swallowed it back. "I don't know if they sexually abused her. But they didn't hit her. They seemed to understand that threatening her with hurting her friend would keep her in line."

Holy shit, Donovan thought.

"I don't think she ever had anything she could take to court. But if … this little girl didn't follow along, they'd lock her friend in the basement and not feed her. We would hear her screaming in her room at night. I'd love to say I don't know what happened, but we all knew." The last word was bitten off, anger rolling off of him.

Donovan understood. Eleri nodded. It was enough of a picture.

It was Eleri who asked again, "So if the kids didn't kill the Merkels, who did?"

Derek's lips pressed together, as if contemplating the best way to tell it. "We'd all gone to bed. We slept four or five, sometimes seven, in a room."

Donovan had read that the house often had anywhere from fifteen kids on up. And at one point, they were stuffed full with twenty-eight children for a couple of weeks. Twenty-eight victims for the Merkels to abuse.

"We were in bed, waiting. Something always happened after lights out. It was a horrible lottery each night," he told them now, leaning forward, his gaze down between his feet, his shoulders slumped.

Donovan had seen it before in survivors. Derek Smith smelled of the awful truth.

"We heard the front door open and we heard noises. Honestly, there were shouts, and then it sounded like bodies dropping."

"Do you think they were shot in the house?" Eleri pushed the story forward.

The kid answered quickly. "I didn't hear gunshots. We heard dragging noises after that. Evan protested a little bit, but he sounded drunk."

Donovan absorbed all of it. Derek was looking up at them now, the story pouring out of him. "Then we heard the front door close. A car started. And that was it."

Donovan leaned a little forward now, hoping Derek hadn't noticed the slight changes to his face. He didn't seem to, and he just kept talking.

"We never heard from them again."

"No one reported it?" Eleri asked, but they both already knew the answer.

"Hell no. We were up all night, petrified. In the morning, though, no one banged on our doors and made us get out of bed. We all gathered in the kitchen. There was a bit of blood smeared on the floor … and An—" he swallowed the name again.

Donovan didn't know what to do with it. There were too many names that started that way. But Derek was still talking.

"The one little girl—the one they always threatened but never hit —she just cleaned up the blood and went about her day. One of the older girls, who was always talking about getting out, about running away, she just pulled everything down from the cabinets and made pancakes for all of us with this little griddle."

"But the girl who cleaned up the evidence?"

"She was eight, and that morning she was so … cold-looking. She got rid of the evidence and none of us said anything."

"Why not report it?"

"Why would we report the best thing that ever happened to us?

We had two and a half blissful days on our own. We watched TV and ate cereal. We almost came and went as we pleased. But as Joe pointed out, if suddenly we were all seen out and about without the Merkels, people would get suspicious. But those were the best two days of my life."

"Do you have any idea who did it?" Donovan finally asked point blank. Leaning forward now, he rested his elbows on his knees, consciously mirroring Derek Smith's stance.

"I think I do," Derek said, looking right at them. "But I'm not going to tell you who."

30

"It's the therapist." Eleri sat forward at the little table, one hand on the file and the other on her computer as though they might escape. But she was the one most likely to leap up and jump away. "Donovan. It's the therapist!"

He wasn't as excited as she was. "How? They didn't all see the same therapist. Or are you suggesting it's a network of therapist killers, getting revenge for abuse?"

"Well, when you put it that way …" Eleri leaned back, her shoulders sloping with her dashed hopes. She'd been so sure for a moment. "Mark Wolkov saw a therapist. Rebecca Talley likely went to one of the women's shelters near her home. I'll bet she at least went into one of the offices, checked in, and got information. Greg Beaman was in therapy for years. And the kids at the home each saw a therapist."

Donovan was shaking his head. "But they're all *different* therapists. And we don't know that Rebecca Talley went to a shelter."

"You're right, of course. It might not be the therapist who's killing people, but that's the common thread between these victims. Every one of them was a threat to someone else."

"That's the thread. Except for the unidentified male…"

She sighed but ignored this hole in her theory. "There must be some way to check medical records from therapy. Like in a hospital, you could just go and pull the records from all the different doctors. You can find everyone who'd visited the ER, for example, regardless of which doctor treated them. And yes, some of it *is* the same therapist."

"Who's that?" Donovan was leaning closer now, once again having perched on the little couch that he was just a touch too tall for.

Eleri reached out, pointing to the screen as if the name hadn't seared into her head. "Doctor Gwen Song."

"What are the connections?"

"She volunteers at the women's shelter *and* she has an office in town."

"We're going to need more than that, El," Donovan said. He gently nudged her.

"Fine." Turning back to her screen, she tapped on the keys for a while until Donovan did the same. Then she huffed out another breath. She wasn't going to be able to subpoena the tax records anytime soon, but she wanted to keep tugging on that thread. It *felt* like the right one.

"Okay, here," Eleri said fifteen minutes later, though not with the same gusto as her initial announcement. "She worked in an office building, in a suite with several other therapists, but the last few years on her own. They ran the gamut from children to marriage counseling. Behavioral therapies…" she was reading off the list.

Donovan nodded. "Okay. It's getting more plausible. We need to connect a few more of the victims, though. Do therapists talk to each other? Or is that some kind of HIPAA violation?"

"I don't think it falls under HIPAA," Eleri said, leaning away from the obnoxious but helpful computer screen and feeling the thread she was tugging on stick and fight back. "But I know there are confidentiality issues there. However, therapists talk to each other as patients. Anything they say to each other in a session would also fall under those confidentiality laws. But my guess is a lot of what they talk about is the patients they have to deal with and the horrible things they've heard and how to process that themselves."

"Okay, so there is probably a network of therapists who know about each other's patients."

Eleri nodded. "It's Astoria. It's small. The therapists here have to all know each other. Don't they?"

"But wouldn't they drive away from here for their own therapy? Maybe not all the way to Tampa, but far enough away that you weren't revealing anything too pertinent about your therapist's neighbors."

"Would they?" Eleri asked. "Astoria is almost in the middle of nowhere. Where would they drive to see this mythical therapist who's close enough to be accessible but far enough away to not know the people they are talking about?"

Donovan didn't answer that. Maybe there was no answer.

"We've really got three therapists," Eleri filled in. "We got Sylvia Lambrecht. We've got Charlie Jay and we've got Gwen Song, who's the marriage therapist who volunteered at the shelter. She's the one the Wolkovs saw."

Eleri looked at everything they had. It had been three hours and a snack since she'd first declared her theory. "I think it's time to get boots on the ground and start talking to these people. Maybe we can find out how well networked they are. What they know, what they talk about."

Donovan was nodding along. "First, though, I think we need to go see Rebecca Talley. We're basing a lot on the idea that she made contact with someone at the women's shelter. It would be incredibly helpful if we knew that she actually did, and with whom. And I don't think the shelter is going to give out that kind of information—not about a woman who's still alive."

Eleri agreed. Rebecca Talley's abuser was dead, but all of the information was likely still protected. Getting Rebecca to admit it would put them light years ahead. She and Donovan headed out the door.

But forty minutes later, she was walking down the front steps of the Talley household, frustrated beyond belief. She climbed into the car, begging for the passenger side this time. She waited until Donovan pulled them out of the driveway—in case Rebecca Talley was watching out the window—before Eleri began to beat her head on the soft back of the seat.

"I don't understand."

Donovan turned to give her a quick look. "I thought you got what you wanted."

Eleri had, in fact, shaken Rebecca's hand, lingering just an extra moment when they first walked in. It was nothing out of the ordinary or suspicious, but she'd seen a flash of the office for the women's shelter through Rebecca's eyes.

That wasn't complete confirmation, but she was confident enough that Rebecca had visited that she'd offered Donovan a slight nod. The question had been, *would Rebecca admit it?* And Rebecca didn't admit it. She didn't even admit that JP had abused her or her daughter.

What she'd offered had been the soft wave of a hand, a shrug that so fluidly dismissed the idea that it was clear she'd thought about the question before and that she was brushing the real answer right under the rug. Rebecca Talley was a shitty liar.

"I got most of what I wanted, but it was inconclusive. I mean, I think she was, at some point, in the shelter, given what I saw. But it doesn't mean she told anybody there about JP or what he was doing."

When Donovan didn't say anything in response, Eleri kept rolling, her frustrations leaking out. "Honestly, the problem isn't what I saw. I'm just not getting anything I can use!"

"Not getting anything you can control?"

Her instant flare of anger told her he'd hit the nail on the head, and she'd best not respond or she'd say something awful. Instead she blurted out, "It's all these family members! They're not our victims, but no one cares. No one will give us any information because they're glad these people are dead."

She couldn't blame them. But now that JP was dead, why wouldn't Rebecca be honest that he'd hit her or emotionally abused her or … something? Was Rebecca protecting her dead husband's reputation?

"Can you get yourself together enough to go visit Gwen Song next? Her office is just down the road."

Eleri nodded, forcefully scooting herself more upright in the seat, making herself take deep breaths. They were at the offices before they knew it, opening a door that let them into an empty lobby. A note outside the next door let them know that Gwen was in with a patient for another five minutes.

They decided to wait. Donovan was sniffing his way around the waiting room when Gwen exited, saying goodbye to a teenage girl before turning to them.

Eleri introduced the pair, and they all offered handshakes, and this time it was Donovan who signaled Eleri.

31

"I'll help you in any way I can." The man spread his chubby fingers wide, his pale, clean palms aimed upright, as though he were an open book. His balding head and round belly covered in a friendly plaid, button-down shirt made him seem as though he were the most welcoming creature in all of the kingdoms.

Donovan could understand why abused kids talked to him. This was definitely the right person in the right job. However, he was locked down tighter than Fort Knox.

Dr. Charlie Jay offered kind smiles, his eyes crinkling at the edges. "Oh, I'm so sorry. I can't tell you that."

"The patient is deceased," Eleri would remind him.

"Oh, I know. But the violation of patient privilege to tell you what I know about them would be a mark against me to the people I see. I didn't see the foster parents, after all."

Of course, the Merkels weren't Charlie Jay's patients.

Beside him, Donovan could feel Eleri getting frustrated, and he was getting there, too. Gwen Song had been a little more open, but still hadn't provided anything useful. Hers had not been the smell that Donovan had traced at several of the sites where the bodies were found.

Upon walking into the office with Charlie Jay—who was not with a patient and was more than willing to talk to them before he went home for the evening—Donovan also recognized that he did not have the scent of the killer.

He was now holding out hope for Sylvia Lambrecht, or maybe for something Eleri would learn from the first handshake. She would tell him when they got back into the car. But, despite the lingering hand clasp with Charlie Jay, just like she'd had with Gwen, there'd been no knowing nod.

"Is there a statute of limitations?" Donovan asked, leaning a little bit forward, hoping his stance would put some pressure on the therapist. But Dr. Jay just leaned back, casually immune to any of Donovan's tactics.

"Now, I have to make it clear: I will become vilified by all my former patients if I tell you anything. I'll lose future patients, too, and I have legal protection here." The last words rose on a note, as if to say Donovan and Eleri should know that.

"We're trying to solve a minimum of six murders committed by a serial killer. One who's still on the loose." Donovan added that last part hoping to appeal to Charlie Jay's sense of morality.

If it was there, it didn't swing this direction.

Now the doctor leaned forward himself, matching Donovan's stance, and even though his expression remained friendly, this was clearly an aggressive move.

Charlie Jay was done. Donovan fought hard to keep his eyebrows from raising. He could see Eleri holding back, too. The doc knew exactly what he was doing. Donovan had to admit, it felt a little rough around the edges to have his own tactics turned back on him. He hazarded a guess that Charlie was the superior player in this game.

"Listen, agents." His voice had changed. The soft, buttery edges had hardened. "I am legally obligated to report any instance in which I suspect, even in the slightest amount, that any harm is about to come to someone. I have reported those things in the past, but they are completely unrelated to this case—"

"Can you give us information about those reports?" Donovan cut him off on purpose.

"I won't. It's all available in police files that you have ready access to." The man didn't budge from his forward stance, facing them down, holding his ground like a champ. "If I felt that any of my patients was presenting a danger to anyone, including themselves, I would be legally obligated to report it. You're sitting right here, and I am not reporting it."

This was it, Donovan thought. Charlie Jay had given everything he was willing to give, and he was not going to let them have any tiny shred more. His next words solidified it.

"I'm going to ask you to leave. If you need me to answer questions, then you'll need to take me to the station or the branch office or wherever you guys do it." He was leaning back now, his hand waving in a dismissive manner. "Come back with a warrant to search my files and I'll turn everything over then. But I can't voluntarily betray my patients' confidentiality."

With a quick glance between them, Donovan and Eleri communicated.

Standing quickly, Donovan held his hand out for a moment, enjoying that he towered over the small, squat man. Not that Dr. Charlie Jay had done anything wrong. And Donovan was forced to admit that were he in this situation—not that he ever would be—he might have done the same. Even imagining himself as a therapist—better yet, as a therapist to children—made Donovan's insides curl. But he shook the man's hand, thanked him for all the help, even though it was *none,* and he and Eleri headed out the door.

This office was deep in a building, and as they headed down the hallway back to the elevator, Eleri looked around. She spotted the closed office doors and empty hall and felt free to speak more openly.

"Not our killer," she whispered. "Not in the slightest."

Donovan rolled his eyes. Now, all of his hopes were pinned on Dr. Sylvia Lambrecht.

32

"Is everything okay?" Avery's voice came through the line, the worry echoing.

"It really is." Eleri's lie rolled too easily. "It's just this case."

She was still trying to figure out exactly what to tell him and what to show him. But the stolen evening for a phone call wasn't the time or the place.

"You just sound a little distracted."

She laughed. "I'm more than a little distracted."

When he offered her the chance to get back to work, she didn't take it. She wanted to stay on the phone. Something about the way he spoke, and the way he reached out and the way he embraced everything about her, gave her hope. But the problem was, while she loved him, he didn't love her.

He couldn't. He didn't know her.

As soon as this case was over, her primary job was to correct that error. But "as soon as this case was over" was a time frame she couldn't predict. So she told him, "We have another interview tomorrow and we're hoping it will reveal something."

She could almost hear Avery nodding along over the line. "I'm sure you'll crack it sooner rather than later."

"I want to believe you're right."

"I am." His reassuring smile was something she felt, even if she couldn't see it.

They hung up after a couple of hours, with Avery claiming he needed sleep for practice tomorrow. Eleri claimed she needed sleep for the case tomorrow. But instead, she picked up a novel, getting lost in someone else's story and letting her brain float away.

When she couldn't quite hold onto that any longer, she played a number stacking game until her tablet dropped from her fingers. She left it there, only vaguely aware of the light fading into the dark of the room as she slipped away.

Eleri woke up at a shocking eight a.m., so early for her vampiric schedule that she was now considering "Florida time." She'd slept eight hours—eight long, heavy, dreamless hours that her body had probably needed and possibly forced on her.

This morning, though, she could have used the dreams. She would have liked to have known more about Sylvia Lambrecht. Eleri had been so convinced it was "the therapist." Then there had been three therapists to check out, and two out of three had completely *not* checked out. There was only one to go.

While she and Donovan had the advantage of his nose, even that hadn't panned out. They couldn't arrest anyone on the charge of "smells like the killer to Donovan," but it would at least aim them in the right direction.

She was about to go out walking around town with him and see if he could just randomly brush past the person he'd scented. The problem was that the smell belonged to the person he *believed* was the killer. The scent had been at both the JP Talley site and then he'd followed it through the woods, finding two more bodies in its wake. If it wasn't the killer, it was definitively a person who understood what was going on.

She got up and dressed, her good mood carrying over as she called Donovan, making the assumption that he, too, had had a good night and was already up.

"I'll take you for a Gator Chomp," she offered, thinking she could eat fruit and oatmeal there as well as in her room.

He laughed. "It all goes on the expense account."

"I know. I'm offering to do the paperwork for it."

"I will take that." He sounded sunny and awake, and not irritated like her.

An hour later, Donovan was clearing his plate and pulling up the directions to Sylvia Lambrecht's office while Eleri paid the bill. "Do you think she knows we're coming?"

Eleri frowned. "Who would have told her? We didn't notify her."

In fact, she was more concerned that, just like yesterday with Gwen Song, they would walk in on a therapist stuck with a patient and have to wait... maybe even all day.

"If there really is a network of therapists talking to each other, don't you think two of them would have mentioned that they'd had visits by the FBI?"

"Do you think they would have had time to mention it in the sixteen hours since it happened?"

"Who knows?" Donovan asked. "I guess it depends on how well connected the network is."

It was something Eleri hadn't considered, but she appreciated the heads up. If Sylvia Lambrecht gave them any indication that she had been expecting them, they would at least know what the network in Astoria was like.

They drove in silence to a small strip mall at the edge of town. It was recently built and nicely kept up, not the kind that would have the restroom around back with a key on a chain connected to half a broomstick. The convenience store at the end was the biggest space.

Maybe the rents were lower out here, Eleri thought. But the parking lot was nearly empty. However, even as she and Donovan got out of the car, a Mercedes pulled up and the driver hopped out and headed into the convenience store at the end of the single story building.

She noted a liquor store and a sub sandwich shop. *Maybe not the best combination to have right next to a therapist.* The only thing worse might be a divorce lawyer, she thought, hiding the slight chuckle. Now was not the time to think she was funny.

They pulled the door open and found a woman sitting at the front desk, her tight black curls pulled in close to her head. Her warm, deeply colored skin was covered in soft freckles and her full lips offered a broad, friendly smile in a shade of red that was somehow both electric and warm.

Eleri liked her immediately. If Donovan sniffed a killer, he gave no clue about it.

"We're looking for Doctor Sylvia Lambrecht," Eleri said.

"Oh!" The woman hopped up quickly in another friendly gesture.

A brightly patterned dress swished around her curvy figure. "I'm Dr. Sylvia Lambrecht."

She immediately held out a hand and Eleri found her grip had the warm sense of comfort and home. Whether Sylvia Lambrecht gave anyone good advice, or helped them solve any of their psychological problems, remained to be seen. But Eleri immediately had the sensation that people would tell this woman anything. She felt like safety.

Donovan introduced them and, though Eleri watched carefully, Lambrecht didn't flinch at the mention of FBI agents.

"Are you here about the murders? In town." She tacked on the last part as if to distinguish it from other murders.

"Yes, ma'am," Eleri replied. The woman was just enough older than her to warrant the title, and Eleri aimed for politeness. This might be Florida, but it was still the South.

"Well, I'm not sure why you're here. And I do have a patient in—" she checked an old-fashioned, red leather-banded wristwatch. "In twenty minutes. But if I can help…" she let the words trail off.

Eleri nodded vigorously. "We'd love to ask you a few questions."

"Then, let's step into my office." Sylvia removed herself from behind the desk and ushered them in. Immediately, Eleri spotted several large, comfy chairs, a love seat, ottomans, bookshelves, and a setting that would make a person feel comfortable spilling their guts.

"Can we start by asking what you know about the murders?" Eleri asked as she and Donovan settled themselves into the squishy furniture.

"Certainly," Dr. Lambrecht told them. "Though I don't know that it's much or that it's helpful."

Then she launched into far more information than Eleri had ever expected.

33

Donovan climbed into the car, his hands clenching the wheel at two and ten. He'd gotten a faint whiff of wolf as he climbed in. But wolves were everywhere, right? He shook it off and waited for Eleri's door to close before he said, "That was telling."

"But she wasn't the killer, right?" Eleri turned to face him and didn't buckle in.

He shook his head. "She knew so much. She said she didn't, but she did."

"But she didn't have any details that the killer would have. Everything she said could have come from newspapers or gossip. We don't even know what rumors are going around about the case."

"I saw it on some Sarasota news channel last night, but nothing major, just that they have a serial killer in Astoria and that the police have handed the case off to the FBI."

"Ugh. That's not helpful." Eleri leaned back but didn't motion him to put the car into drive. They were using the car as an enclosed space for a conversation.

Starting the engine, he waited for the AC to kick in as he tried to organize his thoughts on the case. Sylvia Lambrecht had even suggested that Rebecca Talley had been abused. "I saw her interviewed on TV. She didn't seem that upset that he was gone. After a while, you learn to recognize it—the way somebody flinches, those little deferences when somebody touches them.

Those are signs of abuse. In her situation, I would have counseled her to go to the shelter. There are several good options near here."

It had been the perfect opening, and Donovan had leaned forward. "Do you ever volunteer there?"

"I do." Dr. Lambrecht had smiled and rattled off the name of the one closest to Rebecca Talley's house.

Eleri's thoughts seemed to have followed the same trail as his. "If Dr. Lambrecht was Rebecca Talley's therapist, then she shouldn't have speculated openly on the abuse."

Donovan looked at her now. His body starting to relax as the AC brought the temperature down from a boil. "Do you think she sent Talley to the shelter and she's trying to tip us off with that information?"

"I don't think so." Though Eleri had considered the possibility, she came up negative. "She completely speculated about Talley. That would indicate to me that she's not the woman's therapist and that she doesn't have any kind of advice-giving relationship with the woman. She was just as clear as Charlie Jay was that she's not going to break patient confidentiality. The very fact that she speculated on Rebecca Talley's situation tells me she never saw her professionally in any capacity."

"And the volunteer work, though unpaid, would certainly qualify for patient confidentiality." Donovan agreed with her now. "It's absolutely not her. But you want to know something?"

"What?"

"I think I might have caught a whiff of it when we were walking in."

"*Really?*" She didn't ask why he hadn't said anything. He couldn't. "Donovan, we're still sitting in the parking lot."

Eleri looked at him expectantly, then he watched as her eyes scanned the area in front of them. The low-slung brick building with the cute roofline and the awnings over the doors was mostly empty. "How are your shoes?"

"Pretty shitty for anything other than doing interviews." They weren't wingtips but high-end slip-ons. Donovan had worked his entire career as a medical examiner in nothing but comfy sneakers. He was never going to work his way up to Noah's level of fashion. Noah had looked more like a fed when he was a cop than Donovan did as an actual fed. But he wasn't going to mess up his "nice" shoes. "What are you suggesting?"

"I'm suggesting that we check out the convenience store at the end of the row. We go in, wander, see if you can scent anything. If the person was out in front of this strip mall and they didn't go into the therapist's, then that's the most likely place for them to go. Also, this strip mall backs up onto the Everglades."

She pointed around the edges where he could see trees that faded into swamp. "So if we pull our other shoes out of the trunk—"

"No." He shut that down, wondering when he'd gotten so precious about his clothing. "Even if I put my boots on, I'm not dressed for a hike in the Glades."

"Good point." She looked down at her shirt. "But let's check out the store while we're here. We can come back, if we need to."

"It's probably better if we come back later and maybe don't look like a couple FBI agents walking right into the Glades. It'd be wise to be a little surreptitious."

She opened her car door and Donovan followed suit, regretting stepping back out into the hot, humid air the moment he did it. But it was a very short path to the store. Just long enough for Eleri to look up at him questioningly, and for him to shrug.

The scent was here ... but too faint to follow.

Inside, Eleri debated her way into red Twizzlers and a Diet Coke. Donovan grabbed a snack pack of cheese crackers and a lemonade. They looked exactly like feds getting junk food. And he almost laughed at them.

They checked out, but the store was basically empty. He turned to El, not wanting to step out into the heat and heavy air again. "I didn't want to mention it in Lambrecht's office for the first time, but we need each of the therapists that we spoke with to provide a list of other therapists that they've either worked in an office in a professional capacity or shared patients with or referred patients to."

"Or worked in one of the shelters with," Eleri filled in. "Maybe any other volunteer capacity."

"Exactly." He hadn't wanted to tip off Sylvia Lambrecht that they were looking into the Merkels' murders as well and that they would need to go back at least several years before that.

She'd seemed to find out so much from the papers or the evening news or even the gossip line already, Donovan had wanted to run the idea by Eleri before bringing it up. If the therapists were talking to each other, then the request should drop into all their inboxes at the same time, so they wouldn't be able to tip each other off.

It was always a fine line, asking the questions to get the information they needed without inadvertently trading their own information away in exchange.

"Anything in here?" Eleri innocuously tipped her head back toward the store.

"Nope." But as they headed out the door, the wind kicked up a bit and his nose felt it before he even realized what he was smelling. The scent bloomed faintly, like smelling baking cookies from a distance. Maybe it was strong enough to follow but—as he'd already pointed out—they weren't dressed for that.

Using the back of his hand, he tapped the back of Eleri's, grabbing her attention. He nodded and said only, "It's here."

Immediately, she slowed her pace to something well below leisurely and began struggling to open the bag of Twizzlers. Donovan knew what she was doing and he did the same.

She was covering for him to stop and scan the area, holding the bag up and struggling with it, conveniently turning several different directions. At one point, she even turned around and handed it to him, allowing her a good look back at the front of the store.

As he gave it back—partially opened, allowing her to do even more work if she needed—she said, "Aside from the clerk in the store, no one's here."

"It's not the clerk." The clerk hadn't smelled like the killer.

He huffed his frustration. He didn't even know if the scent belonged to their killer, though it was certainly someone who knew where the bodies were buried. "I think the person was outside but didn't go in."

Eleri—still facing him—walked backwards as she asked, "Do you think we can talk the clerk into giving us the security footage without a warrant?"

34

Eleri sat at the small table in her room *again.* She was beginning to grow claustrophobic. Suite or not, the space felt smaller each day.

The payment of breathing outside air made her not want to do things like go for a walk or even explore. There wasn't time for much leisure anyway. It wasn't as if they could have their discussions on a park bench or at a ballgame.

"Here," she said pointing to her screen, "and here and here."

She ran the video at double speed. The clerk had been so shocked to find out the two people who looked exactly like FBI agents were, in fact, actual FBI agents that he'd handed over the morning's storefront footage without a complaint. He'd been so awestruck that Eleri was almost surprised he hadn't asked for autographs. It was better than the reception they often got.

She showed Donovan the various people she'd picked out. Ones who didn't go into the store. "How far back do we go?"

"Probably a few hours. It was there but faint."

"So it wasn't the people who were in there right before us." Eleri ruled out three of the descriptions she'd written down, as she didn't have names.

"Maybe up to two hours before, but it was outside. And I smelled it before we went into talk to Dr. Lambrecht. So before ten a.m."

"If the person had gone into the store, would you have smelled it in the store?"

"It depends on the air conditioning system. But I don't think they went in, because I didn't smell anything until we stepped out front again."

"So they could have walked by from anywhere, to anywhere." That didn't help. But she reminded herself that, without Donovan they didn't have any of this.

"This one?" She'd gone back a little further.

"Oh." He leaned in closer.

She'd found someone walking along in a hoodie, fingers trailing the brick, as though they enjoyed the texture. Black straight pants and dark sneakers concealed the legs, and the hand was only "not the darkest skin tone." The picture was grainy and rough in black and white.

"Is that odd," Eleri asked, "walking around in long sleeves? I can't even tell if this person is male or female. The coat's so bulky."

"It's not bulky, though," Donovan pointed out. "It's relatively thin. So this isn't an incredibly slim person. I think people who live here don't feel the heat the way people who visit do."

Hadn't she learned that in New Orleans? Grandmere had never been touched by the heat or humidity. She didn't even have air conditioning in her home. At the time, Eleri had thought it was just built with good airflow, and that Grandmere was just born with a good heat tolerance. But now she wondered if it was a spell.

She was starting to wonder if she might be better off casting something on herself. Did she know anything for that? But a spell to keep herself cool in the heat wouldn't solve these murders.

They worked with the information for a while. The unidentified person who had walked along the wall was most likely the person Donovan had scented. Eventually, she gave up and stood and stretched. "I have to get out of here."

"Oh, God. Me too." When Donovan stood, arms up in the air in his own stretch, he towered over her. "Back in ten. We'll go check out Astoria."

The mid-afternoon heat was the worst, but Eleri had dressed far more casually. As they drove past Dr. Lambrecht's building, a sudden and severe rainstorm began. It made Donovan sigh.

"Well that just washed away any trail I could follow." He waved his hand at the grayed-out landscape and the windshield wipers working double-time. They drove through the parking lot and looked for anything that might help.

"There are no other cameras here," Donovan commented. "So there's no telling where that person came from, or even where they headed."

Eleri agreed. It was quite disappointing. They might have seen the killer, but… "All we have is *person.* No gender. No skin tone—"

"We have height!" Donovan put in.

"Assuming they're not wearing thick-soled shoes. But yes, we can get an average."

"Then that's what we go on."

He sounded far more chipper about this than Eleri felt. "We don't even know if that's the person you smelled."

"No. But looking at the footage, it makes the most sense."

The conversation shifted from the incredibly lacking profile to where they might get food. They ducked into a small diner that had brightly colored picnic tables lining the open space inside. The menu offered up egg salad sandwiches and BLTs.

Eleri ate her own sandwich and watched as Donovan put away both his and her bowls of soup that had been served with the meal.

Her stomach was still a little queasy and she suspected it wouldn't fully settle until she'd worked things out with Avery. The way this case was going, who knew how long that would be? The crusts of her BLT sat on the plate, untouched.

She looked up at Donovan. "What's even next here?" She had no idea.

But Donovan looked around for a moment as if making sure he wasn't in earshot of anyone. Then he said, "These people are tortured. Their fingernails are pulled. They're slashed and cut and shot. And *then* they're dumped. So the next thing we need to do is find where the torture is happening."

It was definitely on the to-do list, but normally, the case would have worked in the other order. She'd really considered that once they found the killer, the rest would become clear. It was usually much easier to trace things backwards than forwards. But with all their witnesses clammed up, and the only real clue they had being the possibility of therapists being linked … maybe it was time to figure out what was happening right after the victims disappeared.

"Next up," Donovan told her, "Derek Smith said he heard the bodies hit the floor. If he didn't hear anything like a gunshot or the sound of a fight before that, then drugs are a valid option."

They'd talked about it, but with no direction to search, they'd looked for connections between victims.

"There's no evidence of head wounds—other than the gunshot—on any of the victims," Eleri said. Except Earlene Beaman, but that wasn't related to her murder. "With everything that happened to these people, we ran some basic screens. So it's time we started looking a little more closely."

"We've got samples for Talley and Beaman." Donovan pointed out how easy it would be to run tests, if they could just figure out which ones to run.

"If we can figure out what was used on them," Eleri added, "we might be able to test for it on tissue samples on the Merkels."

"I think if we can figure out how it's being done, then we can figure out who has access to the materials and the ability to do it."

Eleri was starting to feel better. They'd pulled all their threads and nothing had unraveled. It was past time to come at it from the other side. Holding up a finger for Donovan to wait, she called Sheriff Tucker, pleased when he answered after just a few rings.

"Hello, Agent Eames. How can I help you today?"

"Was there a tox screen run on Earlene Beaman when the body came in?" Eleri was working off of the bones, because the body had been saved when no one in her family wanted to have a service for her.

Rebecca Talley had been asking for her husband's body back, but Eleri and Donovan had yet to release it—not until they knew what needed to be checked and tested.

"I believe we did," Tucker told her. "Was it not in the file?"

"No, sir."

"Check with Brzezinski then. She's been the local ME for almost a decade. She would have been the one to run it. Everything I have is copies of what she sends."

Eleri thanked the Sherriff and did exactly that. One of Brzezinski's staff was sending her the information within a few moments.

It was curious that they didn't already have it in the file, but she checked it over, showing Donovan the small print on her phone.

They stayed at the small table, enjoying the feeling of not being stuck in the tiny hotel room for once. She told herself that anybody could walk in and out of the diner and if they got lucky, Donovan might smell something.

It didn't happen.

Twenty minutes later, Tucker called back. "We've gotten ourselves in a rough spot here this evening. We need to hold a press conference and we need you there."

There was nothing Eleri hated as much as press conferences.

35

"You know, you could do this, Donovan." Eleri tried not to move her lips. She stood at the side of the podium where Sheriff Tucker was currently answering questions with jocular waves of his hands. Ultimately, his goal appeared to be to get people to stop asking.

While Eleri's voice carried quite cleanly to Donovan at a very low volume, it didn't work the same in reverse. Her hearing was simply not as good as his—no one's was, except for other wolves. Donovan had to speak loud enough for her to pick up his words without looking at him. He managed.

"But I don't want to."

She huffed. "It's a skill every agent needs."

Eleri was still trying to paste on the appropriate half-smile for the crowd. It was, after all, a murder investigation.

"You're the senior agent. I'm not doing it," he replied.

Ultimately, it didn't matter. Because at that moment, Tucker fielded a question.

"When are we going to hear from the FBI?" the woman in the crowd pressed him.

"Well, how about right now?" The sheriff turned and waved his hand, as though Eleri would come to the podium and wrap up the case.

Unless she wanted to flat out throw Donovan under the bus, she was doing this. She put on her best, most professional face—after all, she'd already put on her best, most professional clothing. If her look didn't scream *I'm a fed* right now, she should be fired.

Lifting her hands, she made a dual braking sign to the audience until they quieted down. With a deep breath and calm expression, she began. "We were called here sixteen days ago—"

"That's over two weeks!" someone in the crowd shouted.

She turned toward the offending voice and used her own skills to find the heckler. Eleri stared him in the eyes and said, in a too-sweet voice, "Very good. Though I suspect most of us here can count."

Then she waited and took a pause before starting over from the top. She intended to let them know that each time they heckled her, they would make the whole thing longer. She listed again their arrival date, then added, "The murder of a body now identified as JP Talley has been tentatively tied to the murder of Earlene Beaman just over a year ago."

She waited then, allowing for questions. She got an earful.

"You're the FBI. So it's definitely a serial killer?"

"We can't say for sure. Not yet." And that was true. The "we" of herself and Donovan could do it, but the FBI could not—though it was damn close. Regardless, she wasn't going to publicly call it and start a frenzy. Another hand went up.

"But it's the ViCAP unit out here. Shouldn't the citizens be worried?"

This time she smiled genuinely. "We're not with ViCAP. We're simply investigating, following every lead so that we can catch whoever did this." Mentally, she patted herself on the back. *Good job, El.*

"What about the murders of Bonnie and Evan Merkel?" This came from a raven-haired journalist with sharp eyes. The woman had calmly worked her way toward the front of the crowd.

"I'm sorry," Eleri sighed. "I'll need you to be more specific."

The journalist smiled and asked, point blank, "Are the murders of Bonnie and Evan Merkel tied to the killings of Earlene Beaman and JP Talley?"

The reporter was hitting the nail on the head. Eleri deflected. "We can't prove it yet."

The tone of the resulting murmur told her that everyone already knew the Merkels' bodies had turned up, and that their demise wasn't accidental. *Interesting.*

Eleri made her braking motions with her hands again. "Well, we can't rule out that any of these murders might be connected, which is why the FBI is here. Our job is still to ascertain if there is a serial killer in the area."

The crowd gasped. She'd actually said the words, but J. Binkley Raymer, her first FBI senior partner, would have been proud of her, from his cowboy hat to his boots. It was a beautiful duck and evade, followed by a jab.

"Are there other bodies that you can tie to this series of murders?"

"We are, of course, pulling old case files and trying to see if others fit this pattern." Again, Eleri ducked, not taking a hit.

The journalist opened her mouth again but, with a tapping motion, Eleri silenced her. Time to wrap this up. "One thing that many of the cases in Astoria have in common—the thing you citizens of town can help with—is that no missing persons reports were filed immediately in these cases. If anyone in your life is unreachable at the moment, or has been gone for more than a week that you haven't heard from, please contact the FBI."

That was enough. She didn't want to say, *If there's someone that you hated, and you're glad that they're gone ...* Hell, it was hard enough to get information out of the relatives of the known victims.

"Thank you so much for coming tonight." Eleri was the last one up, as though the FBI was the be all end all.

When they asked her if she would take more questions, she simply said *"Thank you"* again and turned to walk away from the podium. Tucker hauled himself back into place, official hat on his head again.

He waved the crowd to calm down. "We don't have any more answers to give. But rest assured, the whole team is working on this. We'll keep you apprised of how the case goes."

Will we be doing this every week? Eleri wondered.

This press conference had come without much warning. Tucker had scrambled to get everything together. But at least it was over, and Eleri breathed a sigh of relief.

She and Donovan ducked into the police building—an easy maneuver, since Tucker had strategically called the conference on his own front steps. Following the sheriff back into his office, they headed away from the simmering crowd outside.

Tucker popped up and closed the door behind them. "I know this is taking more of your time, but it's probably better to wait here until everything disperses. Might be twenty, thirty minutes."

Eleri nodded. Twenty or thirty minutes that she and Donovan could have looked at some new pieces in the case. Hell, it had already been two hours since Tucker notified them that he needed them. But if there wasn't pressing, time-sensitive business—and there hadn't been—they really didn't have the right to refuse. They just had to wait out the aftermath now.

There was a knock on the door, and Eleri watched as the sheriff rolled his eyes and muttered, "I told him not to disturb us."

He stayed seated, with his feet up and ignored it, but it came again quickly. The knob turned as Tucker dropped his booted feet under the desk and the door opened to reveal one of the younger deputies. Behind him, the raven-haired reporter stood, an unreadable expression on her face.

She wore red lipstick and black eyeliner and managed to look intelligently professional and just a little bit "goth" at the same time. Were she not trying to get Eleri to divulge all the details of the case, Eleri might have liked her.

"No," Tucker said to the deputy, then looked to the woman. "Sorry, Jesse. No reporters."

"I'm not here as a reporter." She crossed her arms and stayed planted.

"Is that even possible?" Tucker asked.

"I don't know," Jesse replied sharply. She and Tucker apparently went way back.

"Who are you with?" Eleri inserted herself into the conversation, since it was getting them nowhere and she couldn't follow it.

"Astoria News Times."

Eleri nodded, recognizing the name of the local paper. "But if you're not here as a reporter, then why are you here?"

"I need to report someone missing."

36

Donovan had practically bolted out of his chair before realizing that his speed and height would make him seem a threat. He tried to cover it with, "Come on in, take my seat."

He and Eleri had taken both of the only mildly comfy chairs across from the sheriff. The sheriff was leaning forward in his desk now, no longer laid back with his boots propped up, looking like he was about to fall asleep. He was very interested.

"What do you mean, you got someone to report, Jesse?" he said, taking the work out of Eleri and Donovan's hands.

Donovan subtly sniffed the air. Most people, when deceitful—particularly when attempting to play a prank, or to openly lie—gave off a very mild, bitter scent. Jesse didn't have that at all. But from the way her movements changed, she was clearly apprehensive. She didn't answer, just took a slow deep breath as if to gather herself.

"This about Eugene?" Tucker asked before she said anything. He was still leaning forward, still pushing in.

Donovan held his hand up. Tucker might know this woman, but he and Eleri didn't. "Full name, please?"

"Jesse Nash."

"And who are you reporting missing, Jesse Nash?"

"Eugene Nash." Another heavy sigh.

Donovan sensed a connection, and almost wondered if there was a line forming out the door for people to report missing the ones they hated the most. "How long has Eugene been gone?"

"Three days."

"Why didn't you report him?" Tucker demanded, leaning forward.

Jesse merely stiffened her posture and raised one eyebrow.

Finally, Donovan spotted a glimpse of the confident reporter again. She was definitely out of her element back here. Was she just trying to weasel out extra information, though? He didn't know.

"Why do you think I didn't report him, Tucker?" the woman demanded, her arms still folded obstinately.

Donovan's eyes dashed back and forth and spotted the pressed look on Tucker's face, so he asked, "What do we need to know about Eugene? And about why you didn't report?"

Tucker waved his hand to Jesse as if to say, *You tell him, sweetheart,* and Jesse did. "Eugene's a Grade A asshole."

Donovan felt his eyebrows rise and watched as Eleri's did the same. Not the way most people would be talking about their husbands. But what did he know about happy marriages?

Jesse moved to explain. "We got married four years ago. He was wonderful. Everything was fine. I was even happy to become a step-mother to his little girl, Ciara. And that's the real problem here, Tucker."

She looked to the FBI once, but leaned over the desk, pointedly glaring at Tucker. "You don't fuck this up. You get me?"

"I don't understand what there is to fuck up." The sheriff looked genuinely confused.

Donovan waited.

"Eugene's been gone for three days. I didn't report him. Neither Ciara nor I were sad to see him go, and that sounds like what all these missing people have in common." She huffed out a breath. "The problem is that I don't have any legal custody of Ciara. Her mom, who's up in Orlando, is just as bad as Gene."

Her eyes darted away, and Donovan could smell a waft of her shame filtering through the room. "I thought Eugene was one of the good guys. He was, at first. Though I guess he was actually more like his first wife than like me, and I didn't realize that until it was way too late." Another pause, but they all waited her out.

"Floyann had some surgery when Ciara was little, and she was given pain pills after the surgery, and she got addicted. She was a good mother and apparently a good person before that. Now, she keeps going to rehab and trying, but she's not good. And when she's high, she's a terrible mother. Like, she doesn't get Ciara to school, or feed her regularly, or bathe her!"

Jesse was waving her hand, obviously agitated at the ex-wife. "So Eugene got full custody of his little girl. And we met and he was great. He's a wonderful dad. Everything was fine. But you know how it got, Tucker."

She turned to the sheriff again, and Donovan could see that Tucker didn't quite get what she expected him to know. But he nodded. Jesse looked to Donovan and Eleri again.

"The factory went out of business and Eugene had been management over there. Well, just like the rest of them, there was nothing he could do. And with so many jobs going overseas, it wasn't like he could just move to a different job. He didn't find work. I was working all over the country at the time. A lot of travel." She paused and looked back to Donovan and Eleri, as if, again, she expected Tucker to already know this.

"I used to work for an online paper, following serial killers and looking at cold cases."

Donovan tried not to react, but he couldn't help noticing Eleri's tight nod. *Wonderful. A murder hunter,* he thought to himself. But Jesse was still going.

"So Eugene's job is gone and mine becomes our only income. He didn't handle it well. Turns out, he was only a good guy as long as things were good. So things took a shit and Eugene's personality took a shit, too. He was no longer a decent husband. He hit me—"

"How often?" Donovan quickly interrupted.

"Once, about eight months ago. By then things had been bad for a while and I felt sorry for him. But he *hit me,* and I turned around and I planted one right underneath his jaw, sent him backward into the wall. And I guess I must have got them demon eyes my ex-husband always told me I do, but I said if he ever touched me again, I was gonna kill him ... but I didn't kill him!"

She added the last part in a sharp realization of what she'd just said.

"*I didn't kill him.* I wouldn't be in here reporting it to you if I had."

Though honestly, Donovan thought, *that would be the best cover.* Still, any good investigator would find the evidence to pin it to her if she'd done it. And he and Eleri had been graced with gifts that made them better than merely "good investigators."

"Go on," he said.

"It took me a while to figure it out." Jesse looked ashamed again. "But Ciara changed, too. He'd been hitting *her*. He was taking his anger out on his little girl. I can't send her home to her mom because her mom's high all the time! So I left my job and went to work for the *Astoria Times News* so I could be home. It's not paying all the bills. So then he got even madder."

It was a shitty story. One that played out too many times, in too many ways, in too many homes across the country. One that Donovan could think of only in the most logical terms, because to do anything else would let it burrow down into his own memories.

"Anyway, he went out the door three nights ago, and he never came back." She waited, as if there was something they should say.

It was Eleri who popped up with the logistics. "You need to file an actual missing person's report with the police station. We need your home address, and we need to come and interview you and your little girl if we can. Later tonight?"

Jesse nodded. She was probably petrified of not playing good citizen and losing the daughter.

Tucker dismissed her. But as she turned to leave, Donovan's thought manifested, and Jesse issued her last threat. "Ciara stays with me. You try to send her back to her mother because her dad's missing …Just don't."

She shook her head and turned and stalked out the door, but Donovan heard the muttered threat. She probably thought she'd spoken too low, but he caught the sound.

"I will take her and you will never find us."

37

It was after ten before Eleri parked the car in front of the small, pink Florida home that Jesse Nash had listed.

This didn't look like the house where a little girl lived in fear. Then again, they rarely ever did. Eleri's own sister had been abducted when they looked away. And Emmaline had disappeared from a six-hundred-acre horse farm outside of Lexington.

Bad things happened everywhere.

She'd once again changed clothes and she fought not to count how many different outfits she'd managed to wear today. Donovan had changed, too. When they'd gone back to the hotel after Jesse's stunning reveal, Eleri had told him he needed to dress to make a nine-year-old girl comfortable enough around him to answer his questions. It seemed he hadn't quite thought that far ahead. But he'd nodded and then arrived at her door in a T-shirt and jeans.

She didn't know he'd even brought jeans on this trip, but she didn't say anything about it. Instead, she passed him on her own way out the door. "We'd better get a move on."

The drive was short, and they sat in the car for only a moment, gathering themselves for what might be a hard interview. Kids almost always were. But they couldn't sit too long, in case Jesse had seen them pull up.

Eleri threw open the door and walked calmly up the lovely

pebbled front steps before knocking on the door. It opened almost immediately. Jesse Nash had definitely been watching out for them.

"Hey, Jesse." Eleri used her friendliest voice.

"Come on in. We've got snacks set out and more."

There's a nine-year-old at the table. Jesse didn't say it, but Eleri could sense the words hanging in the air: Please remember she's a kid and be gentle.

No matter what else Jesse Nash might be, she was smart. She and Donovan wandered into the neat and slightly overstuffed living room to see a small, towheaded girl sitting on her knees at a coffee table, arranging her M&Ms by color.

Eleri already liked Ciara. Jesse took a moment and quietly told them, "Just so you know, this house was decorated by his ex, Floyann. When I moved in, I didn't want to upset things more for Ciara. It was bad enough getting a new stepmom. And decorating's not my thing. So if you want to draw any conclusions from the way the place looks —aside from the fact that Ciara and I do a regular job cleaning and all that—then understand that your conclusions apply to someone else."

Eleri almost laughed. Jesse the reporter would understand that the two agents were taking in every bit of information and using it to build the case. She held her expression together and simply nodded before moving over to the seat catty-corner to the little girl.

"Are you Ciara?" Eleri asked and almost immediately kicked herself. She hoped the little girl didn't reply, "Do you see any other nine-year-olds around here?" But she simply nodded and Eleri added, "My name is Eleri. And this is Donovan and we're with the FBI. Do you know what that is?"

"It's the Federal Bureau of Investigation. You guys are here to find the serial killer."

Well, Eleri thought, *I gauged that incorrectly.* She immediately adjusted her tone. "Yes, we are. If there is one. We're trying to find them."

"Do you think they have my daddy?" That question smacked Eleri hard, after the way Ciara seemed so adult in response to the first question. There was no terror in her voice, and Eleri filed that away, too.

"I want to tell you that I'm confident that your dad is fine." She watched as Ciara flinched. *Interesting.* If the killer didn't have her father, then he might come back. Ciara wasn't taking kindly to that.

Eleri began to wonder if he'd been abusing the child worse than even Jesse had known. "But I just don't know."

Abused kids tended to love their parents. Many didn't even know they were abused. Sometimes they did, but their life was all they knew of normal. Maybe, if Ciara had seen enough—if she'd seen her mother go down this pathway and not come back, and now she was seeing her father do the same—she was over it. From the way she spoke, she sounded very intelligent. It might not be an abnormal reaction at all.

Eleri dove in with a few standard questions, trying to get Ciara to spit up whatever she knew without it looking like they'd come here just to grill the nine-year-old. "Can I ask what your daddy did for his job?"

Jesse offered a very sympathetic nod to the little girl to go ahead.

Ciara continued to look at the candy she was pushing around on the glass top coffee table, but she answered clearly. "He used to be a good Daddy. And I hope he can come back and be a good daddy again. But people should be good whether they're getting paid or not. Whether they have a job or not."

She huffed. This nine-year-old had clear ideas about what was going on with her father, and Eleri began to wonder how much Jesse might have coached her— or maybe Ciara had simply overheard things and absorbed them.

Eleri questioned everything.

But Ciara kept talking. "After he stopped working, he started yelling at me more. I didn't like it and he would yell at me for things that I didn't do. He didn't even listen when I told him it wasn't me. And then he started breaking things. I had an iPad and he broke it."

Eleri glanced up in time to see the rage on Jesse's face. When the woman caught the look, she explained. "Without him working, we didn't have the money to replace it, either."

"He also broke the kitchen counter. See?" Ciara pointed and Jesse nodded along.

There was a breakfast bar covered in clean white tile and white grout. But even from here, Eleri could see the line that split the tiles.

"He picked up one of the bar chairs and smashed it down on top. I was so scared. I was trying to hide down behind the table." Ciara told the horrifying story calmly, but the corners of her eyes flinched. She was either a very good actress or she was telling the truth. "He was yelling a lot."

Eleri almost asked, *Where's the chair?* But there were obviously three chairs and definitely room for four. So she didn't ask. "Did you tell anybody about how your dad had changed?"

Eleri was wondering if their idea about the therapists was right. This might mean something.

"I told Jesse. And then I was afraid, because I had lied to her before. I told her things were okay when they weren't. But Jesse was nice about it."

The woman rushed over and hugged the little girl. She murmured, "It's okay. I understand."

Ciara laid her head on her stepmother's shoulder.

Eleri could see a few places where the drywall looked like it might have been patched right at fist height. Things had gone down here. And there were only two people in the house now, and this girl sure as hell hadn't cracked tile with a barstool.

Eleri nodded. It was always good when stories notched together tightly. And it was difficult to train a kid into a complex lie. Her gut reaction as well told her that every piece of the story was true. The only issue was that Eugene Nash had clearly lashed out more times than his victims were sharing, and there simply wouldn't be enough time to tell all the incidents.

"Jesse told me if I needed somebody to talk to, that I could talk to my school counselor."

Bingo, Eleri thought. "When did you first start talking to your counselor?"

Ciara shrugged. "Just after school started."

So maybe a month ago. "I'm going to ask you a hard question, Ciara."

Eleri leaned forward, trying to make herself appear smaller and less threatening. "Did your daddy ever hit you?"

Ciara nodded. Her reaction of pulling in and tightening up was the normal reaction of an abused child talking about the abuse and remembering it. "I curled up in a little ball on the kitchen floor last time. I thought if I laid down, he'd stop."

Now, sitting on the couch behind her, Jesse blinked back tears as Ciara's fingers still worked the candies, picking one up and popping it into her mouth and rearranging the colors again.

"When was that?" Eleri asked as gently as she could.

"A week ago."

"How often did he hit you?"

The girl just offered a huge shrug. Kids often didn't quite have the vocabulary or the framework to describe abuse. So Eleri tried to give her the words without framing the answer. "Was it happening more often or less?"

"More." Ciara nodded.

They asked a few more questions before Jesse asked if she could send the girl upstairs to bed. She hugged her and told her what a wonderful job she'd done, and said she'd be up in a minute.

Eleri was working hard to make sure that Jesse could hold to that promise. It seemed Ciara was smart and mature, but maybe it was because she had already dealt with a lot.

Jesse came and sank back down on the couch, her hands clasped tensely between her knees. She couldn't look at them as she spoke. "I suspected he was hitting her. She had bruises. She said they weren't from him. But she's only told me and the therapist."

Eleri nodded. They were treading on very interesting ground. And it got a lot more interesting when Jesse sat up straight. She looked them in the eyes, the reporter suddenly taking back over.

"So, given what you said about the victims not getting reported as missing, that would mean that someone's getting revenge on assholes. So it's either me or the therapist—and I can assure you, it's not me."

38

Donovan hopped back into the car as Eleri climbed into the driver's seat.

"Jesus," he said, "she's put way too many pieces together."

"Has Tucker been holding press conferences without us?" Eleri asked, seeming to ponder how the information might have gone out.

"Could he?" Donovan asked. "Wouldn't we have known? Wouldn't someone have said, 'the sheriff mentioned that in his press conference.'"

He paused, then asked another question. "He can't hold a press conference without us, can he? We're the local reigning authority on this case."

Eleri tipped her head. "He sure called one without our input."

"That still doesn't change that Jesse managed to put together a lot of information." Donovan was trying to figure out how that worked. "Who would have leaked it?"

"It's possible she's got a source in the Sheriff's office," Eleri acknowledged. "But she's also a reporter who's used to following killers. Maybe she just figured out the inevitable conclusion was probably the proper one."

Eleri was onto something. It was just as likely that there wasn't a leak as that there was one.

"Jesse's probably been digging around in this case," he said. "She's a murder investigator, she lives in town, and she might know more about the people who disappeared. That would make it easier for her to put all the pieces together and come up with the same theory we did."

"True," Eleri said.

Donovan's brain kept churning. Jesse had surprised them. "Honestly, she was probably sitting with a jumble of information until we announced at the press conference that one problem was citizens who hadn't reported the missing. Now she sees she has that same situation in her own household, and she knows her daughter only told her and her school counselor."

"At least that's what she believes," Eleri added. "Who knows who a nine-year-old tells her secrets to?"

Donovan motioned for her to start the engine. He'd seen a curtain flicker inside the house. If they sat here talking, Jesse Nash would notice that, too.

Agreeing that it was time to flee the scene, Eleri started the car. As she did, she waved to the house—she, too, thought Jesse was likely watching them—then backed out of the driveway.

As they pulled away, she asked the question he'd been waiting for. "Did you smell anything in there?"

"No. Nothing of consequence. I mean, I can tell you what Eugene Nash smells like now."

With an crease forming above her eyebrows, Eleri turned to him. "You can tell me?"

"No, that was a bad choice of words." Donovan sighed. "I mean, he smells like Drakkar Noir."

"And she *married* him?" Eleri burst out, giving Donovan his first good chuckle of the day, even though it was closing on eleven at night.

"I can tell you things like that, but nothing that would likely make you recognize him, even if you smelled him."

"But *you* can find him again?"

"I can." Of that, Donovan was certain. Now that he had Nash's scent, he could tell where the man had been. "And I can follow the killer."

"Well, alright then. Let's go hit the bar." Eleri seemed way too excited.

"Like this?" They were dressed for interviewing a kid, but as he looked down at himself, he realized he was merely in comfortable clothing. It wasn't like he was wearing a purple Barney T-shirt and sneakers with rainbow laces or anything ridiculous like that. "All right."

But it didn't seem to matter what he said. Eleri was already turning toward the Pygmy Goat, the local dive bar. "We're going where Nash was last seen. Do you think you'll be able to scent him there?"

It was only a few stoplights farther down the road.

"I don't know. It's been a few days, and it depends on how crowded it is. Also, how much the air filters are working or the ceiling fans. If he's been there recently, though, I may very well be able to pick up on it."

"In which case, he's not actually missing," Eleri pointed out.

That would be true. "That puts us back at square one and puts Jesse and Ciara Nash back to square zero."

But that didn't matter until it mattered. Eleri turned in to a bar that was a little more hopping than they'd expected for this late at night. He watched two patrons go in and decided that his clothing would be fine. While Eleri wasn't exactly in what Donovan would call "bar wear,"

She seemed to give zero fucks about it.

She was out of the car, standing on the sidewalk and waiting for him already. They were going inside whether he wanted to or not. He had designated her the senior agent for the press conference, and he was paying for that now.

He climbed out and almost jumped as the car beeped itself locked behind him. Eleri was already pushing her way through the heavy, ornate door. It opened to a room with air that was as heavy as the outside and music that was loud enough to make his eardrums quake.

Eleri must have seen him as he blinked and turned his head side to side. It was a natural reaction, as though he could get away from the repetitive thump. In reality, he was just trying to squeeze some of it out.

"You don't have to come in," she told him. But as Donovan looked around, he realized two of them were far better than one. He pushed past her.

"I'll deal."

While servers were coming to each table, there was no hostess seating customers. This gave them a chance to walk around and surreptitiously check out each corner, as though deciding on which table to take.

After making a loop that smelled only like beer and sweat—and not Eugene Nash—they slid onto the only open barstools they could find. Apparently, they weren't as stealthy as Donovan would have liked. Though they had changed clothes since they'd been featured at a press conference, they only made it three quarters of the way around, before somebody looked up and called out, "Hey! The feds are here!"

Donovan grinned as though it were a funny joke. *What else could he do?*

Now the bartender told them their first drink was on the house.

"Not necessary," Eleri said with a smile. "Neither of us will drink more than one. Caipirinha for me and..."

"Old Fashioned." Donovan didn't add that Eleri probably wouldn't even drink the one she ordered. His tolerance was much higher than hers.

While they waited for the drinks to come, Eleri turned to Donovan. "Do you smell him in here?"

"No. It's too mixed up. Too many people have been in and out since he came through."

She lowered her voice, aiming for a subhuman hearing range. "Do you think the killer has him?"

Donovan didn't have a chance to answer. The bartender was sliding their drinks across the bar and motioning again for them not to worry about it. He'd cover it with the tip.

But Eleri—ever the agent, even when sitting in a crowded bar at almost midnight—pulled out her phone as she asked the bartender to wait just a moment.

"Have you seen this man?" She held up the phone and the bartender only glanced at the photo briefly.

"Eugene. We've all seen him."

"When was the last time?"

The bartender pursed her lips and looked up and to the right, thinking before she said, "Two nights ago."

Donovan was about to tell Eleri that yes, he did think the killer had Eugene Nash. But, if the bartender remembered correctly, Nash had been seen more than twenty-four hours after stalking out of his own home three nights ago.

"Are you sure?" he pushed.

"I didn't work last night, so I don't know if he was here then, but he was here three nights ago, and again two nights ago."

"Alright, thanks." Donovan felt everything crash. Eugene Nash's luck was up, but theirs was dashed. He turned to Eleri. "Now what?"

39

"It's after midnight," Donovan protested as Eleri slammed the car door, shutting herself in the driver's seat. Their timeline just got screwed up and she hadn't even gotten to enjoy her drink.

She had interviews to conduct and—assuming the killer had Nash, which was now much less likely—every hour counted. She replied with a swift, "Watch me not care."

They had questioned the bartender further, asking who Eugene hung out with and if any of them were in the bar tonight. When none of his friends were pointed out, she and Donovan went to the guys down the bar who had noticed them showing Eugene's picture to the bartender. The men were more than just a little drunk and had readily "helped out."

"They gave us a lot of good information," she told Donovan, anxious to follow up on it.

Hands clenching the steering wheel and starting the car, she threw it in gear. They only had so much to go on, but after picking the locals' brains, she found it had now been less than twenty-four hours since someone had seen him. Eugene had to be *somewhere*.

"Why are we chasing a guy who doesn't seem to be part of our case?" Donovan asked as she fought not to speed down the empty streets like a mad dog.

"Because we don't know for certain that he's not," Eleri replied. "He's a prime target."

But Donovan pelted her with more questions. "Is one of our therapists a school counselor?"

"I don't know." Eleri tried to ease up, her hands about to break the steering wheel, her foot angry on the gas. "Look it up."

They'd gotten the lists from each of the therapists about whom they'd worked with—both other therapists and what institutions—and when. The next place they'd hoped to look was any name that showed up on more than one of the lists.

Their other goal had been to figure out *where* the damage might be occurring. The killer had a torture spot, and it wasn't where the bodies had been found. But Eleri's brain hadn't even gotten there yet. She was still hung up on Eugene Nash and would be until he was found.

"Gwen Song was a school counselor, but it was a different school and it was three years ago. She's not Ciara's counselor now," Donovan told her as Eleri followed her GPS to the first house on the list and pulled into the drive.

The windows were dark, the curtains drawn. The only light was one of what looked like it had originally belonged to a line of uplights set into the flower beds—the kind that would have been originally installed when the house was built. The rest were out. But Eleri was in full-steam-ahead mode, even if Donovan wasn't.

"Are you sure, El?" he asked.

"No, but the sooner we find him or the sooner Eugene Nash checks in, the sooner we can take him off our list and get back to following our killer."

Donovan was right. Eugene was almost definitely not part of their case, but she now had a deep-seated itch to find him. If he was alive, she was going to haul his ass into the sheriff and let Jesse Nash press whatever charges she could.

It was past midnight, but she didn't have anything better to do so she found herself walking up the concrete path before she could change her mind. Climbing the four stairs, she was knocking on the door even before Donovan made it up onto the porch behind her.

No one answered. She noticed that he almost put his hands in his pockets. But despite the T-shirt and the jeans and the slight smell of whiskey on his breath, he was clearly trying to remain professional. Clasping his hands in front of him, he did his best to assume a solid, federal agent stance.

She knocked again and was raising her hand to knock a third time when she heard the bolt slide from inside.

A woman in a pale pink nylon gown with a matching robe thrown over it answered the door. Her hair was up in curlers and the little pink tufts of fluff that edged the robe made Eleri almost smile. This woman could have opened the door into four or five decades ago. Almost. Her nails were painted in a thoroughly modern color that matched the toes on her bare feet.

"Who are you?" the woman asked with sleep still in her voice and her gaze.

Eleri dove in. "I'm agent Eleri Eames, and this is agent Donovan Heath. We're with the FBI."

"Oh, my God!" the woman said now, coming awake. "I know you!"

Even though she hadn't known them when she opened the door, Eleri didn't correct her.

"Are you here about that murder case?"

"We're here working several cases," Eleri only slightly lied.

"Oh, interesting," she drew the words out, her eyes were wide awake now.

Eleri didn't mean to venture any further than the porch, so she held up the picture on her phone. "Do you know this man?"

"I do." Her tone had changed, letting Eleri and Donovan know she wasn't a fan. "That's Eugene Nash."

"Have you seen him recently?"

"Unfortunately, yes." Her hand crept up to the fluff at the collar of her gown, her gaze growing wary.

"And you are Gussie Oatman? Married to Leroy Oatman?"

"I am."

"When did you last see Eugene Nash?" Eleri finally got to her main question.

"Three nights ago. He showed up here, madder than a hornet in a sock—"

Not a phrase Eleri had heard before.

"—and he told Leroy he needed a place to stay. So I woke up in the morning to find Eugene passed out on my couch. Needless to say, I screamed fit to wake the neighbors, finding him curled up under my grandma's quilt. And, oh, hell no, he was not staying." Gussie kept talking. "I told Leroy he had to kick Eugene out. He told me Eugene didn't have anywhere else to go, but I didn't think that was true, and I didn't care."

Interesting, Eleri thought. It lined up with Jesse's side of the story, that it was Eugene who'd walked out.

Gussie was still going. "I don't need anybody sleeping on my couch. He told Eugene that it was me that made him kick him out."

She was clearly bitter about that last part.

"And you haven't seen Eugene since?"

"I haven't."

"Do you know where else he might go?" Eleri was sitting on a list of two other names—people he might have crashed with, but she was fishing for more.

Gussie rattled off a new one, which Eleri wrote down quickly and asked what street they lived on. "And would you be willing to repeat all this in a sworn testimony to the police, if it comes to that?"

"Oh, yes, ma'am." The woman was getting into it now, almost excited to be part of a case. She didn't put things together the way Jesse Nash did, just happily volunteered information after midnight and didn't say "I hope you find him."

"Thank you for your time. And I'm sorry we bothered you so late."

Now Gussie was all smiles and dismissive waves. "Oh, don't you worry about that. I understand."

Eleri thanked her again and turned to walk off the porch. Donovan hadn't said anything. Though the door had closed behind them and she should have been comfortable speaking, for whatever reason, on this case, she no longer was. Eleri waited until they were back in the car.

"Smell anything?"

"Eugene. I mean, it's a home, not a bar. They don't have a ton of people come and going."

"Was Gussie lying?" Eleri started the engine, ready to wake up the next people.

"I don't think so. The scent of her and her husband and two teenage boys was much stronger. The Eugene part of the mix was pretty faint."

"Alright, on to the next house." She was already driving them there.

"El, it's going on one."

"Watch me not care," she repeated without rancor. She was

hauling him along, and he was being a good sport. But something told her she had to find Eugene.

She turned the wheel hand-over-hand. Astoria wasn't that big and, apparently, neither was the radius Eugene Nash traveled. They knocked on doors and woke people up at the next house and then the next, seeming to have followed Eugene's path.

He'd stayed with Gussie and Leroy Oatman the first night—the same night Jesse said he'd left. Then, with the second people Eleri had woken up—Simone and Thurston Milia—Eugene had found his lodgings for the second night. This was their fifth house, and Carl Vincenzo opened the door.

"Why are you knocking on my door after two a.m.?"

Eleri almost corrected him that it was merely 1:48 a.m., but instead she just plowed through the usual rigmarole. *Did he know this man? Had he seen him?*

"Yeah. He was at the Pygmy Goat two nights ago." Exactly where Eleri and Donovan had just been. "We had a beer."

"Was Thurston Milia there?" Eleri asked, thinking of the man he'd stayed with when he was last seen.

"Yeah. Seemed Euge had worn out his welcome, so I told him he could come stay with me."

This was the fifth house they'd been to, but they'd only accounted for two of the three nights Eugene had been gone.

Simone Milia had given them pretty much the same response as Lydia Oatman had at the first house. Thurston had let Eugene stay for one night and Simone made sure it was one night only. The men were friends. The wife wasn't.

This was the last place, and no one had seen him after he left the Milia house that morning when Simone kicked him out. Eleri had expected to find that Eugene was here or get a name of where Eugene had gone.

"He hasn't stayed with you?"

"No," Carl told her. "I thought he was going to. But he never showed up."

Next to her, she could practically hear Donovan's ears perk.

40

Here he was, awake and working again at three a.m. For this case, it seemed to be just the way things worked.

Donovan climbed into the back of the tinted-window SUV and began rolling his shoulders. Eleri sat in the driver's seat, not turning her head and kindly not glancing into the rearview mirror. If she'd ever done it, he hadn't caught her.

His muscles stretched as bone shifted. He'd never dislocated his shoulder, but he imagined this was a quick version of what that must feel like. It was certainly a mid-level of pain while it was happening, and a great relief when everything slid back into its new, proper place.

His skin tingled and almost itched. As he shifted, the hair on his arms, legs, and torso had stood up, the way normal people's did when they got cold. Only his hair was thicker, and the shafts pushed further out of his skin. He was already a relatively hairy guy, but with his darker skin tone and black hair, very few people ever remarked on it. Now it had the consistency and quality of a slick, shiny fur.

He rotated his jaw, feeling the mandible shift into its new home. He had tiny notches in his rib cage, near the spine. He knew this because, at night, when no one was in the medical examiner's office back in South Carolina, he'd slipped himself into the x-ray machine and checked. He'd wanted to know how he did what he did.

No one had ever explained it to him. His father had been the only one like him that he'd known for decades—and Aidan Heath made Eugene Nash look like an upstanding citizen. It was only recently that Donovan had learned that his family line wasn't the only one. He had Eleri to thank for that, too.

He rolled his neck, feeling everything settle into its new spot—or its old one. Donovan wasn't sure which form was true.

With a low growl, he alerted Eleri that he was ready.

She looked up, almost startled, absorbed by whatever she'd been doing on her phone. They sat in the dark interior of the car, parked in front of a squat brick building that looked like it had been built in the sixties and that its maintenance had stopped in the seventies.

The whole scene looked different to Donovan now. Everything about him had shifted, even the colors he saw. The scene was very blue-green, almost entirely lacking reds and yellows. The dulling of the color made other things stand out. It shifted his vision further into the distance and caught more subtle movement. It would be a lifelong study to note the differences, but now wasn't the time.

He looked out the front window now, seeing the three-dimensional letters standing out from the front overhang that read "Astoria Unemployment Office."

This place must be a joy to visit, he thought. For someone like Eugene— hitting a personal low and having to publicly show up and admit it—this was yet another hit in a long line of them. Not that he felt sorry for the man.

Eugene was supposed to have been here less than seventeen hours ago. No one had seen him since he left the Milias residence—no one they could ask at three a.m. anyway. When the unemployment office opened in the morning, they could check, but by then, they would be twenty-four hours out. And Eugene Nash had already moved up their list as a potential victim.

Donovan was hoping to pick up the scent.

Eleri opened the back gate of the car, as Donovan was now unable to let himself out—latches were not made for paws and claws. He turned and hopped down out of the back, thinking again how his change made them perfectly dependent on each other.

"Okay, Donovan. What's up?"

Biren! he thought. She was supposed to use his middle name, so that no one connected him with the dog—the dog that was supposedly her friend's cadaver-sniffing dog.

He wanted that whole line to be a joke, but he hadn't quite gotten over it. At least this wasn't one of the scenes where she had to leash him or anything.

He trotted right up to the front of the building, sniffing his way along. He put his nose down into the crack where the brick met the sidewalk. Smells could get trapped down in there. Things that were sticky often held on to them better, and there was plenty of gum or ground-in candy on the sidewalk here. He sniffed his way around.

"Got him?" Eleri asked, maybe a little too anxious.

He tipped his head side to side to say he wasn't sure. Eugene *might* be in the mix, but with so many people having been through, he couldn't be sure.

Following a faint trail, he hoped it would be Eugene, but it quickly switched to something else. Donovan abandoned it and went back to the start point in front of the double doors.

Eleri tapped away on her phone, clearly after something of her own, and let him go about his own business.

Donovan worked back and forth in a wider and wider swath, still hoping to pick up something worth following.

Eleri looked up. "Door handles, maybe?"

It was as good as anything, he thought. Heading back to the double front doors with the wide, gunmetal hand pulls and art deco designs popular from the era, he sniffed at them a little bit. Maybe Eugene was there?

He let his nose follow the frame round, but as his nose hit right at the crack between the two of them, he barked.

"You got him?" Eleri wasn't looking at her phone now.

Donovan nodded. The scent was higher on the doors than he would have expected. Sometimes shoes masked the scent, sometimes they helped. Sometimes the smells wafted off bodies and caught in crevices. Maybe this one had lingered in the space between the doors. He let his nose move up and down, sticking close to the rough surface.

Though he followed it up, putting his paws up high on the door, and got his nose up near five feet into the air, it wasn't there. Back at the middle, he found it trailed away to the left. He traced his way along the side of the building, sniffing at the tiny pores in the rough brick, but didn't find it.

Returning to the middle again, he found the scent and repeated the motion toward the right. This time, he caught it.

He barked to Eleri.

This was a free-standing building. Though others were close, the lots were slightly separated, with a grass alleyway between them. Donovan followed Eugene's scent around the corner, his nose tickling with something else he recognized.

He followed it to the edge of the sidewalk, where he hopped off and felt his paws squish. The grass was starting to collect dew in the early morning hours. Donovan didn't mind. He still followed the scent caught in the brick. It lingered, mixed with other people and now with cigarette smoke.

For a moment, he'd thought it was gone as he sniffed up and down the side of the wall. But as he stepped back and forth, trying to find Eugene's scent on this side of the building, his paw stepped down on something squishy—cigarettes.

The butts were also wet with dew, but that would hold the scent to them. Dropping his head, Donovan inspected each one. They lay in a haphazard pattern and it made sense: pick up an unemployment check, feel shitty, head around the corner for a smoke. Lastly, drop the butt into the grass.

Donovan sniffed the first. It didn't belong to Eugene, nor did the second third, fourth, tenth, or eleventh.

But the twelfth one did.

He looked up to Eleri and gave another short, sharp bark.

Eugene Nash had been here. According to his friend, Eugene was supposed to swing by around ten, kill a little time during the day, and then hook up with Carl when he got off of work. But Eugene had never showed.

Donovan sniffed at more of the cigarette butts. Only one belonged to Eugene.

Where did he go after this? Donovan wondered. He lifted his nose to sniff at the wall again.

That's when he caught the other scent that had been tickling the back of his brain, but he hadn't placed it.

Now, he turned back to Eleri and gave her the signal of two sharp barks before he took off running.

41

"Wait, Donovan!" Eleri called out.

He had already ducked between the buildings and was heading into the Everglades.

She had her boots on, because she'd wanted to be ready if they found something. It had become more likely when they didn't find Eugene Nash alive and drunk at a bar or at any of his friends' houses.

"Wait, Donovan!" she called again, and she saw up ahead that he stopped, turned, and looked back at her. She'd passed between the buildings now, stepping into the open space behind them. There was no parking lot back here, and her feet squished into the wet grass.

Still running after, she caught up to him. "Hold on."

When she'd been at home recovering, she'd thought this might be necessary one day. It seemed a simple enough thing to work on and removed enough from where she'd been and what she'd done, that she'd made it a hobby. Other people crocheted or painted—Eleri checked her family's Book of Shadows and worked on useful spells.

She'd copied the text and brought the herbs. She'd been working on it before she fell asleep some nights. Today, she'd stuffed the sachet into her pocket, almost forcing herself to remember.

Having no idea if it would work, she pulled it free and held it up by the strings, as though this should impress her partner. He could probably smell it and probably wondered why she'd brought a sock drawer freshener with her. But she placed the hand stitched bag she'd taken from Grandmere's so long ago into her hand. As she clenched it in her fist, she said the word she hoped would activate it.

"Dico." She said it again. *"Dico."*

Then she held it out.

Shit. She had not thought far enough ahead. Donovan was supposed to *wear* it. But he would not take kindly to her looping something around his neck. He hated any type of leash or a collar.

Never mind. She grabbed the chain on her own neck and looped the ribbon ties through before offering up the Latin command for *speak* again. She would have to wear it herself and hope it worked.

Donovan knew enough to understand—too much med school, too much time talking with Wade and Art and Will at the de Gottardi/Little farm with the only other wolves he'd really ever befriended.

Eleri looked him in the eyes as he clearly questioned her actions and her sanity.

"I'm hoping to understand you now." She could almost see his one eyebrow go up, a dog's quirk on his face, but he easily understood the idea. "Say something."

The sound that came out of his mouth was an odd bark/growl combo.

"Holy shit." She felt her own grin. "You scented the killer!"

He jerked back and even she could read the surprise on his face.

"It's a spell. I've been working on it."

"Since when?"

"Haha, I totally understood that!" She jumped up and down, definitely looking ridiculous in her knee-high rubber boots, sweating in the Florida heat in the middle of the night.

"Good for you. We've got to go." His tone was droll and she loved that she could hear it. This was what magic was for: small helps and pushes. Not for anger and fire, not like the Queen's Staircase.

"Yes, sir." She offered a salute, but unless he had eyes on his butt, he didn't see it. She took off, following behind him, already knowing that she wouldn't be able to keep up. The only thing that allowed her to maintain his pace was that he stopped so often to sniff at things.

Her turned his head and offered an odd, low whine.

"The killer has Eugene Nash?" she asked and got one bark in reply.

She heard *Yes,* in her head, but she always heard that anyway with one single Donovan bark. It was a code they'd worked out long ago.

She had known for a long time that she had the power to cast a spell of this magnitude. And she wondered now as she spoke to him, was she the one hearing him, or was she emitting sounds more like a dog? After all, she was wearing the sachet intended to go around his neck. No one was out here, so did it matter?

Her feet pounded into the ground, sometimes slipping and throwing her off balance. She had her gun strapped to her hip and she peeled her jacket as she went. It was far too heavy to be wearing it in this weather, let alone running in it. She'd worn it to cover the firearm, but—again—with no one out here, little mattered.

The unemployment office, much like Sylvia Lambrecht's house, backed up onto woods. Planned and planted with oaks and maples, the ground sloped quickly away to Cypress and algae. Eleri could feel the soil's sturdiness change under her feet. The earth had been built up in areas where the buildings were constructed, a specific effort to make the ground solid enough to build on and high enough to avoid flooding. But as she left manufactured ground, she stepped into wilderness.

Donovan paused, sniffed at two trees, and kept going. Eleri fought to keep up. In the dark of night, it was difficult to follow a very black dog. But so far, he'd stuck to what appeared to be a decent path.

"Wait. Donovan, Wait!"

Again, he turned and looked at her.

She'd seen something and needed to turn around and go back. The earth was wet, almost wet enough to slide back into place when it was gouged or damaged.

"Here." She pointed to what she'd seen. "Is this a drag mark?"

Donovan had approached her, coming close to the rut she'd found that could have been a heel mark from a person being tugged backwards. He put his nose down to it and sniffed. "Yes, it's him."

"And he wasn't walking," Eleri added.

Donovan shook his head side to side.

"So the killer definitely has him, and you can smell the killer, too." She just had to confirm all of it.

"Yes," Donovan told her, before turning away again, loping along the path, and forcing her to keep up.

Her feet moved in a steady rhythm as did her thoughts. Her eyes looked for roots and ruts, and she tried not to trip, but her brain had thoughts about what the killer's place might be like.

Holding people hostage was expensive in terms of money and time and effort. People often thought about kidnapping, but if you kidnapped someone, you had to feed them. If you didn't, they didn't last very long. You had to bring them water. You had to have a place for them to be where you could either tie them down or lock them in and they couldn't escape. Because if they easily escaped, then they weren't very well kidnapped, were they?

If you did manage to hold on to them, it was a fact of nature that they were going to need to urinate and defecate. That was going to happen wherever you kept them. Very few people were content to deal with the smells and the cleanup. So Eleri figured these people were maybe drugged and damaged to the point where they couldn't quite perform the usual bodily functions.

They also wouldn't be able to fight back before the killer started working on them. She'd checked the bodies for binding marks on the wrists and ankles and found none. There were very few defensive wounds, too. In several cases, it seemed there were none. Most people would fight back if someone was coming at them with a knife. All it took was a raised arm or an innate last-minute turn to deflect and the knife marks wouldn't have ended up where they did.

The story from the foster home supported this, but the empty toxicology reports didn't.

Eleri kept chugging along, trying to pace herself. Donovan didn't have to. Her thoughts still followed another path. *What if I were the kidnapper?*

If she was going to keep one of these people—and if she was going to inflict this kind of pain—she would need access to drugs and syringes. She would also need access to a room, likely one with a drain in the middle, and access to water. And she would probably need water pressure high enough that she could hose it down. Where would that place be?

Donovan put his nose to the ground again. Then he looked back at her and barked.

Eugene Nash, though he had stormed out of his home three days ago, had been missing slightly less than twenty-four hours. He was still in the typical missing persons "golden window" time frame, but with this killer, Eleri didn't know if that would be enough. JP Talley's time missing would make her think the killer kept them for several days. That would bode well for Nash. But if the death was relatively quick—just getting the victims far enough away to do the damage—then Eugene might already be dead.

She was running headlong into a mess. Donovan had claws and fangs and power, but she was the only one with a gun and the authority to arrest. She had no idea if this killer was following her imagined protocol or had designed their own, but she was about to find out.

42

Donovan pushed forward, the ground softer and wetter the further he went into the glades.

Eleri was right. Eugene Nash had been dropped like a sack of dead weight. He'd smoked a cigarette back by the building, the smell and the scent of him and the cigarette embedding itself in the rough brick, and on the butt of the cigarette. It had waited there, lingering through the day, for Donovan to pick it up.

Then the killer had come into the area, again the scent faint—so faint he hadn't been sure. Back here, it was clear the killer and Nash were traveling together, and Donovan came to the conclusion that there hadn't been much of a struggle. If the two had exerted themselves, the killer should have left behind a dose of pheromones, fear, or excitement. Donovan had smelled none of that.

In fact, it occurred to him now as he ran after this person, that he'd never scented any of those changes. Was he was dealing with one of the coldest-blooded killers that he might ever have come up against? All the best fighters have learned to slow or still their reactions. But this? It was so low on the scale that the abduction had the same scent profile as someone doing their job. And he'd not smelled anything else from the killer as he made his way through the glades, where everything was rich and loamy. The only extra information that filled his sinuses was the exertion of the killer dragging the body along behind them.

So far, what he was scenting was alive. Given what they'd seen on the other bodies, Donovan fully expected him to be so at least for some time. It wasn't possible to inflict pain on a dead man, and the autopsies had clearly shown that the wounds and pulled fingernails had occurred while the victims were alive.

There would be no point in changing MO now. At least, Donovan hoped not, because that would work in their favor. And, honestly, while he was on the path to save Eugene Nash's life, he couldn't say he would lose any sleep if Nash lost a few fingernails along the way.

Stopping for a moment, consciously remembering that Eleri struggled to keep up with even his casual gait, he turned to look behind him. Though he couldn't see her, he could hear her crashing through the brush.

As he waited, he anxiously looked up ahead. The path was fading away as he traced it. Most people didn't come this far into unused land. But there was enough to follow and he could occasionally find ruts where the feet had been dragged and the marks leading him forward, even as the scent did.

He was impatient. Eleri was slow, and Eugene's life might hang in the balance at the other end. But Donovan didn't have breadcrumbs to leave for his partner to follow along. If they got separated, that could be trouble for either of them. In fact, if he was seen wandering alone out here, he might be shot. He looked enough like a wolf, and enough like a threat, that anyone who killed him might only get a slap on the wrist from the Wildlife Commission—but Donovan would still be dead.

He wasn't going to do that to Eleri. He stopped to let her catch up. She came into view, jogging along steadily, keeping pace as best she could, given the rough terrain. She was in good shape, and he had to appreciate the effort. After all, she was only human.

She motioned him on and he took off again, nose to the ground, snuffling as he went. The scents he picked up were the same. It simply confirmed he was on the right path. The foot tracks were backwards—the killer had been dragging Eugene Nash, who was also facing backwards. Given the spacing, the killer probably had his hands hooked under Eugene's arms. Drugged people were dead weight, and dead weight was the hardest to carry, even harder than someone actively fighting back.

Adrenaline spiked his own system even if it didn't spike the killer's. They had to be getting close. He'd covered enough ground, and it made sense to drag someone back into the Everglades to torture them. No one would hear them scream. The untrod swamps weren't usually the places people came for hiking or exploring.

Some did. But it wasn't that common, and the killer could rest assured that the odds of being found were low. The scent profile proved it: The killer and the victim were the only ones who had been back here. *They were close.*

Finally, two plus weeks into this crazy case, and it took another victim to get the killer found. But if they saved Eugene Nash, then they could close this with a solid green checkmark in the box.

Periodically, Donovan lifted his head, scanning the area in front of him, making sure that he was alert for any dangers coming at him. Because what he could smell was the past, not the future.

This time, he caught sight of the corner of a small wooden building. The wood was aged to blend into the surroundings quite readily. The little Cypress hut would be perfect, and the scent was leading him right toward it.

Though he wanted to turn and bark to Eleri, he knew that making noise would give them away, and giving them away could get them killed. The killer did, after all, have a gun. If they were smart, it had a suppressor on it. So they could easily take Eleri and Donovan out, hide the bodies in the bog, and the agents would never be found.

Donovan slowed, waiting for Eleri to catch up and silently, mentally warning her to stay back. Then he remembered the spell, and turned to offer a low growl. It was a sound that shouldn't register as out of place out here in the Glades—nothing that would make their killer look up from their devious work.

Eleri immediately understood.

It was a damn fine spell, he thought as she dropped low, crouching onto the balls of her feet and slowly stepping forward. Now, the two of them stalked their way in, his nose periodically going to the ground, though his eyes stayed alert for movement.

Eleri, with her gun drawn, walked slightly sideways, making herself narrower, something Donovan couldn't do in this form. Unfortunately, Eleri—the human—would be the main target. Most people didn't worry about a wolf bearing witness to their activities. So he stayed in front, buffering her the best he could, and slowly, quietly they cased the small cabin.

Donovan scented blood.

43

The scent was strong here. Donovan almost didn't have to sniff to follow it. He found tracers of the killer everywhere, but it was Nash he was following on a straight line in.

There was no front porch on the small, weathered cabin. The front door itself looked as though it didn't seal tightly. The wood siding had likely once been beautiful, but had warped unevenly as it aged, leaving gaps. This place would be a nightmare if a storm hit, or if it ever got cold. On hot days, it was probably a sauna. Given what the killer did to the victims, that was probably a positive in their book.

Nothing was dead inside the cabin. Even in the darkest, coolest hours of night, it was still hot. Anything dead would be decomposing, and Donovan would have picked it up.

Slowly he crept along, his sensitive ears perking. Donovan aimed wide, hoping for a warning before anything dangerous came their way. But he picked up no other sound than Eleri, a few nutria, and a handful of large, wading birds—only the things that should be in the Everglades, and not the killer.

Turning around, he let another small, odd roll of vocals come out of his throat and hoped Eleri and her strange witchcraft understood. She nodded that she did.

He couldn't hear the killer inside. He wasn't close enough to detect a heartbeat, but he didn't hear movement, though that might mean that he and Eleri had been discovered and the killer had hunkered down and stopped moving.

If Eugene Nash was inside, he was likely drugged, as there was no thrashing or thumping. Donovan would have heard that.

Eleri nodded at him again and, with a small motion of her hand, she told him to go forward. He wondered if her speaking spell held or if she was just agreeing with the general idea that they should be careful.

They slowly worked their way in toward the cabin with no windows. It lacked decoration and the roof was sagging but, even close enough to see the grain in the wood, Donovan heard nothing.

The smells trailed in wild rivulets around cabin. The killer had been here frequently.

Taking a sniff, Donovan felt a faint odor tickle the inside of his nose. *JP Talley*. This was it. This was where the work of murder was being performed.

Another sniff, another step, and he was close enough now. The blood he scented was Eugene Nash's. In fact, he could smell the decay starting to set in. It coated the coppery scent of fresh blood, letting Donovan know this hadn't happened within the last hour.

Decay began almost instantaneously after a death. There was something about the change as the heart stopped beating that left a trail. Though Donovan's senses were keen in this form, he was starting to wonder just how much blood was in there. The smell had assaulted him far back.

Eugene Nash's was fresher. Talley's had taken a little while longer for him to pick up, and there were more scents layered underneath. Dark and dried, dead copper pinged along his neurons. The bodies might be gone, but the question was: Was the killer huddled in a corner, gun waiting, ready to shoot Eleri as they walked in the door?

Donovan couldn't tell. The scents were strong. Could he pick out the killer's live smell and separate it from all the trails and tracers swirling around?

Eleri had flanked the cabin, seeming to look for small gaps in the wood that would allow her to peer inside, but she hadn't seemed to have found anything useful. Her finger raised to her lips, her hair catching glints of red light despite being pulled back. The curls formed a far too friendly puff at the back of the base of her neck for the job that she was performing.

He watched as she moved to the front door and Donovan trailed her, taking the other side. She stayed near the hinges, gun held at the ready in her dominant hand, the other reaching across for the knob. He noticed she didn't even try to twist it, just pushed on the door and watched it swing inward.

They both braced, but nothing happened. He sniffed and shook his head. Now that the door was open, it was clear no one was here. In fact, the smell wasn't even strong enough for Nash's body to have been removed all that recently. Several hours ago, maybe, but not just before they arrived.

Donovan looked up at Eleri and gave another of his low growl/whines that went through several syllables.

"Dead?" she asked, her tone soft in case the killer was still around.

Donovan entertained the possibility someone might be watching. Could the killer have come back? Could they be hidden, ready with a sniper rifle?

Donovan nudged Eleri inside and out of any line of sight. They ducked low, finding themselves in an almost square wooden box. The air hovered, still and hot and rich.

Some of blood had washed away. Other smells lingered, mostly urine and sweat and fear. People who were afraid pissed their pants on the regular, he knew. But the lack of human feces told him that they hadn't stayed here long enough for that to happen. *Interesting*.

The torture might last for hours, or even beyond a day, but it hadn't gone much beyond that. The victims weren't given a reprieve. They were tortured until they were at death's door. And then they were dead.

"It's a good design," Eleri said, "—for probably not having been designed for this at all."

After all, what was *designed for this?* Donovan didn't want to know.

He wanted to sniff each corner but, though the space was probably the coolest it would get, it was still a hotbox. He could see Eleri plucking at her shirt. He offered another growl. *Let's go out carefully.*

She hugged the inside wall, peeking out the door with her gun and just half of her face momentarily—fast enough to scan the area, quick enough to not present a target.

He did the same. They looked at each other and automatically shifted positions. They'd told him at Quantico that when he and his partner had worked together long enough, they would anticipate each other's movements. He and Eleri had been that way from the start. Though it had taken him a while to figure out that was most likely because she was reading everyone's mind, whether she knew she was doing it or not

Eleri moved lower down in the door frame as Donovan lifted his head higher and they did it again. It was as safe as they could be. They saw nothing, and he heard and smelled nothing to indicate they were in immediate danger.

Slowly, Eleri rolled her way around the door frame, probably getting splinters in the process. But she led with her gun and stepped outside, staying plastered low against the building. She couldn't turn sideways to protect from a threat if she didn't know where it was coming from, but she followed all the protocols she'd learned from the FBI.

Long minutes ticked by as they waited.

Sweat rolled down Eleri's temples, but her gun didn't waver. Eventually, she lifted her free hand, palm up. "There's nothing, Donovan."

He offered a nod and breathed out a sigh of relief and put his nose back to the ground. They didn't want to disturb the cabin any more than they already had. This time, he followed the scent of the dead body. Once again, the killer had flipped it on to its back, probably hooked arms under Eugene's shoulders and dragged him along.

They followed a little slower now that he knew there was no life to save. Donovan turned to face Eleri behind him.

"The killer's gone?" she asked.

"Hasn't been here in recent hours," he replied. And they began to move with much more freedom. They followed the scents in silence.

After a while, the sun was up and they'd traveled far enough to make him wonder if the killer had been here when they had been back scoping out the cabin. It would be a long walk back to the car, but the scent of decay was growing stronger.

They were close.

44

Eleri examined the body of Eugene Nash. At first, she just stood and looked, one hip cocked out as she did a preliminary assessment of the scene.

The body was crooked, the head at an odd angle, not quite what she would expect if his neck was broken, but definitely uncomfortable enough to be clear he was dead.

One hand was twisted all the way around, the arm broken. His hand lay palm up in the soft, muddy puddle. His legs bent and listed to the side, almost as if he were trying to pose like he was running. But Eugene Nash wouldn't do that anymore.

She wanted to feel bad for him. She wanted to feel bad about the bloody fingertips. He'd had the same three nails pulled that had been missing on JP Talley and Earlene Beaman.

She still thought only taking three was odd, but it seemed a particular form of torture, not to pull them all.

Dark slashes crossed Nash's torso, bold and bloody—fabric, skin, and muscle sliced cleanly through. Being trained as she was, Eleri knew she was catching glimpses of bone. In another area, she spotted the fascia of the abdomen—still, not fatal cuts. Lastly, he had a bullet hole in the middle of his shirt. Right to the sternum.

She wanted to call Donovan over, to let him get close and sniff. Instead, she pulled out her phone, took a picture, and then added a filter. With the altered coloring, it did look like residue on the shirt, indicating the killer stood very close by when firing the fatal bullet.

With his head tilted, the entry wound to his temple was aimed skyward. The exit wound would be soaking in the mud and the muck. It mattered to her, even if nothing more mattered to Eugene now. It looked as though the killer had placed the head carefully, to be sure the gunshot wound was straight up and easy to see.

Interesting.

"I'm going to call this in," she told Donovan. "It will take them a while to get out here." Then she motioned to the ground around the body. "Let's keep your paw prints out of the scene if we can."

He tipped his head, and she could almost hear the sarcasm in his gaze. He'd been carefully walking the perimeter. Now he turned and growled back at her as she searched for Tucker's number.

"I'm going to see if I can follow the killer out."

She paused. "Wait, is that what we want to do next? Leave the body here and trace the killer?"

She heard him, clear as day. "If you call the sheriff, they'll descend on the scene. And if we get close, the killer may spook."

It was a rough call. The appropriate format was to call the authorities, establish a perimeter, and not leave the body once they'd found it. But… they *were* the authorities, and tracking the killer was far more important.

There was nothing they could do for Eugene Nash now. And if predators came along and took pieces of him, well…

"Hold on." With her phone held out at various angles, she walked a circle, taking pictures of the body, both with flash on and off. She hated pictures, but if something happened, she would need this for reference.

Once she'd done everything she could with just a gun and a cell phone, she motioned Donovan to lead on. He tracked slightly wider and wider circles around the body until he found the right spot, whatever that was.

She was left following along, though she was soon able to easily pick up signs here and there that let her know that they were on the right path, even if she wouldn't have gotten here by herself.

She passed a clear footprint. *Not a large looking foot,* she'd thought, even as she quickly snapped another picture. On television, they always took a print and instantly declared it a Nike size 11 men's. But that wasn't realistic. Snow, dirt, and even concrete expanded and contracted as it dried and changed, and the sneaker companies often shared treads. Though exact size couldn't be determined, general size could, and this had been a little bit smaller than she'd expected.

Unfortunately, it might not mean anything. Small people sometimes had big feet and vice versa, and there wasn't much extrapolation that she could do. She could only say that, statistically, it was likely that the killer was shorter and smaller than she had initially estimated.

She looked up to see that Donovan had moved further in front of her and she jogged to catch up. She'd never re-holstered her weapon. If they were following the killer, they might be getting close. Donovan likely wouldn't pose the kind of threat that someone would shoot at, but she couldn't be sure. So she kept the gun close.

Aside from a few moments where he would stop, lift his head, and sniff the base of a tree or such, Donovan just kept plodding forward.

Eleri felt her energy waning. The adrenaline had kept her going while looking for Eugene Nash, but finding his dead body had slowed her down. That she was petrified of the killer being in front of them or above or behind them, and knowing that she would have to react quickly to stay alive, should have kept her on high alert. It didn't do the job well enough.

The energy feeding her legs and keeping her moving was slowly draining away. She needed food and water, and none of that was an option right now. She also had no idea how far she was from society, only that she was a long way from the car. Possibly, she was three feet from a restaurant or two hundred miles from the nearest civilization. She pulled out her phone to check and found her signal wasn't strong enough to grab an accurate location.

Figures.

So she followed Donovan, who seemed to need nothing more than to keep pushing forward. She hadn't carried her kit. It was too heavy. While she would have loved to flag the edges of the crime scene and cordon it off with yellow tape, she'd simply abandoned it. The killer could loop back and move the body. Or predators could come and munch pieces of the freshly dead Eugene.

She and Donovan might be faster than they thought they were. They could catch up and get murdered right here in the middle of nowhere. She clearly needed food. She was getting morbid.

Eleri looked up at the bright sky. She had no idea where she was, so she kept walking aimlessly forward until she almost bumped into Donovan. Stopping suddenly, she looked at him as he shook his head. He'd stopped. "What?"

He offered another vocal roll that said, "I don't know." And he turned and walked back past her, heading back the way they'd come. He put his nose to the ground again and retraced their steps.

He walked so close to where she stood that she stepped backward into the brush, getting off what little invisible path there was. He made it three feet past her, then he stopped and did it again.

This time, he sniffed left, heading a few feet into the brush. Eleri watched as that clearly yielded nothing, and he headed back across the path, checking out the brush and undergrowth to the right. Looking confused, he turned a full circle and spiraled his way out with his nose to the ground before coming back and sitting right in front of her.

He looked up, gray eyes worried. His voice started with a low growl and twisted into a worried roll. "Eleri, the scent just disappears."

45

"You should get some sleep," Sheriff Tucker told her.

Eleri knew the wear and tear was showing. Still, she said, "Thanks, but I'm good."

The fact was, she was doing okay. This wasn't the first time she'd been up for more than thirty-six hours straight. And leaving the scene as the body was processed would have left her with second-hand information.

They were only several hours behind the murder itself. Whereas Talley's body had sat in the glades for a while before it was found, this time, they'd been right behind the killer.

Having been awake for so long and having marched who knew how many miles through the thick underbrush that made every step harder, Eleri wasn't willing to leave the scene now. But she was more than willing to let the crime scene techs take over. She was more than content to let them take the pictures and swab the body. They rolled it over to check his internal temperature to back calculate time of death.

One of the techs—who had to be dying in that Tyvek suit—looked up and waved to get Eleri's attention. "He's ninety-two point nine degrees. Given the high ambient temperature, I would put his TOD at about four or five hours ago." Then she grinned. "Is that what you expected?"

"It is." Eleri dug up whatever reserves she had and smiled back.

They purposefully hadn't told the team what their suspected time frame or MO was, in the hopes that the techs would look at the scene with fresh eyes and maybe draw some conclusions that they hadn't.

The tech pointed to Nash's hands. "The pulled nails appear to be the same configuration as what some foreign countries do to prisoners of war. It's a known torture technique. I looked it up."

"Good work," Eleri told her. *Good tech,* she thought. That would have been news to her had an analyst not found Dexter Allen and linked it already.

She surveyed the scene again and took a sip of her sports drink. She wasn't really thirsty, but she needed it to stay hydrated and awake. After tracking the killer's scent out away from the scene until it disappeared, she and Donovan had turned around and retraced their steps.

They'd come back to find the corpse undisturbed. No one had discovered the body while they'd walked away. But that wasn't surprising. Who was out that late or that early? Who would be this far back in the Everglades on a path that had been created by a killer dragging a body? Someone would have had to randomly stumble across the corpse in the last few hours. So Eleri had supposed it was likely safe, and they'd bypassed by the body a second time, skirting wide around the scene to not leave prints, leaving Eugene Nash where he lay.

They'd headed back to the hotel under the guise of changing clothes and allowing Donovan to change into someone the sheriff would listen to. But there had been no sleep. They'd simply changed into dry clothing. Lord knew she was already dressed for traipsing through the muck in the mud. The sun was fully up by the time she called sheriff Tucker and told him what they'd found. Then they'd headed back out, stopping at a coffee shop drive-thru. She'd arrived with a frothy coffee drink in her hand, icy and cold. It had disappeared quite some time ago.

The sheriff might not have fully believed them, because he took one look at the body and only said, "Son of a bitch," before tacking on something about Eugene Nash deserving the end he had come to. Then, Tucker pulled out a satellite phone and issued more instructions to his team.

The extreme spottiness of cell phones back here was an interesting thing, Eleri now contemplated. It meant people didn't traipse out this way much. If they became injured, how would they signal for help? Which meant the killer could work under greater cover. Even if someone did catch them in the act, who could the witness alert? As far as the killer was concerned, it was a stellar choice.

The crime scene team had now picked the body up and moved it onto a backboard. Eleri didn't envy them having to haul the literal dead weight out of here. It was one of the last things to do. The techs had already photographed everything and taken plaster casts of all the impressions at the scene, as well as Eleri's shoes. As the first two left, the remaining techs started collecting soil samples. It was almost two p.m. and Eleri was beyond ready to leave.

The same tech with the great comments earlier came up to her, this time seemingly shy. Eleri didn't get it. It must be because she was an FBI agent.

"Can we get a cast of the dog's paw?"

Ah, a request that Eleri should have been ahead of. "I can get you one."

But she didn't like thinking what that would require. "Do we need it? It's clearly not the killer's print. And only the one dog was out here."

She said it nicely, though her thinking was a little more sarcastic. *Actually, it's a wolf. But whatever.* Clearly, she needed food and maybe more caffeine. And about fifteen hours of sleep before she even contemplated telling Donovan she needed a plaster cast of a shape he was no longer in.

The tech nodded and Eleri tried to be more polite. "I'll call my friend today and ask her if she can get that for you."

Though, while Eleri would blame the outcome on her friend, ultimately it would be up to Donovan. He probably wouldn't want to do it. She was just grateful that no one had yet asked to meet the dog.

"Well, if we rule out the dog," the tech said, more confident now, "and we take your prints out, there's really only one other set of prints. Well, there's the sheriff and there's your partner, but they stayed well out of the scene."

Eleri nodded. "Anything preliminary to report?"

"Standard hiking boots tread and the ground is so soft, it's hard to read."

"What size would you estimate?" Eleri figured this tech, Glenda, would have the right of it.

She was clearly moving into her area of expertise and speaking more freely. "It looks like a women's size eight or nine or a men's size seven, maybe six."

"Small foot for a man," Eleri commented, "or average for a woman."

The conversation stalled and the tech went back to the scene, getting down on her knees again. Eleri didn't miss the work right now.

The problem with glades—with woods in general—was that it was incredibly difficult to lift fingerprints. There were likely plenty on Nash's body, but the blood alone would obscure most of what the killer had left behind. If they got lucky, the killer had touched the blood before it dried, and then left a clean print in Nash's blood somewhere else.

But from what Eleri had seen, there wouldn't be anything that obvious.

"We should head out." Donovan got her attention, tapping her arm as though to pull her away.

"They're not done," she sighed. She didn't want to miss anything.

"They're done enough. We need food and we need sleep. And then we need to get to the medical examiner's office tonight to do the autopsy."

Shit, she thought. She'd momentarily forgotten about the need to do the autopsy when no one else was around. Her tics and odd actions were a little easier to cover. If she got a moment, she could touch the bones and close her eyes and just say she was praying. There were far more excuses for her actions than for Donovan lifting a liver to his nose and taking a good deep inhale. Once she'd even seen him lick the air around it. If he then declared they needed a tox screen that he was correct about, things would get very, very suspicious. They had to do the autopsies at night, when no one was watching.

Tucker must have overheard Donovan. "He's right. Go back and get some sleep."

Tucker had a vested interest in them getting to the autopsy tonight. He'd be wanting the report. Even if the case was truly in their hands, Eugene Nash was his people.

But as she turned and walked away, Eleri heard the soft voice of the tech she had been speaking to. "Oh. Oh! This is interesting."

46

Donovan held the electropherogram in his hands as he studied it.

Eleri had somehow managed to push the DNA results through very quickly. The lab had it back to them in the amount of time that it took for the machines to work. It was incredibly rare to get a result back this fast.

It was also incredibly rare to see the thing that had made the tech declare the results interesting on site. She'd pulled up a plug of soil and swabbed it and run an assay on the sample. It had turned up *two* blood types—an O positive and a B negative.

Though he and Eleri had been leaving, they'd immediately gone back to see what the tech had found. Then they'd quickly tried to leave the scene again. Beyond the tests getting ordered, there hadn't been much they could do, until now.

Turning to Eleri, he held out one of the papers she'd just printed for them. "This is a mess."

When reading DNA graphs, the key was sharp peaks. This one had rounded hills.

DNA matching was dependent on pairs of genes that showed up in an individual. A person could have one spike, indicating they had two copies of the same gene. Or they could have two spikes, indicating the gene came in two varieties, different versions from their mother and father. "Look here. This has almost four spikes, and so does this. And this."

DNA graphs didn't sequence the entire genome. They looked for a handful of key genes with high variability. Hopefully, everybody had the gene that made their liver function. The things that distinguished people were the ones that could vary quite a bit.

"Wow," Eleri looked at the results, the other pages clutched in her hand. "There really are two blood types there."

He watched as her eyes flicked to the side, doing exactly what he had just done—checking the time.

"I liked that tech. What was her name?" he asked.

"Glenda," Eleri answered. "And yes, she's good."

She'd been smart enough to test the soil around the body in several places. She'd collected from several depths as well, even after Eleri and Donovan had left.

In almost every level Glenda had sampled, the test reacted to both blood types. But it was stronger on the righthand side of the scene and much weaker on the left. The mix showed different concentrations at different depths, too. She'd collected three soil samples from the right and two from the left. Each had been converted to a DNA test and an electropherogram produced. Those from the left side of the body showed a graph that Donovan held up now, comparing it to the first one he'd showed Eleri.

Knowing that she could read them, possibly even better than he did, he only labeled whose blood they were. "This is Nash." He shook the one printout slightly. "And this is the sample from his upper left side near his shoulder."

"It's definitely mixed," Eleri said. "Not too badly, though. You can see Nash in the spikes, but there's definitely someone else's blood there."

"Now look at this righthand side near his hip."

"That's a complete mess. Honestly, because we have the pure graph of Nash's blood, I think I can see him in there. But if I were called to testify in court, asked that Nash's blood was definitely included in this sample? I wouldn't be able to say it with any level of certainty."

"Agreed." Donovan sighed at the thought. "And you know what that means?"

Eleri nodded and he let her call the sheriff this time. Maybe it wasn't quite as bad as calling the man at eight a.m. and telling him they'd found the dead body of the man they'd been looking for. But waking him up on that same night? Eleri certainly had the tact to handle it better than he did.

Donovan listened in as she told Sheriff Tucker their suspicions. And he heard the man's voice over the phone. "You have got to be shitting me."

47

"I'm sorry. What's the redhead's name?" Eleri asked Sheriff Tucker, almost just for something to say. She figured if she was going to be out here all night, she needed to know the person's name.

"That's Luna. Glenda and Luna are two of our best." Despite the fact that the heat was only slightly less in the dark than in the daylight, Tucker sipped hot coffee.

"They were here earlier, too," Eleri said, wondering how many times she could return to the same spot in the woods in one twenty-four hour period. Hell, it hadn't even been fifteen hours since she'd pulled up short, seeing Eugene Nash's body. "You aren't going to let them rest? Or bring in somebody else?"

She stood to the sidelines, her own Tyvek suit unzipped to let the air flow. This dig she wanted her hands on. But Tucker turned his whole head to give her a dirty look.

"You've seen how big my town is. We don't have spares."

She laughed. At least she thought that was the appropriate reaction to what Tucker had said.

The two blood samples in the soil had yielded clear evidence that there was extra, human DNA. It was highly possible there was another body *below* the first. It at least meant that someone else's blood had spilled or their bodily fluids had leaked in large enough quantities to taint the soil below Nash's corpse.

As they'd looked at the graph just a few hours ago, from the comfort of the hotel room, Eleri had asked Donovan, "Did you smell it?"

He'd blinked. "I *did*. I didn't recognize it for what it was, though. I mean, there's always plenty of decay out in the woods. And I knew it was human. But Eugene Nash's body was right in front of me, so it didn't occur to me that I was smelling two different corpses."

"Wouldn't old decay smell different from new decay?" It did to her, but she didn't have his sensitive nose and she didn't know what his answer would be. For all the time she and Donovan had known each other, this was a conversation they hadn't quite had.

"It does. But the new decay is so strong. Think of it like ..." he paused for a moment, "like getting a steak dinner. You don't smell the broccoli. It's there, and if you paid attention you might detect it, but you don't *notice* it."

Eleri nodded. He was right. Normally, you could smell broccoli, and you could smell the potato. But with a steak was in the middle of the plate, the meat was what you noticed. And Donovan would use a steak as an example.

Eleri turned to Tucker now. "You always see people on the internet saying you should bury a dead dog over a murdered body. And I wish people would do it." Leaving a body over another body would have stumped them if not for Glenda's catch.

Tucker had laughed along beside her. He was not in a Tyvek suit, not rotating in to work the dig on his hands and knees like the rest of them. He stayed at the edge, telling everyone he was in charge of the Klieg lights. No one had argued.

"Yeah, people don't realize the cadaver dogs are all well-trained to human scent only. They won't alert for the dead dog."

Eleri nodded along. If a cadaver dog alerted, then he smelled human flesh. But this was a new one. "So the killer obviously knows now that *we* know this is someone who's been operating for a minimum of seven years. But only in the past year have their bodies been found—"

"That we know of," Tucker interrupted.

"True," Eleri replied. It was plausible several other bodies from this killer had been found but not connected. She added, "But no one with pulled fingernails. No one had stab wounds and gunshot wounds, unless you simply didn't report them into the database. But I know you did."

Eleri had looked through Tucker's files and he was shaking his head. He'd uploaded every death he had into the system as soon as he could. She knew it. As much as he seemed like an old-school cowboy —so often running around in his shit-kicker boots, and tugging his pants up—he was intelligent and well-organized.

Definitely the right person for the job, Eleri thought.

Tucker sighed. "Maybe he got nervous, or simply decided to use a previous burial spot."

"Or they led us here, and they wanted us to find this one, too." Eleri thought the second option was more likely. Whoever this killer was, they'd operated for quite some time without getting caught, without anyone even realizing a serial killer was in their midst.

The myth about serial killers was that they were charming and intelligent. And the fact of the matter was, it wasn't that killers were charming and intelligent—it was that the non-charming and non-intelligent killers usually got themselves caught before they could rack up too high of a body count. But that understanding would extrapolate backwards, too. If they had this many bodies, then they definitely were good at evading the authorities.

The scene went quieter for a while, with Tucker watching and Eleri thinking it was time to get back in and do her part. She hadn't slept enough, but neither had anyone here. It wasn't an excuse, but damn, the heat was harsh.

She zipped up her suit and the motion must have caught the Sheriff's attention. He rocked back on his heels, his hands in his pockets, looking too casual to be at the scene of yet another body. "I'm not getting that autopsy report by morning, am I?"

Eleri laughed, glad she liked this guy. This would be a lot harder if she and Donovan were playing tug-of-war with the local authorities. "Hell no, you're not. But look at it this way." She waved a hand toward the dig. "It'll be later, but you'll get the bonus of two reports!"

Glenda and Luna—Eleri was glad she now knew the woman's name—were hunched over the hole the four of them had dug. Donovan had sat back on the sidelines, peeled one glove, and was chugging a bottle of water. Eleri was stepping forward to make herself join them when Glenda looked up.

"Agent Eames? We've got it."

48

Donovan woke up to bright light streaming through the cracks in the curtains. He could almost feel the heat of it. Even though, intellectually, he knew the heat wasn't getting into the room, the day had started feeling hot just from looking at it.

He was in nearly Central Florida at the edges of the Everglades, and his back felt like he'd twisted it with a wrench. He'd done mostly the same work as Eleri the night before, but his partner had done this work in the past far more often than he had. As a medical examiner, people had brought him *wet* bodies—bodies with tissue still on them. Bodies that had come from beds in nursing homes, or murder scenes, but usually not from underground. When the bodies did come from underground, they were usually what was referred to as *dry*. Those went to the forensic anthropologist, not him.

But now his partner was a forensic scientist, and she wanted to be hands-on. Sometimes that meant she wanted *his* hands on it, too. He understood. The more hands that she controlled, the more she could direct, and the easier it was to make sure the body was brought up exactly the way she wanted it. He understood and had used her in the same way more than once.

Now, though, as he rolled over his back felt as if he'd developed sudden-onset scoliosis. It hurt to reach out for the bedside table and tap his hand around until he smacked his phone.

They'd been wearing kneepads. Eleri made certain of it. The

two techs—Glenda and Luna—were already well-equipped and did this often enough that they were probably waking up and going for orange juice mimosas this morning in chipper little moods. Donovan wanted to look at his knees and see if they were bruised all to hell and back ... or if they would even still bend.

He told himself he wasn't getting old. Anyone who didn't normally work on their hands and knees, reaching down into a three-foot hole and carefully brushing away dirt for hours on end, would feel this way. *Wouldn't they?*

He tracked the phone in front of his face, trying to move only his arms. As he dialed his partner, he appreciated the good hotel, glad that he couldn't hear her phone ringing next door. It was well past two p.m. and his stomach grumbled—usually a welcome, normal sound. Now he wondered how he was going to get this creaking body to some food.

Eleri didn't answer. He wondered for a moment if maybe she was stuck in bed, wrenched into some horrible position where she couldn't even reach her phone. But he knew Eleri wouldn't be like that.

He was stuck. He wasn't quite brave enough to just twist himself upright so that he could do something that would make the pain lessen. So he called Lucy, not expecting anything.

A smile bloomed on his face when, for once, she picked up. He immediately asked the question that agents ask each other. "Where are you at?"

"Manistee-Huron," she replied, jolting Donovan's attention.

They'd had a case up there a while ago. In fact, Walter had followed them there from where she first met them in LA. Lucy was known as Walter Reed in the homeless camp where they'd first met her, but she was no dummy. And Eleri and Donovan had tripped the ex-MARSOC soldier's sensors left and right.

"What are you doing there?"

"Westerfield sent me with GJ." This was news. She'd been on an entirely different case a while ago, and Donovan asked about it.

"We closed that. Westerfield said he'd been waiting for when we had some down time. He wanted me and GJ up here because we knew the area. And because GJ knew the coding in the files."

That is an understatement, Donovan thought. GJ didn't just know the coding, she was the one who'd cracked it. But Lucy was still talking.

"We've been going back in the building and re-searching the rooms and pulling out any files. He also had us looking for hidden rooms."

Donovan thought the place had been closed up this whole time. The experiments that had been carried out—on children, and apparently by the government—had been unspeakable. "Who are the documents going to?"

Shouldn't they go to the children? The children who'd been held there were long since grown up. Most of them deceased. He slowly lifted his free hand and put it over his eyes, as if to block out the world he'd seen in the state park. And then the images of the aftermath of what had been done. That had been a truly difficult case. One of the first points where Eleri had learned that what she could do could hurt more than help.

Eleri had almost been killed on that case. It might have been the first time that Donovan had realized that they weren't just playing at some adult version of the Scooby gang out solving mysteries.

But Lucy's voice sounded concerned. "I don't know where the files will land. We're taking them back to Westerfield and we're following up with the kids and with their kids." She paused. "When GJ and I showed up, Cory asked us if we were keeping tabs on them, and I immediately said no, that's not what we were doing." She paused again. "But now? After seeing what's in there, we're not so sure."

"Did Westerfield say anything?"

An indelicate snort traveled down the line to him in response to that stupid question. He could admit that part. "Good point."

Westerfield was often close-lipped. For the most part, Donovan felt the assignments he'd been sent on had been necessary, and that he and Eleri had done a good job of closing them and taking harm out of the world. But following up on the kids from the Axis Project, and then the Atlas derivative of it, was more an invasion of privacy than a case that needed to be solved.

He asked Walter a few more questions, wondering if maybe there was a murder tied to it or some other reason for this to have landed in FBI hands. "Any other reason for Westerfield to be after it?"

"Not that I know of. Donovan, we don't have anything to *solve*. It feels like we're just on recon for something that should be closed, not opening."

He wanted to ask more questions—to ask how Cory and Amanda were doing and whether the baby had turned out okay, whether it was healthy and walking by now, whether it had turned out like Gwen and Faith—but his phone beeped at him.

"Shit, Lucy, I've got to go."

"Of course. Have fun finding your serial killer." She signed off and Donovan smiled, but he still couldn't move his back. Walter never had a problem with him leaving suddenly. Then again, she did it to him as often as he did these days.

As much as Donovan questioned Westerfield, he was supremely grateful that he had given Walter the opportunity to become an agent. It had changed everything for her.

Donovan tapped the button, letting Walter go and picking up from his partner. "Hey, El. What's next?"

"You're not going to like it."

49

"You two just like doing the autopsies yourselves?" Dr. Brzezinski asked.

Eleri wished she could say that was the case. And it *was,* but it just wasn't anywhere near the whole truth. "We do. We've worked together for some time. It allows us to have access to everything unhindered, and since we don't know our way around, I know we would get in your way."

"Well, that's not a problem. Just remember, we're happy to have you during the daylight hours, too," Dr. Brzezinski offered.

But when Eleri only nodded, Cara took the hint and headed out the door.

That was the part that Eleri hated. She wished she could just say, "Look, Donovan's going to sniff the organs, and I'm going to commune with the bones. If you're good with that, then we're good." But she couldn't risk exposing herself that way, and she would never risk exposing him.

Eleri had, however, let Brzezinski and her tech get Eugene Nash's body onto the table. On the second table, to the side, was the skeleton they'd pulled up the night before—the body that had been directly beneath Nash's.

Eleri's preliminary assessment was that the buried body was maybe ten years old. Thus, it might not be part of the case. She'd have to look more closely, and she'd need to check more information about decay on buried bodies in the Glades. It wasn't an assessment she could truly make right now.

"Who's first?" Donovan asked.

Eleri hadn't commented, but she had noticed he wasn't moving quite as fluidly as he usually did. She wasn't either. Standing for hours over an autopsy table was only going to make her lower back, her neck, and her knees feel worse, but there wasn't much she could do about it. They needed the information.

"Nash first," she said, thinking he would be the easy case. She grabbed a dental kit, pulled the body's mouth open and pushed the tiny, rectangle-shaped image receptor inside.

At least it didn't hurt Eugene Nash to bite down on it. She held two fingers under the man's chin, waiting without speaking until Donovan took her place. They moved with a fluid ease, each knowing what the other wanted. She grabbed the x-ray gun waiting on the counter.

They repeated the motions for three different shots.

"Is it enough?" Donovan asked.

"I can't imagine it's not. I don't have to make perfect matches. We're already quite certain we know who it is. We just need a legal identification." Eleri plugged the gun into one of the computers, grateful it had a USB cable. The equipment here was so old it didn't have wireless connections.

"I'm taking the body," Donovan told her as he wheeled it to the other side of the room. He pushed the table at an angle into the machine, the way Brzezinski had shown them, and took shots of the torso, arms, legs, and skull. The images would make a puzzle set that could be put back together to create the equivalent of a full body scan. Then he hit the computer to get a look at them.

Eleri already had the dental x-rays on the screen. Tucker, in his anxiety to get this case closed, had been supremely helpful. They already had the films from Nash's dentist by the time they'd showed up. As Donovan took over, she was finishing up.

"We have a legal match," she said. "This is definitively Eugene Nash."

Donovan only nodded. Neither of them had doubted that would be the case. But as the screen loaded with the images he'd just taken, he pointed to one shot. "Look, there's something in his throat."

Eleri tipped her head. Trachea or esophagus was hard to distinguish in a head-on scan, as the two tubes lined up, front to back. She looked to Donovan. "Where do you think it is? Esophagus or trachea?"

"I don't know. But we'll find out soon."

Without saying anything more—Eleri would write up the report on the dental match later—they began with more photographs. Next, they peeled and bagged his clothing. Eleri ran blood samples from the stains on the shirt. When the body lay naked on the table, they inspected it again. Almost without speaking, Eleri pointed out the slashes and cuts.

"It's shockingly identical," she offered and watched as Donovan agreed. "But how would it be *that* identical to what's on JP Talley? It's precise—*too* precise. It would indicate the victims aren't fighting back in any way. They aren't even trying to get away."

"But the point is the pain," Donovan countered. "So doing this when they are unconscious doesn't make any sense."

She agreed. The cuts—the precision and the consistent placement —looked as though the victims were completely incapacitated. She was struggling to wrap her head around it. "Is the killer cutting them up and doing all of this to make it *look like* torture?"

"If the cuts occur when the victim is alive—" Donovan countered, "he would have to make the victim unconscious, which would spare them the pain, and then kill them."

"It doesn't line up." Eleri agreed with him on that count. "These bodies don't exhibit any signs that they died in pain."

"But look..." Donovan countered, pointing again to the slashes on the torso. "Nash was clearly alive when this occurred, and he was alive for a little while after. You can see how the body reacted to the cuts. It tried to start healing the wounds. That means it's ante mortem, not even quite peri mortem. As if the killer let them sit with the open wounds for a while."

As Eleri thought for a moment, Donovan moved his face down close to the body, closed his eyes, and sniffed. "He was scared. There's a lot of fear here. So he was aware during the cutting."

Of course. *Because no case they got could be easy*. She picked up one of Nash's hands and rotated the arm. "But there's no marks from wrist restraints."

Donovan checked the feet. "No ankle restraints. Nothing in the cabin to restrain anyone, either."

She sighed. Tucker had spared two guards to watch the cabin, though Eleri would have preferred a camera setup. They were waiting for Westerfield to send them someone to set that up. But even so, Eleri figured the cabin was likely burned. The killer had to know they'd found the place.

"Are you ready?" Donovan asked, scalpel at the ready in his gloved hand.

When she nodded, he began the Y incision.

Forty-five minutes later, they found what was in the trachea.

50

Eleri sat in Sheriff Tucker's office, wanting to obsessively check the door and be sure it was shut tight. She leaned forward over his desk as if that would make it less likely for her voice to carry. She didn't want to be overheard. There were enough rumors flying already.

Tucker was looking over Nash's autopsy report. It was seven a.m. and it had been a very long night. She and Donovan had performed two autopsies and would soon head back to the hotel and finally get some sleep.

But first, Tucker needed some answers. A disturbed look crossed his face as he asked her, "Nash's own pulled fingernails were in his throat?"

Eleri figured anyone who wasn't used to this kind of work would certainly be disturbed by that. She nodded even as she corrected him. "They were in his trachea. He breathed them in rather than swallowed them. But this is new. It wasn't the case with Talley or with Earleen Beaman."

Tucker shook his head. "Y'all weren't here for that autopsy. But Brzezinski would have found fingernails in the throat if they were there."

"I've no doubt," Donovan said. Eleri was glad he was making it clear to the sheriff that the reason Brzezinski wasn't on their autopsies had absolutely nothing to do with the quality of the woman's work.

"Does this mean our killer is escalating?" Tucker asked next, throwing out a term she'd come to hate in her profiler days. But she knew what he meant.

Eleri only shrugged. "On the one hand, yes. The murders are coming closer together, and that's almost always an indication of what people call 'escalation.' However, that's also what we see on organized killers who kill to relieve urges. I don't think this killer has urges. I think this killer takes out the people he finds who fit his profile."

When Tucker continued looking at her, she went on. "And it might not be an issue of escalation—it might just be an issue of information."

"What do you mean?" Tucker asked.

"Well, we have organized serial killers—the ones who make plans and carefully choose and stalk their victims. And they're very hard to catch, because they've planned for everything. They clean up after themselves, they don't leave a lot of evidence behind. In fact, a lot of them get caught decades later because they clean up according to the evidence level of the day. Eventually, new technology comes along and something left at an old crime scene can get pulled back out. For example, the Golden State killer left DNA everywhere, not knowing that he shouldn't. But a disorganized killer, or an opportunistic killer, has a certain kind of victim. And when they get the chance to make a kill, they take it. Some of these guys are good enough that they do last a long time, but they don't tend to have what we think of as that psychopathic inner urge to kill. That's what creates the time frame we see in a lot of serial killers—how often does the person need to kill someone to relieve the urge that's built up in them."

She took a deep breath, but Tucker was still wanting more. "Oftentimes," she continued, "as they go along, each kill gets less and less satisfying. So the time frames get closer and closer together. That could be what's happening here."

"If you look at the slate of murders that we have, we do seem to have a ramp up." Tucker tapped on the papers he still held.

Eleri didn't quite agree. "But this killer appears to be killing based on getting information about who's abusive."

"You really think that theory is going to hold?" Tucker asked.

Eleri almost opened her mouth, but she could feel Donovan answering.

"We do. It appears that every single one of these victims was reported to a local therapist as being an abuser just prior to being murdered."

"Even Nash?" Tucker sounded surprised. "I knew I didn't like the guy, but … and what about Talley? Talley was an upstanding citizen. He didn't abuse anyone."

Eleri and Donovan looked to each other, and she could almost feel the slight twist of his facial expression that said, *You take this*. He wasn't about to tell Tucker that he'd walked into the house and smelled the fear. She smiled at Tucker. "One of the things Donovan and I are trained in is body language. Rebecca Talley flinches if you touch her from behind. It's a classic abuse sign—"

"Flinching when you're surprised is?"

"The way she does it, yes." She wished the Sheriff had more training in that kind of thing. "You learn to recognize it after a while. Her nervous, quickly-positive response style indicates someone who cooperates because they think bad things are going to happen if they don't. That smacks of abuse."

"And when you asked her straight out, she told you JP abused her?"

"No, she didn't," Eleri admitted. But then she looked Tucker in the eye and made sure he understood. "But she was lying through her teeth."

"Where would she have reported it? Wouldn't think an abusive husband would want his wife seeing a therapist."

Donovan chimed in, as though they needed to defend this to the Sheriff. "Exactly. But GPS data from her phone puts her in the small office for one of the local women's shelters on her way to and from the grocery store."

"But you can't confirm that yet?"

Was the sherriff being overly skeptical about this? Then again, maybe it was just due diligence.

She decided not to take it personally. "The shelters won't release that kind of information while Rebecca Talley is still alive. So they're not going to tell us until we get a warrant."

"And you're getting one?"

"Working on it," was probably the best answer she could give. It was tempting to say *No, Donovan and I have other ways of tracking this killer*. She couldn't just blurt out, "I can tell you without a warrant that Rebecca Talley went in one day because I could feel her on the door frame."

It bothered her that a reasonable portion of her job was back-filling steps she had already taken so that she could prove her evidence without explaining how she and Donovan worked.

"What about Nash? He was an asshole, but who reported him?" Tucker tapped on the folder in front of him again.

"It looks like Ciara told her school counselor about him five days before he disappeared."

"Son of a bitch." Maybe it had been performative questioning. He sure seemed to believe them now. He let the report fall to his desk with a smack. "All right. Tell me what the big deal was with the other body."

51

"It's the other body that actually makes our killer look like they might be escalating," Donovan said. There were so many things he couldn't tell Sheriff Tucker, like Eleri had put her hands on the bones and was quite confident the person had been tortured to death. But the images were vague. Most of what she'd gotten was more like the first set of bones, the ones that they still had not identified.

"There's a single nick mark on the ribs that's consistent with the slashes this killer is using. It does look to be in a slightly different place. What we noticed is that the more recent marks are very, very similarly done. Definitely indicating that we had the same killer in those cases. This one, was slightly different. There's a gunshot wound to the chest, but not to the head." To Donovan—and Eleri—it made perfect sense. Apparently, not so much to the sheriff.

"Are you sure this is one of your victims?"

Donovan nodded. "And we'd like you to allow us to include it in our own case."

That was the crux of this argument. They could get into a tug of war with the county over who owned the body to investigate it, and that wasn't anything either of the agents wanted to deal with. It was easier to present the clinical evidence and hope that Tucker decided to give it to them.

He probably would, Donovan thought. But it was his personal goal to convince this man it was in his own best interests to let the

FBI handle it, because fighting with Tucker would interfere with the investigation. Though Donovan would have initially taken this route, he had learned from Eleri some time ago that the softer, gentler path was almost always the way to go when dealing with live people. He was trying it now.

"First, this makes sense, given the new findings of the fingernails in the trachea. It would mean that the killer's MO changes over time. Which we expect." Tucker nodded along as Donovan explained.

"The shot to the chest—" Donovan pointed with a finger, tapping on his own sternum, "matches the current cases. It's in a relatively similar location. And, in a lot of cases, there's not a lot of evidence of knife wounds on a skeleton. But the mark that's on this rib does match."

When Tucker didn't seem convinced one way or the other, Donovan kept going. "We have no idea about the fingernails in this case, just like we don't in many of the older cases where we only found bones. But—" Donovan leaned over and pointed at the printed report he'd handed Tucker, but the sheriff hadn't read yet. "The main issue is that Nash's body was directly on top of this one. Think of the Everglades and how big they are. How many great places there are to hide a body… and this was not on a known pathway—"

"So how did you find it?" Tucker leaned forward again.

Even though they'd told the lie once before, it made Donovan go on alert and his heart rate kick up just a little bit. Tucker questioning their methods was the last thing they needed. "Eleri found it. She was out with her friend's dog."

He hated saying it, but more than that, he would hate being found out. Just the thought made Donovan hold his tongue.

Tucker let out a sigh. "That's a good dog your friend has."

Donovan breathed a sigh of relief.

"He is," Eleri said with a half-smile.

Steering the conversation away from "the dog," Donovan added, "The location of Eugene Nash's body makes me think the killer wanted us to find it. We—" Donovan then pointed between himself and Eleri. "—firmly believe this body is part of our case. And we believe that this killer has been operating with impunity and completely under the radar for some time. Now that they've been found out, they're anxious to have all of their crimes put on display. If there are more hidden bodies, I suspect we'll find them soon."

"You think more bodies are going to come floating to the surface?" Tucker asked, clearly upset by the idea. "How many could there be?"

"We don't know," Eleri answered with a shrug that looked perfectly normal to Donovan. She was so good at appearing perfectly normal, whereas he was still working on his skills for covering everything up. When he'd been an M.E., he'd shown up, done the work, bossed his few employees around, and written a report when he was done. He spoke to as few people as possible along the way.

Here he'd gone and taken a job in which diplomacy played too large a part for a man with few diplomatic skills. But he was getting better.

Tucker sighed and picked up the folder he still hadn't opened and then dropped it again. "I'm not going to argue with you. If you want to keep this body as part of your case, go for it. Please hand it back to us as soon as you know it's not."

Donovan could feel the relief whoosh out of him. Though he wanted to jump up and pat himself on the back, it was hardly the reaction for the tiny office. *Maybe later*, he thought, but as he let go of the tension, he realized he was bone tired. He and Eleri had been up the entire night, and they hadn't had a full sleep since they'd been out to track Eugene Nash. During that time, they'd processed two crime scenes—or one crime scene twice, depending on how he looked at it—and performed two autopsies.

He needed food and a full eight hours.

Tucker started to hand the file back, but Donovan put his hand out to stop him. "It's yours. We'd like you to look it over, see if there's anything we might have missed. Plus, we'll need you to see if you can help us find a match."

Donovan was about to stand up when Tucker asked the question, "How old is this body?"

"Ten years, give or take." Donovan nodded along as he said it. The estimates were always difficult. The further back the dates went, the wider the range got. And the stranger the soil they were dealing with was, the wider the estimates got. There were seven body farms in the US where scientists studied human decay at various climates, seasons, and conditions. And none of them were in the Florida Everglades.

"I'll look into it today," Tucker said, clearly trying to call the meeting to an end. "Is that everything?"

The man sounded exhausted. The last thing he'd ever wanted was a serial killer in his midst. He probably suspected every one of his neighbors now. Though Donovan couldn't understand the feeling—because he'd never been connected to a community, not the way a normal person was and certainly not the way a sheriff would be—he could see that it was wearing on the man. Still, there was one last thing.

"Actually, Eleri and I have a strategy that we'd like to propose."

52

"We need a break," Donovan announced from his spot on the small couch in his hotel room. "I'd like to take the evening off, go out, get a nice meal and just not deal with things for about four or five hours. Then I'd like to get a full night's sleep."

They'd slept most of the day, but once again, it hadn't been the kind of rest his body needed to catch up from the deficit they were both racking up.

"Can we combine our break with a little work on the case?" she asked.

"Which part of *break* did you not understand?"

Wow. Look at him. The guy who had once lived a life that only consisted of running in the woods and going to work was now chastising his partner over taking one lone evening fully off—and doing it with snippy tones over the phone.

"I'd rather not," he continued. He needed to turn his brain off for a while.

"Well, here's what I'm proposing." She sounded far too chipper for the person ruining a break they both needed. "There's a little circle on one of the islands that's all posh and full of art galleries and nice restaurants. Let's go there. Let's have dinner."

He was immediately suspicious that she hadn't mentioned the work part. "Where is this?"

"Lido Beach. It's not that far away. And what I'm proposing is that we go check out the dunes where they found the Merkels' bodies."

She said it with a smile and a cheer that he couldn't match. He didn't have the energy to say no. If they were going to be out at the shoreline, they might as well check. "I guess I can live with that. Just walking on the beach?"

"Kind of."

He didn't like her tone. There was more to it, but he understood. They'd been here for several weeks and, aside from the fact that he could smell the killer in various places, they still had no idea who the person was. Hell, if he could just brush past this killer on the street, they could identify them, match up some fingerprints, and go home.

He suspected it would all go down in a flurry when it finally came together. But the flurry had not yet happened, and they hadn't even gotten close. He was still bothered by the way the scent had disappeared in the middle of the woods. *Who did that?*

He knew drug-sniffing dogs could smell cocaine inside three layers of plastic shoved inside a barrel of peanut butter. His sense of smell was likely just as good. So, who could cover their scent so damn quickly that it seemed to vanish? Who could do it without leaving a clear trail of whatever the solvent or more potent smell was? Because there had been no other scent there. Other smells and other people had mingled in that area, and Donovan had to assume the killer looped back around to some more populated area, but the killer's signature smell had just vanished.

"No jeans," Eleri told him.

He wanted to reply that he didn't need to be reminded to dress like an adult but, then again, he'd worn scrubs and sneakers to work for an entire decade. And he *had* shown up dressed inappropriately to the situation several times when they first began working together. So he tried to take it in stride.

Ten minutes later, he was knocking on her door. Then he spent another ten minutes waiting for her to emerge from the bathroom. He tried not to look at the papers spread across the table. He was *not* working.

When she finally stepped out, he pulled his head back in surprise. "A dress?"

She shifted her bare shoulders as if to say, "So what?" What she did say was, "The weather's really hot and I don't want us to look like FBI agents casing the scene of a crime when we're out there."

She'd managed that in spades, he thought. She wore sandals and had pulled her hair up into a ponytail, the reddish-colored curls poofing out behind her. "Well, you do not look like an FBI agent."

He so rarely looked "official" that he automatically assumed his own look tonight wouldn't be a problem. Cutting off any further comments, Eleri grabbed her keys and headed out of the hotel and down to the car, automatically taking the driver side. "Get in. I found us a restaurant."

Well over an hour later, they'd arrived at Lido Beach and completed the full circle on the center of the island. Eleri pointed out the restaurant. "That one!"

Donovan noticed the line outside the door, but Eleri being Eleri had managed to snag a reservation, and they walked past the line. Inside were mirrored walls, bouncing lights, and the scents of the best Cuban food he'd smelled in a long time. It was all he could do not to growl with delight.

Eleri immediately ordered some Cuban champagne lemonade cocktail. And Donovan didn't ask about her alcohol intake on a case. After all, he was the one who said they were taking the time off. If he liked beer at all, he would have grabbed one.

Though they tried not to discuss the case while they waited for the paella to show up, it was impossible not to. Eleri asked after Lucy and GJ, and Donovan caught her up about the other two agents looking into the Atlas project. Eleri had frowned at him but, true to the desire to be "off," she'd not pushed.

Donovan had then asked after Avery, but he already knew most of the story. He'd been there for a lot of it. So the non-work conversation ran out long before the paella arrived.

"Tucker said he has a few options for me to check for matches." Eleri broke the imposed no-fly zone first.

Glenda and Luna had been thorough. Though the skull had been missing a handful of teeth, they'd searched and found another nine in the soil around it. They'd even taught Eleri a thing or two.

"With the water tables rising and falling all the time and being very near the surface, the bones here shift. I'm from Oklahoma," Glenda had said. "If we exhume a body there, we can see what position it was in when it was put into the ground. But around here, the water moves the soil more, and the pieces get more scattered."

Donovan and Eleri had considered that when writing up the

report, but he didn't mention it now. He only told Eleri that Tucker probably had the actual missing person in the batch. The only one the Sheriff hadn't found was the male in his early twenties.

Donovan had his back to the restaurant. Behind Eleri was a mirrored wall, and they both naturally stopped talking as the waiter approached. The big, sizzling pan was placed between them, and Donovan felt his face want to open up. Though this was no nearly raw steak, the scents were so tantalizing that he could tell his nose flared.

He watched as Eleri's eyes had widened for a moment and he made the effort to keep his bones in place. The food was fantastic and it managed to keep them off the subject of death and serial killers as they lingered over the meal.

Eleri's drink, though alcoholic, had to have long since worn off before they headed out. They took the bridge back to the mainland and over to the bay at Sarasota.

In a lot of Sarasota, the beach was rocky, but there were patches of white sand and dunes. Eleri knew exactly where to park. She led Donovan onto the dark path and up to the beach, directly to the place where the crime scene tape still cordoned off the area.

Though Eleri had stepped out of her sandals and looped her fingers through the straps to walk barefoot—or maybe just to look like a tourist—she'd headed straight to this spot.

Donovan picked his way over the dunes, the loose, cool sand not a friend to his sneakers, as they started to check out the scene. He could smell it even before he ducked under the tape. The bodies had partly risen to the surface, much the way Glenda had described. The ocean scent assailed him from all sides.

The sand still stank of decay.

Eleri was walking around, destroying a crime scene that was too fluid to actually be destroyed. Looking down into the pit, she let the moonlight be their only guide. Maybe she didn't want to bring any more attention to them than picking their way under the yellow tape already would.

But she stepped forward and her foot shifted.

"Eleri, stop!" he called out. Though it might be too late.

He'd smelled it.

53

Eleri's arms flailed as her feet slid out from under her.

There was nothing to grab onto. Her hand whacked into the sand as she went down, trying to turn herself around so that she could scramble at the side of the sloped pit. But every effort proved useless. She simply kept sliding down into the sand that was wet with ... *what?*

She told herself it was just ocean water. When she reached the bottom and finally managed to stabilize herself, she stood in the empty space where the bodies of Bonnie and Evan Merkel had been extracted. Her heart was pounding from the scare. Her feet were wet and cold. She was breathing heavily, but she managed to get herself upright and put her hands on her hips.

She looked up to Donovan to give her a hand, but he was turned away his nose up.

Had her epic, dramatic fall into a grave not been enough to get his attention? He'd said something which she hadn't quite caught while she was pinwheeling her arms and trying not to yell like a fool.

Turning one way and then another, Donovan still paid no attention to her. Eleri reminded herself that the bodies had been wrapped in a tarp and were relatively well desiccated. That meant the wetness on her feet was not likely bodily fluids that had leaked out. Plus, it had been seven years since the Merkels died and were placed here. So anything that had leached out, had likely long ago been carried away by the rising and falling tides.

After she talked herself down from her stomach turning, she called up to Donovan. "Hey, dude! Can you help me out?"

But as he turned back, she caught a wild look in his eye.

"Eleri. I smell it."

Both intrigued and exasperated, she leaned forward, trying to put one hand on the dune to brace herself against the loose sand, which was about as stupid an idea as a person could have. She held the other one up toward Donovan. She couldn't have a conversation about what was stealing his attention while she was still standing in a grave. "Help me up!"

Unsure that she'd ever be able to scramble her way out on her own, she continued to hold her hand up. This time, at least, he did carefully lean over and extend one arm down to her.

Again, the sand shifted, making movement difficult. Anything she braced against immediately moved. But Donovan did most of the work, practically pulling her to the top.

Eleri looked up at her partner, his wrist still firmly clenched in her hand, and finally asked, "What did you smell?"

"The killer was here, Eleri."

Of course he was. She'd just fallen into the hole where he'd buried a few bodies.

So Eleri looked around as she cleared the top edge and stepped several feet away. She was on the other side of the hole from where she'd started. As far from the shoes she'd probably flung to hell when she slipped as she could be.

"Thank you," she offered absentmindedly to her partner as she started walking around the edge looking for her missing sandals.

"The killer was *here*." He repeated it with more emphasis.

Maybe his brain wasn't working, or maybe hers wasn't. But she pointed one empty hand down toward the pit. "There were bodies in there. We know the killer was here. And I just stirred it up."

She felt her mouth twist again at the thought. If Donovan smelled it, something had lingered in the hole she'd just stood in with bare feet. But her partner gave her a dirty look.

"No. It was recent."

"What? Why?" She did need to get her head twisted back on straight.

"Maybe the killer came back to admire their handiwork. Maybe to be part of the crowd or to watch the police bring up the bodies," he suggested, though he still was looking off into the distance and not at her.

Eleri couldn't see her sandals anywhere in the dark and pulled out her phone for the light, instantly spotting one. "I don't think there were any crowds when the police pulled up the bodies. Maybe news reports, though. People gather for that. Are there a lot of smells?"

"There's enough. A lot of people have been through here, but I can't tell if they gathered all at once. It might also be from people walking by, kind of like us."

"Not like us," Eleri interjected quickly. "One—we're supposed to be trained and—two—I'm enough of an idiot to fall into the hole."

"Sarasota police didn't put any cameras out here, did they?" He still hadn't looked *at* her.

While she wouldn't be excited about having her epic slide into the sand caught on film, Eleri would gladly trade it for getting a glimpse of who had been here. But she looked around, too. "I don't think so."

As she found her second sandal, he added, "I don't think so either. After all, we're the primary investigators, and we didn't put any cameras on it."

Given that Nash's body had been left on top of another corpse, Eleri began to think they should have cameras everywhere. Was it worth it to put them here? Would their killer come back a second time? She and Donovan would have to ponder that later.

Donovan muttered a string of words that Eleri couldn't quite make out except for the last one, which was most decidedly *Dammit*.

Picking up her sandals—and having embarrassed herself enough for one night—she decided she'd seen what she needed.

"What?" she asked, more than ready to go home, or back to the hotel, which was the best she could do for now.

"Eleri, it's not fresh, but it's fresh enough. We need to come back and we need to follow that trail."

54

Donovan put his nose to the ground, both excited and frustrated. This was supposed to be an evening *off* work, but Eleri's side jog to the burial site had turned into far more than the expected look-see.

It was well past midnight. They'd headed back to the hotel, changed Eleri out of her "I'm not an Agent" dress and him into his leisure/changing gear. Then they'd driven the hour back. Now he was following a path down the beach.

He'd caught the scent and—especially on shifting sands and in a high wind area like this—he couldn't simply wait twelve hours and come back later. It might have dissipated by then. He also wasn't familiar with scenting along beaches. Anything he'd picked up when chasing down the good folks at Miranda Industries had happened relatively soon after they'd been there. He didn't know how long a scent could cling to sand and reeds.

He wanted Eleri to research it …

This time, she'd cast her spell on him as they'd climbed into the car at the hotel. She'd tied the little sachet to the chain of her necklace once again, and he'd turned to her and asked, "Is it working?"

She'd given him a truly sour look that clearly said *"Dumbass."* What she said out loud was, "I don't know. You're still speaking English. Ask me again when you've got a different face."

He'd had to smile. It had been a stupid question. But now he spoke up and made one of the odd noises he hated—a growl that changed pitch and volume. It sounded almost as bad as the dogs that everybody claimed could say *I love you*. But in this case, she seemed to understand.

"Good lord, Donovan. I don't know where I'll find that information." But she turned up the brightness on her phone and started tapping as she trailed along behind him.

They were probably a thousand feet further down the beach when she said, "Donovan, apparently nobody's done a study on how long a dog can track a scent on the beach."

Well, that was what he'd expected, even if the answer was useless. He added it to his ever growing list of things people should research to make his life easier. He motioned to Eleri as he followed where the scent shifted. It almost congealed, becoming thicker as it moved away from the beach. The little dunes that bracketed the paths with reeds and cattails caught the wisps of it and it clung. He followed relatively easily, his speed picking up as he headed toward developments, and the sand beneath his paws turned to wood and then pavement.

The killer had walked along here openly, not hiding anything. That meant he was confident they didn't know who he was. Sadly, he was right.

Donovan turned back to Eleri and emitted another odd series of whines and growls.

"Alright," she said, "I'm on it."

They needed to know if any of these storefront businesses had cameras. Though he couldn't quite tell when the killer might have come through, it had to be within the past few days.

Slowing his pace, he put his nose down to the pavement and up against the brick and siding. The past pulled at him now with slightly stronger scents. He needed more and wanted to get more detail from it, but it was old.

He needed a good, clean pocket of it, something stronger. It had been so clear back in the woods, following the dual scents of the killer and Eugene Nash. But he hadn't been paying attention then, had he? Given that he was tracking, not reading, and thinking he could catch up to the killer, he hadn't cataloged any of the details a scent could tell him.

Now that he had it again, it was too faint. Was it male or female?

Agitated or calm? He'd been trying to get more information but, right now, it wasn't here. Only the faint scent of sweat lingered, and most humans smelled like that most of the time.

Eleri diligently followed along, this time in boots that were out of place on the beach and the street but would merge seamlessly if the trail led them into the woods or glades or anywhere the soil was wet and boggy.

Another block later, Donovan pulled back, startled. He turned around, sat down, and stared at Eleri. He didn't even have to say anything. The scent had disappeared again.

"What?" she asked, leaning closer, very much looking like she was having a conversation with her huge dog right in the middle of the street. Well, she pretty much was.

"Into thin air," he told her, then retraced the steps. When he tried it again, he was flummoxed, but unsurprised that the same thing happened. If he was watching the killer video, he would expect the person to simply dissolve or poof into nothingness.

When he checked again and convinced himself that the impossible truly had happened, Donovan once again did what he'd done in the Glades and started at the vanishing point, circling out in wider and wider spirals. Aside from crossing the path—where the killer had walked into the vanishing point but not out of it—there were no other scents to pick up. The killer had simply come here and disappeared.

He looked around and tried to see if there were any cameras nearby, but the houses here were older. Probably very high in value, given their proximity to the beach, but they weren't the kind of big-money homes that would have anything other than a doorbell cam.

The streets were overgrown with untended palms on either side, the fences chain link, and the houses one-story stucco. Somehow, the area either hadn't attracted developers or the citizens had held them at bay.

He made a sound to Eleri, more frustrated than ever. This was supposed to have been his night off. It was well past the middle of the night and they had nothing to show for it. He was not going to be able to get anything resembling a normal night's sleep, either.

He was trotting up a residential street, looking like a two hundred pound wolf. He didn't even have a scent to follow. So he aimed the direction that would get them back to the car.

He trotted his way down the street and onto the boardwalk back to the public beach. But as the concrete under his feet shifted to wood, his nostrils flared.

The scent was both unknown and familiar.

There was a wolf on the beach... *now.*

55

Donovan told himself it was normal for a wolf to be in Sarasota. In his loner days, he would have followed them, too. So he hopped back into the car and changed form. Eleri agreed that it didn't necessarily mean anything dangerous, but the nagging feeling that it did hadn't let up.

The drive back to Astoria at five a.m. had been quicker than the way out, given the lack of traffic, but it was still tedious. He told himself everything was fine. On the road, he could slough off the sense of unease the scent had sparked in his core.

But then he'd opened his hotel door and stepped on the white envelope. Although Eleri was at her own room, she was only next door and had barely put foot on her own carpet. "El?"

His tone must have grabbed her, for she'd stepped backward and turned her head to give him an odd look.

"Do you have an envelope shoved under your door?"

She looked down, as though she might have missed something so glaring. She shook her head, and he whispered, "El, get over here."

His eyes had narrowed, and time had passed in an odd heartbeat and then she was at his side. "What is it?"

He shrugged. He wanted to tell himself it was fine. "Probably a hotel bill?"

She gave him an odd look. "The reservation was in my name.

Anything from the hotel should be at my door." She paused. "Also, we were last here close to midnight. Was it here then?"

No. A strange time of day for an unmarked envelope to slide under his door. Strange for anyone to even know what room he was in; the hotel had stayed mostly empty. Who would have seen him coming and going?

He swallowed tightly.

"You go shower," she'd told him. Then added, "Give me your key."

He'd seen her duck back into her room before he followed the instructions. Now, as he stepped out, dressed in the clothing he'd hastily grabbed as his chest had clenched, he found her standing over his little table, letter on the table and her kit in hand.

His clothes were damp against his body, something he usually hated. But right now, he didn't have the bandwidth to be upset about it.

She'd waited for him, not opening it. Now she held out a pair of gloves toward him, and she used the tongs to flip it one way and another, showing him the envelope was completely unmarked. It was only white, no writings or markings aside from the black powder Eleri had used to lift fingerprints from several locations.

"What does it look like?" he asked.

"It's the same fingerprints repeating. Looks like one hand of one person."

When he nodded, she slid the edge of her metal tongs into the gap at the edge of the envelope flap and began to painstakingly lift it. This was the part he hated, the part where diligence and meticulousness paid off later. Right now, he simply wanted to know what it was.

Why the hell had it shown up just after he'd scented a wolf?

The two had to be related, if only because of the odd timing of both ... didn't they?

A small eternity later, she had the flap open. Eleri put her gloved fingers inside, pulling the paper out and opening it.

Leaning over her shoulder, his eyes quickly scanned it. And it wasn't so much what was written on the paper as the letterhead that had his blood running cold.

56

Eleri stared at the paper, the numbers glaring back at her.

She'd sat here, itching, impatiently waiting, as Donovan took probably the fastest shower in history. While she'd prepped everything she could—dusting for prints and getting the flap open, she hadn't opened the envelope. The letter was under *his* door, after all, not hers.

Now that it was open, and staring them in the face, she couldn't untangle her feelings. So she tried to watch both the paper and her partner at the same time.

When he looked up at her, she said only, "Coordinates."

Handwritten strings of numbers spelled out a latitude and longitude. Only she had no idea where these points crossed. It could only be somewhere someone wanted them to go.

Donovan spoke the overly obvious part. "The letterhead is *Miranda Industries*."

"Hold on," Eleri said. She was already looking up the coordinates point. "It's just a little way south of here.

"Is it a Miranda Industries office building? Wolves? A body?" he asked.

Eleri tilted her head and raised her eyebrows. "The question is: Is it a *trap*?"

"Probably. They send us coordinates. We show up."

"So, we're being stupid if we don't consider it a trap. Or is it a warning?" She had no idea. "Do we recognize the handwriting?"

She didn't.

"Not at all," Donovan told her, not helping. Then he grumbled. "I was going to go to sleep."

Once again, they'd been up all night, out into the wee hours tracking down a murderer. Now it should have been time to sleep through the hottest part of the day.

"Do we move?" he asked, shifting the topic suddenly.

But she followed and added, "Because clearly they know where we are … right down to the room number."

He nodded. "Given the timing, they not only know where we're staying, they know where we are at any given time."

He was right. But Eleri wasn't sure about packing up and fleeing. "Somebody followed us here. If we start a flurry and move right now, it will be obvious. We have to assume they're still watching."

"I'm not thinking about taking everything right now, just maybe stuffing a change of clothes into our pockets. We head out the door like it's a normal day and get another hotel room. Not for long."

"That works," she countered. *"If* they've got people watching us, but not following us constantly."

"You don't think we can shake them?"

"No. I don't. It's Miranda. They're huge. You know how, at Quantico, we were taught to tail people on the freeway by trading in and out with different cars, so that we wouldn't get noticed? I suspect Miranda Industries can do that even better than we can … though, it still might be worth trying," she conceded.

The conversation paused for a moment as her brain churned, trying to untangle what had just been handed to them and why, and then make a good plan—not a shitty one—for how to evade their stalker. Donovan must be doing the same thing because he, too, fell silent.

At last, she put words into the empty space. "I think we start by getting a single, two-bedroom suite." Their current rooms didn't connect and Eleri didn't like the idea that they could be so easily divided. It hadn't occurred to her when she'd requested the rooms that they would be anything but the hunters when they came down for this case.

She was thinking fifteen different directions at once. Who could have left this note? What was at the coordinate point? Were they in danger? What if they left? What if they stayed?

She glanced at her phone again, wondering if it had any answers, but she held it up to show Donovan. "The location of the coordinates is in the middle of the Glades."

"It's going to be tricky to get in to."

"And tricky to get out of," Eleri added. She understood Donovan's desire to just shove some extra underwear into his pocket and disappear.

However, the plan made her more than a little squirrely. Maybe fleeing was something he was used to from a childhood on the road. Here, she didn't even like leaving the room during the day. She'd only felt comfortable enough to leave her things behind because the hotel was so bland. As far as she'd known, no one had any idea they were staying here. Even the local townspeople pestering Sheriff Tucker didn't seem to follow them, and she'd seen no one familiar in the lobby.

But now, she felt her chest clench and her back straighten at the idea of leaving her suitcase here. What if someone came in and rifled through it? She had things of Grandmere's with her, things for spells, things she needed and things she couldn't bear to part with.

Her thoughts rolled and tumbled as if in a snowballing path that she couldn't stop.

Donovan interrupted her. "Can you cast a spell on us? Get us in and out without being noticed?"

"Probably." She hadn't even thought of that. She'd pushed her magic so far down that she'd only cast on them to listen to him when he was the wolf. Touching the bones wasn't magic, it was just part of who she was, the skills she'd had since the day she was ten and her sister disappeared. But she *should* think of it. This was her job, to protect them in the best way she could. This was the reason she'd been invited into NightShade and the reason she and her friends were alive after the last case. But it was the same reason she'd shut down everything and started from scratch, and this shouldn't push her new boundaries.

She would need Grandmere's bowl and the herbs. Bringing all these treasured and necessary items was part of the reason she packed such a huge suitcase. She tucked away the little sachets in case they were away longer than she intended. She wouldn't want the spell to wear off. The cloth bags were the same ones that Grandmere had hand-stitched so many years ago.

Honestly, they were things Grandmere had most likely intended to hand down to Emmaline, the more powerful of the two Eames daughters—an heir apparent to a throne neither of them had known about. But Eleri couldn't think about that now. "They'll be looking for us."

"I know," Donovan said. "But how do we not leave?"

There was no good answer to that.

There were so many things about this that Eleri didn't like. The Miranda Industries printed at the top of the white paper alone was enough to make her blood run cold. The thought that they were being watched and that she might be put in the same position she'd been in before was enough to make her stop breathing. She was being tested, but would it push her beyond the limits she'd set?

Serial killer or not, she was *supposed* to come to a small town in Florida and use the investigative skills she'd learned at Quantico, and perhaps some of the others she'd grown into over the past several years. But she wasn't supposed to be stalked by a powerful international conglomerate that wasn't just running drugs but artifacts and wolves and more.

Just knowing that something was hunting them—had followed them here—was making her wonder just how far she was going to get pushed. Would she react in a way that she couldn't control?

Her blood ran cold, but her heart raced.

57

"I don't like this." Donovan watched as Eleri clenched the steering wheel.

He'd thought that driving would give her something to do, but the anxiety rolled off her. He sat in the passenger seat next to her, fully human and still able to smell it. It wasn't fear—he didn't think she was even that concerned about what they might find at the coordinate site—but she was worried as shit about something.

Now wasn't the time to ask.

They'd headed south on Highway 31 and swung a left on 74, heading further into the heart of the Everglades. Now it was time to start looking for a place to park. They'd have to walk the rest of the way in.

There were roads back here that disappeared into nothing. The occasional houses warranted a school district. But mostly it was open land, and Donovan hadn't had time to learn who held the deed.

"Text Walter," Eleri told him, pointing as though that would make her command more understandable. Then she quickly added, "Text GJ and Christina and Noah and Wade." Then she added, "Not Westerfield."

There was a pause in her words, a moment that told him Eleri somehow considered their boss separate from the others—and not because he was their boss.

"Do you feel anything else?" he asked, hoping she'd picked something up from the letter or from a touch of the door frame on the way out. But she'd said neither of those things. He'd held out hope that she would simply sense the truth as they got closer. Now he knew she sensed something about their Special Agent in Charge.

She shook her head, though her words contradicted the motion. "I do. I just can't sort out what it is."

"Well, I can tell you the whole thing with sending Walter and GJ back to Atlas is weird."

"It is," she agreed.

But Donovan caught the odd look on her face, even though she stared straight ahead at the small amount of traffic passing in the Florida morning light. He knew she had more to say, and he waited until she let it out.

"I've wondered for a while. He's been sending us into these cases and withholding information."

"On this case?"

"I hadn't thought so." He watched her teeth clench and felt his own clench for her. She waved her hand in front of them. "But …"

So far, his own feelings had been nebulous, forming little balls in the pit of his stomach, but only when he thought about them. This note changed everything.

"I mean," Eleri circled one hand at him, the other still clinched on the wheel tight enough that he thought if she were larger or stronger, she might have cracked it. "He sent us to Miami, and then to Nassau …",

"Maybe he didn't know about Miranda and the wolves," Donovan countered, but he believed the same as Eleri. He was mostly curious what her arguments were, and if she'd been thinking the same things he had.

"How could he *not* know? I can see how you and I individually didn't know. I didn't even know people like you existed until I met you. I knew Wade *for a decade* and didn't know. And *you* didn't know there were more wolves until you met Wade. But Westerfield knew. He just didn't tell us. Our first assignment together, he gave us no information about each other at all!"

Donovan let her keep going. She was speaking thoughts he'd been holding back for a while. Though who he was holding them back from, he didn't know. Maybe himself …

Eleri's voice got louder in the otherwise quiet of the car, which was only broken by the whir of the AC. "Allison worked for Miranda industries! How would Westerfield—with his fingers in every paranormal pot in the US—not know about Miranda?"

Donovan had no devil's advocate question of his own, but he was now adding to her ire. "He knew about the de Gottardi/Little farm for a long time. He recruited wolves from there specifically."

"Like Wade," Eleri said, her words urgent, as though they'd been lingering for a long time, and were finally coming together.

"Do you think he led Dr. Marks directly to them?"

"Jesus," Eleri said, the word gushing out somewhere between a hard *no* and a *maybe*. "I want to say, not on purpose. But plausibly."

Now, Donovan thought with Walter and GJ tracing his and Eleri's old steps through Atlas and Manistee Huron … "What's Westerfield doing, having them follow up with Cory and Amanda? Maybe scoping out new recruits?"

Or was there something more to it? Donovan had been diligently tapping out a message and clicked onto every name Eleri had cited. He made sure that this was a group conversation via text and that they all knew that not only were Donovan and Eleri running headlong into something they had no idea about, but also so they each knew they weren't the only one with the information. A network was better than a handful of individual agents.

It was GJ who wrote back immediately with the same question he and Eleri had just been asking themselves.

— Did you tell Westerfield?

— No.

Donovan texted back just the one word, letting the implied answer hang.

— I wouldn't either.

The words made Donovan suck in his breath. It was a harsher indictment than anything said in this car this morning. It was enough that he and Eleri—who constantly worked in each other's pockets—would have the same paranoid thoughts. That GJ had immediately come back with the same concerns magnified every argument in his head.

His stomach dropped as he held his phone up directly into Eleri's line of sight for a moment.

"Oh crap," she said.

"Yeah. We're not the only ones." They'd all been thinking it.

— Too many coincidences. GJ wrote back.

— Too many times. We've all been dropped into something that turned out to be larger than we were told.

Donovan's thoughts ran away with him now. Things that should have been known. Things they should have been warned about. It had all been easier to chew and swallow back down when he thought it was only his imagination running wild.

"We have to be close," Eleri said as another new message popped up on his screen. From Christina.

He held it up for Eleri again. "Holy shit. Look at this."

58

Eleri watched as Agent Christina Pines knocked on her window and peered into the car with a confused look on her face. As she turned to look into the Glades as though searching for something, Eleri rolled down her window.

The agent startled at the movement.

"Christina!" she called out, happy to see the other agent. They'd all been a bit concerned about her.

But the other agent only peered around, a confused look on her face. Her pink ponytail bobbed with the movement as her head turned and she checked everything around her. Her hand came down and rested on the edge of the car door where the window had disappeared, almost as if checking that it was really down.

"Christina!" Eleri was now just as confused as Pines looked.

Eleri was about to call out again as, beside her, Donovan started cackling.

"It works, El!" He almost couldn't get the words out, and she didn't understand what the hell he was talking about or why he was so damn gleeful.

Then she watched as he reached for the twine around his neck and lifted the sachet she'd given him over his head. He waved and called out, "We're here, Christina!"

As Agent Pines jolted at the sight, Eleri pulled at her own sachet, which she'd once again looped through her necklace. "Sorry, Christina! This is new and we were not sure it worked—"

"Until now!" Donovan was almost in tears and she would have been mad, but at least he was enjoying himself.

"Well shit, Donovan! This means we just drove down the highway in a seemingly empty car!"

He laughed again. "Hopefully no one noticed. I mean, at least I suspect there's no cameras on the roads back here."

"Jesus, you two gave me a fright," Christina exclaimed, now looking at them in the car and laughing too. "Yes, whatever you did, it works."

"I asked Eleri for a spell to 'keep us from being noticed.'" It was accompanied by another full belly laugh.

But she wasn't quite as gleeful as Donovan. Maybe he was just punch drunk from not getting any sleep. But Pines let the incident go and turned right back to business. "So what are these coordinates?"

Eleri wasn't quite ready. "Are you on a case? Did you just happen to be down here in the area?"

"No and yes. I'm on leave." Christina shrugged, but she'd been on a lot of leave lately, and Eleri was beginning to wonder how that worked. Christina seemed to have caught on. "I have seniority over you guys. I've been with Westerfield a lot longer and he understands he can give me leave, or he can lose me. I'm about three inches from retiring."

Eleri hardly thought Christina was of an age to actually retire, but she understood the sentiment. She didn't ask the woman, *Well, what would you do if you left NightShade?* because apparently, Christina was already answering it for herself.

"I came down here to check out Miranda Industries." Then she paused. "Actually, I was tracking one of the Dauphine sisters and wound up too close to Miranda for comfort."

Eleri sucked in a breath. Somehow, with everything that had happened at the de Gottardi/Little ranch and everything that they had learned, the Dauphine family was no longer her own personal nemesis. Now they were everyone's.

Her grandmother had been a Remy, and the Dauphines and the Remys had a blood feud that went back centuries. But now, it felt strange to have her fellow agents not just on her side but carrying their own fued with them.

"Have you found anything?"

"Gisele is supposedly down here, and Miranda has a stronghold outside Miami. So I started looking for connections. I found a few, but that's too tangled for anything fast. Right now, let's check these coordinates. What do you have?"

Eleri had placed the letter into a plastic evidence bag, and she held that up now for Christina, not willing to leave what they had behind at the hotel. She also had the boxes of bones in the trunk of her car. Now that someone knew exactly where they were staying, the locks would not be enough.

"Interesting." Christina flipped it over, saw the backside was blank, and asked the same thing Eleri had asked. "Do we recognize the handwriting?"

Both of them shook their heads, and Eleri added a hopeful, "Not unless you do?"

Christina shook her head, pink hair curling around her neck in a sweet, cheerful mood at odds with the determined look on the agent's face. "Well, let's go in."

Eleri shook her head again. "As you can tell, I can cover Donovan and myself, but I wasn't prepared and can't cover you."

It was Christina's turn to crack a wide grin and laugh at her. "Eleri, I can cover myself."

It only took a moment to realize that this was completely true. While Christina had no powers to make herself actually invisible, she could make anyone who'd seen her forget they ever had. And, if they ran into anyone who might know something, Christina had the power to make that person just *want* to spill the beans. She was beyond useful here.

One quick glance to Donovan, and Eleri could see that he agreed.

"Then let's get going before the day gets too hot," he said.

Within moments, they'd locked the car. Eleri had stopped and tried to subtly put her hand on the warm hood, not wanting to motion to anybody watching that the trunk maybe had something valuable in it. She quietly cast a spell, so that everyone would simply look past the car and not want to get into it.

They couldn't afford to lose what evidence they had. She couldn't imagine explaining to Sheriff Tucker that they'd gone looking for an international company that trafficked in werewolves and had lost the evidence on his serial killer case.

As the three headed into the woods, Christina led the way, her digital compass out in front. Eleri trailed close behind, her head still reeling that Christina just happened to be so close.

They'd walked for less than fifteen minutes before Donovan put his hand on her arm to stop her.

59

"They were here," Donovan whispered as Eleri turned to look at him, an odd expression on her face.

Whatever she'd done with her spell, they had no trouble seeing each other, but she'd tried to alter it a bit so Christina could see them. Only, it hadn't fully worked. He stepped forward and touched Christina lightly on the shoulder.

The other agent startled a little, but then turned her head slightly, as though listening to the sounds of the plants and animals around her. Christina didn't want to look like she was having a conversation with no one. Not that anybody should be watching them out in the middle of the Glades. But then again, Donovan knew better than to draw random conclusions.

They were all being overly cautious as they had no idea what they were dealing with. Donovan had already considered putting cameras up near the cabin they had found and then adding more along the trails in the Glades. So why wouldn't their killer use cameras, too? The price and availability no longer limited them to law enforcement agencies.

He whispered in Christina's ear, letting her know what he smelled, and she nodded. Slowly, she stepped to the side and visually swept the area to her right, but it was a move to let him take the lead. In a moment, the other two were tucked in behind him, Christina still holding the compass out in front of her.

Donovan watched as Eleri stepped in close to Christina and he heard her whispered words. "I wonder if he'll lead us to the same place the compass does."

Under her breath, Christina muttered back, "At this point, I would imagine so."

The small team trekked on, Donovan still in point, pushing further into the odd foliage. The going was slow. The footing was alternately firm and soft. Things scurried away, leaving the path clear but making noise to let him know they could sense him and were irritated by his presence.

He suspected that, if he ran into a dog, it would bark at him. He knew all the things dogs caught scent of and barked at, but this was the first time he'd considered invisible humans as an option.

"Is it recent?" Eleri asked softly and he knew she was asking about the killer's scent trail.

"A few days old," he replied, wishing he were in his other form and knowing there was no way to change now. "But it's built up. They've been here several times."

"Several times recently?" Eleri asked.

Donovan sighed. It was a good question, just one he didn't know the answer to. There were tracers going both directions, some stronger, some weaker. Sometimes one right after the other, but of differing levels as well. "Relatively recently."

It was the best he could do, but it didn't smell like a path that the same person had been walking for years.

"I wish I had my stick," Eleri muttered from behind him, sounding as though the heat were making her crabby.

It was in the trunk. Donovan knew they could have brought it along, but they hadn't thought of it.

"There are lots of sticks around here," Christina said softly, still remembering not to move her mouth too much.

"Ah, no," Eleri was almost laughing now. It was no ordinary stick, though that's what she always called it. "It's a custom T-bar with a point on the end. Straight shaft, like rebar, but smooth."

Eleri was talking about a rudimentary tool commonly used in forensic searches. No matter how wonderfully someone packed the ground or disguised the grave, as the body decomposed, it shifted everything. The dirt was always softer over a body, and often the shape of the loose dirt even resembled the shape of the hole. Finding a square or rectangular patch of soft soil was usually a dead giveaway of a grave.

It would have been a pain to carry a full metal rod with her the whole way, as her "stick" wasn't lightweight. Donovan had a second thought that it would have been good as a weapon should they need it. His gun was on his hip—in fact, all three of them were carrying—but it wasn't always the best weapon.

"Then again," Eleri said, "all the dirt out here is weird. Who knows what I'd find?"

Donovan wondered along with her.

Then it hit him. He paused, his hands outstretch as he smelled the air. He could feel and hear the shuffling behind him as the two women also came to a stop.

Letting his face shift ever so slightly, he took another deep breath.

First, they'd looked for the coordinates.

Then they'd been following the killer's trail.

Now, he sniffed and turned to face the other two. Christina wouldn't know, but Eleri did.

All Donovan said was, "Our killer was here."

60

Eleri was sweating, though if that was from the heat and humidity of the day or because of what she was looking at, she couldn't tell.

The small cabin stood much as the other had—old, weathered construction. This one was originally wood but had metal and other random materials tacked onto it, as though it had been repaired repeatedly over the years. With pieces newer and older, nothing matched. The roof was a conglomeration of odd shingles, most of them seeming original. They ran at an angle from one side to another, the little space not big enough to warrant a peak.

This tiny building was even smaller than the first and had barely enough space for two people to lay across the floor, though Eleri guessed that usually only one of them was lying down.

She watched as Donovan stepped forward, sniffed the air, and then reached for the door. Christina quickly stepped in front of him, stopping his hand and for a moment. Eleri frowned. Then she remembered that, if anyone was watching, seeing the door swing open by itself might have been more than a bit disconcerting.

As Donovan stepped back, Eleri moved into place behind Christina as the other agent drew her gun. Then she put her fingers through the small opening that served as a door handle. It was a risky move, and Eleri tensed until a moment had passed and the other agent's fingers remained intact.

She'd told herself it was safe—that Donovan would have sensed something if Christina was about to lose limbs. But this perfectly human—if abominable—case was getting stranger by the day.

There was no lock and no place for one, and Eleri sucked in another hot breath as Christina swung the door open. It took a moment for her eyes to adjust, but she could readily see that the inside was just as bad as the outside.

The only new material was a tarp, folded in several layers and thrown across the floor. It had once been bright orange but was now mottled and dark. Some of the stain was dirt, probably, but most of it was blood. Eleri didn't need Donovan's nose to confirm that.

She watched as her partner lifted his face into the air a little bit. He stepped closer and sniffed. "Same guy—it's our killer."

Not that she needed confirmation. They had already determined that the last cabin hadn't been the site of all the murders. Though this one didn't look fresh at all.

For a moment, the three of them peered inside, probably all their brains working like hers to catalog everything and check for anything out of place, any cue or clue that could help solve the case. But she didn't find any magical scrap of cloth or see any vision that helped. In a moment, Christina made a motion with her hand and the three of them moved.

In tandem, they circled the place, though none of them dared step foot inside. Eleri, her own gun firmly in hand, slid to the left as Donovan and Christina headed right.

She wondered if anyone was watching. Could they see the bushes move as she stepped into them? Or were they now truly invisible to the human eye? She had no idea.

This was one of the spells she had worked on during her weeks cloistered away at Foxhaven. But with no one else around to tell her if it worked, she'd been running on her own best guesses. At the time, she hadn't really cared what the spell could do, only that she could cast it with ease. Control had been her only goal.

Now, she looked up into the trees and checked the surrounding trunks for the small black dots that indicated digital spyware. But she might have looked right into a lens that was well-enough camouflaged that she hadn't even seen it. Though she searched for tech, she found none. But it didn't mean they weren't here.

The cabin, for all its old shabbiness, had no gaps that she could see. The killer, whoever he might be, was smart. He was organized and prepared. Having a second kill location was important, in case one of them was ever found.

In fact, if Eleri were their killer, she would want two spaces that she could use interchangeably and a third that she checked often but that remained untouched. If anyone found one of the two used locations, they would lack a full spectrum of information, because half the kills had occurred elsewhere. Her third place would look like the other two, but anyone who had been there would be able to say that no, it was not the place the killer was using. But she would have vetted it and made sure it was acceptable for future work.

This case was taking too long. What she needed was something of the killer's. She thought about cutting a corner from the tarp inside, but then it would be too obvious that the cabin had been found. Also, the tarp had clearly run with the blood of more than one victim long ago, so it might give her strange mixes of information.

Slowly creeping around the back of the cabin, Eleri looked up at the side for anything she might be able to use. The day was bright enough to see well, but the canopy overhead was thick and she wasn't getting the best light. Eleri pulled out her phone and turned on the flashlight feature hoping it wasn't bright enough to alert anyone, but would be enough to let her see the siding more clearly.

She was hoping for a hair or something obvious. Honestly, even if she found it, she wouldn't know it was the killer's. Because this was the back—nearly opposite the door—she figured the victims didn't come back here. And they likely didn't do the repairs.

A small, square piece of wood had been tacked over what Eleri figured must have been a hole or a leak of some sort. The wood looked relatively new, the nails thin. It was a chance she had to take.

Glancing around one more time, she checked for cameras that she still didn't find and listened for footsteps that she still didn't hear. There was only herself, Christina, and Donovan. Reaching out, she tugged at the small piece, working it back and forth until the nails loosened.

It took too long, despite her best efforts, but eventually, she held the thin piece of wood in her hands. There was nothing she could do about the nails sticking out; they made it impossible to slide the evidence into a pocket for safe-keeping. She would have to carry it back with her.

She could only hope the piece would yield what she needed.

61

Eleri put her hand on the doorknob to her hotel room and stopped dead. She had not expected the zing that shot up her arm. She jolted at the image—six feet tall, dark brown hair, male, blue eyes, friendly smile.

The door had opened for him.

She now jolted, letting go of the knob as though it were hot and watched as Donovan and Christina jerked back along with her, maybe because of her reaction.

She'd dragged her ass up the back stairs of the hotel to her third-floor room, as they'd not wanted to be seen by hotel security. She was tired and beyond ready to sleep. She'd even already offered Christina the pullout sofa in her suite.

But now she would rescind the offer.

"Someone's been here," she said, wide awake from the burst of adrenaline. "Not just someone, Donovan. I think it was our wolf."

Donovan was already nodding. He'd been exhausted, too, but he must have caught the scent. It was just a reminder that they couldn't let their guard down at all.

"*Your* wolf?" Christina asked.

"We ran into one on the beach," Eleri answered as she scanned the doorframe and checked the digital lock, unable to see if it had been hacked.

"Actually," Donovan corrected, "I think he's maybe been around before that. But he trailed us at the beach."

"Did you find him?"

"No, we didn't interact at all. We didn't even see him. I just knew he was there."

As the other two talked, Eleri twisted the knob and carefully pushed the door open, expecting to find the room ransacked. But it appeared untouched. Then, as she stepped foot into the room, she could feel it. Nothing was out of place, but everything was.

Donovan let Christina in then pushed the door shut behind them. The last thing they needed was tourists coming by and seeing them scoping out their own rooms. Or worse, a reporter.

Quickly drawing their weapons again, the three moved through the rooms with precision. Christina was now wearing both the sachets around her neck. The spell had been an easy transfer, and Eleri was pleased with the work. So now it appeared just the two of them walked into the room and cleared it. It was a quick job. Only the bedroom and the bathroom required doors to be opened.

As the three reconvened in the middle of the room, declaring the space clear, Christina began to lift the sachets from around her neck. But Eleri looked at Donovan as he said, "Don't take them off."

"Everything has been touched," Eleri whispered, trying to talk in a low enough tone that no listening devices or cameras would pick her up, but loud enough that Christina could hear. She figured Donovan —now actively sniffing at the air—had found the same things she had.

"We need to check your room, too," Eleri declared. "And then we leave."

She hadn't been ready for this. It was well after three and the day was boiling. She needed a bed and sleep in a place that hadn't been violated. She suspected none of that was coming anytime soon.

For a moment, she told herself that no one was here now and she took a deep breath. In that few seconds, she remembered she'd put the bones in the car along with all of the other actual evidence, and she was grateful for her foresight.

When she opened her eyes, she looked around and cataloged what she could.

All the DNA electropherogram prints had been left on the table. They could be easily reprinted; they were just paper. But someone had lifted them and not put them quite back into place. She'd packed the files from the sheriff's office and left behind the copies of the autopsy reports.

With another thought, Eleri stepped quickly into the bedroom and placed her hand into her suitcase. Immediately, she could feel that her clothing, too, had been rifled through. At one side, there was a black bag with ribbon drawstrings that contained a hammered bronze bowl and was packed with herbs. There was no magic wand, but it didn't take a genius to see that this was a suitcase of a practiced witch.

"We need to check your room," she said again to Donovan.

"I'll stay here," Christina volunteered, "and see if I can find surveillance."

Eleri didn't acknowledge her—if there were cameras or listening devices, it'd be better if she didn't. Instead, she and Donovan stepped out of the room. Their actions had most likely made it clear to anyone watching that they knew the place had been touched.

Donovan's room was much the same, nothing out of place, but he said he could smell the invasion. She could sense it.

After a few minutes of careful searching and finding that just about everything had been touched, they stepped back out into the hallway and Donovan began to speak in a low voice.

Eleri followed his thought process and agreed. If there were devices inside, they probably weren't in the hall. The hotel already had cameras at the end of the hallway. It was one of the things she'd liked about the place and probably something that their FBI liaison had taken into consideration when choosing this hotel for the reservation.

"We're moving," Donovan said softly, and Eleri nodded in agreement. "Then let's get started."

Three hours later, they had a new rental car—another SUV with the kind of space Donovan would need if he had to change. They hadn't checked out of the old hotel room, but had packed and carried everything down the steps, not letting Christina touch any of it. Though Eleri would have loved the extra set of hands, they couldn't risk having their new third person spotted.

At last, she'd settled softly onto the fluffy couch in a new hotel room, a large suite with two rooms attached. She'd reserved it and the car on another card, not bothering to go through the Bureau. She didn't suspect anyone there, but … she didn't trust anyone now, either.

She gave Donovan the main bedroom, leaving herself and Christina taking the other room with two twins. Eleri felt better having Christina stay with them. Another set of eyes and ears and talents was more than welcome, now that they weren't just solving a serial killer case.

They'd already checked and cleared each item they brought for listening or tracking devices and they had the new car and they were on the other side of town. But she still didn't feel quite safe. She knew, though, it wouldn't be long before her body would demand sleep. Even then, it likely wouldn't be restful, because she'd stolen the small piece of wood from the cabin.

"So," Donovan said, "the coordinates were clearly a ploy to get us out of the rooms, so that this wolf could go through them."

Eleri nodded. But Christina was quick to point out, "But it wasn't *just* a ploy. It was usable evidence in your case, right?"

Christina was right, Eleri thought. "It was a trade."

"One that we didn't agree to," Donovan pointed out.

Eleri only smirked. Whether they'd agreed to anything in this case —other than that they would investigate it—she wasn't sure.

"But if it's a wolf," Christina said, "then they had to know that Donovan would smell them upon return."

It was an interesting thought. One that Eleri, with her sleep-deprived brain, hadn't considered.

"But they wouldn't know that Eleri would sense them, too," Donovan added, somehow still on his feet and having enough energy to pace the room.

"Does that matter?" Christina asked. "If Donovan can tell they were there, do they really need both of you?"

"Well," Eleri said, thinking back to what he'd found in her suitcase, "if he didn't know it before, he certainly knows now."

The question was, *what did he want?*

62

"I think we go back to the therapists," Donovan said after they told Christina everything they had found. He hoped to hell her fresh eyes would see something new.

He and Eleri always pushed each other, sometimes flat out playing devil's advocate, looking for holes in a plan to make it worthy before they enacted it. So Eleri, of course, asked, "We just go back and ask them the same questions again?"

"Take me." Christina raised her hand to volunteer, her smile ridiculous.

Donovan immediately looked to Eleri. "That might not be a bad idea."

But even as he said it, Eleri added, "I think having two FBI agents in your office is nerve-wracking enough. Three would be—"

"—but it doesn't matter," Christina interrupted. "If you're willing, I can keep them calm."

Yes, Donovan thought. Christina had been through a lot trying to make the use of her powers ethical and he often wondered if she would live out her retirement sitting in a pediatrician's keeping the children calm and happy.

"Also," Christina said, "I can make them talk—but it sounds like you don't suspect any of them."

Donovan shook his head, and in nearly identical motion to Eleri's as she said, "We don't. They've all checked out."

Donovan was practically talking over her, saying the same thing. "Their alibis seem tight. None of them is the killer."

Christina nodded. "Do you think it could be a network? Different people report to different therapists, and the therapists get someone else to kidnap the person?"

"I don't think so." But even to his own ears, he'd answered a little too fast. Donovan knew he really should give the idea more merit. But the fact was… "There's a single scent signature."

"And coordinating it to this level would be rough," Eleri chimed in, and then paused. "Unless there's a network of informants and only one killer."

They needed to turn that rock over and see if Christina's idea would work, rather than dismissing it out of hand. His brain was running in circles. The day had worn on and they still hadn't slept.

They had ordered food to the hotel room, none of them willing to leave after the incidents of the last twenty-four hours. Even though they didn't want to draw anyone's attention to the fact that they were there, they had to eat. Delivery seemed the safest option—the chances that the delivery person or anyone at the restaurant they chose was in on the killings should be low.

Anyone paying attention to the old hotel would see they had moved out, but they continued to pay for the rooms. When the maids showed up, they would know. But that might be a while. They'd flipped the Do-Not-Disturb signs most of the time, because boxes of human bones weren't good for anyone to find.

When the knock came at the door, the three agents used excessive caution. Eleri stationed herself around the corner with her gun drawn. Christina stayed near the hinges, protecting herself with the wall. And Donovan barely cracked the door open, not willing to put an eye to the peephole, knowing that the movement would tell a predator exactly where his head was. While he was confident that Eleri and Christina were capable of many things, he did not believe for a second that the other two might even be able to undo a gunshot to the head.

After deciding the delivery boy was not the killer, Donovan reached out and accepted the bags. The three of them ate burgers and fries and slightly melted milkshakes that tasted better than they should have. And then, as he'd begun falling asleep in the armchair,

Christina asked a few pointed questions about the investigation and then waved the two of them off to bed.

He barely managed to strip down before falling between cool sheets, sniffing everything, as though to make sure the strange wolf had not walked through *this* hotel room, touching everything. Donovan was out almost instantly, but his dreams were fitful and stole his rest.

He was small and his father yelled at him. Aidan Heath's lips pulled back, gums and long teeth bared, as he yelled at a much younger Donovan to shove everything he owned into a garbage bag.

Once again, he'd demanded impossible tasks. There was no way Donovan could possibly collect everything in the five minutes he'd been allotted. Long before age nine, he'd sorted his things by their level of importance. In the dream, he worked fast and scared, always wondering if this would be the time his father left him behind like he'd threatened so often.

As an adult, Donovan had often thought that would have been a much better option.

He woke up to gulping breaths, reminding himself that he wasn't that boy anymore. But there was nothing like a vivid dream to remind him what Aidan Heath had really been like. Donovan hoped the man was dead. When he fell back asleep this time he dreamed of his mother.

And this time he woke up hating her and wondering, *Where was his brother?*

63

Eleri woke with a groan. A princess-and-the-pea situation would have been much preferable. Instead, the wood block not only created a lump under her pillow, it also caused all sorts of nightmares.

She'd seen the piece get hammered into place at the side of the cabin. That was about the most useless of information the block could have shared. Again, she saw the killer had long, slim fingers, unfortunately, in gloves. She couldn't even see the skin tone because in her dream, the night had been dark and she had only been able to discern that the color of the arms was neither very, very pale, nor very, very dark. It wasn't much to go on.

More usefully, she'd seen Eugene Nash's corpse dragged through the woods. His body was slung up in a harness, making it easier for the killer to handle. That at least was interesting. If they could find the harness, they should be able to track DNA from the blood.

Still, the harness wasn't the smoking gun to find this guy, but it could be helpful in the future. She tucked away information.

The killer sometimes dragged the body by facing backwards and sometimes slung part of the harness over their shoulder and moved forward, still dragging the backward facing body.

Was the killer big or small? She still couldn't quite tell. But seeing through the killer's eyes, she had learned that pulling Nash along had not been an easy feat.

When Eleri and Donovan had been chasing the scent through the woods, the killer had not been just a few steps ahead of them. The body had slowed him down enough that they would have caught up.

Awake from the mire of her dreams, she rolled over and reached under the edge of her pillow, feeling around for the wood block and expecting yet another zing of information, but none came. Maybe the little wood block didn't connect her to the killer in quite the way she'd expected.

When she'd come into the room, about to pass out, it had become clear that she couldn't slide the wood under her pillow with the three nails sticking straight up. For a moment, she'd considered jamming them down into the mattress to keep it steady. But in the end, she'd opened her small multi-tool and used the pliers to bend the slim nails inward. Though it was the only work she'd done on the block, she wondered if she'd done too much. Or maybe it simply hadn't held too many secrets in the first place.

Eleri rolled the other way, wood still clutched in her hand, and saw the other bed next to her was empty and made with the sharp lines from the hotel staff. Either Christina was a meticulous bed maker, or she'd never come to sleep at all.

At least she crawled into pajamas that were fit for company because she did have a roommate—and also because they never knew when they'd be interrupted in the middle of the night. Now she carried the block out into the main area. A blanket and a crisp, white pillow lay over one arm of the couch.

"Oh, Christina, you didn't have to sleep out here!"

"It's fine. I only slept for a few hours." The other agent didn't even look up and just waved the concern away.

Donovan sat beside her on the couch and Eleri saw that one of them had pulled the small dining table over. They'd dug the travel printer out of its box and new pages adorned the tabletop. Christina had asked if she could see Eleri's phone the night before and Eleri had let her. She trusted Christina not to look at her texts, but in the end, did it really even matter? She was willing to trade her privacy for a way out of this ridiculous case.

Checking the clock hanging over the small kitchenette, she saw that it was four a.m. She'd slept a good, sturdy night since they'd gone bed so early—or so late, depending on how she looked at it. But now she held up the wood block. "I slept with this."

"Interesting."

"No," Eleri sighed, "not very. I got about exactly jack all."

The look on both of their faces said *bummer,* as she set the wood block on the edge of the table.

"Well, I had some luck."

"Look what Christina found." Donovan pointed to the printouts on the table. "She pulled the GPS on your phone."

Eleri nodded. It made sense. They often left Donovan's phone in the car, once he changed. Wolves didn't exactly have good phone pockets. So hers tracked every place they'd gone.

"Look." He stood up, leaning over one of the pages and put his finger on the map. There was a red line running oddly across it. "There are a few interesting things, but look...This is where we started, at the side of the unemployment office. You can see here where we loop around." He pointed to a dot. "This should be the cabin."

Eleri saw where she'd noted the location when they were out following the trail. Donovan pointed to another dot.

"This is Eugene Nash's body."

Eleri tipped her head to look at the map. She'd noted that location as they stood over the corpse. That had been the first time they'd seen it, before they'd notified the Sheriff. It was farther away than she'd expected. But then again, she'd not had any idea how far they had gone, just that she should keep going.

"Here, we've looped around to the other side. We made a good arc on that trek."

Almost a semi-circle, Eleri thought.

"Remember I said I thought we were closer to civilization. See?" He pointed. The end of the line, where they had doubled back, was just shy of a campground and not far from the outskirts of town.

"Look what we were close to." He pointed to a building near the end of the red line. "Sylvia Lambrecht's office. And over here ..."

He was moving to the next map before Eleri had a chance to absorb that.

"Look here. This is where we were yesterday."

She wanted to blink. *What even was yesterday?* The way things were going, it was now the middle of the night. They'd officially hit three weeks on the case and they didn't even have a suspect. But Donovan's excited musing made her wonder if he had something.

"See? Here's where the second cabin is." He pointed to the red dot where Eleri had marked yet another spot.

"So we came this way." He drew his finger down the roadways. "Remember I said I picked up the killer's scent better around there, but he didn't come to the cabin the way that we did?... See, we went south, and then we went east, and then the small road turned back north and we walked northwest. Heading back the way we came!"

She'd known that. They'd come up north on one of the small roads into the Glades, but once again, she hadn't realized quite how far they'd moved. Then when they'd walked north—she could see by the red line now—they'd come back close to the edge of Astoria.

Donovan was pointing out the same thing. "Look whose office is a *very* short distance from that cabin."

Now, Eleri was fully awake.

64

Donovan stood on the doorstep in a white, button-down shirt and dark slacks. In deference to the heat, he wore no jacket or tie. He figured he looked more like a Mormon than a fed, but they hadn't wanted to come in bearing the full weight of the *Men in Black* suits.

Dr. Jay wasn't their killer. Donovan had smelled the killer several times, and it simply wasn't this man. But Donovan had spent several hours combing over those stupid spider maps, and the trails that led back to these offices.

Dr. Charlie Jay and Dr. Sylvia Lambrecht and even Dr. Gwen Song *had* to know the killer—whether or not they knew they did.

Christina stood next to him, her straight dark skirt much like Eleri's. He wasn't used to seeing the women dressed this way. Both usually preferred the sharp-creased, dark slacks that were definitely more "fed-looking." But he could only imagine the skirts were in deference to the heat. For a moment, he was envious.

As the doctor pulled up behind them in a small, beater car, Eleri turned around and opened with her best smile. "Thank you for meeting with us, Dr. Jay. We really appreciate your help."

He stepped forward, the briefcase in his hand as battered and worn as the car. "I'm happy to help however I can. I'm assuming you have new information?"

He was fishing, but Donovan wasn't going to take the bait, nor was he going to go off script when the three of them had a plan. "We wanted to start off by letting you know that you're not on our suspect list."

Eleri picked up the thread smoothly. "But we do think that someone you know might be."

Looking around as if to see if anyone was watching, Charlie Jay put his key into the lock, wiggling it slightly as if it didn't quite function. He motioned them all inside the office where he flipped on lights and changed the atmosphere from dark and gray to welcoming and sunny.

He had come in early to meet them for this conversation prior to seeing his patients. Donovan scoped the place out while Eleri introduced Agent Pines, but he'd managed to be looking the exact right direction to see Charlie Jay's classic response to Christina's handshake. He instantly relaxed. Donovan wondered if his fellow agent could put someone into a hypnotic coma with just a touch, or maybe even just a look or a thought.

Now with the nerves completely gone, Dr. Jay was effusively open. "Come on back. My office is the most comfortable room, and I've got plenty of places to sit."

Donovan remembered from the last time they were here, and in a moment the doctor and all three agents were settled into big comfy seats, Eleri and Christina side-by-side on the couch.

As Charlie Jay leaned back, enveloped in one of his own super-puffy armchairs, he laced his fingers and crossed his leg over the other. His body language position was at odds with the concerned look on his face. "Now, explain to me what you meant, because I'm not sure I follow."

It was Christina who nodded. "I want you to share with us everything you know."

"Of course." Dr. Charlie Jay simply agreed, though any decent therapist would have repeated his statement about doctor/patient privilege. Christina was already working on him.

Donovan leaned forward, joining in now. He lobbed the first question. "When you see your own therapist, what do you talk about?"

"Everything about me. Issues from my childhood. Sometimes things that patients tell me bring up feelings about myself or my past.

Sometimes we talk about my marriage." He didn't even look surprised at all the things that came out of his mouth.

Donovan kept pushing. "Do you speak about your patients?"

"Not generally, no."

"But your patients have problems that bother you ..." Donovan didn't ask this time. He fed the doctor the line.

And Dr. Jay answered in kind. "Absolutely."

Christina blinked. Donovan wasn't even sure he saw it, but Charlie Jay ticked up a notch. "I've talked to the two other local therapists. That's really all we have. I mean, there's a school counselor, but she's not licensed. There were a few more—Gwen Song was in a group practice. But Astoria is a small place. Honestly, convincing people to get therapy is difficult. Convincing people in rural areas is harder. And it's not cheap. The group Gwen was with couldn't find enough business and they left, but she was willing to continue part-time because she wanted to stay in town."

Did she now? Donovan thought. Though he knew Dr. Song wasn't the killer, he was suspicious of everyone.

Charlie Jay was continuing to mouth-vomit his story, and Donovan tried to stay focused. "But when something comes up with a patient, I tell Sylvia and Gwen. We tell each other about patients ..." He paused for a moment and then jumped in with, "for advice! It's appropriate medical care to seek second opinions!"

Donovan just nodded, though he didn't know anything about that when it came to therapy. "Tell me, do you ever share patients?"

"Oh, sometimes. Sometimes I get someone and I think I'm not the best person to help them. That maybe Sylvia or Gwen is."

"Why would you think you're not the best person?" Donovan was sniffing the air but also trying to control the conversation. The goal was to let Christina focus on keeping Charlie talking and for Eleri to be able to see if she could pick up anything.

"Well, many therapists—you might even say *most*—are therapists because they've come through some kind of trauma themselves. They want to understand and they want to help others. Gwen went to school after fleeing an abusive marriage. For Sylvia, it was her mother."

"What about her mother?"

"She was horribly abusive, physically and emotionally."

"And for you?" Donovan waited for a hesitation, but there was none.

Charlie Jay now seemed more than pleased to spill his guts. Donovan hoped Christina closed his memory of this session, so he wouldn't panic later that he'd given away anything he shouldn't. "Drug addiction. As a teenager, I was on the wrestling team. We had to keep our weight down. I don't know if you know what Florida's wrestling team is like, but we win championships. So the coach started giving us cocaine to help keep his winning streak alive."

Holy shit, Donovan thought, but yeah, every single member of the group had had an abuser. *Son of a bitch.*

Christina leaned forward, her mouth forming a soft smile that Donovan knew was out of character for her. Her expression suggested she was offering an ice cream flavor or asking for his favorite memory. But what she asked was, "When you find a patient who has been severely abused, who do you tell?"

65

Gwen Song had said much the same thing in her second interview as they'd gotten from Charlie Jay. They'd managed to get to her by lunchtime, killing the hours in between with a much-needed breakfast and a trip back to the hotel.

They'd reexamined all the paperwork—all the files from Tucker, all the printouts, the emails, and the interview notes—but Eleri found herself disappointed that nothing had popped.

Then Dr. Song's story dovetailed with Dr. Jay's quite neatly. It was good backup, but they didn't learn anything new at her interview, other than that Charlie Jay had been truthful about everything.

Dr. Song had lamented the breakup of the group practice. She'd laughed and shrugged. "Maybe we shouldn't leave psychologists to build business plans."

But she'd grown up here and wanted to stay behind when the group dissolved. "I got a later start on my career than most others. I was in a fifteen-year marriage, before getting myself out—that took several more years—before I even went to school. So I'm more than happy to work part time."

When they ran out of questions, Eleri thanked her for her time, and they reversed their welcoming handshakes from the way in, letting Christina leave last so she could push the woman to retain only certain memories of the interview.

They burned the time between Gwen Song's appointment and

Sylvia Lambrecht's with a nap. This time, Christina used her bed and Eleri was grateful. She'd been afraid she was the reason the other woman had slept on the pullout couch.

Not wanting to wrinkle her clothes or overheat—despite the fact that the air conditioning was doing its very best—she changed into her pajamas and immediately passed out. Two hours later, Christina was shaking her awake.

"Eleri. I'm sorry to wake you, but we've got to go."

It was damn near the best sleep she'd had in a week. The paltry information from the wood block had not been worth the hours of rest it had cost her. And she still wasn't caught up, but she did feel better. Needing to brush her teeth and hair, she begged for one of the bathrooms then talked through the door as she got ready.

"I forgot to tell you earlier. I did get something else from the wood block, though I'm guessing it's useless." She'd already told them that she couldn't ascertain skin tone or size but that she could rule out extremes. "There was a harness made of the kind of webbing that you use for tie downs on trucks, but not as wide."

"What? The killer wore a harness?"

"No." She pulled the wide comb through her curls and added product. "It looked like the kind climbing harnesses are made from. In fact, this might have started life as a climbing harness, but it was reworked."

When she was dressed, she opened the bathroom door to speak more freely, but saw the frowns on their faces.

"Why would they wear a climbing harness?"

"Remember how Eugene Nash was dragged backwards through the woods, his heels digging into the ground?" she explained, hoping to do a better job this time. "And we thought the killer had grabbed him under the arms and pulled him along?"

She watched as Donovan nodded, buttoning up his shirt again. Even he had changed clothes and fallen back asleep. Christina sat on the couch already ready to go, somehow having done all the same things Eleri did, but simply much, much faster.

"He didn't just grab them under the arms and pull them, he used a harness. He put the body into the harness—or maybe had it on them before they died? I don't know. But the harness gave him leverage so he could drag the body easier. In fact, I bet if we go back and look at the body, we can find some marks from it."

Donovan was nodding now. "If there's bruising, then we would know he used it when they were alive."

They should have seen that during the autopsy, she thought, but then again, these cases were so convoluted that harness marks very well might have been obscured by blood and cuts and other bruising if they didn't know to look for it. "If we look at the pictures from the earlier ones, we might be able to find it there as well. On JP Talley and Earlene Beaman at least."

"Excellent!" Christina declared too strongly. "When we get back, we'll go through the photos ... again."

Eleri felt her mouth quirk at the other agent's well-feigned excitement and she reminded herself that Christina was free to leave at any time. At least she hadn't so far.

Once again, they carried everything back and forth to the car as they went. No one wanted to do it, but the thought of leaving evidence to be stolen or rifled through was too much. She'd bagged the bones in groups in brown paper, since plastic could introduce mold and mildew. Then she'd put all the bones into a single box to make it easier.

Because they'd all napped when they came back to the hotel this time, they'd at least not unpacked. So Donovan had simply picked up the briefcase they carried. Despite the effort, no one was willing to let any of it out of their sight.

Eleri had done her best to hide the hotel room and to hide her obvious witchcraft materials inside of her suitcase. Though everything was still there, the goal was that anyone looking simply wouldn't see anything Eleri didn't want them to. But a wolf might smell some of the things she had burned in the room. Nothing she could do about that but hope that the spellwork covered scents, too.

They simply couldn't risk the wolf getting another chance to steal from them, even if he hadn't done it. So, hands full, the three of them piled back into the SUV. This one was silver instead of black and Eleri appreciated the lighter, more reflective color in the Florida heat, wondering who would ever buy a black car in this state.

They let Christina drive as they talked on the way to Sylvia Lambrecht's office.

"They really triangulated the town," Donovan said. "With Dr. Jay toward the south and Dr. Lambrecht toward the northeast. Song's office is a bit more central, but definitely on the west side."

Eleri wondered if that was intentional. If the therapists were dividing up the town like pie, or if they were circling the wagons and closing everyone in.

As they entered Dr. Lambrecht's office, Eleri hung back, letting Donovan handle the introduction of the newest agent. Christina once again worked her magic, her calm voice making Sylvia Lambrecht calm, though Eleri almost laughed this time. Dr. Jay had noticeably calmed when Christina pushed him. Dr. Song had begun talking in long, effusive sentences instead of her usual give-nothing-away tone. But with Dr. Lambrecht, Eleri simply wasn't able to tell the difference.

Sylvia Lambrecht had that kind of personality that probably made her a perfect therapist. The tone and cadence of her voice was naturally soothing, her smile naturally welcoming. Everything about her was non-threatening and comfortable. With the woman's attention on Donovan and Christina, Eleri trailed her fingers along their furniture in the lobby area. Much like Dr. Jay's space, all of the effort had been put into her office, where her clients could be comfortable. The lobby was merely a place for paperwork and waiting.

But as Eleri ran her fingers along the edge of the front desk—completely unoccupied now, as Sylvia's part time assistant had already headed home for the day—she felt the rush.

Her head swirled with images and for a moment and she felt dizzy. *The killer had been here.* She could see Eugene Nash through their eyes, walking into the unemployment office. Walking out angry and shoving a paper into his pocket. Heading around the side of the building and lighting a cigarette... alone.

Eleri gripped the edge of the desk as she felt the moment the decision was made. Not the decision to kill Eugene Nash—that had been made some time ago. His death was already a given in the killer's mind. But she felt the moment it was decided to take Eugene *now*.

She sensed Donovan turn and look at her and knew that he sensed something was off. But she must have been upright, because he motioned to Christina and walked with Sylvia Lambrecht into the office, closing the door behind them, leaving Eleri with her visions.

Eleri's world narrowed to the things she saw as she traced the wood edge of the desk. And as she watched, Eugene saw the killer approach and he looked up and said, "Oh. Hi!"

66

The interview with Sylvia Lambrecht moved quickly, though Donovan was worried.

Eleri had stayed in the lobby, obviously having gotten something off of the front desk, though Donovan had no idea what. Still, the last thing he wanted was for Dr. Lambrecht to notice or try to do something about it. Eleri would stand there as long as she needed and get whatever she could. But the wait until Eleri opened the door and quietly joined them felt interminable.

With Dr. Lambrecht's attention focused on Christina, the way the other agent was controlling her to do, Donovan shot Eleri a look as if to ask, *What did you find?*

She offered only a small shake of her head in return. It was enough to tell him that he would learn later. He hated waiting, but what else was there to do?

"And when you have a severely abused patient, what do you do?" Christina asked.

"Well, I counsel them on ways to get out of the relationship. When it's a kid, they often can't, not without calling child protective services."

"Do abusive parents send their children to therapists?" Eleri asked with the kind of tone that let Donovan know she found that unlikely. But she'd inserted herself cleanly into the conversation, so that

Sylvia's memory of her being part of the interview wouldn't have to be fabricated by Christina.

"Sometimes the emotionally abusive ones do. They don't see it as abuse at all, and they send the kid to me to 'fix them.'" Sylvia held up her fingers in air quotes. "But it's more that a therapist is always a therapist, and if I'm talking to a kid and I learn something, I try to help."

"What about with adults?" Christina pulled them back to the planned script. The idea had been to interview the three doctors with as similar a process as possible, allowing the agents to compare any differences in the answers.

"I try to hook them up with whoever can help."

"That's not you?"

"Well, I certainly can help them learn healthy coping mechanisms, but there are no real healthy coping mechanisms for physical danger. I can help them figure out what to pack and make plans. I can help them figure out how to hide those plans from their abuser." Then she interrupted herself. "It's most necessary to keep my patients safe. I can also tell them how to hoard their money and how to stay safe in the relationship until they're able to leave. But I can't show up at the door and arrest their abuser, if you know what I mean."

"Ah," Christina nodded with her "I understand" expression firmly in place. "So you bring the police in."

"Sometimes."

While Sylvia babbled on about how and when she did this, Donovan was listening with one ear. His other was attuned to Eleri, but she was now sitting quietly, adjusting herself into a simple listening-but-not-judging position.

Obviously, Eleri was fine. Whatever she'd seen would just need to wait.

Then Sylvia mentioned referring patients to the shelter. Gwen Song had also mentioned the shelter, and now both the women referred to their own time helping there. Charlie Jay wouldn't have been allowed beyond the doors as a male, but he'd also mentioned referring patients.

"I tell them that if they go to the hospital, the doctors there can help them press charges. They can call for me and I can help with that as well. I tell them how to get in touch with the shelter without alerting their husband. Things like that."

The three of them had sat through nearly the same interview twice before today. Though Christina was new to the case and the information, she deftly kept track of which answers were similar.

Donovan had expected more variance. More loopholes. Hell, he'd half expected someone to grin secretly and whisper that he or she could have the abusers "taken out" if they so chose.

But they'd gotten nothing of the sort.

He was struggling to stay focused.

"And when you find out that a patient has been abused, who do you tell?" Christina mimicked his earlier words almost exactly.

Sylvia Lambrecht's dark brown hands folded in her lap in a calm and comforting position. "It's very hard to hear it when someone has been abused and my heart breaks for them, though as a therapist, you really shouldn't let that show. Charlie and Gwen and I get together and we pour out our troubles. Technically, it's 'seeking a second medical opinion' and it absolutely is that!" she clarified. "But sometimes, it's just help for us. I don't think people realize that we carry everything they hand over to us. It's hard to set down the burdens of others, especially when we want to help and they're resistant."

The sadness in her eyes was clear. The woman was a born caretaker.

They'd already asked questions the first time about Jesse Nash, about Earlene Beaman's sons, and about Rebecca Talley. But Donovan figured, now that they had Christine here, and the words were flowing freely, they should ask again.

For fifteen straight minutes, Sylvia told stories. She animatedly told tales she'd heard from Charlie Jay. She talked in detail about what she'd seen in her own office, what she told Gwen, and more. As before, with Dr. Song, it all fit neatly with the previous interviews.

No one here was covering anything up—not that they could, with Christina's influence. But Donovan felt more than confident that none of these therapists had a killer for hire. If they were triggering the events that lead to the abuser's deaths, they didn't know it.

With a quick look to the other two, he raised his eyebrows slightly, to ask if they were done here. Both the other agents offered subtle nods.

One by one, they stood up, shook Sylvia Lambrecht's hand, and said thank you. When it was Donovan's turn, he watched as her other hand came across the back of his in a comforting, two-hand clasp.

Her skin tone, though a different color, was the same depth of hue as his own. He didn't know why it caught him right then, to think of that.

He'd never thought of his own mother, Amisha Bannerjee, an East Indian woman from Calcutta, as anything other than just his mother, but he'd inherited his darker skin from her. Despite the fact that the three of them were here, and that they wielded whatever powers they had, and that Sylvia Lambrecht was operating under those powers—in that moment, Donovan felt as though *he* were under *Sylvia's* spell. Her warmth and genuine desire to help bled through the simple touch.

As he looked down at her hands, though, he noticed something. Involuntarily, his fingers clenched slightly, holding her hand in his now firm clasp. He rotated his wrist, moving her hand so that the one she'd placed gently across the back of his was turned up so he could examine it.

"Can I ask you a question?" It was stupid. He could ask her anything. Christina was still here. Dr. Lambrecht would have to answer truthfully.

Christina would now have one more thing to remove from the doctor's memory. It was important that all three interviewees from today remember only a calm, simple interview with the FBI agents, even though none of them had spilled the beans.

But he had to ask. "Your fingernails—the middle and third ones—...I'm sorry, I just noticed."

For some reason, he felt the need to be polite, though she would never remember him asking. Still, he knew that memory studies showed that people who lost their short-term memory still remembered the *feelings* that they learned from the encounters. So he was trying to be gentle about the defect.

Sylvia smiled, not insulted by his question. "Yes. I lost those nails once."

Stunned, he moved his wrist again, trying to get her hand in better light.

He saw then that thumbnail was the same. The same three fingernails the victims were missing.

"They grew back," she told him easily. "And they look pretty good. But you have a sharp eye and you caught it."

He did have a sharp eye. With a cool smile, he covered the sudden lightning bolt of knowledge that they'd stumbled upon something important. "When did this happen?"

67

They'd exited the office calmly, but once the doors were shut, the car became a hive of activity. Despite the sweltering heat they closed inside the vehicle with them, Donovan felt the conversation burst around them. Christina at least had the foresight to crank the AC and blew hot air on them.

"She has the same fingernails missing that we've seen on our victims."

"Does that make her the first victim?" Christina asked. "Her mother was abusive. Did Sylvia survive the damage, but her other victims don't?"

Donovan turned to Eleri for the answer. "Wouldn't you have picked that up when you touched her?"

"I should have, unless she's hidden it from herself in some way. Though I have seen repressed memories from some people. But I don't think that makes sense in this case. I mean, she acknowledged that it happened when she was in the military and she was a POW."

Still, the zing of excitement hit him hard, as if they'd finally hit some critical mass of clues. They were finally holding enough pieces to see what the picture should be.

They asked stupid questions, reiterated information. But it was important. He had learned, both in his own work, and specifically in courses at Quantico, that they had to re-sort everything around new information. If they jammed it in where the old information dictated it might go, they could miss something.

"The missing fingernails match with our interview with Dexter Allen," Eleri pointed out. "That gets us back to before any murders."

Next, Christina asked, "Do you think they were POWs in the same place? Or is fingernail pulling just a common thing that happens when our military personnel are captured overseas?"

Donovan shrugged. He truly had no idea. The military had never been on his radar. Growing up with a man who made instantaneous demands that swayed the family one way or another, Donovan was not one for taking orders or jumping at finger snaps. He hated authoritarians with a gut reaction that bordered on rage. In fact, he had said as much multiple times to Special Agent in Charge Westerfield when the man had initially tried to recruit Donovan into the FBI.

It had been the lure of solving cases on a grander scale, and the promise of studying criminology and interrogation at Quantico—a privilege afforded only to those who could find a route inside—that made him say yes. Donovan had to admit, he'd always been overly curious. He told himself that he would be able to hide what he was for his weeks of training. And he had managed it.

But now, as always, he found himself faced with information that he didn't know enough about. He asked Christina, because he already knew about Eleri. "Were you in the military ever?"

Before she could answer, Eleri motioned Christina to start the car. Sitting in the parking lot for too long would only raise suspicion. And the three FBI agents dressed as such, despite the heat, might already be causing questions.

Checking over her shoulder, Christina backed out without the rearview camera. "The closest I ever got to the military was the FBI."

Like Eleri, Christina had come into the Bureau of her own accord. Westerfield had found her once she was already an agent with exceptional case-closing rates and a few odd stories from the field, unlike Donovan, who had been plucked from civilian life.

"These three therapists are the key to this case," Eleri said, motioning downward with one finger to help make her point from the backseat.

Donovan agreed, and he finally got to ask about what he'd been waiting for. He told Christina, "Eleri saw something when she was in the front lobby."

"I suspected as much." At the time, Christina had had her focus on Dr. Lambrecht and had not seen Eleri wandering about and touching everything like a toddler, or maybe like a psychic.

Eleri leaned forward then, not quite tall enough to make it into the space between the two front seats, as the car was rather large. But she tried. "The killer was in that office."

"When?" Donovan asked.

"I don't know. But the sensation at the edge of the desk was strong enough to get a real connection. I watched as he followed Eugene Nash. Then as he spotted Nash coming out of the unemployment office."

"So the killer was in there recently. But I didn't smell them." Donovan was confused now.

"Has the office been cleaned thoroughly enough? Maybe it was long enough ago that the scent is gone," Christina offered as she took a turn onto one of the main roads.

But Donovan was shaking his head. Eleri could touch and sense the killer, but ... "If Eleri got a sensation that strong, and from Eugene Nash's disappearance a few days ago, I would think I would still be able to smell the killer."

It was inside. The scent *should* have lingered long enough. Why hadn't it?

"Maybe the desk was new," he tossed out one option. "Maybe Dr. Lambrecht just bought it and it happens to have traces of the killer on it." He was grasping for ways that Eleri had found something that he hadn't. But Eleri shook her head.

"I don't think so. It matched the other furniture in the lobby. And all those pieces look like they've been there for a while. There was something about it. I don't know." She paused. "I think the killer had been there. Maybe it was recent, just not recent enough for you to smell it in human form. But I watched the killer sight Eugene Nash and make a decision that now was the time to take him."

Christina was watching the road, heading back to the hotel, as had been the plan. None of them were eager to stay in the heavy and restrictive clothing. And they needed a place other than the car where they could speak freely.

"If we go back tonight," Christina asked, "can you touch the desk again? Maybe see who the killer's next target is?"

"I don't think so. I get the feeling I bled that connection dry. I stayed and I left my fingers on the desk until I was getting no new information. Then I gave up and came into the interview."

Donovan had figured as much, but it was disappointing to hear that there might not be additional information to tap into. He huffed a breath. He couldn't figure out why Eleri had found something recent and he couldn't *smell it*. He hadn't smelled the killer *at all*.

Just then, his phone pinged and so did Eleri's. It was telling that Christina's device remained quiet, a reminder that they had invited her to this case and that she'd come in voluntarily. Also a reminder that they were keeping that information from their boss, who still didn't know they were working with a third agent.

Because she was driving and because she didn't get the message, Donovan relayed it to her. "The agents got the cameras set up at the first cabin. They're working on the second one. We should begin getting preliminary footage very soon."

"Then we stay in the hotel and start watching," Eleri declared, having moved past the missing scent that Donovan simply couldn't let go of.

68

"Turn here," Eleri told Christina as an idea hit. She checked her bag to see if she had the sachet and when she found it, she looped it through her necklace.

"Eleri!" Donovan said quickly. "Don't do that where people can see you!"

Quickly, she flipped her head side to side, checking out the windows and wondering if anyone might have been looking into the backseat of the car. Luckily, the windows had been tinted by someone who was a little overzealous. "I don't think anyone can see me back here. But on the plus side, if we ever decide we want to kidnap somebody, we might have found the perfect car."

When Donovan just sighed at her attempt at humor, she conceded. "It's a very good point. I'll pay more attention in the future."

When he didn't respond again, she asked, "Can you even hear me?"

"Yes, I can hear you." He sounded exhausted and he probably was. She wasn't at her stellar best, either.

"I want to go back to the old hotel, Christina. I wanted to check in and see if anything is there. See if our guy's been back."

Donovan only nodded from the front. It was probably the closest she was going to get to *That's a great idea, Eleri!* right now.

"You shouldn't go in alone," Christina said as she took the last turn.

"I don't have enough for all of us." She'd only made the two sachets for her and Donovan. Clearly, she needed to make more rather than relying on Christina's abilities to cover for herself.

"I know. And I can push the people who have seen me. But I still haven't done a definitive test on how well I show up on cameras, or whether I can erase myself from people who see me on footage, maybe even years later." She pulled into the lot at the old hotel. "But that just means I sit with the car while you and Donovan go up together."

"I don't like splitting us up." Eleri was thrown back to a problem they'd had in the past. Three agents meant there was no good way to keep people safe in partners, especially if they needed to go different directions.

Christina wasn't having any of Eleri's worries. "It's a car. I'm locked in. Unless someone fires a bullet through the window *at my head,* and I don't see them coming—which is honestly the same danger as any given day—" Christina added, "then we're going to be fine. What are you looking for, anyway?"

"I don't know. I just wanted to see if he came back. I have a feeling…" That was enough for them to operate on, Eleri knew. She'd hate if she was wrong, but she couldn't shake the idea of checking in on the old rooms.

A few minutes later, Christina had snaked her way through the lot and pulled in next to their old rental SUV. Like the hotel room, they hadn't let it go.

The new SUV looked enough different from the old one that Eleri hoped they wouldn't immediately be recognized. It also hadn't been driven to this hotel before, so hopefully no one was watching and thinking, "There they are."

Donovan got out and Eleri—hopefully completely invisible to anyone watching—climbed awkwardly over the seat and out the door that Donovan had casually stood by, leaving it open for her. She carried a second sachet for him and patted her pockets down for the keys to the rooms.

As Donovan couldn't examine the old rental without being spotted, Eleri walked carefully around it and gave the car a once over. There were no obvious key marks, no signs of forced entry. It looked as if it had been left alone. After a few days of sitting in the exact same spot, it might likely garner attention, but no notices had been tucked under the windshield wiper. Maybe they'd find paperwork from the hotel under the door.

Donovan meandered slowly across the parking lot, looking at his phone to disguise his abysmal speed. Eleri bolted to catch up as he used his key card to let them in the side door and then into a stairwell.

Quickly looking upward and around, Eleri checked the corners and saw Donovan doing the same. "No cameras."

"I don't see any," he agreed, but they both looked around again and realized they could duck under the staircase. Eleri stepped easily into the space and watched as Donovan had to duck low to keep from bonking his head.

She handed him the second sachet and stood waiting as he slipped it around his neck. Within a moment, he simply faded from view.

"That's pretty cool," she said. "I hadn't watched it work before. Didn't know if it was instantaneous or not."

But then she realized *she* couldn't see her partner either. "Dammit." With a few blinks and a head shake at her mistake, she grabbed the amulet around her own neck and offered a small incantation. Once she opened her eyes, Donovan was there again. She hoped she was the only one seeing him and that she hadn't undone the whole thing.

"Now we can see each other." She started up the stairwell, the air inside the small space disturbingly warm. The hotel had not invested in keeping all of the nooks and crannies cool—certainly not the places they hadn't expected the guests to be frequenting.

At the top of the staircase, they had another dilemma—but Eleri didn't know what to do about it. There was a camera at the end of the hall. Anyone in the hallway would see the stairwell door open, and no one there. Still… "I think we'll be out of sight. Listen at the door? See if anyone is nearby and might see it?"

He did as asked, placing his ear to the door only for a second before saying, "Shit, Eleri, it doesn't matter. We have to open the room doors, too. And those are in sight of the cameras."

He looked around quickly. Still spying no cameras in the stairwell, he pulled the sachet off and handed it back to her. "I'm going to have to be seen going in."

She put her hand firmly on his arm, blocking him for a moment. "Let's think it through, first. It'll alert anyone watching that we're still here. Though they might have seen us already coming and going—well, they already saw you coming into the hotel. But if they're watching all of that, then they've made the new car and they would notice that neither of us are coming and going at the rate we were before."

She sighed, hoping he understood the word salad she'd just spewed.

He seemed to. "So assuming we've already been made, just by coming back here, what do we have to lose by going and checking the room?"

"Fair," she conceded. There was no good way to sneak in. She'd liked the hallway camera coverage when they'd first checked in. Now it was working against them. They'd also been planning on calling the front desk and getting footage of when their visitor had slipped the paper under the door. With everything going on, and their need to make up for lost sleep the day before, they simply hadn't done it. Maybe Donovan could just stop by the front desk on the way out.

With a nod, Donovan shoved open the hall door, letting the cooler air of occupied spaces wash over her. If anyone was watching today's footage, or anyone had been standing there, they saw only the one man walking down the hallway.

She trailed along then stepped back to wait as he used the key to open his own room and step inside. It was mostly empty. The bed was still made from the last time the maids had been in, but Eleri didn't know when that was. It was another thing they'd missed in their quick cleanup—that someone would be coming in and checking the rooms periodically. "We didn't put out the Do Not Disturb sign."

As he quickly took care of it, Eleri touched everything. In the bedroom, touching the pillow brought images of the young woman, brown hair slicked back into a bun, stripping sheets and putting new ones on. At the sink, she saw the same woman wiping the counters and faucets. But when she ran her fingers over the small side table, Eleri got a jolt.

69

"He's been here," she said.

"Since the last time?" Donovan asked her, standing in the middle of the hotel room, a frown of concern on his face.

Eleri nodded. "I don't know what he did … but I think he was here relatively recently."

Donovan swept his hand, open-palmed, around the room in a broad gesture. "Then he knows we're not here anymore."

The place was too sparse. In an effort to leave nothing of value behind, they'd barely left anything at all.

She nodded in agreement as Donovan said, "I guess that tells us what we needed to know. He did come back."

"We need to check my room, too, though." Eleri let Donovan lead the way out of necessity. She was itching to run to the next room and throw open the door, but she wouldn't show up on security cameras.

A few moments later, standing in her old junior suite, the feeling was even stronger. "He spent more time in here."

Donovan put his hands on his hips, looked around, and tipped his head. "I mean, that makes sense. This is where all the evidence was last time."

Eleri started touching things. The door handle gave her a jolt, as probably he'd touched it on the way out. So had the maids.

She was ducking into the bedroom to see that her bed had been once again crisply made and clearly abandoned as Donovan called from behind her. "El?"

Turning, she saw him holding another white envelope. "Where was that? On the floor?"

He pointed downward. "I think it was left on the table and maybe blew off as one of the maids walked by or closed the door."

Eleri saw that he held it oddly between two fingers in a pincer grip. From the upper corner she would get maybe a quarter or an eighth of a fingerprint from him, but he hadn't disturbed any other evidence by grabbing it.

"Should we open it?" he asked.

"I don't think we can." She didn't have her kit. She wanted to fingerprint it thoroughly. She needed to open it without leaving her own prints and smudges. The last letter had yielded prints that matched nothing in the system, and she expected nothing else here. But she had to be sure that they didn't have two—or more—intruders following them and breaking into their rooms. That was a possibility if Miranda Industries was orchestrating this.

Eleri had carefully asked a friend to run the first prints she'd lifted, leaving no trace with the FBI. She'd still not addressed why she felt that was necessary. "So we take it back to our current hotel and then we print it, we open it, we do a full evidentiary run."

He nodded and once again swept his hand around the open and empty room. "Is there anything else here? Because I don't smell anything specific."

"I don't think so. It's just so weird." She tried to string her scrambled thoughts together in a way she could understand. "He came here. So he saw the room was empty, but he left us a note. So he's still trying to contact us, and he thought we would come back."

Donovan nodded. "He probably had the note ready before he arrived. Maybe he was surprised that we were gone."

"I don't know. He did a good job breaking in. The digital key didn't seem to have been tampered with. So he either knows how to crack it, or how to talk his way past the front desk." That was a thought she'd been keeping at bay since the last break in.

This was now a hotel that no FBI agent could use again in the future. It clearly didn't have proper security. Though, she thought, would any agents be coming back to Astoria?

She was still trying to create coherent, linear chains of thought when her phone rang. Automatically, she lifted the phone to see that it was Sheriff Tucker. But in that same moment, the reflection on the screen showed the upper corner of the room behind her and she shook her head as she tried to come to terms with the fact that she truly erased herself from sight. It should have been cool. It was disconcerting. And that was yet another disturbing thing to untangle.

"Hi, Sheriff."

He wasted no time. "We're having another press conference tonight. Seven p.m."

Eleri looked at the screen. It was already six. That was hardly any warning. She wanted to ask, *Are you sure that you need us?* But obviously he was. They were the investigators in command. He, the local acting authority, was merely there to help them. She wondered if she should tell him, *You can't call any more press conferences without my permission.* But for tonight, it didn't matter. He must have already notified the press.

"Same place?" she asked.

"Courthouse steps this time. A little more prominent. Better background. You have anything you can add?" he asked.

"I can share what kind of evidence we have." She considered for a moment. It would take a little forethought to figure out what she could and couldn't reveal. She needed to say the right things to get the crowd on their side as well as get them to come forth with any evidence. "All right. We'll be there."

Donovan wiggled the envelope, still firmly grasped by a tiny corner and his two fingers. "Think that means we have to be done here?"

Eleri nodded at him, the yarn in her brain even more tangled now. "So that means that our guy—our wolf—still has access to our rooms. He knows we're not here now. Last time, he seemed to trade information—though we didn't agree to the trade, per se, he did give us an incredibly useful clue."

"But he used the time to check out our rooms." Donovan shook his head. "I see no clear agenda there, either. But we need to get going if we want to be ready for that press conference."

Eleri held up her phone and took a picture, then commanded. "Flip it around."

She got a picture of the back of the envelope as well and immediately sent them to Christina with the words: "Found this. We're on our way down."

Donovan raised one eyebrow at her. "Christina's barely a hundred yards that way." He pointed out the window where the parking lot could be seen. "Did she really need a picture?"

"Yes," Eleri told him solemnly. "I'm beginning to think we need to start documenting each step, in case we don't show up at the next one."

70

Donovan stood back, hands clasped casually in front of him. It was difficult to look cool and aloof in the Astoria heat, but he was doing his best despite the sweat rolling down his spine. He was listening to Eleri make statements that held a wealth of information but told nothing of value.

"Yes," she told the crowd, once again using two hands to make a braking motion to calm the irritated. It didn't work. "We do have new evidence and we are making progress on the case."

"Do you have any suspects?" Jesse Nash called out.

Donovan recognized the raven dark hair and the strong voice.

Eleri filled the empty reply neatly. "We don't have anyone in custody at this moment. We are certainly keeping our eyes on things and working to keep the community safe … to make sure that nothing more happens to anyone else who lives here."

Donovan's eyes tracked back and once again found Jesse Nash easily. As Eleri's last few words were broadcast from the microphone, he watched as Jesse's lip quirked. *Yep,* he thought. *No one was upset that these people were gone.* At least not their immediate family members.

There was still a bit of a hue and cry over Talley's murder, as people seemed to think he had been some pillar of the community. Rebecca Talley half-heartedly had joined in, maybe thinking it was easier to go on with her life letting people believe what they already did. His standing in the community might make him—in death at least—more of a benefit than a detriment. Maybe it was just too much trouble correcting people.

Donovan fought the urge to roll his shoulders and crack his neck. He'd left his mouth in his practiced flat line that was neither pleased nor disapproving and definitely said *Don't approach me*. He appreciated the late Florida sunlight that afforded him the sunglasses that hid his eyes darting back and forth. This was what he'd imagined when he'd finally signed on the dotted line for Westerfield, though without the heat and the humidity.

The crowd pushed Eleri with questions coming on top of each other and forcing her to pick one out. Donovan heard them all distinctly but understood that others didn't.

"If you don't have anyone in custody, then the killer is still loose. So how can you keep us safe?"

"It sounds like you don't have any suspects at all!"

"Who are the suspects? The town people deserve to know!"

But the one that grabbed him was, "What about the cabin?"

Jesse Nash. It was all he could do to keep his head from whipping her direction.

Where was this woman getting her information? The next thought followed quickly on the heels of that one: How could they harness Jesse Nash and make her information work for them?

Without moving his head, he flicked his eyes to Eleri, still standing at attention at the lectern. Her soft smile stayed in place as she thanked everyone for their very thoughtful questions.

What a load of shit, he thought. At least she delivered it beautifully and he was aware that it needed to be done. Making people *feel* safe was part of the job. But he'd always been a bit literal, and they weren't *keeping* anyone safe until they figured out who was killing them. Then again, don't hit your spouse or your kid and you were probably going to be fine. He was constantly biting his tongue not to tell people that one.

Eleri ended with, "Please be aware, everyone is afforded due process. We don't want to take anyone into custody until we're certain we can make the charges stick. However, we do have our eyes on the community, and we have a much clearer picture of how this killer has been operating. Rest assured, we expect to make an arrest shortly."

Slick. "Shortly" could mean anything. But with that last word, she closed it down, gave the crowd one nod, and stepped away. Whatever it was they wanted to ask, she wouldn't be answering it.

Once again, Sheriff Tucker stepped back up to the lectern and offered his homey, charming answers. He did a much better job of calming the crowd, which was rapidly growing more agitated.

Eleri slid into place next to Donovan, her expression not giving away the cringe they both surely felt inside. As soon as Tucker called it, they casually darted from their post. They ducked into the car and drove in circles as they headed back to the new hotel room, making sure no one was tailing them. At least, no one from the press conference was. Not the reporter, Jesse Nash. Certainly not their new tail, whoever the wolf might be.

When they arrived back at the hotel, Donovan felt gummier than ever. The combination of the humidity followed by walking into the air conditioning made his clothing press in on him. It wasn't a sensation he liked. He wanted to hop into the shower, but Christina sat at the table, the letter now opened before her.

They'd left her here, not wanting her seen. The longer people didn't know about a third agent working the case, the better. In fact, the therapists wouldn't even remember that she had been there.

He'd had the chance to be on the receiving end of her powers more than once and had watched as the room caught on fire around him. He'd felt the oppressive heat, heard the crackle of the flames that licked out at him, and smelled the materials burning… when no such thing had happened. He didn't doubt her ability to do exactly as she said she could.

Now that he thought about it, maybe next time they should hide her in the crowd and see what she could glean. But she was holding up the envelope, which she'd carefully dusted with black magnetic powder. Donovan could clearly see the fingerprints she'd illuminated and lifted.

"Same guy as last time?" Eleri asked and Christina quickly nodded. Then, using the long tweezers, she lifted the page from the table, once again revealing Miranda Industries letterhead. The same handwriting—should he have doubted the connections—had only a few words.

GM Corp is a subsidiary. Follow the shells.

71

"Wait." Eleri blinked her eyes. "GM Corp is a subsidiary of Miranda?" She was trying to wrap her brain around it. It wasn't working all that well. Why was Miranda Industries insinuating itself into her case? It was bad enough that she was anywhere near MI, let alone that she was somehow now tangled with it.

She was tired. She needed sleep. She wasn't the kind of person who needed a regular sleep schedule to function, but she needed more than what they'd been getting recently. After several weeks of this, it felt as though her brain was rebelling, trying to remind her that she needed to at least do better.

Donovan was nodding at her. "It is. We followed the shell corporations, and Miranda is the parent." His fingertip was perched on one page, as if holding it down, or holding the connection together. Maybe he needed sleep, too.

But it was Christina who filled in the words. "That nice house, and maybe even the hold he had over his wife? JP Talley wasn't just a big shot locally. He was relatively high ranked at GM Corp."

"We didn't pay attention to his job," Eleri said. "It passed initial inspection and seemed irrelevant to this case. He was killed because of the way he treated his wife."

Christina shrugged. "It might honestly still be irrelevant to this case. Are any of the other victims associated with Miranda Industries?"

"I don't think so."

But she didn't know, did she?

"Earlene Beaman was on disability and the Merkels worked for the state, running the foster home. So, no, on the surface at least, no one else was working for Miranda."

"But if JP Talley was a big shot at one of their subsidiaries, that might very well explain why you're suddenly getting letters on MI letterhead a week later. One of their top brass goes missing under unusual circumstances and Miranda has to make sure that they've covered the trail."

Eleri agreed, though she didn't like where it was going. "Miranda has to make sure the agents investigating the case of their top brass guy are..." Eleri let the sentence trail off, not sure where it went. Had they figured out it was unrelated?

Noah Campbell had been with them the first time they'd infiltrated Miranda. At the time, he'd been with Miami Dade PD. But, true to form, SAC Westerfield had recognized his skills and quickly recruited him to the FBI—right into the NightShade division.

Now, when she thought of having the might of the FBI at her back, it seemed far too small to make her feel safe. Not against a behemoth like Miranda Industries. All three agents were clearly dealing with difficult thoughts regarding the information they'd gotten.

"I don't think you did anything wrong." Christina looked to the other two agents as if knowing they needed the assurance. "I don't think you missed anything, and I don't think this actually has anything to do with our killer. But it does tell us why and how a wolf from Miranda industries began trailing you around."

"That doesn't make me feel any better." It was easy to see the other two felt the same way.

"He didn't ask for anything in exchange this time," Donovan pointed out.

"I don't know..." Eleri said. Things were so tangled, she had to work everything out each time she opened her mouth. "Last time we got the note, we had no idea it was an exchange until we got back and found what was wrong."

She didn't like where this might be going. "So, we won't know what we traded away for this information until after we find it missing."

Donovan and Christina looked at each other, realizing they might have already missed it.

72

The morning light felt bizarre as Donovan woke up. It wasn't the norm lately. He hadn't slept well, though that was appearing to be the norm. He groaned, though no one heard it and it didn't do anything.

The night had stayed unusually hot, and they'd cranked the air conditioning. He'd spent the entire night wrestling with the covers, alternately crawling under them and throwing them off, vacillating between too warm and far too cold. Now, he tossed them aside, not caring about the mess as he pulled on some clothing.

In the main room, he found Eleri and Christina sitting at the little bar, eating bowls of hot oatmeal. Eleri didn't even offer him one. She knew better. Donovan passed both of them as he aimed for the coffee pot. He'd rather have Cheetos for breakfast or he could simply wait and eat when the offerings were better.

"What's on the agenda for today?" He asked and received the very snarky answer of, "Find the killer and go the fuck home."

Eleri had clearly had enough of this case. He had, too.

"Not going to find the wolf who's been trailing you?" Christina tossed out the question and then stayed quiet.

Eleri gave a long, drawn-out sigh. "I mean, I figure we have to do that, too. But I don't want to."

"We can't just leave it behind and forget it ever happened." Donovan knew he didn't have to tell her.

They had a wolf from Miranda Industries trailing them. They might go home, but he had no doubt they could be trailed there, too. And, at home, they were in entirely separate places. Eleri's wealthy family owned at least three large pieces of property and maybe had homes in other cities as well. He didn't know.

He would go to South Carolina, just outside of Gadsden. It was one of the few places he was confident that the Eames-Hale family did not hold property. And Christina? Hell, he didn't know where Christina lived these days. He didn't think they'd be safe with Miranda Industries on their heels.

They at least needed to know who was following them and why. "Okay, but what's really on the agenda?"

This time Eleri gave a better answer. "We have footage from the cabins to watch."

The cameras hadn't been up for quite a full day, but if they got lucky, it could speed everything up with identifying the killer. He nodded.

"I want to recheck the bones, too." Eleri gestured toward the box where the lid didn't quite fit because she'd stuffed the skeletal remains of several bodies into it instead of just one.

"And someone needs to interview Jesse Nash. We need to figure out where she's getting her information."

"Should we make an appointment with her or just show up?" he asked.

Christina was dressed, Eleri was still in her pajamas. It might be a statement, he wasn't sure.

"I think we just show up," Eleri said. "If she is getting information from unusual sources, then we don't give her time to prepare or cover them up. Plus, we take Christina."

He watched then as his partner turned to the other woman. "If that's okay with you?"

He and Eleri had learned, maybe the hard way, not to assume that anyone was willing to use whatever skills they had on command. Christina merely nodded, ate two more bites of her oatmeal, and set the bowl and spoon down with a small clack. "It's what I came to do."

"We're grateful," Donovan told her, finally getting a sip of the still-too-hot coffee. "It's made a huge difference."

Christina's eyes darted away for a moment and Donovan wondered what she was thinking. When she looked back, she said,

"I'm here and I'm happy to help. I was in Florida on my own accord—trailing traces of Miranda. Anything I could find. I was looking for wolves and Dauphine sisters. And, honestly, I was trying to find any connection back to the de Gottardi/Little farm."

"You think it's all interlaced?" Eleri asked.

"I have no evidence of that, but I don't see how it can't be." Christina looked between the two of them and Donovan knew his expression told her that he agreed.

He didn't want that to be the case. But with everything they'd seen, it seemed almost impossible that the problems weren't related.

"So when I saw you were here, it made sense to offer to help."

"But you didn't know JP Talley and GM Corp were connected to Miranda?"

"Not at all. I just answered your text."

And yet, somehow, Donovan thought, *they'd reached out blindly and stumbled into another connection.*

Christina still looked apprehensive, her gaze now darting between Eleri and Donovan. Her next question revealed just how worried she was.

73

"Do you think *I'm* the reason the wolf from Miranda industries found you?" Christina asked them, her normally no-nonsense tone filled with concern.

"No," Eleri jumped in quickly. "I don't think that for a second. Donovan and I had the sense we were being followed from almost the beginning of this case. We were brought in within hours of the sheriff finding JP Talley's body. It wasn't long after that I first got a zing from the door handle on the car … as if someone was paying attention."

Eleri remembered one time before when she'd been convinced she was being followed—the case in Manistee Huron. And she'd been correct. When she looked back, though, she could say that instance had ended well. She did not have high hopes for this one.

She kept talking as she hand-washed her cereal bowl and set it in the tiny dish drainer beside the tiny kitchen sink. "I don't think any of this traces back to you." Then she switched subjects. "Let's each pull up some of the camera footage and start checking. Maybe we'll get lucky."

An hour and a half later, they'd gone through just about everything. The FBI team had set up three separate cameras triangulating each of the cabins. So the two arrays were basically the same. The agents had watched views from all three on high speed, knowing they couldn't afford to miss if the killer had stepped into view from only one angle and turned around and left before a second camera caught him.

Eleri didn't have hopes for the first cabin to reveal much. Finding Eugene Nash's body had almost guaranteed that they'd gone past the cabin. The killer would most definitely consider it burned. If he was operating the way she thought he would, there would be a third cabin—one that Eleri and Donovan didn't yet know about. So she was holding out her hopes for the one southeast of town—the one they'd been given by the Miranda wolf.

"Oh, look at this!" Christina's voice was far too cheerful to have spotted a killer.

But Eleri leaned over and looked at Christina's screen. The image was black and white, the FBI not having sprung for full color—not that Eleri thought it was necessary.

"What are these birds?" Christina asked them as she pointed to the screen, a smile on her face.

Eleri didn't know. She wasn't much of an ornithologist in general, and she certainly couldn't tell from a black and white image what a full-color Everglades bird would look like.

Donovan had taken all the footage from the cabin where Eugene Nash had been killed and was watching it at high speed, since they didn't expect to see much there. He had, however, seen several mid-sized cats go through. And like Christina had, he called the other two agents over to watch.

"That's in the Glades with us?" Eleri didn't like the idea of sharing space with large cats—Florida Panthers—that she couldn't see.

"They probably don't like the smell of me." Donovan grinned.

What should have taken them maybe two hours, had taken almost three as they gleefully tried to identify wildlife, none of which had included a serial killer. Eleri had seen hikers coming through.

"Look," she pointed now to her own screen, drawing the other two away from the seemingly colorful birds. "There are people back there, three of them."

They were far enough in the distance that she really could only see legs and boots. "Someone got close enough to this cabin. But if someone was inside screaming, they would have come by to help. Don't you think?"

"No one was in there when they went by," Christina pointed out. They hadn't seen the killer dragging a new victim in, and the agents that installed the array should have checked the place out. "But if someone was ... Is that a nearby trail?"

"I didn't smell any nearby high-use paths when we were there. We were really pushing our way through the brush." Then Donovan paused and asked, "Do you think it's the killer, coming by to check on the place?"

"Like he knows—or at least suspects—it's been compromised, so this is a casual drive by?" Eleri thought about it for a moment. "But this is three people. We have a singular killer."

They knew that because of Donovan's scent-tracking ability, and because of Eleri's ability to get impressions by touching objects. So while it was nothing they could claim as prosecution-level evidence, she was more than confident they had a single person, working alone, at least for the killings. She mused a little further out loud. "But if one or more of the therapists are tipping the killer off, then maybe this is a way of checking on the cabin. They come out in a group."

Though Eleri didn't believe any of their therapists were the kind to go trekking their way through the Glades, she couldn't say for sure that they weren't. She watched the footage again, and again, taking a sip from her coffee mug, only to find that it was empty. And so were her ideas.

She'd have to wait and see if it happened again before she could decide if it really was a group checking up on the cabin, or just somebody who'd gotten a little too close to a killer's lair. She was stuck on the idea that, had someone gotten close enough to hear screams, that would seem very poor form for a killer. Then she asked, "Don't they see the cabin? Wouldn't they want to come check that out? It seems fully out of place in the Glades."

But neither of the other two agents had an answer. Ultimately, they had to abandon the footage and simply wait until more came in. That would hopefully make things clearer, especially if the hikers came by again.

If they were really lucky, it would reveal the face of their killer.

Half an hour later, she was dressed and the three of them had piled into the SUV. Their first stop was Nash's home. The car wasn't in the driveway, and it appeared that Ciara was at school for the day. They checked in next at the *Astoria Sun Times* building, but didn't see Jesse Nash's car there either.

"What now?" Donovan asked. "Do we just drive around town and look for her car? Do we stake out her house?"

Eleri wasn't much for living in the car, eating fast food, and not having a place to go to the bathroom. "Please, no. Not that."

"Can you find her then, Eleri?" Donovan asked.

"Maybe, but I don't have anything of hers to use."

In a moment, Donovan had turned around and handed a business card into the backseat.

Jesse Nash - Reporter - Astoria Sun Times.

Eleri raised one eyebrow at him. "You know, honestly, it has her phone number on it. We could just call her and see if she'd meet us now. As long as we don't give her enough time to prepare or hide anything, it'll be fine."

But even as she made her snarky comment, she saw where Jesse Nash was.

74

"Everyone has cabins out here." Jesse Nash said it as though it were common knowledge.

"You have one?" Donovan asked in quick reply.

"Well, no, I don't. Not *everyone* has one, but they're not uncommon. People used to live back in the Glades and honestly, some still do." The reporter was looking at them like they were the crazy ones.

"Are there trails and paths to them? Is it like cabins at the National Parks?" Eleri asked.

"It *is* a national park." Jesse narrowed her eyes.

The reporter had come home relatively quickly after they'd driven away looking for her elsewhere. Now it seemed she wasn't really keen on being accosted in her own living room.

Donovan didn't care. Christina could take care of that. As he watched, she leaned forward and placed her hand on Jesse's knee and simply said, "Don't worry. No one's upset with you."

Jesse's entire stance changed. She breathed out an easy sigh and her spine unstiffened. "The deal is, there are a lot of cabins. Most of them are probably not habitable and a lot of them are way back where nobody goes. Back where you wouldn't stumble upon them, even if you were out for a hike one day. The Everglades is a national park, and some of the cabins are grandfathered in, and some were just left to rot."

"Okay," Eleri said, carefully putting out a hand to let it rest on

Donovan's knee, as if to say, *Maybe don't be so harsh this time*. "But why would you think that there's a cabin involved?"

"I'm right, aren't I?" One side of Jesse's lips quirked with the realization.

"Obviously, we can't tell you any information about the case," Donovan stated, now more grateful than ever for Christina's ability. Otherwise, Jesse would be running off to write an article about the cabin the killer was using. Honestly, at this stage of the game, she might be able to get herself some national press.

When no one else talked, Jesse felt compelled to fill the space. Whether it was her own urge or one Christina had given her, he didn't know. "It just makes sense. The victims are tortured."

Donovan noticed Jesse didn't flinch or react much at all, despite the fact that her own husband fit that category. Whatever he'd done, she was no longer a fan by the time he'd gone missing. From what Donovan understood, her life and his daughter Ciara's life were almost undeniably better without Eugene here.

Jesse kept talking. "That kind of thing can't happen at whatever place the victims are being taken from. I know it's not. There have been no crime scenes in anyone's homes. In fact, there doesn't seem to be a crime scene at all, except for the place where the bodies are dumped." She took a breath and kept going. "And it is public knowledge that they weren't killed where they were left. So—A to B to C—they have to have been killed somewhere else."

She looked between them and took their blank expressions as a cue to go on. "If you torture a person like that, they're gonna scream." Jesse raised her hands as if indicating her own roofline. "If that had happened to Eugene, here, the neighbors would have called it in. We get noise complaints if the kid on the other side of us plays his music too loud. So while it's possible that Eugene came home sometime while Ciara and I were out, and may have been taken from here, nothing actually happened to him here. There was no evidence of blood. Trust me. I'm not that good of a housekeeper."

This time, Donovan almost laughed, but he fought to keep his expression neutral. Apparently, the fewer emotional outbursts someone had, the easier it would be for Christina to clean it up afterwards.

"This isn't being done anywhere in town. This killer has been active for at least seven years, and not been caught yet. So he's not an idiot."

They all paused for a moment when Jesse ran out of steam about why she was convinced there was a "kill cabin" involved.

Donovan decided to go fishing. "What other theories do you have?"

She looked as if she wanted to hold back, but Christina offered a soft, subtle nod and Jesse's mouth opened and the words came out. Donovan wondered if Jesse was somehow able to push back on Christina's forces a little better than the average person. He had known what the other agent could do, and he knew he wouldn't have been able to resist. If Jesse could, he'd be jealous.

"So I mean, I'm an investigative researcher, not a murderer," she qualified, now leaning fully back against the couch, draped backward almost as though she'd been drinking. One hand waved casually through the air, as if that would make the FBI agents take her statement for truth. "So I'm good at finding things. I don't know the details, because *nobody's releasing the autopsy reports yet.*" The last line was ground out and directed at them. "But we know that they were cut—not really stabbed, but sliced. We know that they were shot, usually more than once."

Jesus, Donovan thought, for someone who couldn't get her hands on the autopsy reports, she still knew a lot.

"I haven't been able to find anything about the killer shooting them—other than that it's an effective method for killing a person." Again, her attitude bled through the tone of her voice. It probably wasn't her usual, professional tone, but the real one without all the filters that Christina had removed. "The cuts? I couldn't find anything specific about that either. Other than the fact that people in Florida get stabbed. *A lot.* I couldn't link anything specific to these cuts or the way they were cut."

She knew the way the victims were cut?

"It was the fingernails that were weird. And the fact that they all had a *few* fingernails pulled, but not all of them. So I went searching for that." Now she leaned forward, elbows resting on her knees, hands dangling, but still gesturing animatedly. "It turns out, that's something people used to do to prisoners of war. Apparently, some fingernails are more painful to pull than others."

Jesse nodded at them, knowing she was onto something.

Donovan almost lost it. All their big breaks in the case were nothing more than a smart Floridian could put together with some local knowledge and internet access.

After a few moments, Jesse tapped out. "But even with the amount of information I have, it's not solid enough to write an article. Even the *Astoria Sun Times* won't let me ramble on with my speculations, though I think I'm pretty good."

Though she wouldn't remember later, Donovan worked hard to refrain from offering up any facial expressions that might let her know just how right she was. He didn't want her to get a feeling later that she should continue to pursue this line of thinking.

Eleri called a halt by thanking Jesse for her time. Christina stood up and shook Mrs. Nash's hand. They all watched as Jesse blinked and looked confused. She told them *thank you for coming by,* as though she didn't know why she was saying it, but that it must be the right thing to do.

"You know, I'm really tired. I think I'm going to take a nap on the couch before I have to go turn in my report for the paper."

She was curled up in the corner before the agents even let themselves out the door. They headed down the walk and quietly climbed into the car, Donovan taking his now-usual place in the passenger seat with Christina behind the wheel. Turning the key, Christina started the engine and began to back out of the driveway, but Donovan put his arm out to stop her.

"I don't think we should leave."

75

"Are you serious?" Eleri couldn't quite believe what she'd heard as she leaned forward from the backseat.

Donovan cranked his head around. "True, actually hiring Jesse Nash could be a nightmare. So maybe we don't *hire* her. Maybe we offer an exchange of information."

"But why would we do that?" Christina asked, her voice almost flat. "We already got all her information, and we can get more out of her anytime we want."

"It's true. But she's already figured out the things that took us a couple of weeks to put together, and she did it without our information."

With that argument, Eleri began to understand what he was going for, and she watched as Christina's facial expression changed, too. They'd been as surprised as he at the conclusions Jesse Nash had managed to put together.

Donovan looked between the two women, as they still sat in the car in the driveway. "None of us is a native Floridian. Unless you are, Christina?"

"Oh, hell no," was a very quick reply that made Eleri almost laugh.

"Well, apparently, native Floridians are all very aware that there are cabins back in the Everglades. We could have been looking for one much earlier. In the end, we only found it because we stumbled across it!" His voice was rising.

Eleri realized he was right. It had been three weeks since JP Talley's body had been found and they'd made plenty of progress. But they were definitely hindered by not knowing their way around, by having to learn or stumble onto everything that a native might already know. Jesse Nash not only was a native to Astoria, she was someone who already had her fingers in all the pots.

"The question is," Donovan continued, "what do we trade?"

"I think we ask for her help and in exchange we give her exclusive rights to the story." Eleri tossed her first idea out.

"Once the case is solved," Donovan added, as all three seemed to be in agreement.

But it was Christina who added, "I suspect she'll want to release that story before anyone else knows."

Eleri looked to Donovan, who shrugged back at her. "As long as we have our suspect in custody, it should be fine. In fact, we might be able to use her to get the community watching for someone once we know who this person is. She can help spread the word once we have a BOLO."

"Then, I think we're fine," Christina conceded, still not having started the car.

"Do we tell Westerfield?" Donovan asked next.

Eleri was surprised by her own vehement feelings of refusal, though she tried to present a logical argument rather than an emotional one. "We go off the books so much. I don't think we have to, if we're not paying her with FBI money. We pay her with information and a chance to scoop other outlets, so there's no reason to tell him. It'll simply show up later in the reports." She thought about writing up reports for three weeks' worth of investigation. And that was if they solved this case tonight.

"So we go back in and set this up?" Eleri asked, looking around the small space. What an odd decision to have just made. But a good one.

"Just you two. She needs to remember this," Christina said, pointing out an obvious concern.

Donovan and Eleri climbed right back out of the car and the two of them went up the drive, leaving Christina behind, the engine running to keep her cool. Though, hopefully this would be fast.

When Donovan knocked on the door, he hit it extra hard, likely remembering that they'd just left Jesse asleep on the couch. It took a few minutes, but the woman finally came to the door, a little rumpled-looking.

Twenty minutes later, they had a deal. Jesse's new job was to do the things that they couldn't. Her first assignment was to gather all the rumors she'd heard around town about the killer into one place.

"Write it down and email it to this address." Eleri held out her card. Even though she was certain she'd given Jesse one before, she couldn't remember if that was something Jesse should or shouldn't remember.

The reporter could be invaluable in this way. They needed to know what the locals were saying and whether there was anything they needed to refute in the press conferences or maybe bolster.

"The next thing we need you to do is have the town networks help look for abused spouses and children." Eleri asked it neutrally, trying not to openly acknowledge that it was likely something that Jesse had personal knowledge of. But because of that, she was the perfect foil. She could walk into the shelter and ask her questions. They would tell her what she wanted to know, and they wouldn't hold back or think things were or weren't important to tell the FBI, because they wouldn't know they *were* telling the FBI.

Jesse looked at her phone and offered a quick reply. "Is there anything else you need to tell me now? I appreciate this, but I'm due to meet my boss at the office in a little bit. I have a report to turn in and I need to do it in person."

"We'll contact you if there's anything else."

"And I can read the autopsy reports?"

"Yes," Eleri told her, "and you can do your research, but you'll need to keep us apprised of your theories and anyone who makes your suspect list. And if you leak or print anything before we give the okay —you'll be prosecuted by the FBI."

"Oh, I won't. But I want to see those autopsy reports." She paused, looking pointedly at the two agents still standing between her and her own front door.

"We're glad to have you." Eleri shook Jesse's hand one last time, then started to move. "We're blocking your driveway, but we'll leave right now."

As they climbed back into the car with Christina, the other agent almost didn't wait until they had their seatbelts on to pull backwards out of the drive. "We got a ping from my cameras!"

76

"Damnit!" Donovan almost yelled the word as they opened the door to their hotel suite.

There had been someone in the hall when they'd exited the elevator and he didn't want to alert any of the other guests. But he was feeling less like a guest and more like a guinea pig.

This hotel was naturally busier than the last. Obviously, the last place had been their first choice, and there weren't that many options in Astoria to begin with. But as soon as he'd opened the door, he'd smelled the wolf. He wasn't the only one who knew instantaneously.

"It's only noon!" Eleri exclaimed. "We left at 9:30. That's a small window for him to have targeted that we weren't here!"

"Well, we'll get to see him now!" Christina was almost gleeful, until they looked at her oddly. "Remember, I said I had the place set up? Well, I put a small camera near the door."

"You what?" Donovan asked, turning back toward the hall door that they'd closed behind them. He was thinking a thousand thoughts at once. The room looked untouched, but he easily smelled the man who had come through here, so he knew the place had been broken into. Eleri had trailed her fingertips along the furniture as she always did, and he'd seen her flinch several times. She was maybe even seeing specifics.

Christina was the only one who was calm. She'd plopped down on the sofa, opened her laptop, and started tapping away.

Out in the hallway, Donovan checked for other people. When he saw none, he asked, "Where's the camera?"

"Right by the door frame!" He could hear the grin in her voice and still managed to not put all the pieces together. He looked both ways, stepped into the hallway, turned back, and looked at the door frame. Then he closed the door and looked at it again.

"Hi, Donovan!" she called out and, as he glanced inside, he saw her waving to her laptop screen.

"Christina, there's nothing he—" He broke off the last word, finally realizing what she had done. Still standing in the hallway, he flipped off the door frame where he assumed she'd hidden her camera and listened to her inside the apartment as she laughed. At least someone was having a good time.

He stepped back in. "Is anything missing, El?"

"No. Except maybe a white envelope."

He stepped back into the suite, closing the door behind him, and having a moment where he considered just slumping against it. But agents didn't do that. It was dangerous.

He had no doubt that a trained agent could hear him through the door and know exactly where to shoot to kill. *He knew how to do it.* It was a skill he'd had to fake *not* having at Quantico before he got recognized for his supersensitive hearing. He'd simply taken the slap on the back from his training partner and nodded, saying, "Damn, that was a lucky shot!"

But it hadn't been. And he didn't lean on the door now.

Eleri opened the door to hers and Christina's bedroom and Donovan made the three large strides it took to get to her. As they stepped inside, Christina was still tapping away at her laptop.

He sniffed the air, even as he noted for the first time that this room, like his, didn't have any spare space. The beds were fulls, not twins, and they took up just a little extra of the floor for it. The headboards were padded and comfy, but they, too, seemed to fill the space, as did the end tables. He saw Eleri's suitcase on a fold out rack pushed up against one wall. There was no extra space to maneuver here. But even so, he turned to look at Eleri exactly as she said it.

"He didn't come in here."

Together, they turned and beelined directly across the suite, Donovan reaching for his door handle, before pulling his hand back almost as though it was hot. Better if Eleri touched it first.

He waited. She only shook her head. When they stepped into the room, he saw that nothing had been touched. But more importantly, he smelled that his intruder hadn't even stepped in here, either.

"So weird," Eleri said. "Almost respectful."

Just as he started to relax, Christina joined in again, her eyes not leaving the screen. He suspected she was rolling through whatever footage her invisible little camera had picked up while they were gone. She said, "Last time, he got us out of the room to check it. Maybe this time he got us *into* the room. You need to go down to the car and get your evidence."

Damnit!

They'd made the conscious decision to leave the boxes in the SUV and do a quick sweep of the room first. But now, with the knowledge of what they'd found—and what they hadn't—he'd forgotten all about it.

Donovan pounded down the staircase at the end of the hallway, not caring about the noise. The stairs were faster than the elevator. He started to cross the parking lot at breakneck speed.

Still, Eleri held out her hand as if to stop him. "Don't run. It's either there or it's not. It's not like he's going to steal it directly in front of us."

Then again, Donovan thought, *Christina could do that.* He didn't think this wolf could, though. *He* couldn't. And the other wolves he'd met? Well, they were *wolves*. The thought surprised him that it was the first time it had crossed his mind, but there was no reason there couldn't be a wolf with more powers than he had.

77

Eleri held her breath, thinking as Donovan must that she would open the car and find it empty. But at least she had the knowledge that Christina had caught their wolf on camera.

She and Donovan had only known that he'd been in the room, and they still hadn't seen the camera itself, as Christina had hidden it so well. She wondered if the wolf had stolen their evidence. And then she wondered, *Why would he?*

They tried to walk calmly across the parking lot in case anyone was watching, and surely, someone was. Eleri yanked at the car door, cracking it open, her chest expanding and her heart releasing. She saw everything intact and in the same place.

Lifting the lid on the box, she waited for the hit of recognition that someone else had been here, but it didn't come. While she wasn't quite ready to reach inside and check every single bag and count the number of bones, her initial instinct told her that it hadn't been touched.

Behind her, Donovan slid in close, placing his head just inside the door. "He hasn't been here."

It occurred to Eleri that Miranda was huge, with branches all over the globe, and probably its own agents everywhere. So she asked Donovan, "Has anyone else been here?"

The flicker of his eyes told her that he'd not quite considered it yet, but he was able to quickly shake his head. "Just the three of us."

"Thank God." She wasn't sure if she said it out loud or just in her own mind. She reached in and tucked her fingers into the handles of the bone box. She'd have to inspect them all again—just to be sure. Donovan held his hands out, letting her turn and place the box into his care. He was one of the few people she would trust to carry something as precious as skeletal evidence.

Then she reached in, grabbing another smaller file box where they'd stashed all their reports and copies, and the bag for the things they couldn't leave in the car. She slung it over her shoulder. They awkwardly made their way inside, hands full of evidence, fumbling key cards to gain access.

This time, they took the elevator. It was barely three in the afternoon and she was starving. Her day was already shit. It had been better when she wasn't getting to bed until four or five or even seven in the morning and slept through this part of the day.

She was sweating now, not having felt the heat in her mad dash down the staircase and to the car. But now she needed a nap and food and an attitude adjustment.

They stepped back into the suite to find Christina still in the same place.

"Put that down. Come over here." She gestured to them until they moved into place, flanking her on either side and watching over her shoulders.

She pulled up the footage from the doorway. "Watch."

While Eleri and Donovan had been running to the car, Christina had been finding something valuable. She had installed one camera on the outside of the door facing the hallway and another on the inside, scanning both the main room and straight out the window.

Eleri now began to wonder if she wouldn't see someone outside looking in. Or, God forbid, even a Dauphine sister levitating herself up to the third floor to appear beyond the glass.

"Here." The image Christina pulled up disrupted her awful thoughts.

He had dark brown hair and brown eyes. He was tall with a medium build. The image had more details than Eleri had gotten from touching what he touched. She could see his face. His face looked kind, but his expression looked as though he owned the room. The last bit made her angry.

"Do either of you recognize him?"

Eleri watched as Donovan also shook his head. "I can't smell him through the camera."

At least that made her smile. "He looks like what I saw. But I never did get a clear image from touching things. And no, I don't recognize him from anywhere else."

She watched as his face moved out of frame a little. Christina had placed the camera just to the right of the door, on the side with the handle, generally meaning anyone who came in would lean that way. She'd managed to snag quite a few clear shots of his face.

"Look where he comes in." Christina clicked a few buttons, shifting camera views. Eleri and Donovan watched along with her this time as the wolf came through. Though he trailed his fingers along a few things, he managed not to rifle anything. Christina put it to words.

"Unless there's more going on here that we don't see, he didn't take anything. It's like he just came in to be sure that we were us and that our things were actually here."

"Do you think he was looking for the evidence?" Eleri asked, now even more concerned about protecting it.

"Maybe. Do you think GM Corp wants JP Talley's autopsy report hidden, or even his body, for some reason?"

Eleri froze. She hadn't considered that. Anyone working for Miranda likely had secrets. His murder might be tied to the abuse, but the evidence might be of concern to Miranda.

"We have the autopsy report. Best-case scenario is that he gets his hands on a copy." But she and Donovan hadn't put in everything they'd found. They couldn't. If he was after some evidence on the body, the autopsy report might not be enough.

She hadn't even thought to check up on the corpse. *Jesus.* Brzezinski would have said something if they'd found anything. But Eleri was already picking up the phone, grateful when the doctor answered.

"Agent Eames!"

"Eleri, please." She'd made the correction once before but wanted to make it again. "I have a weird question for you..."

"Weirder than the rest of this investigation?" Cara covered the concern with a small laugh, but Eleri didn't miss it.

"Yes, actually. Can you check on JP Talley's body and see if it's been messed with?"

"Messed with? I don't think anyone's touched it since y'all did the autopsy."

"I'm hoping that's the case." Behind her, she could hear Donovan and Christina muttering about what even would be in a body that would trace back to Miranda Industries.

"Is he a wolf?" Christina asked softly, and Eleri saw Donovan shake his head no.

"We would have recognized that right away, so it's not about hiding that."

Eleri spiked a thought at that. Had JP Talley been a wolf, Miranda Industries would have been watching the Talley girls.

Changing background noises made it clear the doctor was talking as she walked through the medical center. Eleri heard as she answered a few questions along the way, a warm, friendly attitude bleeding through all of it. It was moments like these that Eleri wished that she didn't simply come in on a case, blaze through town, mark it closed, and leave. She got the impression that she and Dr. Cara Brzezinski might have been friends under other circumstances.

"All right, hold on. I'm pulling him out of storage."

Eleri could hear as the latch clicked. The DeSoto County Medical Examiner's Office still had the old wall of square doors with imprinted metal plates. When she'd been there, Eleri had noticed some of the numbers had worn off and she could see, in her mind's eye, the 429 on Talley's locker. Not that there were 429 spots, that was simply the label.

She heard the old metal tray rattling as Brzezinski pulled it open. It had warped a little, and even with the weight of the body, it didn't quite lie flat anymore. But the doctor hadn't gasped that it was empty.

Eleri heard the squeak from pulling the tray all the way out. Dr. Brzezinski would be able to see Talley now, head to toe. So at least there was nothing glaring and the doctor told her the same. "No, I don't see anything."

Eleri was breathing a sigh of relief when the doctor said, "No. Wait."

78

Christina had stayed at her laptop, still hammering on the keys, as Eleri and Donovan dropped into the nearby chairs, both of them a little stunned.

"They'll call us back if they find anything. Should we go now?" Donovan asked.

"Of course we *should,*" Eleri answered immediately, feeling the sting of not being able to act. "But if I lay my bare hand on that body or you lean over and sniff it, it's going to be way too obvious."

"We can ask for privacy."

"No, we can't. They can be nice about it, but there are windows on the doors to the surgical suite. So we can't guarantee someone won't see unless we are the only ones there. And that means we wait until night."

Cara had told them that when she'd pulled Talley's body from the fridge, it had been put in facing the wrong way. They were always placed toes out, because the refrigeration unit was old and had differing temperature ranges. It was colder against the wall, so they put the bulk of the bodies back that way. That meant head in/toes out.

"I'm sorry I didn't notice at first!" Dr. Brzezinski hadn't needed to apologize, but she had. "I was expecting something crazy, like a shark bite out of his side, or even a missing toe tag, or a different corpse!" It had taken her a moment to discern what was weird.

Eleri pointed out that if Talley's body had been rotated, that meant someone had taken him entirely out of the refrigeration unit, moved him, placed him on a table and maybe run some tests. When they put him back, they'd not realized they did it the wrong way.

"That means somebody broke into the facility," Eleri sighed as the pieces came together. "Because, if one of the employees did it, they would have put the body back correctly."

Donovan agreed. "I have a hard time imagining one of the employees at the DeSoto County Medical Examiner's Office is somehow linked to Miranda. I was the ME at a small, slightly underfunded county office much like this one. And I was not that good to my staff—not like her. I'm still confident I would have known if one of them was helping someone else rifle through the corpses."

"Maybe the Miranda guy came in and bribed one of them." But as she heard the tone in her own voice, she realized she wasn't quite so sure. Given Donovan's history, and that Brzezinski was far warmer than he'd been—therefore more in tune with her team—Eleri thought that was much less likely.

"I think that's too far of a stretch. It would require someone to be disloyal to Dr. Brzezinski, and I don't see that happening." When Donovan said it, she agreed.

So they'd settled on the theory that the wolf from Miranda Industries had managed to break in, but there wasn't anything they could do about it yet. Dr. Brzezinski had promised to call back after a more thorough search, which Eleri figured would take at least ten or twenty minutes and wouldn't be surprised if it was several hours.

"Now what?" he asked.

"Food," Eleri told him. Though Christina had been nose down into her laptop, that made her head pop up.

"Absolutely." She and Eleri hadn't eaten anything since the oatmeal that morning.

Donovan made himself useful by figuring out who delivered. The options in Astoria were slim. They were basically stuck.

As Donovan rattled off Christina's burger order, Eleri's phone rang and she motioned to both the others. Dr. Brzezinski's voice came. "The marks are subtle, but they are there. Our locks were picked."

Eleri had noticed that, like most everything else in the office, the locks were ancient. Not digital, but key and tumbler.

"I've got my admin on it right now. We're getting them replaced."

Not that it would make any difference, Eleri thought. She had to assume that whoever had come in had finished the job. They would want to do everything the first time to minimize their chances of getting caught. If they hadn't reversed the body, no one would have known.

She didn't say any of that to Dr. Brzezinski, though. They couldn't afford for anyone at the ME's Office to leak the information that the case was getting stranger and stranger.

"Do y'all want to come in and look at the body again?"

"We do," Eleri said. "But we're on top of a bunch of other things right now and we don't know when we'll be able to come in."

Donovan asked a question that she hoped wasn't as strange as it sounded. "Can we come in later at night? That seems to be when we have free time."

Their previous night-time autopsies at least should make that request less odd, and Eleri breathed a sigh of relief when the doctor agreed.

"I'll need to get you the new key—Hold on—" Cara must have gone old-school and put her hand over the mic, which didn't quite cover all of the sound. The exchange was rudimentary, but Dr. Brzezinski came back on. "We'll be completely rekeyed, external and internal offices, by six tonight."

"We'll definitely be later than that," Eleri said. It would have to be. If people were there, the two of them couldn't do what they needed. "We'll come and get it from you. But I don't even know if it will be tonight, so don't stay late for us or anything."

"Oh, okay?" There was a question at the end.

She realized then she'd just given something away: A tampered with body wasn't the most important factor on this case.

Dammit. She couldn't take it back, so she said goodbye and hung up. Trying to relieve some of her self-directed anger, Eleri shifted topic. "What's next?"

"I'm checking footage," Christina offered.

"I'll help with that," Donovan said. The food was still half an hour to forty-five minutes away.

Eleri sighed. "Two of you is enough? Because I want to check the bones."

Christina raised an eyebrow, but Eleri replied, "I haven't looked inside the box in several days. I don't even know if we still have all the pieces. If someone took one, I only know that it happened between three days ago and now, which clearly isn't good enough."

The others quickly agreed, Christina and Donovan staying side by side, computers open as they scanned hours of footage.

Eleri went into her bedroom, looking for space. It wasn't large, by any stretch, but the bed was a flat surface bigger than anything available in the main space. She left the door open and hollered out. "Don't worry, Christina. I won't put anything on your bed."

"If you make it first, it doesn't bother me. Trust me. I've had worse things in my life."

That garnered a loose chuckle from Eleri, who realized she needed it. Pulling the covers taut, and disliking the wild design on the comforter, she looked around for options. The colors might obscure small things. A uniform background would be better.

From her kit she pulled out a lightweight foil blanket. Silver wasn't the best, but she would use the dull side and it was better than the comforter. First, she laid out the full skeleton of Earlene Beaman, checking every bone, counting and arranging. When she found everything intact, she put Earlene's bones carefully back into their labeled bags and laid out Evan Merkel.

There was nothing unusual there. All of his bones were present and accounted for, too. She put him away and laid out Bonnie next. It was tempting to assume a spot check was good enough and everything was here. But she'd learned that lesson more than once and she counted.

This time she pulled out their unknown victim. He, too, was laid out appropriately with all parts still there. But as she went to put all the pieces back in the appropriate bags, she touched the skull.

79

"It was the same things as what I saw last time," Eleri told him as they finished the last of the burgers.

Donovan wadded up the paper, stuffing it down into the sack. The whole room now smelled of meat, cheese, and French fries, and he could almost still feel the fizz of cola in his nostrils. Not his favorite thing. But right now, the hit of caffeine and sugar was worth it. He could smell the artificial sweetener of Eleri's drink each time she set it down and jostled it.

Eleri explained to Christina. "I saw a bonfire, him, and a few friends. An old car. And him having sex with some blonde girl."

"That's it? Doesn't sound very helpful." Christina frowned.

"Yeah. I did see the faces more clearly, so that helps. I didn't need to see that last part the first time, and I sure didn't need to see it again."

Donovan almost laughed at Eleri's irritation of being unwittingly led into someone's sex life.

"So what's next?" he asked. They'd hit the point of having both too much and too little to do. They'd all agreed they couldn't go check on JP Talley until the facility was closed.

"Well, we do have another twenty-four hours of camera footage from the cabins," Christina pointed out, her tone somehow both hopeful and doubtful.

It was a job that needed to be done, but Donovan groaned. "Can't we get an analyst to do it?"

"We could. But do they know what they're looking for?"

"Humans!" he answered too quickly and Eleri quirked an eyebrow at him.

He realized that no, they weren't just looking for humans. They were looking for things that maybe only they would recognize. Maybe a wolf, and not just any wolf, but a specific wolf. It was also possible all they would see was a ripple in the atmosphere. What if it was someone like Christina?

"Fine," he huffed out as the three of them set up quietly next to each other, each tapping away on their keys. "Same as last time?'

"What did the lab results say about the cabin you found first?" Christina hadn't been here when they found it and Eleri had taken a surreptitious sample.

"It showed evidence of Talley and Nash and Beaman. And another blood sample that's still unidentified."

They hadn't taken evidence from the southeast cabin, not wanting to disturb anything. But Donovan thought, if their killer had a sense of smell like his, that cabin was burned, too. If they had a sense of touch like Eleri's, then they would know exactly what samples had been taken. He could only hope that their killer was a perfectly normal human being. With everything he'd seen, he didn't lay odds on that.

Eleri and Donovan split up the footage from the southeast cabin and Donovan managed to get through his at a relatively high rate, somehow finishing before either of them but still bone tired and exhausted. He'd barely moved a finger and yet it had mentally worn him out.

Relaxing a little bit, he leaned back and tried to figure out what the forward-moving plan was.

"I'm going to check the list that Jesse Nash sent us." Though he wasn't keen on staring at a screen anymore, it needed to be done. It had pinged their email while they were scrolling through the footage.

Jesse was fast. Maybe it was just a preliminary list or maybe she had simply already cataloged everything and this was complete. But as he opened the email, he saw the list was relatively extensive.

Eleri had already forwarded her copies of the autopsy reports, so

Jesse Nash had more to chew on now that she was done with her initial assignment.

After a quick scan, he forwarded a copy to Christina—who was still off Jesse's radar—and began to read it. It was a thorough list. Jesse Nash noted not only what the rumor was, but who she had heard it from and when. There was more than one mention of "the Ghost of the Glades" and Donovan rolled his eyes before opening his browser and googling it to see if it was a real thing.

Apparently, it was not only real, most every Florida town had a "Ghost of the Glades" just like every landlocked town had "the old haunted mansion." He had to admit that one didn't look promising.

Jesse had even made notations that she didn't fully trust the sources on this one, but he was glad to see that she'd included it rather than pre-weeding out what she sent. The second rumor had come from the Rotary Club and was telling people to lock their windows. This group seemed to think that women would be abducted from their own homes.

Blazingly inaccurate, Donovan thought. Even with the limited information they had, at least people should have known that they were safe enough. But as Jesse noted, they clearly weren't following any actual facts.

Another rumor said that JP Talley's company had him killed.

Interesting. At least someone understood that Talley's job was not quite as it seemed. He mentally filed that one away. Another bullet point suggested that a handful of people—particularly Jesse's friends —believed that Talley and Nash got what they deserved and speculated that maybe the Merkels were the same.

They all knew that Earlene Beaman was no contender for mother of the year and Donovan saw an asterisk followed this one. "These people are all my friends. These are the ideas that I hold, and I may very well have influenced them."

Donovan had no doubt of that.

Another note suggested that the killer was either Craig Renfro or the ghost of Craig Renfro, coming back to get revenge. He was just googling Craig Renfro from Astoria, Florida when Eleri began to motion excitedly. "I've got it. Oh, my God. You will not believe this."

80

Eleri waved the other two agents over excitedly, not quite sure yet what she had found. "Look!"

Donovan and Christina almost skidded into place next to her, bumping and jostling her on the couch where she sat as they each took one side and the three of them tried to peer at the small laptop screen together.

Someone was clearly coming toward the cabin.

Eleri had been scanning slowly enough that she caught the movement as it entered the view. The person was dressed in dark greens and blacks, not quite camo, but the clothing was certainly doing the job of keeping them from being easy to spot.

From this camera, they could see that their person of interest was coming toward the cabin from the northeast; other than that, they could only see movement. Even the outline was difficult to make out as the timestamp showed it was close to midnight.

"Is it a woman?" Donovan asked.

Eleri could only watch and find out. Slowly, more and more of the person came into view. The cameras were relatively high in the trees, hopefully keeping them out of the way of animals and any standing water. So she'd first seen the top of the head. "I think so. Looks like dark hair pulled back into a bun."

The entire view was dark and Eleri had needed to rewind just to be sure what she was seeing when she'd spotted it. Now with the three of them there, they let it play out to its natural conclusion at regular speed.

She wanted to hit the button, move the images faster and see where this person went. Were they really aiming for the cabin, or were they on an unlucky route caught by FBI cameras? But they needed the details.

"Do you think it's just a hiker?" Christina's words could have come from her own head, but the person had moved further, stalking their way in, and Eleri now was forming a different opinion.

"Not really," Eleri replied and pointed to the screen. "Look at what she's wearing."

Moonlight streamed through occasional gaps in the canopy, revealing dark clothing, almost military in color and design. The glimpses showed hips and narrower shoulders and confirmed the hair in a bun at the base of the neck—a woman.

Medium build. Small hands? Small feet? Eleri wondered.

"It is an odd outfit for a hike," Donovan finally chimed in. "But it's not enough to say it's *not* a hiking outfit."

Eleri had to concede that she might be making it more than it was. The long sleeves could be protection against bites and stings. The dark colors wouldn't be comfortable in the broad light of a Florida day, but this was late and it was under the canopy of the Glades. *But the Glades were full of poisonous snakes, panthers, and even alligators. Why would someone be out alone at midnight in dangerous territory?*

As they watched, the person moved forward in an almost marching movement, something about it tickling the back of Eleri's brain.

"Holy shit," Donovan said. "She went straight to the cabin."

There was no indication in the way she moved that she was checking out something she'd just spotted. The direct line she stalked indicated she knew exactly where she was going.

The person disappeared from sight as they circled the small building, moving around back. Eleri had hopes that they would find her in view on the other camera for this timestamp and she jotted it down nearby.

It took quite some time to watch through all the footage. But it quickly became clear this was someone who was familiar with this cabin. The person was not surprised when they opened the door and found the tarp across the floor. There was no repulsive reaction to what the agents had seen as obvious blood stains.

This was someone checking on the place. This was not a random hiker who found a small building and was fascinated by it.

It wasn't until they watched the third camera view that they saw the hiker took a different trail out than in. And they finally got a good look at her face.

"Holy crap!" Eleri yelped.

But Donovan was quick to reply, "Yes, but that's not the killer."

"Why?" Christina asked him.

"I told you," he answered her directly across Eleri sitting in the middle. "We've been to her offices. I smelled her and I smelled the killer. They're not the same."

Christina flopped back onto the couch then, all of the tension draining out of her. "Is it possible that when you smelled the killer you smelled the wrong person?"

That was an interesting thought, and it made Eleri question the assumption as well. They'd followed a scent that Donovan had found, a profile that Donovan had declared the killer. But was that what it really was?

"Yes." He wasn't questioning it at all. "It's the scent of the person who originally abducted Eugene Nash. It's the scent that was at the scene where JP Talley's body was found. It's the scent associated with dragging Eugene Nash alive through the woods, to the north cabin, and then dragging his body further through the woods to the drop site."

"It does pose an interesting problem," Eleri mused. "Maybe someone else actually did the killing, and that scent belongs to the delivery person."

But Donovan wasn't having it. "There wasn't another scent at the cabin, so who would the killer be? And it's not her, either. The greater the number of people involved, the more likely they are to get caught. You're suggesting that this triumvirate has worked, not only undercover, successfully, but ultimately *unknown* for over seven years. And you're suggesting that someone—with no discernible scent—waited at the cabin, let this person bring Eugene Nash, then killed him, and let the other person drag him away."

She had to agree. When he put it that way, it was beyond highly implausible. "There were no other scents in the cabin?"

"No," he insisted. "Well, yes, but I recognized Eugene Nash, and I recognized JP Talley. The other scents, aside from animals and decaying wood, and general forest smells, were blood signatures."

"So we still have a killer to find," Eleri sighed. "But it looks like we just found our accomplice."

81

They'd rushed out of town to rent more cars, this time in different shapes and colors. They still hadn't made it in time to catch the doctor, much to Donovan's disappointment. There simply hadn't been time.

By the time they'd seen the footage, they could have plausibly rushed to Dr. Sylvia Lambrecht's office to watch as she closed up for the day. But their SUVs had been seen around town and their presence would be obvious.

He'd almost shaken his head as Eleri rented the two new cars with her own personal card. They were now the proud owners of not one, but four, rentals—one of which was simply sitting unused at their original hotel holding space with the also-unused hotel rooms.

They decided, relatively quickly, that the best course of action was not to arrest Sylvia Lambrecht immediately, but to follow her. That meant effectively staying hidden. So they rented a cream-colored, mid-size car designed to blend in and a smaller, energy-efficient model in blue so the three cars could run an appropriate tail operation, hopefully without alerting Dr. Lambrecht.

Donovan had his doubts. All three cars were shiny and well-kept, not necessarily something that happened often in the Florida weather. And it didn't seem to happen a lot in a small town like Astoria. Though there certainly were plenty of people here who were wealthy enough to spend their time keeping their cars shiny—people like JP Talley—it wasn't the norm.

But the agents couldn't take a chance on an older car. If anything died on them while they were tailing the doctor, they would lose her. Therapists were trained to be observant to the nth degree, and Sylvia Lambrecht had also been in the military. So, even with three cars swapping out regularly, the doctor still might catch on to them quite quickly.

But it didn't matter. Because as he finally swooped by the office, it was already past seven p.m.

"She's gone. The place is closed up." They had the phone lines open between the three of them, all heading in slightly different directions in an effort to find the doctor.

"I'm headed to her house," Eleri said through the line. "Is it clear at the office? Can you get out and check around, see if you can smell the killer?"

Donovan did exactly that, because most of the small strip mall was already closed or so dead that no one was paying attention. But, aside from a few old, lingering traces, there was nothing new.

He attempted to make himself look like he was simply checking in the windows to see if anybody was still in the office. Then he'd looked around the whole place, finally heading down to the convenience store, where he grabbed himself a soda.

By the time he was back in the car, Eleri had already arrived at Dr. Lambrecht's house.

"She's here. It appears she might be in for the night."

"I don't get any traces of the killer here at her office, nothing I haven't smelled before." Had the killer come by since last time, the scent should be much, much stronger.

Christina had been driving the big silver SUV, tooling around town. But now that Eleri had spotted the doctor, the question was, what should they do?

Eleri's knew. "I think I'm stuck here for the foreseeable future. I'm just going to stake her out for the night."

"You should have a partner." He didn't like the idea of her being stationary and by herself. Escaping and evading someone was easier on the move.

"I should. But how do we make that happen? I'm almost obvious enough already. I'm in a car that one of the neighbors will recognize with a person sitting in it." She paused. "Maybe I can cloak it? If someone comes and joins me, though, that will be even more of a red flag to the neighbors."

"And to Sylvia, if she looks out the window and sees you," Christina added.

"At least the houses are set far enough back from the street. They've got cute little fences and slightly overgrown foliage. I think I'm well enough hidden that no one's really going to notice me, but I wouldn't do anything else to draw attention."

"Are you set for a while at least?" Donovan asked, not liking the idea of leaving his partner out in the dark night, on the street, with a killer on the loose. Then again, he didn't doubt Eleri's ability to defend herself, he only disliked the idea that she might need to.

But she was right: There was little option for them to join her.

He was nearly back at the hotel when he decided he didn't care. This killer tortured their victims. Safety was primary. To hell with it if it blew their cover. "Christina, can you meet up with her? Cover yourself as you walk in?"

"I was just thinking the same thing. And then I can cover the both of us."

"I do think I can hide the car," Eleri said, at least not balking at getting a partner she'd just said wasn't a good idea. "I don't have many supplies here, but I still think I can do it."

Grateful for that, Donovan reminded them both to check in as he pulled into the parking space at the hotel.

"I also don't like us being split up, but I think it's the only option," Eleri said. "We need someone at the hotel, too. And maybe you can get some sleep."

"I'm already here." He was walking in the front door and waving to the desk clerk as they were signing off.

For the first time on the case, he was truly alone. He rode the elevator up to the room and stood at the door cautiously, wondering if they'd been invaded again and what he might do if they had been. Had the Miranda wolf somehow lucked into them being separated?

Donovan held his breath and his heart stopped beating as he waved the key card and clenched the doorknob, not sure what he would find inside.

82

His breath let out in a comical whoosh as Donovan realized he smelled nothing. No one had been in the room, except him, Eleri, and Christina—not since the last time the wolf had come in.

They still hadn't figured out if anything had been taken—or left behind—but they had swept the place for bugs and tech. Everyone who used bugs knew that there were sweeps to find them.

Anything wireless sent a signal, anything wired had a wire, and therefore, it could be detected with electromagnetic or radio frequency scanners. The question was, did new tech exist that evaded the sweeps? He wouldn't put that kind of information past Miranda Industries.

Now, as he finally relaxed, Donovan wished he'd thought to pick up food But it seemed wrong to head back out at this point. With his two partners doing the serious work, climbing back into the car for a burger run would put him somewhere he wasn't supposed to be. What if they needed him?

So he checked the small fridge and the cabinet, grateful that Eleri had stocked it. He still had the orange soda he'd bought for cover at the convenience store. He added handfuls of cheese crackers to his diet as he sat down and pulled open his laptop. He was supposed to sleep but that wasn't going to happen. He needed to be rested if he was going to be trading out with them, but this case had been full of nothing if not bad sleep cycles.

Checking emails, he decided to be useful and replied to Westerfield's check in for a Situation Update. He'd let Eleri handle the last few, since they were growing more and more unpleasant as the case dragged on, but this was something he could do now.

After updating their boss—still leaving Christina out of the story—he checked with others. First, he texted Lucy, then checked in with Eleri and Christina. They'd opened the phone line, managing to sound supremely bored from watching the front corner of a house that had gone dark.

“Do you think she has this early of a bedtime?” Christina mused wryly.

So there wasn’t even anyone wandering around as a shadow behind curtains or blinds, he thought. Having nothing to add to that, Donovan didn't know what to say. The boredom of a stakeout quickly shut the phone line down, allowing Eleri and Christina to get back to the overtly casual job of watching. They had to be ready to leap into action if anything did happen.

Needing to fill the time, he messaged GJ as well. He’d just set his phone down when it rang and he picked it up, a little surprised.

“Hey, Donovan.” Despite the late hour, GJ was chipper as always.

“You got Lucy?” he asked.

“Of course. Walter’s right here beside me.”

“Hey, Donovan,” Lucy spoke up. If GJ’s tone was soda, Lucy was whiskey.

Though he’d messaged, it was GJ who’d dialed instead of simply replying. “What’s up?”

“I didn't want to put this in writing anywhere …” The younger agent drew the words out, indicating that something was, in fact, up. “We've got the journals—”

“And Westerfield knows we have the journals,” Lucy added in. “We already had to report that.”

Something about her word choice made Donovan's ears perk up.

“GJ’s working on code-cracking.”

“Didn’t you already crack those codes?” Back when he and Eleri had been on the case and GJ had been handcuffed to the pipe behind the hotel toilet.

“These are different. In fact, each set of books was kept in a different code. And yes, I think I've got it.”

"There were stashes in different locations as well," Lucy added for him. "More than what you found when you first worked the case."

"Is it all documentation from Axis and Atlas?"

"Yes. And it's not pretty." This was Lucy's dead serious tone, not GJ's generally happy disposition.

"Okay?" Donovan drew the word out as if asking what was next.

"It was an interesting report, but we're not sure we should hand the translations to Westerfield."

There was a pause on the other end of the line as Donovan stopped dead. He had just written his own report in which he'd omitted an entire agent. Were they *all* holding back?

"It's damning information," Lucy went on. "It's like they were trying to create people."

Donovan knew. He'd been there. He'd seen the facilities. And he understood—or maybe he understood better now than he had at the time—that the Axis and Atlas projects had been trying to create a new breed of human. "Are you suggesting …"

He paused, not even quite willing to say it out loud.

"We knew they were trying to make a new species that would survive a possibly apocalyptic future," GJ filled in. "But it looks now as if they were also trying to build individual people with specific talents. And Westerfield seems to want this information badly."

"Are you suggesting that Westerfield might not be *finding* agents but *creating* them?"

"No." GJ's response was quick and sure enough to give Donovan an easy sense of relief. "I don't think he can. I don't think he has the tech. The problem is that we marked off Axis and Atlas as failures. The kids died, the facilities closed. But some of the kids *didn't* die. And I think there might have been more kids in other places. More than we found back then."

Her words shocked Donovan to his core. Although why he was surprised, he didn't know. They'd already found two separate locations. Two separate projects having been built, one from the other, and he and Eleri had just assumed they'd found the whole thing.

"We don't think Westerfield *can* do it." Walter emphasized the word *can*, once again, disturbing Donovan.

"But you think he wants to?"

The silence was answer enough.

They stumbled through a few more words but there were no good outcomes and nothing they could answer tonight. Donovan couldn't tell them whether they should or shouldn't hand in the translations. But he did ask, "What's the alternative?"

"We tell them GJ couldn't crack it."

That would be easy enough. "Do you think Westerfield would know it's a lie if you tell him that?"

"Well, that's part of the problem, isn't it?" GJ offered up.

But even as they'd almost agreed to sit on it, Donovan's email popped up. "Shit. I've got to go. Something just popped with the case."

He said his goodbyes, not liking the conversation he was leaving and hoping the email he opened was better. So he hit the button to see what Jesse Nash had to say.

83

Jesse Nash had been busy. Donovan opened the email to see that she'd managed to do more than just correlate all of the rumors she'd heard today. Apparently, she'd also already made her way through all of the autopsy reports. This email told her thoughts on each of them.

Earlene Beaman - everyone knows she was horrible to the boys. Child Protective Services took them away more than once. And every time the children were returned, everyone knew it was a bad decision.

JP Talley -

Most people didn't know the truth about him, but apparently Jesse did. While visiting the shelter, she'd encountered a very timid and nervous Rebecca Talley asking similar questions.

- he abused her. She showed her bruises to the woman at the shelter and got instructions on what to pack in a go-bag and how to hide money and ID from him.

Evan and Bonnie Merkel - Everyone was shocked when they disappeared. Everyone suspected foul play, and everyone believed them to be good, upstanding citizens who did the Lord's work by taking in horrible children that no one else wanted.

That was interesting, Donovan thought. The Merkels, at least, had managed to have everyone snowed, even if JP hadn't quite pulled it off. But the killer had still found out.

He made a mental note that it might be the Merkel case that

would tell them what the line of communication was. It might draw a line from Sylvia Lambrecht straight to their killer.

Unknown Victim - You should check your records and see if this is Craig Renfro.

The name rang a bell with Donovan and he quickly flipped back to Jesse's earlier email. There had been rumors that the murders were perpetrated by "the ghost of Craig Renfro." Jesse Nash wrote more.

Craig Renfro disappeared just over five years ago. I remember it, though I had to look it up to see the exact year. He was young, early twenties, and fits the description in the autopsy report. He had been stalking a young woman, not yet eighteen. Once the family put up a restraining order, people came out of the woodwork quite confident he had been after her for some time, maybe a few years. She disappeared. Craig was the number one suspect. And he did a shitty job of denying that he'd killed her. Her body turned up two weeks later and it was clear that she had been raped and murdered.

A week later, the police announced that they had enough information to arrest and indict Renfro. But right before they got to him, he too disappeared. Only his body never turned up. At least, I think, until now.

Donovan began to wonder why it wouldn't have been identified.

He flipped through the attached images Jesse had sent. There were more than a handful, and he realized he needed to examine them more closely. As long as Christina and Eleri didn't ping him, he had the time.

Most of them were documents, clearly scanned old paper versions. He made it through a few before realizing he needed to forward it to Christina, though it was possible Eleri had already seen it and shared it with her. Then again, their eyes should be on Dr. Lambrecht's home.

Saving all the photos that Jesse had included, he sent them via text, thinking it might get the women the information they needed faster—at least for now.

A ping came back quickly, with the blond woman's pic and Eleri's question: "Who is that?"

— That was Melanie Shipman. Donovan texted back quickly with the information. She was Craig Renfro's girlfriend. He went missing within a timeframe that could make him our unidentified skeletal remains.

— It's him.

Eleri's text was fast and too simple to have any doubt. The phone rang and he answered. She didn't even say hello—her eyes were probably still on the house as she talked. "Remember when I said I saw him having sex? That's her."

"Jesse sent us the information that she put together from the autopsy reports. Obviously, there's nothing medical there but—as we expected—she has her finger on the pulse of the town. So the police had a warrant for Renfro's arrest," Donovan explained. "He raped and murdered her."

He heard the pause and understood that she was probably reacting. She hadn't been pleased at what she'd seen when she thought she'd been privy to the guy's sex life. That what she'd seen wasn't consensual churned his stomach. He had no doubt she was swallowing back bile.

"What?" Eleri's voice broke the silence, but she wasn't speaking to him. Then she told him, "We're leaving the car. It appears Sylvia Lambrecht left the house a while ago, and we've been watching an empty house."

"How did that happen?"

"We have to go!"

No! But the line was dead. They weren't supposed to leave the car. Not without him.

— Don't leave without me.

He tapped it out even as he was already on his feet. Unfortunately, he was too far away to hinder their progress. And sure enough, he received a quick reply.

— There's two of us. We've got this. Will meet up when you get here.

But even as he gathered everything up and prepared to race out the door, his phone chimed again. An FBI analyst warned him one of the cameras at the southeast cabin had gone down.

An interesting coincidence, he mused, getting ready to relay the information and then realizing that Eleri would be getting the same pings.

He was down the steps and out into the parking lot where he climbed into the large SUV that had been left for him. As he started the engine, the phone pinged again. Another camera had just gone out.

84

"She's not here."

Christina confirmed their suspicions about Lambrecht. Eleri had even gone so far as to place her hand on the back door and try to mentally search the home. She completely agreed. What she wanted right now was Donovan's sense of scent. He could come here with his fast nose and faster legs and just follow their missing suspect.

"I think she's been gone for a while," Eleri said, believing the woman had slipped out the back door some time ago without them noticing.

Christina only nodded along, though Eleri had hoped she would give some reason the idea was wrong. It wasn't.

These little neighborhoods on the outskirts of town had *cul-de-sac* streets that reached back into the trees like fingers. Though some of the houses backed up against fencing and other houses many, like Sylvia Lambrecht's, backed into the trees.

She and Christina might have a difficult time tracking the woman. As Eleri wished once again that Donovan was here, she wondered if they could spare the time to wait for him. Christina stalked her way around the back yard, checking for evidence, and Eleri thought about where she'd seen a house like this before.

Donovan had a home that backed up onto the National Park. He'd chosen it specifically because it allowed him to change and slip out the back gate undetected. If Sylvia Lambrecht was their killer, or even just in league with their killer, maybe this had been by design.

"Can you follow her?" Christina asked.

"I think so." Her answer was as solid as it could be. This wasn't the kind of thing that Eleri had practiced for. She'd always had Donovan; using her own measly skills for tracking hadn't been a priority. But a spell to follow someone had been in the Hale Family Book of Shadows.

Wondering if the Dauphine family had a similar working spell, Eleri figured they must have something they would use it for tracking. Her great-great-Grandma Hale's practical magic had seemed more domestic. The spell she'd seen for following a cheating love was at least three "greats" back on the Hale/Llewelyn tree.

From the other side of her ancestry, Grandmere also had following spells, though she hadn't specifically taught Eleri how to track a criminal with magic. Eleri found herself mashing together spells and incantations from the old Book of Shadows and the craft-voodoo cross Grandmere had practiced.

So now she thought she could probably follow Sylvia Lambrecht.

Christina still stood in the middle of the backyard. Eleri motioned her new partner up onto the back porch with her. They both still held their guns out and ready, aimed toward the ground near their feet, just in case Eleri had forgotten the danger inherent in this situation.

She pulled her sachet out of her pocket—the one made with herbs pilfered from Grandmere's closet. The spell she'd started from was one first recorded in the Hale family Book of Shadows from a Massachusetts jail cell. Once again, Eleri looped the sack around the chain at her neck and said to Christina, "Cover yourself. We need to not be obvious. They're taking down the cameras."

"So they knew to look for them, and they found them."

"We can't afford to be seen."

Christina nodded and Eleri watched her partner close her eyes and take a deep breath. Though Eleri saw no change, Christina looked up and said, "Ready to go. You know I could have covered you, too."

"I know. But, in case we get separated, and you can't find me... and because I want you to save your mental power for anything we might run into. I went ahead and did my own."

They were going in blind, but Christina had been an agent far longer than she. The only reason Eleri was senior on this case was because Christina wasn't even officially here. She cast a second spell intended to illuminate footprints, and then she and Christina traipsed across the backyard, no longer worrying about what the neighbors might see.

There was no fence, only the boundary of where someone stopped mowing the grass. They stepped into higher foliage, realizing quickly that the dips and ruts in the ground created small gullies where water ran in small quiet rivulets.

Eleri had not worn proper footwear for this. She hadn't even been dressed for a stakeout. But she was here now and it appeared someone was at the cabin taking out the FBI cameras. If it was Sylvia Lambrecht, they had a smoking gun.

Again, her phone pinged with a message from Donovan saying he was on his way. She updated him about where they were and what they were doing—it was the best she could do. They couldn't wait.

The two of them followed the faint glow of footprints, the information patchy, the glow sometimes hard to discern. Eleri tried again to reinforce her spell, though it didn't work. It would have been better with her hammered copper bowl and a true flame, rather than the one she'd used from a lighter yesterday morning. But there was no time to go back to the hotel room and cast it properly.

"Oh, look." She found a solid footprint in front of them. The spell had illuminated this one well. She stepped to the side, just as she and Christina had been doing, moving gingerly around so as not to tamper with the evidence.

"That's the best one yet."

Eleri agreed. A full footprint was carefully captured in the mud. Even without Eleri's spellwork, it was painfully clear. "It looks like the same tread we got from the scene where Eugene Nash's body was found."

And the print belonged to a smaller foot. *Interesting*, she thought. Had the killer gone into Sylvia Lambrecht's house via the back door, and was now leaving? Were they wrong and Sylvia Lambrecht was actually still inside? Or did the doctor and the killer simply have similar shoes?

As they slowly and carefully followed the trail, probably getting further and further behind the killer, who was likely moving fast, Eleri wondered if Sylvia would double back and run into them.

They'd both been quiet for a while, but Christina spoke up softly. "I thought it was interesting that Sylvia lived on the southeast side of town, far away from her office."

"It's not that far. The town's not that big," Eleri said.

"And that's what I thought, too," Christina told her. "But now we're following a path out of Sylvia Lambrecht's backyard, straight into the Glades, and look what direction we're going ..."

85

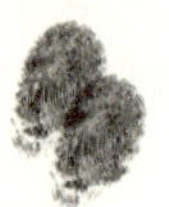

"What do you mean she wasn't here?" Eleri wanted to scream her frustration to the heavens, but they couldn't afford the noise.

Donovan had arrived to meet them in the Glades in human form. Thus he didn't have his full scenting capabilities, but he was always better than most people. He'd headed straight to Sylvia Lambrecht's home and found the house still empty. He'd reported in and quickly headed out the back to catch up to them, following the path Eleri and Christina had left.

He had done exactly as Eleri had thought, scenting the trail—though only passably, given the current shape of his nose—and following along at a much faster pace than she and Christina had been able to move, given their limited tracking ability. They'd messaged back and forth along the way, her phone pinging and lighting up in the dark of night. She could only hope her spell covered that, too.

As soon as Donovan had come into view, she'd immediately asked, "Are you visible?"

"Nope!" He'd shaken his head with a grin and held up the sachet around his neck. Given that they could all still see each other, she couldn't tell if it was still working. Either way, she would need to cast it again when they got home tonight. She had no idea how long the spell would last.

She and Christina had kept plowing forward, letting Donovan with his longer legs and easy stride catch up to them. They were almost to the cabin, though no one appeared to be there. Unless their killer was waiting inside.

Eleri held out her hands, motioning the other two to stop. She closed her eyes, took a deep breath, and tried to peer inside the cabin. *She saw nothing*. Not empty space, not dim light, just nothing. The cabin would be dark in the middle of the night. The tarps they'd seen, in spite of having been brightly colored once upon a time, were now stained and dull and wouldn't even be visible. There was nothing visual to grab on to.

"I think it's empty," she said.

Donovan caught on. "You're not sure?"

"I can't see anything. So I have to assume that means there isn't anything inside the cabin. But it could mean that I'm just not seeing what's there."

They proceeded forward with caution. Donovan seemed to have something he wanted to say, but they were so close and she felt him holding back. Now was not the time.

Eleri looked up into the trees where the cameras had been placed. They were gone and a quick sweep showed an obvious disturbance of the dirt beneath each. Someone had come through and definitively removed the devices.

Within moments, they surrounded the small cabin, weapons drawn, now no longer held down at their sides but pointed toward the sky in a two-fisted grip, ready to aim and fire on a moment's notice.

Donovan moved around the back by himself as Christina and Eleri flanked the door. With a nod from Eleri, Christina reached out across the doorway, hooked her fingers, and quickly pulled the door open.

Eleri prayed that her friend would not get those fingers blasted or chopped off. But Christina moved too fast for anyone to get any jump on her. As the space was revealed, Eleri jumped into the opening, weapon leading, only to find it exactly as she believed, *completely empty*.

The team turned their attention to the surrounding area, waiting to see if they were being stalked or even just watched. But when they found nothing, they took a few more minutes to clear the area.

Sylvia was no longer here. Or, Eleri wondered, had she dressed in the dark gear again, allowing herself to blend in with the night. Was she just beyond the trees, watching and waiting to make her move? Or maybe she was just waiting for them to leave, so she could trek her way back home after checking on her kill cabin.

"Can you tell where she went?" Eleri asked Donovan as she reached out and tapped on his arm.

He shrugged a little. "I'm not as good in this form, but I think this way."

"A different way out than in," Christina pointed out, her weapon still gripped tightly.

If all was right, and they couldn't be seen, they could at least get the jump on Sylvia if they ran into her. At least Eleri hoped so. None of it was guaranteed.

"Let's follow her?" It was more a question than a command from a senior officer.

"I'm not sure I can. I can get traces, but I'm not close to the ground and I just don't detect as well in this form." But then he turned around and looked at the two women. "But I'm not even sure that matters. I've been trying to tell you, Sylvia Lambrecht wasn't here."

86

Donovan sat in the hotel room, watching as the glow from the windows changed as the sun rose. He couldn't remember the last time he'd been more frustrated.

They'd followed the path back to Sylvia's home as best they could. They used Eleri's spellwork, Christina's tracking ability, and Donovan's nose. It had taken all three working together, since they weren't just tracing the old trail backwards. In the end, they'd looped around to connect up and go straight up the backyard.

Eleri had tried to take pictures of the glow she had cast on the footsteps, but her witchcraft didn't want to capture on film.

They'd carefully tracked their way around the outside of the house, finding someone inside, relatively confident it was Sylvia Lambrecht. When they reached the front of the yard, they headed down the street and all climbed into the SUV, where they could keep an eye on the house while they talked.

"Whoever it was left from Sylvia Lambrecht's house," Eleri emphasized. "Then they went *back* to Sylvia Lambrecht's house. And Sylvia Lambrecht was missing from her house when we followed that person into the Glades."

Eleri was insistent, but Donovan was equally forceful. "But it *wasn't* Sylvia Lambrecht in the woods."

"Then I don't know who it was…" She'd sighed out the phrase and Donovan felt her frustration matched his.

When they continued to watch the house for a while and nothing happened, they'd considered leaving one of them behind to monitor the woman. But, unless she skipped town, they'd be able to come back and find her. This was, after all, Astoria, and leaving town was her only option to truly stay hidden. However, Sylvia had to have a sense that things were closing in on her.

"What do you think her chance of fleeing is?" Donovan asked.

"It's a lot lower if we bug her car," Christina pointed out.

Luckily, Donovan carried a few devices in the bag in the backseat of the SUV. He pulled them out, showed off the handful and asked, "Where can we put another? Might as well use them."

"Something that will trace her if she leaves the house." Eleri pointed out that the garage was not attached, which meant Sylvia would need to either leave via a doorway or a window or dissolve her way through the walls.

The small team of three snuck back to Sylvia's house, moving past several others, since they'd all tried to park non-obviously. Donovan reached up and stuck a device at the top corner of the back door and then another on the front door. Christina and Eleri got Sylvia's car with not one but two pieces, in hopes that if she found one device and removed it, the other would remain.

The devices were sensitive enough to let them know if either door was opened. "I didn't see any other outside doors. You?"

Eleri and Christina both shook their heads at him and they made their way back across the lawn and to the street. He hoped like hell Eleri's spell was holding, because if it wasn't, what they'd just done was more than obvious.

As of now—unless Sylvia could somehow dissolve through walls and disappear—they knew where she was. So they'd returned to the hotel, talking about getting some sleep. But, despite watching the trackers not move at all well into the early hours, they'd only catnapped in cycles.

Nothing had pinged, though Donovan believed it would happen soon. Sylvia Lambrecht would surely need to be in the office today.

At one point after watching the trackers do nothing, they'd pulled up the view from the cameras around the cabins. Because, as Christina had pointed out, whoever had taken them down had probably been in view of them prior to grabbing them. Sure enough, though it took a while to find, it was clear that their perpetrator had come into the woods and straight toward the devices.

They showed up on the image.

"Donovan," Eleri exclaimed, "that *is* Sylvia Lambrecht."

Though it was dark and the image grainy, the face was clear. She looked directly at the camera.

"But it's not her," he insisted. "I've smelled her and I've smelled the killer. The killer smells like a different person."

"But your sense of scent isn't as good when you look human … do you think maybe you missed it? We can see Dr. Lambrecht taking down the cameras about thirty minutes before we got there."

"It's not as good. You're right. I can't really track well with my nose like this, but this person—" he didn't call her Sylvia, "—she lingers long enough to take down the cameras. I would have smelled Dr. Lambrecht if it was her."

"Do you think she has the ability to alter how she smells?" Eleri asked now, clearly spit-balling ideas.

But Christina shrugged. "Why would she even do that? You and I both wear perfume sometimes, but Donovan can easily detect that. It doesn't change who he thinks we are."

Donovan nodded and Eleri had to know that, for him, that was easy. He could name most fragrances and had no trouble detecting the scent of the person underneath.

"Is it Sylvia Lambrecht and somebody else was there and the scents are getting tangled?"

He shook his head at her, trying not to get exasperated with her intent. She just wanted to figure out what wasn't working. "That would be two distinct scents from two distinct people."

"But Sylvia Lambrecht came to the cabin, and she looked directly at the camera. We can all see her."

He threw his hands up. "I don't know what to tell you. But the visual and the scent information don't match."

"Nope, it doesn't make sense." Christina sounded as though she were still puzzling through the problem. "She would have to have the ability to change out her full human scent—something that Donovan believes is not possible. The other wolves I've met also think it's not possible. *And* she would also have to know she was being followed by someone who could detect that in order to know to change it."

Eleri let out a harsh sigh, clearly beyond frustrated. Donovan was, too, but somehow Christina kept a cool head.

"Let's rewind the video further. See if maybe someone else was there."

Donovan tried to reason that… Maybe he was smelling someone who'd been there just before this Sylvia-looking person had. And maybe Sylvia could mask her scent, so he was smelling the first person.

The footage from each camera cut off abruptly as she took it down. One of the remaining cameras caught sight of her taking down the first camera. They all watched as she dismantled it. She bashed the camera itself apart against a rock, making sure it was completely destroyed. Then she broke the strap and mount and threw each in separate directions.

"That explains why we couldn't find much of anything," Eleri lamented. She'd complained about having nothing big enough to get a fingerprint off and not being able to find the vast majority of what was missing.

They watched backward through the footage, finding a point where, much earlier, Sylvia Lambrecht had come through and traced the path around the cabin. She'd been checking the place out, and she looked all around, frowning when she spotted the cameras.

Her steps had been sure and steady, tickling something at the back of Donovan's memory.

"See. She *was* there earlier. The last two people at the cabin were both her, but I didn't smell Sylvia Lambrecht at all and I *did* smell the killer." When no one responded to him, he added, "She spotted the cameras. Why didn't she take them down then?"

"I'm guessing height," Eleri commented. "When she came back, she had that small ladder with her."

"So where did it go?" Christina asked. They hadn't found it at the scene.

Eleri peered at the screen, forcing her attention to the stupid little ladder that had made odd marks in the soil beneath each of the trees.

Donovan paid close attention, too. Anything could become the evidence that could lead to mistakes down the line or break the case.

"I don't get it." She sighed heavily as she turned to Donovan. "I'm not doubting you. I'm really not, but I can't make it work!"

"We're smart." Christina still sounded cool and collected. "One of us has to be able to solve this problem. Sylvia Lambrecht has been on video coming to this cabin on more than one occasion. We haven't seen anyone else come through. And we had cameras on the place until before we were there. Sylvia Lambrecht has a history as an abused child. Well, all the local therapists do …"

Donovan tilted his head. "Is that unusual?"

Christina shrugged. "Wasn't it Charlie Jay who pointed out that therapists often get into it because they've been through it themselves?"

"There's only three in town. It's not a statistically significant sample," Eleri joined in, even though they were still off track. It didn't surprise Donovan at all when she pulled it back. "Everything is perfect—except for the scent."

She motioned at the laptop, shaking her open hand. The image they had freeze-framed was of Sylvia Lambrecht stalking her way into the clearing. She was looking up at the camera with the obvious intent of taking it down. For a moment, no one spoke.

Then Christina grinned. "I've got it!"

87

"She's a twin!" Christina blurted out as Donovan looked to her.

He saw the idea settle in for Eleri even as it hit him.

"If you want to be a criminal," Christina offered up, "especially a particular variety, having an identical twin is absolutely your best option."

They both looked to her, nodding.

Donovan picked up the thread. "You would have eyewitnesses stating where you are and giving you a solid alibi ... until somebody figures out that you have a twin."

"Also." Eleri looked excited. "Initial DNA evidence won't separate the two. We have to know that the sample belongs to a twin and run the analysis specifically checking for variations in twin DNA. Now, their fingerprints would be different. But the only real fingerprints we have in this case are the ones from the damn wolf who left us the messages."

Donovan and Christina followed along with her reasoning. There had been no fingerprints associated with Evan and Bonnie Merkel's disappearance. Nothing had shown up at the house in the initial investigation reports that hadn't been part of the elimination process.

JP Talley's clothing had been soaked in blood and hadn't shown fingerprints, either. And, as those were the primary markers distinguishing twins, nothing would have let them know there were two people involved.

Donovan looked to the other two after he'd turned it over a bit. "If Sylvia Lambrecht was abused as a child, then wouldn't her twin have been, too? Giving them both the same motivation?"

No one said anything. It was clear they all agreed that their killer believed they were ridding the world of bad people, saving the victims of the abusers. Donovan had to admit that it was a morally gray area. FBI agents were expected to be black-and-white thinkers. Break the law, do the time. Commit a crime, simply be wrong. But the idea of twins made pieces of the case snap into place.

"Can we pull fingerprints off the cabin itself?" Christina asked the room.

"The wood is too faded. It's weathered and has too many bumps and ridges. The tarp is a better bet ..." Eleri looked to the other two.

"That cabin also is burned. Now that the cameras are down, it's probably in our best interest to take it apart for evidence. Soon," Christina pointed out.

Again looking to the other two, Donovan asked, "What exactly is on our to-do list?

"Take apart the cabin for evidence," Christina immediately repeated.

"Find Sylvia Lambrecht's twin," Eleri put in.

Donovan quickly made notes and added his own. "Figure out how the damn scent keeps disappearing, and confirm Craig Renfro's identity."

Christina frowned. "If he was a missing person that Jesse Nash knew about, why wasn't this confirmed before?"

"He didn't match anything at the time, and no one went back and re-opened the case until now. At least that's what Sheriff Tucker said." Eleri looked back and forth between them.

"Renfro was wanted at the time … Do you think it was covered up?" Christina asked.

Donovan felt his head jerk upright. Another puzzle piece slipping into place. "So they believed he killed Melanie Shipman, and then when he was murdered, they simply listed him as missing and left him that way? Protecting his killer?"

Christina shook her head, her eyes darting from side to side as she shrugged. "It's an option."

The sheriff couldn't have known then that the Renfro case would be re-opened and carefully examined as part of a serial killer investigation. Then Donovan added another item, speaking out loud as he typed. "Jesse Nash told us that she ran into Rebecca Talley. But we need to go back to Jesse and ask her exactly who she talked to about Eugene. That's going to give us an idea of what the path is from Sylvia to her twin."

The other two nodded their heads.

"We also have to watch footage from the other cabin," Eleri added, even though they'd all pretty much agreed the killer wouldn't be back.

The sun was fully up and no one had really yet slept, but Donovan figured they were all too wired to do so. Nothing had pinged from the trackers yet and it was seven a.m. "When does her first patient arrive today?"

Clearly, the other two didn't know either.

"Lambrecht could walk out the door at any moment or not leave her home at all. In the meantime, let's see if we can find her twin." Eleri motioned all of them to get to work.

All three immediately logged into every database they knew of, looking for Sylvia Lambrecht's identical sister. But before anyone found anything of value, one of the trackers pinged.

88

Eleri tipped her head in close, staring at Christina's screen. Though they'd been watching the very data for several hours with nothing happening, now the tracker on the front door showed that the door had swung open.

Then, within two minutes, the other trackers showed the car backing out of the driveway. The two trackers on the car not only gave them a backup, should Sylvia find one of them, but the tech that they had was good enough to know that the two trackers were now moving in tandem.

In order to remove them from the car convincingly, two people would have to stand on opposite ends of the vehicle and remove the trackers simultaneously. Anything else and the agents would see the discrepancy. The AI would read the change.

They'd really covered everything, Eleri thought—except the twin. "Everything's good, as long as it's actually Sylvia Lambrecht in that car."

On the other side of Christina, Donovan began tapping on his phone again. At Eleri's questioning look, he readily explained. "We asked Jesse Nash about the rumors around town and we asked her about the autopsy reports and the victims. But we didn't ask her about the therapists. I'm asking her now."

"Good call," Eleri told him. Jesse Nash, and in fact all the locals, might already know far more than they did.

"She sure doesn't miss Eugene," Christina commented under her breath.

Eleri agreed. "Do you think she's our killer?"

"She's not," Donovan piped up from the other side, most likely referring back to the scent that he'd uniquely identified as the killer. He was frustrated about that, but she didn't have any answers.

"I was just kind of making a commentary on the kinds of people this person is taking out." Christina corrected the flow of the conversation.

"Rebecca Talley has put on a pretty good show of grieving for JP," Eleri said.

"I got the feeling she actually misses her husband." Christina was still glued to the screen, even though she was fully in the conversation, too.

"Why?"

"My guess is she was hopeful that she could turn things around. That's a normal phase. They hope that when things get better outside the home, they'll get better inside it, too."

Eleri didn't ask where Christina's confident answer came from. She was just grateful that at least one of them wasn't so easily distracted.

"I asked Jesse for the rundown on the therapists," Donovan announced after boldly pushing a button on his phone. "Anything she knows about all three therapists off the top of her head."

"Did you tell her we could use it ASAP?" Eleri asked. "I don't want Lambrecht skipping town."

Donavon nodded that he had. So far, Jesse had been good. Eleri was beginning to wonder if the amount of work they were giving her would interfere with her writing for the newspaper or taking care of Ciara. Then again, this could legitimately fall under the category of her writing for the paper, because ultimately, it would fund her big scoop story on the murders.

Twelve minutes later, the twin trackers turned up right at the front door of Dr. Sylvia Lambrecht's strip mall office.

"Crap." Christina flopped back into the couch after the expletive. "We can't track Sylvia anymore."

Eleri tipped her head one way then the other. "True, but I don't know how we could have without breaking into the house. I honestly don't even know what she might carry every day or all the time."

"Wallet." Christina tossed out the one word as if it were a done deal.

But Eleri quickly countered, "Not everyone carries theirs all the time, and if they do, it's likely because they use it all the time. So she might very well notice a tracker in it."

"Do we send someone to the office to watch her?" Christina asked next.

"I don't even know," was Eleri's reply. She was still concerned about them splitting up.

Though watching the office wasn't going to be a big deal, the problem was that the very nature of the business was that anything could become a problem at any time. They all sat and watched the stationary trackers for a few more moments before Eleri spoke again.

"I do think we need to do a drive-by at some point later, just to be sure she's there. Though, if she's going to skip town, she's going to skip town. I'd really love to watch her for a few days."

"Sure, but watching means watching." Donovan pointed out something that wouldn't have made sense to anyone else.

"The problem is there's only three of us. And I don't know that it's Sylvia we need to be watching." Not that she knew who the person she should be watching was.

"She might be the conduit to the sister. Or the sister could have wised up and fled town already," Christina pointed out. "She knows about us. She found the cameras, which honestly means Sylvia probably knows, too. The two cabins have been made."

"Yes, she knows there were cameras, but I'm guessing by the way this has gone on and how well she stayed hidden, she's not dumb. That would mean she knows we have her face. Or at least, her sister's face." Eleri didn't like it even as she said it.

"So the twin is likely already in the wind is what you're saying." Donovan huffed out an exasperated sigh.

"It's entirely possible," Christina added, still flopped back on the couch in a near position of defeat.

Eleri didn't like the small feeling in the bottom of her gut—that they might have finally figured out who this killer was and then lost them before they had a chance to apprehend her. But if that was the way it was, then they would simply have to track down the twin, wherever she'd fled to.

Eleri felt the vibration in her pocket almost before she heard the dual pings from hers and Donovan's phones. Her lips pressed together at the thought of reporting to Westerfield right now, of all times. She quickly formulated a "can't talk, too deep in the case" response.

But as she picked up the phone to see what it was, she heard Donovan say, "Yes!"

As she glanced at the screen, now curious rather than wary, she saw what her partner was talking about.

Jesse Nash was fast.

89

"Are we abandoning the trackers?" Donovan asked as he pointed to the screen.

"Not really," Christina offered and then she tapped on the screen and let them know she was setting a code that would alert them all, should the trackers move.

That made sense to him. "Where can Lambrecht go without the car?"

It wasn't rhetorical, and the three of them looked at each other for a moment and began listing the options.

"The convenience store and the small furniture shop next door."

"If she's willing to walk in the heat, in her professional clothing and her heels, then there's a good number of places near enough to get to on foot," Eleri pointed out.

"Around the edge of the office she can head up into the Glades. Up towards the north cabin," Christina added.

Donovan thought none of those were good options for them. They would be great ways to lose the therapist. "Do we have an excuse to call her just to hear her voice and know that she's in?"

"We can think of something. However, do we even know that it's her?" Eleri posed.

"I don't understand."

"She's got this twin sister ..."

He was shaking his head that the sister might be filling in at the office today. "Seems to me it'd be really difficult to swap out. I mean, as a therapist, that would be a lot of information to keep up with, wouldn't it?"

He wasn't an identical twin himself and he hadn't had friends who were identical twins. So he couldn't really say, only that he heard stories of it or seen it in ridiculous sitcoms. "You don't think her patients would notice?"

Eleri shrugged. "If she spends her time asking questions, maybe not. If they're not expecting a switch? Well … we sure didn't."

"True." There were so many options in this case that his head was about to split open. But he was hopeful it was the moment right before all the pieces lined up.

"Is there anything we can do about it right now?" Christina asked.

At that point, Eleri and Donovan looked to each other and shrugged. "I guess not."

"So let's see what Jesse Nash sent." Donovan pulled up the email on his phone. Like the last one, things were grouped clearly. "Dr. Charlie Jay. Bachelor's from University of Central Florida. Doctorate in clinical psychology from Baylor."

Donovan read off the years of graduation. "Looks like he finished early, at a young age. And Jesse noted that he'd had a variety of drug problems."

"Charlie already confessed that himself." He kept reading. "License lost, license reinstated. Interesting, but straightforward. The Jay family is originally from LaBelle."

"Hold on," Eleri said, folding up the screen on her own laptop and typing in the information. "That's about an hour south of here. East of Naples."

Donovan kept reading. "She thinks he moved because of the drug problem once he got clean."

"To get away from the temptation, or to start over where people didn't know him?" Christina asked from her laid back, closed-eyes position on the couch. Maybe she would be the first to get some real sleep.

"Jesse doesn't say." Donovan moved on to Gwen Song. This time, the universities and degrees showed up much later in Gwen's life. So far, things matched what the therapists had told them, but with extra information, like which schools she'd graduated and where she'd grown up.

Eleri and Donovan commented at the time. "Both Dr. Song and Dr. Lambrecht are from families around here."

"Charlie Jay is from close by, though not here. Do you think that's important?" Donovan looked at the women.

But Christina—without opening her eyes—shook her head. "This is Florida. Though we all think of it as a vacation destination, for the people who live here, it's home. In any small town around the US, it's not uncommon to see families who've been there for at least four generations."

"But a lot of people do move away," Eleri pointed out.

"And a lot eventually come back to where they started and a lot never really leave." Christina still hadn't moved nor opened her eyes.

"These three all went away," Donovan pointed out, "and they all three came back. You don't think those numbers are a little odd?"

"I really don't," Christina replied, "because we're only talking about them because *they're here*. So they are pre-selected to be in that group. That's why I don't think it's significant to the case."

Donovan had to concede her point. He went back to reading the email until he commented, "Interesting. Song's ex is in the state pen."

"Still?" Eleri asked, and the sincere query in her voice made Donovan think it through.

Gwen had commented that she escaped an abusive relationship and then gone to school afterwards. It had been a number of years since she'd left him. Donovan would have appreciated it if a person could get locked up that long for abusing a spouse, but he had a hard time believing the man would be in jail for long. He read a little further. "Apparently he is now in on an entirely different charge for aggravated assault. Several charges, actually."

Eleri commented, "Good thing she got out when she did."

Sylvia Lambrecht was last on the list. Never married. The military service in her background matched what the doctor had said. Her mother, Jesse noted—as she had so many times, because she simply knew family histories around town—had been in and out of various marriages, as was Sylvia's father.

There was a note at the bottom, with Jesse's own thoughts added in. Donovan read it. "I honestly don't know how Sylvia practices here. I would assume there'd be a conflict of interest in treating family members or maybe even someone you have a personal history with. Between her mother's and her father's various marriages, Sylvia Lambrecht is related to the Marches, the Songs, the Skipperkeys, the Shipmans, the Redmons, the Nguyens, and the Schwimmers ... at least."

Donovan's eyes snapped up. "Shipman?"

90

She'd been right, Eleri thought, as the three agents began to scramble.

"If Sylvia Lambrecht was related to the Shipman family, that might be the link on the first of our known cases."

It took them forty-five minutes to dig up what they needed, during which time she was grateful that the tracker didn't move. She sincerely hoped that Sylvia Lambrecht was sitting in her office, helping someone else get right in the head, even if she herself was clearly not.

"Here." Christina swung her screen around as she talked. "Melanie Shipman's mother, Eliza, is Sylvia's mother."

"They're half-sisters." That was big news to Eleri.

Christina continued. "Eliza was married to Melanie's father, Edmund Shipman, for eight years. They have Melanie and a son, Greg."

"She's noticeably younger than Sylvia." Eleri tried to work it all out. "But Sylvia Lambrecht is Black. Melanie's not."

Donovan motioned up and down to Eleri and his own skin tone. "I'd argue that Sylvia's mixed race. Her mother looks more white."

Eleri nodded along. Edmund Shipman was probably also very pale, because Melanie Shipman was a blond-haired, blue-eyed doll. Looking at the two women's pictures side by side, she now saw many facial similarities. But she wouldn't have thought to look before finding the relationship. She'd have to step up her game on that.

"So Melanie Shipman is Sylvia Lambrecht's younger half-sister. Melanie gets herself a stalker. The family does everything they can—restraining orders, police intervention, et cetera. Still, Melanie winds up murdered. And then Craig Renfro disappears within the month." Eleri could almost hear the small soft snaps of puzzle pieces fitting together. "And we get our first known murder by our killer."

"Do you think Jesse Nash figured out that the unknown victim is Renfro?"

"We haven't confirmed that it is Renfro yet," Eleri pointed out. Though she could admit that, for themselves, they were convinced.

"Maybe now, after JP Talley and the Merkels were found, and the community knows they have a serial killer, Lambrecht wants to be acknowledged. Can we use Craig Renfro to draw her out? Make it public that the body is identified as him?"

"It might work." Christina shrugged, finally lifting her head.

Eleri thought it sounded more than plausible. She turned to look at Christina's screen. Though nothing had alerted, she felt the compulsive need to check. She saw the two trackers still sitting in front of the office.

But just as she thought it was all coming together, Donovan said, "Wait. Where was Sylvia Lambrecht during the window for Renfro's murder?"

"In the Army… so she's not our killer," Christina said.

Eleri glanced up quickly, almost laughing at the way Donovan's face twisted as if she could actually see him biting his tongue to say, *I've been telling you, she's not our killer*. Instead, what he said was, "That's a problem."

Eleri and Christina both looked to him, the seriousness of his tone weighing heavily.

"We just pulled all these family records, everything that's related to Sylvia Lambrecht," he explained. "We found connections to the Shipman family and several others. There were marriage and divorce records for Sylvia's mother, and her father, all through the county records. It's what we *didn't* find that's more important right now."

Suddenly Eleri felt the weight of Donovan's revelation, too, even before he said the words.

"There's no record of Sylvia's twin."

91

The three agents began to scramble again, tapping furiously on keys, accessing databases and records.

Eleri turned to Christina with an odd thought she hadn't considered before. "Is that your personal laptop?"

Christina caught on easily and Eleri realized that Christina would have thought of this well before she had. "I've been using my personal laptop almost exclusively for the past several years. I left my FBI-issued one at home before coming on this trip."

Eleri nodded slowly. Christina was definitely ahead of her on the game. "But if you're accessing databases …?"

"I'm accessing public records. And I'm accessing things that I have bought personal access to, certain hubs, that kind of thing. So yeah, I don't quite have the full range that you guys do."

But it was safer, Eleri thought, understanding that, as Christina was on leave, she would definitely want to fly under Westerfield's radar. In that moment she wondered, *Did Westerfield know that Christina was here?* Was he wondering how long they were going to try to hide another agent?

With a nod of acknowledgement, Eleri turned her focus back to the task at hand.

"Is Sylvia adopted? Sometimes they split up twins at birth." Christina offered a hypothetical scenario.

"It doesn't work." Clicking a few things, Donovan pulled up saved pictures of Bernie Lambrecht. He pointed to the screen. "He's listed as Sylvia's father, and he looks like her."

Eleri could see that he did. She pulled up a picture of Melanie Shipman. "They look too much alike."

"Okay, so not twins split up through adoption issues. Maybe they were split up at birth, though." Christina seemed to be thinking out loud.

"Could they have put one twin up for adoption?" Donovan asked as though following her trail.

"Probably not, but it could happen." Christina created a scenario for them. "Again, the older the case is, the more likely it is that things were missed. Technology just wasn't as good thirty or forty years ago as it is today. What if the family thought they were having one baby, and couldn't afford a second?"

Again, Eleri conceded. That might happen—but it was unlikely.

"It doesn't matter." Donovan sounded disappointed "Hospital records will tell us."

Eleri found herself grateful that Dr. Lambrecht was unmarried and they didn't have to trace her back through a series of name changes. She herself would not change her name if and when she got married, she added mentally, if only to help the people investigating her death solve it a little easier.

"Oh, dear God," Donovan sighed. "Finally!"

But his excitement faded as the page he'd found loaded and he read off, "Live birth, singleton."

The agents looked at each other, Eleri feeling like her brains had been through a blender, with all the various things that had popped up. "That doesn't make any sense. We saw Sylvia and you smelled someone else."

"A sister who happens to look very much like her?" Christina posited, sending them on another document chase.

This one took longer, because they had no idea if the sister would be older or younger or by how much ... and because, ultimately, there was no end. Only that they'd exhausted all the options and found nothing.

"Do you want to message Jesse Nash again?" Eleri finally asked.

Donovan did.

Eleri didn't like giving the reporter the task. Jesse wouldn't miss the fact that they were getting close to something as their questions became more specific. Eleri consoled herself that the reporter had already agreed not to print anything about the case until and unless the FBI agreed.

"The question is, does Jesse—who has her fingers in everything—possibly also have her mouth in everything?"

The other two looked back at her, but Eleri kept going. "She could be talking to everyone. Can Jesse really be trusted? What if she purposefully shares information to try to get ahead of the FBI, or maybe even withholds something. What if she mistakenly lets information slip when she talks to one of her many local friends, as things obviously came up and Jesse just talks!"

The way the reporter had quickly brought together the initial information about the rumors from around town showed that Jesse did talk. But Eleri didn't know how much.

Donovan didn't know either, but he added, "Right now, Jesse is our best lead .... And I already messaged her before you had your questions."

Almost before Eleri could concede anything, his phone pinged. Donovan looked up at them. "No. Jesse doesn't know of Sylvia Lambrecht having any sisters besides Melanie. And she wants to know why we're asking."

This time, it was Eleri who tipped herself back onto the couch. She had to slow down. She was thinking so fast, everything tangled. Every time she organized her jumble of thoughts, a new idea was tossed into the mix.

Eleri and Donovan argued back and forth, sometimes switching sides, arguing that they *should* tell Jesse why they wanted to know, and then that they *shouldn't*. Christina remained quiet, until at last she spoke up.

"All those arguments are valid. But can you just check, Eleri?"

"What do you mean?"

"The question here isn't really why or how or what damage she can cause if we make a mistake. The question is, *Can we trust Jesse Nash?*" She looked pointedly at Eleri this time. "Is there any way you can *see* the answer?"

92

As the afternoon went by in a blur of activity, a case that they had slowly been chipping away at was beginning to chunk off in larger and larger pieces, Donovan thought.

Sylvia Lambrecht's car had not left the office all day. When it did, they hopped in their car and rushed over, confirming that Sylvia was, indeed, inside the home—or at least the woman they believed was Dr. Sylvia Lambrecht.

They'd spent the day digging up information and chatting with Jesse Nash. They did not tell her about the scent changes that Donovan had noticed, they'd merely explained a little of why they were curious about Sylvia Lambrecht.

— There's evidence that she was at an important location at a particular time.

Donovan texted, then added more. — However, there's also sufficient evidence that she wasn't there at that same time. Identical twin is the premise we're working on right now. Any help you can provide would be grateful.

— On it.

That reply had come from Jesse Nash a while ago. Honestly, Donovan had believed he would get a text right back and that Jesse might just crack the case for them. But it didn't happen. He hadn't heard from her since then.

They'd eaten hasty, drive-through meals, and he couldn't tell if his stomach was churning from the food or the case itself. He asked, "Is there *any* evidence for a sister?"

"I think we can conclusively say there's not a twin." Eleri obviously didn't like the idea either. It had seemed so sound. "If there is, she's so well hidden that no one can find her. That just feels impossible to pull off."

It brought them back to square one. "So then she's changing her scent. How?"

This time, Donovan partially conceded. "I've never seen or heard of anything like it."

"You've basically smelled people all your life, right?"

"Early on, I didn't know what it was. I didn't even understand that I had an unusually good sense of smell. But later ... Yeah."

"I'm messaging Wade," Eleri told them all.

Luckily, it took almost no time to get a text back. Donovan was grateful, but the reply was, "Never."

Eleri held the phone up for the other two agents to see. "Well, that didn't help."

"So she can't change scents..." Christina offered up slowly. "Is it possible she can change her face?"

Donovan could see that Eleri froze, too, and he felt it in his own body. "I've never heard of that. But ..."

Eleri gestured to Christina. "Christina can make us think whatever we want. Christina can make us see someone else when she's there, right?"

Slowly Christina nodded. "So they *could* change faces but—if they're like me—they don't have to. They just need to make us think that they're Sylvia Lambrecht."

Donovan didn't put anything past most anyone these days. Hell, he could change his own face, just not to that. He looked to Christina. "How would you make it happen?"

"This is why I erased myself from video footage," Christina began to explain, "rather than making you think there's somebody else. I did that a few times in school—made everyone think I was this one popular girl. I always got caught. I couldn't quite pull off all her mannerisms, and the real Brittany was actually somewhere else at the time."

"Can we send the footage to an analyst?" Eleri asked. "Christina pushes *people*, so maybe someone else would see it as it actually is. They could see something different than we do, maybe."

Eleri was already tapping away at the screen, and Donovan saw she was noting timestamps where Sylvia's face was clear on the image. "Can you push everyone who watches a video, even if you have no idea who it might be in the future?"

Christina thought for a moment. "I don't know. I usually work with store footage and erase myself from the employees' minds. It's not the kind of thing that somebody might come back and watch years later, or that someone new would come and watch."

"It's still worth a try." Donovan grew impatient and Eleri sent it over immediately along with a photo of Sylvia to see if it was a match.

When no analyst immediately pinged back with a video image, saying *No, this woman is not on that video,* Donovan began to get restless.

"You didn't sleep last night, did you, Donovan?" Eleri asked.

He shook his head no. None of them had, though they'd all managed a few catnaps. The day had passed in a flurry of action.

"We're all going to crash soon. If we don't control it, we'll all burn out together and we'll miss Sylvia when she leaves the house." She looked to Donovan.

"You want to go first?" He tried to beat her to the punch, but Eleri only laughed.

"I was hoping someone else would. I feel wired."

"I think we all do." Christina shrugged. "But I'll give it a try. Wake me up if anything happens."

Christina didn't come back, and the quick loss of small noises from the other room told Donovan that the dark and quiet had done the trick and one of them was finally getting some rest. But, thirty minutes later the screen pinged.

Sylvia Lambrecht's back door had opened.

93

"We should have put cameras on the back of the house," Donovan lamented loudly, only moments after the ping came through.

They would have to head to the southeast side of town, immediately. Luckily it was all of five or ten minutes away. Unfortunately, as he glanced through the suite, he thought of the boxes of evidence. Was there time to take it all with them?

Only then did he realize he'd left it here when Eleri and Christina had been watching Dr. Lambrecht's house. When they'd told him the house was empty, he'd simply hopped into the SUV and come after them, not even remembering to carry everything along.

Even if they didn't pack everything up now, they still likely wouldn't get there in time. As evidenced by the last time they tried to trail her, Sylvia Lambrecht prepared fast and she knew her way around.

Though Donovan was in sneakers today, it was the only thing he could say he had going in his favor.

"Go wake up Christina," he told Eleri, but his partner paused.

"She's the first one of us getting any sleep." She started to look at the phone but he didn't quite make it through the calculation of the number of hours that they had been awake with only occasional catnaps in between.

"If Sylvia Lambrecht's back door opened and we let you sleep through it, how would you feel?" he pushed.

At that point, Eleri conceded, though it was clear she was growing tired, almost to the limit of her endurance. He was feeling exhaustion settling in himself.

"Wait." He held out his hand to stop her. "Do we take the evidence?"

Now was not the time to mention that he'd forgotten it before, though she'd probably noticed the backseat was empty. She hadn't said anything at the time and she shook her head now. "We can't. There's no time. I wish there was some place to lock it up. We know the guy from Miranda can get in, but I guess he didn't take anything the last time, so he probably won't take it this time either…"

She let the sentence trail off as if she were defeated by the idea that there wasn't much she could do about it. There were too many balls in the air and they had to pick which ones to catch.

At least one thing was decided, he thought. Before he knew it, Eleri was emerging from the bedroom with Christina in tow. For someone who'd barely fallen asleep, she looked alert.

"Let's go," she told them. Though even as they were heading for the door, she stepped the other direction and tapped a few keys on her computer. Then held up her phone and said, "Now I've got the trackers here, too."

Christina waited until they were in the SUV with Donovan at the wheel, trying not to peel out of the parking lot, before she said, "The back door closed immediately after it was opened."

"Is it possible she didn't really leave?" Eleri asked as Donovan kept his muscles tight, trying not to speed through the nearly empty town in the dark.

But as he glanced over, he saw Christina tipping her head one way then another. "I guess she could have opened the back door, looked into the yard, then simply closed it. But the last time the door opened at this time of night, she went out into the Glades."

Donovan agreed: It was worth the race to see what was happening. He wished they could fly under the radar better. The big car might be memorable to anyone paying attention.

Finally on Sylvia's street, he parked in a different spot from before, not wanting any of the neighbors to get too used to seeing them. He only then thought that, if they had been smart, they would have brought the little car. But they hadn't been smart, and they were here now.

He and Eleri slipped the spell sachets around their necks and the three of them climbed out of the car. A quick survey of the house revealed nothing. But as Eleri stepped into the mulch of the flowerbeds and touched the siding, she jerked her hand back.

"She's home."

Had they come out here for nothing?

Even as he thought that, Christina pulled out her phone. "Shit. I missed the notification. The back door opened and closed again, just … three minutes ago."

"Did she just check the backyard?" He turned to look at Christina.

"She was gone for over twenty minutes. That's not a backyard check." The other agent hadn't even looked up from her phone, as if trying to make heads and tails of the new information.

"What would she be doing?" Donovan couldn't puzzle it out either.

Eleri looked up at him. "If there are two of them, who knows?"

They quickly entertained the possibility that the two women were merely doppelgangers—unrelated, but so close in looks that they could pass as twins. The likelihood of finding one's doppelganger was low, Donovan knew, but not zero. But the likelihood that your doppelganger would also share your zeal for murdering deserving victims was insanely low—but also not zero. "Let's knock on the door and see what happens."

They started to walk forward, but Christina stopped them. "Hey, idiots, you're invisible!"

Shit, he thought, that would do no good. Inadvertently playing ding dong ditch with a killer was not his idea of sound investigation. So they stepped into the tree cover and made sure no one was looking as they removed the sachets.

A knock brought Sylvia Lambrecht to the front door. She had a robe wrapped around her body, slippers on her feet, and a confused look on her face.

"Dr. Lambrecht…" Eleri started, but Donovan looked down.

On Sylvia's legs, he saw black tactical pants.

Eleri gathered her thoughts. "We came by to check on you. We're concerned about the killer—"

"The killer?" The woman stepped back, surprised, and clutched at her robe.

Donovan stepped forward. *Was this Sylvia Lambrecht?* He sniffed at the air as Eleri spun a story about the doctor having known the families of the victims.

"You think he's coming after me? Because of what I know?" The fear on her face and in her scent was genuine. "I don't really know anything."

She frowned at the agents who'd barged onto her front step after dark. But Donovan tried to surreptitiously step a little closer.

Eleri caught on and she stepped up, too. "Can we come inside for just a moment? I don't want to let the bugs into your home."

Without waiting for a reply, Eleri crowded them all into the front hallway, as if forgetting her manners. But she kept going, covering for Donovan. "It's just a small working theory."

"But what about the other therapists? They know things, too. Dr. Song, Dr. Jay?"

A tight-knit little group, Donovan thought as he tried to slowly filter the scents. Something was bothering him.

When he figured it out, he did everything he could to keep his eyes from bolting wide. He made a subtle motion to Eleri that they were ready to go.

Whatever had happened, it was clear this woman smelled of the Everglades. She'd been for a run just before opening the door, and all the fragrant flora of the trees and bogs had left their traces on her.

Eleri quickly extracted the agents and told Dr. Lambrecht to lock her doors. She apparently felt no guilt about leaving a little paranoia in her wake.

Outside, Eleri nodded toward the peephole as they heard the deadbolt slide into place. Donovan held his tongue until they were a few steps away and then turned and whispered in a hiss.

"She was with *him*!"

Eleri and Christina stopped walking, but Donovan put a hand on each of their backs, propelling them forward. If anyone was watching, he didn't want them to see anything unusual.

"I picked up the scent. It was faint. Maybe he touched her or got close ... the wolf from Miranda industries. *I smelled him on her.* And it was recent." Donovan rambled through the explanation as he saw

Eleri open her mouth. He tried to pre-guess what her question would be, and he said, "Maybe fifteen minutes ago."

Now, with the other agents as stunned as he was, they moved down the sidewalk, heading back toward the SUV. Only as Donovan stepped toward the tall bushes where he'd parked the car, hoping to keep it partly covered, did he smell and see the man leaning against his vehicle.

94

Eleri felt her insides clench as the man from Miranda Industries stood there in human form, leaning against their SUV.

He hadn't introduced himself, just said, "So I see we agree."

Donovan stepped up, nostrils flaring. Thankfully, he was a good four inches taller than the man. "What are you doing here?"

"I have one job: Find JP Talley's killer and make certain that the killer didn't do it for any reason my people need to be worried about."

At the term *my people,* Eleri's jaw tightened and she saw her two fellow agents try to hide their own reactions. "His death doesn't appear to have anything to do with your *industry,*" she said.

She'd put emphasis on the last word, but that was stupid. She remembered as soon as it rolled off her lips that he'd sent them information on letterhead. Nothing like feeling stupid when facing down a man who had entered your home and violated your possessions.

"I apologize," he offered softly now and, though he didn't clarify, it sounded like he was apologizing for exactly what she was thinking about. "I simply had to know what, exactly, you were investigating."

Donovan splayed his hands wide, almost in a gesture of welcome, but not quite. "Well, now you know."

A brief pause followed, the wolf indicating that perhaps he was done with that line of conversation. "I'm assuming you're about to make an arrest."

Eleri merely blinked at him. If she had been the only one in the conversation, she would have held for silence. But the others didn't.

"Do go on." Christina stepped slightly forward.

Eleri watched in amazement as the wolf opened his mouth and told them, "Doctor Lambrecht is your killer. I just ran into her in the woods. She saw me, grew frightened, and she turned around and ran back home."

"What was she doing in the woods?" Christina's tone was too dulcet for the question.

"I don't know." He shrugged in a way that told Eleri Christina had pushed him.

Tapping her partner on the shoulder, Eleri silently asked if she could take the next question. Christina stepped softly aside.

"How did you find Dr. Lambrecht?"

"I was in the Glades. Miranda has several locations, small operations that we keep fairly hidden." He spoke the words with the calm assurance of someone proud of their work, but very quickly, his expression became stunned, as though he knew he shouldn't have let that out.

Interesting information, Eleri thought. Then she saw the subtle change in him as Christina pushed him further.

"I stumbled across the cabin. It was obvious what it was used for. Anyone seeing inside wouldn't even need my senses to know that. I followed the scent outward."

"And?" Eleri asked, wondering what this other wolf would say.

"I trailed it as far as I could. It vanished." He turned and pointed back to Dr. Lambrecht's. "In the Glades, near that woman's backyard. I followed it again and again. The police tried to hide their reports, but even only knowing the general area the other bodies had been found, I was able to find and follow the scent. One of the paths led to her office. It's clear that she's the killer and whatever it is that you can do," he waved his hand to Eleri and Christina, seeming not to catch on that at least one of them was doing it right this moment, "you must know what you have. It's time to make an arrest."

Eleri was impressed that he'd come to almost the same conclusion they had, but he was missing a very important part.

"And if we don't arrest her?" Christina asked.

It was one of those moments. Had it been a game, Eleri would have slapped her partner on the back and said, "Good play."

He tipped his head. "I guess it doesn't matter. None of the other people she's killing relate back to us. I can clear Talley of being blackmailed or anything of the like."

"Miranda's secrets died safe with him," Eleri said and watched as he said "Yes," quite smugly and followed it with a too-quick reaction of surprise.

"Are you going to erase this?" she whispered to Christina.

"Oh, yes." With a deep breath, Christina slowly let her air out. If Eleri had no idea what Christina could do, she would never have recognized the signal. It might just be the only thing that kept her from frying his brains or erasing his entire childhood.

The man shook his head and asked, "So are you arresting her?" as though the conversation hadn't even happened.

Eleri shooed him away from the car. "We've got this in hand."

In tandem, the three of them climbed in.

He had excellent hearing, so they couldn't talk just because they'd closed the car doors. Donovan drove down the street, leaving him in the rearview mirror. Eleri looked back to see he climbed into his own car, looking just a little confused before driving away.

"Dammit!" Donovan smacked the steering wheel. "I wanted to take him in."

"But how could we?" Eleri asked. "He's here for information about Miranda. I'm assuming he's a relatively high-level operative. And look what happened when JP Talley—who had a mid-level management position at a small corporation hidden through three shell companies—died. If we take that wolf, I suspect the wrath of Miranda comes down on us. Hell, Westerfield doesn't even know Christina is here."

"Yeah," Donovan agreed, "but I still wanted to take him in."

Eleri understood the feeling. It was frustrating to restrain herself simply for the sake of better judgment.

"Where am I going?" Donovan asked, still driving away.

Eleri waved her hand forward. "Might as well go back to the hotel. He already knows where we are. If that's where he's going, we should probably get there first."

"So is it time to arrest Sylvia Lambrecht?" Christina asked. "Do we have enough evidence, or what can we fabricate that will support it to Sheriff Tucker?"

Eleri was opening her mouth to say something when Donovan added, "You should know something else. She smelled like Sylvia Lambrecht. Not like the killer."

95

Eleri flopped back onto the hotel room couch.

Donovan had sniffed the place and declared that the wolf had not been here. She touched pieces of furniture and hadn't felt him either. Christina checked all of the evidence.

Finally convinced they were in the clear, she was now completely and utterly exhausted. Everything had caught up to her and she was going to pass out on this slightly too-small couch that had likely been chosen because it made the small room appear somewhat larger.

"I don't get it." Irritation ate at her. "*He* said she was the killer. He said he ran into her behind the house, then she turned around and came back. Whatever she'd been going to do, he'd thwarted her. He's the only reason she was there when we got back."

"But it wasn't the killer. That was Sylvia Lambrecht." Donovan held firm.

Everyone was frustrated. Donovan's one odd piece of evidence was the lone holdout keeping them from immediately arresting her. Eleri had no doubt they could find a few fingerprints on the tarp in the cabin, and that they needed to go dismantle it right away.

She hated to admit it, but it was plausible the Miranda wolf had saved them from letting her destroy it. If Eleri had been the killer, and she knew the cabin had been made, she would have been hitting the tarp with bleach as soon as she could. Hell, it might already be done.

They could have called in a team to process the scene, but she kept thinking they would get to it themselves before the FBI could send the proper people from Tampa. It had taken a while to get the cameras up, and it would take at least as long for the complex job of processing the cabin. She wished now that she'd already pulled the trigger on that. They might have missed their only chance.

"Well, hells bells," Donovan muttered, the odd Southern phrase sounding weird from him.

"What?" Eleri and Christina asked in stereo, the same air of defeat in their tones.

"Jesse Nash messaged back with an idea." He read it off. "If no one has seen the two of them at the same time, then it's possible they're Batman."

Donovan had almost laughed, but Eleri thought that wouldn't change the human scent.

"Or it's MPD." Donovan almost laughed at his own suggestion as Christina asked, "What's MPD?"

"Multiple personality disorder," Eleri replied quickly. "Though it's now diagnosed as dissociative identity disorder or DID. And it's not real."

Donovan stopped his angry pacing and turned to stare at her. "What?"

Eleri shrugged back, not moving from the couch. "It's not a real thing. Ninety eight percent of therapists will tell you that it doesn't exist. It's just an interesting and dissociative ploy for attention. Do people actually adopt alternate personalities? Sure, but is it really a fractured personality where some of them don't know about the others and coexist at different times in the same body? No. It's not real."

Donovan looked to Christina, his expression a clear query saying, *"Do you believe what she's saying?"*

Christina obviously didn't have an opinion.

"Fine," Eleri conceded. "There are a few therapists who swear that it exists and that they found someone who has it. But in most cases, it's been shown that those therapists were actively seeking patients with DID. And therefore most likely they helped their patients generate it, whether consciously or subconsciously."

Donovan still stared at her rudely.

"What?" she asked, finally feeling awake.

"You're *really* going to tell me that something like that doesn't exist? You call me a werewolf. You're a witch. And Christina—" Christina just raised her eyebrows at him. "And I'm sorry. I don't even know what we should call you. Are you psychic? You're not psychokinetic, you're ..."

"Who knows?" Christina's hands lifted palm up, almost approximating a shrug but seemingly too tired to fully get there. At least she didn't seem offended.

"No one in this room has any right to say something doesn't exist. And I hate to say it, but it explains everything."

96

"Can multiple personality disorder actually make her change her human scent?" Christina asked, almost incredulously. She'd already shifted around and was sitting at her computer screen again.

Donovan didn't know the answer and Eleri was still shaking her head at him, as though MPD or DID was as fictional as they themselves were supposed to be.

At last, Eleri conceded, "I'll grant you that it does make sense."

Christina looked up from her screen, where she'd found something.

"I've read that, with DID, one personality might need glasses and another doesn't. Or one personality might have an allergy to a certain food and break out in hives. Then, when the personality shifts, the hives instantaneously disappear. So honestly, at least as far as the rumors about it go, I don't see why changing their identifying scent wouldn't be on that list."

Donovan thought it made sense. There was not much literature at all about ultra-human scent. For one thing, most humans couldn't smell it. And two, the dogs that could smell it, didn't have a good record of communication, explaining to people what they were noticing and what they weren't.

Still standing—although he'd managed to stop himself from pacing—Donovan held his phone out toward Eleri as if it were the diagnosis. "This is our working theory right now."

"Okay, fine," she muttered. She hadn't really moved from the couch.

"So what do we do with it?" Christina asked. "Can we go arrest Sylvia Lambrecht?"

"No," Donovan said. "We follow her."

"More importantly, we need to dismantle the cabin and collect evidence." Eleri suddenly popped up off of the couch. "We need to go do it now. A fingerprint should match her, if it's truly DID."

Donovan felt his eyes roll, not as a response that her idea was stupid, but as a physiological reaction to being as tired as he suddenly was. Eleri was already standing, shaking her head, even motioning to Christina to get up.

"The Miranda wolf followed her. She went out into the Glades to do something just a few hours ago. It's possible the cabin is still standing and it might still be full of evidence."

Donovan considered that. If he were the killer, he would have gone to the cabin first. The cameras proved that the place had already been found. Destroying it might be the way to go.

"If it's got her fingerprints on it, maybe on the tarp in someone's blood…" Donovan added. "That's all we need."

Eleri and Christina nodded, both of them now looking far more awake than he felt. Eleri made a sweeping motion with her hands. "Get dressed. Get your kits. We're going now."

97

As they approached the cabin, Donovan heard the noise.

They were still a distance away, but he motioned to the other two agents. Invisible though they should be, he wasn't certain that their sounds were covered, too. "She's there," he whispered. "We have to move faster."

The three had been creeping forward softly, keeping eyes out for every signal. But he heard someone at the cabin already. Probably Lambrecht.

If they snuck in slowly, they could lose everything by warning her. Or they could come crashing in and maybe get the evidence before it was gone. He picked up his pace, pulling out in front, not wanting to get separated from the other two, but they simply couldn't run as fast as he could … even on human legs.

For a brief moment, he thought about changing form, but he wasn't quite far enough away to make the difference in distance. And while his fangs were ultimately useful, so was his trigger finger.

He kept going. His lungs felt close to bursting far too early in this outing, probably from the overwhelming lack of sleep for the past several days. He didn't even have to sniff. The scent came to him.

"Kerosene!" He hissed, alerting everyone as the volatile chemical reached out and tickled his nose. He wanted the other two to know what they were up against. He somehow ran faster, gun still firmly in hand.

Did she hear him? Did she see the movement of the trees as he sped past? Had the spell failed?

Because as he arrived, he found Sylvia Lambrecht with a kerosene can at her feet and a matchbook in one gloved hand.

Fucking gloves! he thought. They were here to get fingerprints.

She whipped around, her gun in her other hand, aimed right at him, fast.

He sucked in a breath and drew to a stop. The silencer on the barrel told him a lot of what he needed to know about the murders. Her stance was low in the knees, her aim true, her shoulders steady.

It all clicked then: the military background, the abuse she'd suffered as a child. This woman—whatever she thought her name might be—was not the caring therapist who helped others. She was a soldier.

As he watched, the stance relaxed a little bit and the eyes swept side to side, confused. Eleri's spell was failing, but it hadn't actually failed, yet.

Sylvia Lambrecht couldn't quite focus on him. She tensed again, stance sharpening, gun swinging around.

Now he slowly moved his own weapon to a steady, two-fisted grip. He had no doubt that she couldn't quite see him, and he equally had no doubt that a bullet was more than capable of hitting him. If he'd ever believed himself immortal—and his father's actions had sure made his lineage seem that way—Donovan's time in NightShade had made it clear that none of them was.

Heart pounding, feet planting hard, he stopped his forward motion and raised his gun. Maybe she could see the gun. Maybe she could see a feather of movement in the air.

She stopped, her grip wary.

He could shoot her and take out their killer right now. All his doubts about who was behind this had fled. Now that he was face-to-face with her, now that he was in range, he sniffed in deeply and knew this was the right person. Whether Sylvia Lambrecht was the wrong person or not, the woman in front of him at this moment was their killer.

But if he took her out, and they failed to find evidence, it could start a whole other thing. It wouldn't be Ruby Ridge or Waco, but it would be something Westerfield would have to completely cover up.

She was dropping her stance again as Eleri and Christina came up behind him, pounding through the underbrush. They cracked twigs as they went, making Lambrecht's head snap back and forth one more time. They all three watched as she cut a tight circle around the cabin, checking for intruders that she knew were there but couldn't see.

Lowering the gun, she cautiously went back to the matches.

Next to him, Donovan felt everything change as Eleri ripped the sachet from her neck and yelled, "No!"

98

She was breathing heavily, hands out, gun held high in the air.

The most important thing right now was to preserve the cabin. Eleri knew they needed the evidence in there to tie up this case.

In the dark, it was difficult to see the woman dressed in her tactical gear, though this time, as quick as they'd been, the three of them had made an effort to dress much the same.

"FBI!" she called out and could feel the change behind her as Donovan and Christina both became visible in the middle of the dark night.

Sylvia's gun had been aiming at unknown things but now trained directly on her.

This wasn't the first time Eleri had been at the business end of a loaded weapon. Her senses were all on high alert. She could feel Donovan and Christina behind her, aiming their own weapons.

It was a standoff. If Lambrecht took her, they would take Lambrecht.

"FBI," she repeated, reverting back to ingrained habits. "Sylvia Lambrecht, you're under arrest."

The gun didn't waver, but the head tilted. "You've got the wrong person."

"What's your name?" Eleri asked sharply, not quite the therapist this woman's other personality was.

One eyebrow went up as if to say, *Do you really think I'm going to tell you?*

Eleri had heard of alternate personalities having all kinds of bizarre names, from *kitten* to *gup-gup* and even movie star monikers. Maybe someone that they'd seen on screen as a child and wished to be. But the most common were other versions of their birth name.

"Sandra?" she asked. "Sarah? Sylvie?"

The facial expressions suggested that she was off base. She shouldn't risk it, but she did. For a brief moment, Eleri closed her eyes and searched.

"What are you doing?" the woman demanded, and Eleri almost chuckled.

Maybe all she needed to do was act out of accordance with the organized engagement that this soldier clearly expected. When she opened her eyes, she had it. "Sophia."

A small, nearly imperceptible stiffening of every muscle in the woman's body told her she'd hit.

"Sophia Lambrecht, you are under arrest for the murders of Eugene Nash, JP Talley, Evan and Bonnie Merkel, Jennifer Volkov, Earlene Beaman, and Craig Renfro."

Again, Lambrecht stiffened as Eleri included the last name. Despite Sheriff Tucker's insistence that there were no local dental records for Renfro, and that no one knew where he had come from as he'd moved to Astoria only a few years before he disappeared, Eleri found she now had confirmation.

Renfro must have been the first murder—Lambrecht's revenge for a beloved younger sister. And the first lesson that she was capable of taking evil out of the world.

"You're under arrest," Eleri repeated, though Sophia's stance didn't change.

"No, I'm not." The woman's voice even seemed to have different musical notes than Sylvia's. But none of that was important, as Eleri felt the air shift and change around her.

The warning retort was replaced with a sharp sucking sound.

There was no sound of a hammer. The trigger made no noise and the silencer covered most of it. But Eleri could feel the air parting as the bullet whizzed toward her.

99

It all happened so fast that Donovan wasn't certain what was actually going on. But that was normal, once the first bullet flew.

Eleri shifted fluidly in space as though knowing it was coming. The only way that was possible—given the speed of a bullet, as Wade had so astutely informed him—was to react before the trigger was even pulled.

It was Christina who screamed briefly and crumbled to the ground.

As Donovan and Eleri reacted to the hit of their fellow agent, he felt his organs shift with the shock. Christina was down, bleeding heavily from a head wound. Her arm was thrown across her torso and she was not moving.

Medically, he tried to assess the situation. As he looked over his partner, he heard the scrape of a match and hiss of flame. Behind him, Sophia Lambrecht lit the cabin. The fire rumbled and crinkled like old brown paper as the cabin flared to life. The kerosene sending a skyward whoosh of heat.

Then, in another blink, Sophia Lambrecht was gone.

He heard her crashing through the woods as she ran away.

Eleri dropped to her knees, yelling, "Go!" at him and pointing in the direction their perp had run.

"I'm a doctor," he countered her command. He should stay with the wounded.

"You're also the fastest. And I have to preserve the crime scene."

Shit, he thought. He didn't necessarily agree with her. Christina needed an actual doctor, and his leaving might kill her—but staying and arguing almost definitely would.

Donovan pivoted. He hated leaving the two others behind. He ran, following the sounds echoing off the trees and reverberating through the damp air, racing as fast as his human legs would carry him.

Behind him, he heard Eleri. "I've got you, Christina. Hold on tight."

Then the air shifted around him again and he heard the chant as he crashed forward through the brush, knowing that he wasn't going to be fast enough. He didn't know this place, and he couldn't scent his quarry.

Behind him, Eleri's voice—now with a resonance he didn't recognize—chanted words he didn't understand and called on gods he didn't know.

Was she doing something else and letting Christina bleed out? Or was the spell to stop the bleeding? He didn't know. He crashed five more steps before feeling the first raindrop.

Maybe Eleri could do both—save the evidence and take care of Christina. Donovan focused his attention on the woman still pounding through the Everglades in front of him and somehow, despite her smaller size, gaining distance.

In that moment, Donovan made his decision. While still moving forward, he reached down, pulled his shirt over his head, and tossed it behind him. His shoes went next.

100

Eleri stayed at the scene, directing the rain as best she could even as she tried to rip the cabin door from its old, rusted hinges.

Christina lay on the ground behind her. Eleri mentally checked and saw her partner was still alive, so she reached into the cabin. She could feel the flames licking at her. Accelerants were no easy matter. She prayed hard as she stuck her hand inside, grabbed the edge of the tarp, and felt the burn on her fingers as she yanked it out into the downpour. Maybe she herself was already wet enough that it wouldn't scar. The rain would ruin half of it, she knew, but she had to get the fire out.

The cabin was old and rickety, and as she tugged at the pieces, the story became clear. The victims had been drugged—a paralytic they hadn't tested for. Sylvia Lambrecht was a psychiatrist, not a clinical psychologist. She had the ability to get her hands on such medications and the knowledge of which ones would work. Her victims had been alive, alert, and unable to fight back through all of their torture. In a sick way, Eleri found it fitting.

She could only hope Donovan had better luck than she was having here. The cabin was falling apart in her hands, the kerosene burning it despite the downpour she'd wrought.

Behind her, Christina spoke up softly, as if in pain. "Someone's coming."

Eleri was smart enough not to look at her fellow agent for confirmation. She swept the area as her hand went to the butt of her gun and she dropped the tarp to the ground.

Her weapon wasn't silenced. It would let everyone in earshot know where she was and what she was doing. But if she needed to shoot, so be it. Even through the rain, she felt the change in the air, all of her senses open and blooming. She held her breath as the woods shifted and the fire on the tarp slowly began to douse.

She wanted to fight with the flames and save anything she could from the small cabin, but it wasn't possible with someone approaching. Had Sophia Lambrecht returned? Was it maybe Sylvia wandering the woods now?

But it was Donovan coming back, dirty and barefoot, one sneaker dangling from a finger, the other missing. His T-shirt was inside out, shorts now wet and plastered to him.

He'd changed, and run, but he was back now, empty-handed. She looked up at him as he yelled through the rain.

"She disappeared again."

So she became Sylvia. Eleri hadn't bought his theory before, but now maybe she did.

The cabin continued to burn even as Donovan told her, "I should have still been able to trace Sylvia, but I couldn't." He held his hand up toward the sky as if maybe the rain was at fault and her attempt to save the evidence had thwarted his chance to get their perpetrator.

Behind her, Christina had slowly gotten to her feet. Her head wound was still bleeding. The bandage Eleri had wrapped on her was soaked from rain, but mostly doing its job.

"We need to get Christina to a hospital," he said. "And then we have to find Dr. Lambrecht."

Eleri agreed, watching as the rest of the cabin burned and realizing it was futile. She picked up the tarp from where it had fallen into the mud her rainburst had created. Now, with only one small flame in the corner, she stepped on it to put the last of the fire out. Parts of it were already burned away, wavy edges crisp and black, but parts of it were still intact. It had been folded into quarters and she prayed that was enough.

Looking up, she called off the rain.

Donovan was already next to Christina, helping her along. "Can you walk?"

But Christina was brushing him off angrily, suggesting that she didn't need a hospital. So now, with one of their agents severely injured, and no suspect in custody, Eleri folded the still warm tarp and tucked it under her arm.

The three defeated agents—one of them barefoot—walked two miles out of the Everglades.

101

Donovan had Eleri drive the SUV back from their outing, his bare feet too sore from the walk to drive.

Pulling out his phone, he saw the message from Jesse Nash. *Jesus,* he sighed, scrubbing a hand over his face. Once again, he turned around to check on Christina, who was sitting up in the backseat of the large SUV. He was being obsessive about watching her, but he didn't like that head wound.

Eleri assured him the bullet had merely grazed her head. But he was concerned that both women were brushing off a head shot.

"Go to the hospital," he told Eleri.

"No," Christina replied again firmly. "It will set us back."

Honestly, Donovan thought, *it would only set Christina back.* They could leave her at the hospital. Not that he wanted to.

"Hospital," he said again to Eleri, and at least she nodded and agreed with him. Then, to quell further arguments, he relayed Jesse Nash's message.

"More rumors. This time the rumors are that the killer is taking out abusers," he quoted, then added his own commentary. "Jesse has listed at least three different people making their cases public. Probably hoping for help."

"Seriously?" Eleri asked sharply and he felt the car jerk to a halt at the stoplight far too fast. Once again, his head swung to Christina in

the back, who flinched with the motion. Eleri apologized then added, "They are *baiting* the killer?"

"Sounds that way."

"Did Jesse at least tell us who these people are?"

"Yes," Donovan nodded. "Ashli Jenkins. A woman in the trailer park, whose husband only comes home once in a while from working on an oil rig. Jesse noted that he's on the rig right now. The second is more subtle, just rumblings from one of her social functions. She's not sure if the rumors started with the wife or if somebody else thinks the wife is abused and is putting it out there. But the woman is Julia Flores, and the concern is that her husband is keeping a tight rein on her, locking her in the house and so on. And the last is a high schooler shouting to anyone who will listen that her stepfather has been sexually abusing her for years. And that would be Jennifer Song."

"Song?" Eleri and Christina both said at the same time.

Donovan nodded. "God bless Jesse Nash. She was thorough. She says Jennifer is a cousin of Dr. Song."

"Wow, that family has some monumentally bad luck," Eleri stated.

Donovan understood that trauma like this tended to carry down through generations. His own history was part of the reason that he never intended to get married or have kids of his own.

"That gives us two wildly disparate targets." Eleri took a turn, getting close to the hospital.

Christina noticed and again protested. "It's a head wound. It bleeds a lot. It looks worse because of the rain. I'm fine. You—" She turned to Donovan, and he felt the strict stare. "Get me back to the hotel, put some steri-strips on me, and bandage me up. We're going to have to split up, and that means we need all of us."

In fact, Donovan thought, it meant they needed more than just who they had, but they would have to make do.

102

Eleri stood on the Song family's front lawn. Time was of the essence.

Eleri had refortified the spell on the sachets and Christina had covered herself as usual. Still, Eleri wasn't sure if she was watching out for Christina or if Christina was watching out for her. The head wound had to be monitored, but Eleri was going to close her eyes anyway—if anyone could see her, it would cause trouble. The family might flip out that the FBI was there, or maybe someone watching would try taking a shot. So many options.

"Ready?" she asked Christina.

The other woman nodded, acting as though she wasn't wearing a large, nude-colored elastic wrapped around her skull, making her look like an escaped patient.

Thank God no one could see her, Eleri thought. Stepping forward, she placed her hand on the doorknob. The visions she got were swift and awful. Ever since she'd learned the information she was getting was real, she had not been able to remove herself the way she used to.

The stepfather was doing more than just abusing Jennifer. It took a moment in which Eleri fought to unclasp her hand, but her stomach churned and her fingers spasmed, clenching tighter, as though she were unable to sever that connection herself.

The stepfather was hurting everyone in the house in some way or other. When she finally was able to let go and step back, she leaned over, hands braced on her knees as she took deep, gulping breaths. It might be true that no one could see her, but if she left a pile of vomit on the doorstep, that would be found.

Hands touched her shoulder. "Are you okay?"

She breathed in through her mouth and out through her nose, not the right direction, but the one that calmed her stomach right now. Eleri held up one hand, as if to say, *No, but I will be.*

She took three more slow, deep breaths, then stepped off the porch. All she could manage to say to Christina was, "If Sophia Lambrecht is vetting her victims, then this one is legit."

Christina didn't push for more details and they climbed back into the small, compact car. They tried to switch out vehicles as often they could, so as not to be spotted driving back and forth across a roughly empty town in the middle of the night.

But the sun would be up soon and Eleri had to take the wheel and get them to the next potential victim's house as soon as possible. Christina was not allowed to drive—an invisible driver was not acceptable, nor was one with an obvious head wound. At this point, only a small spot of red had seeped through the bandage, and Donovan had deemed that acceptable. Eleri sent him pictures and told Christina to sit still and that she was going to damn well go to the hospital if Donovan said so. Luckily, Donovan had not said so.

She was grateful she hadn't had to wrangle her partner into the emergency room. Unhooking the sachet from her necklace, she turned the key and asked Christina to check in with Donovan. In a moment, she heard the return ping and her partner read, "Still nothing."

Donovan planned to sit outside Sylvia's house with the windows down, so he would hear if the doors opened and anyone went out the back. Right now, they were expecting Sylvia Lambrecht to go out the front door, start her car, and head to the office for the day.

"Tell him we're on our way to the next one," Eleri said, again grateful the town was small. She was at Julia Flores' apartment before they knew it.

When they arrived, she stealthily headed up the steps to the front door of the unit, placing her hand on the doorknob again. She saw lots of kids coming and going here, and that the physical violence was almost entirely directed at Julia. The kids were spared, but not from seeing it. The apartment was too small for that.

Eleri and Christina stalked back down the steps, rattling the metal framework as they went. If anyone was up, they'd wonder what the hell ghost had invaded the building, but the agents didn't care. They had at least parked around the corner of the building, so that no one would see an empty car suddenly populate with two FBI agents before it pulled out.

As they headed away, the sun was coming up.

"Are we going out to the trailer park?" Christina asked.

They had probably forty-five minutes before they could expect Sylvia Lambrecht to leave the house. The problem was, if she did leave and Donovan followed her and she knew it, they would have trouble. If she left and Donovan lost her, they would have trouble.

"The guy from the oil rig is not supposed to be in town."

"Do we trust that?" Christina asked her.

"If we trust Jesse Nash. She's been reliable so far. She wouldn't give us misinformation, unless she was actively trying to get him killed." As the words came out of her mouth, Eleri realized it was something she hadn't considered before.

Jesse Nash, like Sylvia Lambrecht, was an abuse survivor. She had been through the situation herself and might feel for other victims. But Eleri didn't have time to follow that train of thought.

"We need food. If Donovan's going to get any, we have to bring it to him." She changed the subject as she pulled into a drive-through for egg sandwiches and high-diesel coffee for everyone.

Within moments, they were on Sylvia Lambrecht's street, flanking the house from the other side. Donovan had already pinged them that she was up and moving about.

"Can you deliver Donovan his breakfast without being seen?" Eleri asked, and only after Christina was walking down the street, bag in hand—that Eleri could clearly see—did she wonder if maybe everyone else just saw the food crossing the street. They really had to be sure that they had this straightened out. Unfortunately, there wasn't time now. She just had to trust that Christina was covering everything.

Eleri watched as her partner hopped into the SUV, closing the door and chatting with Donovan for a few minutes. It looked like he leaned over and checked the bandage and Eleri wondered what else they might be speaking about.

It sucked being the third wheel, but Donovan had been the third this whole night, and Eleri wouldn't begrudge him any social time he got—even if she had to watch them talk without her. Christina quickly came back—her food was in this car, after all—and the three of them sat, phone lines open, eating their breakfast and occasionally pausing when Donovan told them to, so he could listen.

Donovan's voice hit them as Eleri saw the front door open. "It's go time."

She and Christina were facing the wrong direction to simply pull out and follow. It made more sense for Donovan to take the first part of the run. Even as Sylvia climbed into her car, Donovan drove past, getting ahead of her to hide what he was doing. The question was, had any of the information that had filtered to Jesse Nash already filtered to Sylvia Lambrecht?

103

The day had been long and tedious. Donovan had even slept in their car for a bit. Sylvia Lambrecht had arrived at her office and—based on the traffic at her front door—had seen patients all day until after five.

Because he'd been on duty the night before, listening in case Lambrecht fled, Eleri and Christina sent him back to the hotel in the middle of the afternoon, hoping he could sleep. It was the best they could do, but he was grateful and felt much better afterwards. When Sylvia had left the office, she'd driven to a nice restaurant to pick up dinner and headed home.

Eleri had shown up in the middle of the night, after she and Christina had taken their turns at catching a nap, and let Donovan sleep through part of the night. Eleri didn't have Donovan's sensitive hearing, but she did have the trackers. If the back door opened, she would know and she would wake them all.

Unwilling to leave, he'd leaned the seat back in the SUV and fallen into a deep rest. At six the next morning, he almost felt human. He told Eleri he was awake before he fully was, but he had parked in a different location, facing the other way now, so that it wouldn't be his SUV that followed Sylvia Lambrecht to work.

Sure enough, their quarry stepped out dressed for the office and Eleri followed right along. Halfway across town, Donovan traded out with her, trailing the doctor all the way back to the strip mall at the north side of town. Eleri traded back in a different car and demanded he leave.

"Go back and sleep," she'd told him, even though he protested. "Check out Christina's wound and get whatever rest you can. You've had the least of any of us. If you have to run, you're going to need your reserves."

That, at least, was an order he understood. Two hours later, he was opening one eye to check the time, grateful for blackout curtains and wondering if he should go back to sleep, when his phone pinged.

— Now. Sylvia Lambrecht went to the restroom at her strip mall. And she didn't come back out.

Eleri told him they were out of the car and checking up on the situation.

— She's in the Glades and we're following. Come find us.

104

Donovan padded along, picking up the scent of Eleri and Christina easily.

It had been awkward driving up and then changing on his own, but this was how he'd wanted to come in. He'd thought being the wolf would be easier and faster. Now, with his nose to the ground, he wasn't so sure.

He'd parked the SUV around the side of the mini mall, counting on the dark windows. Using his fingers he'd opened the passenger side door, leaving it cracked, before climbing into the back of the SUV. He rolled his shoulders, shifting his face, and let the changes take place.

It had been just as awkward climbing into the front seat in wolf form as it had been in human. If he'd been smart, he would have opened the back door, but ... lesson learned.

He'd taken off into the loamy soil, wet with the water that dripped and ran through the place, rich with the scents of flora and fauna. Heading around the back of the building, he sniffed at the bathroom door to catch the scent. The scent here was already Sophia.

He'd taken off like a shot, offering a sharp bark as he went, wondering if Eleri and Christina were close enough to hear it. He alternated keeping his nose to the ground and letting his legs eat the distance. As Eleri had pointed out during so much of their downtime the day before, of the two potential victims they had looked at,

Jennifer Song's house was closer to Sylvia's home and Julia Flores' apartment was closest to her office.

But though he believed he had it figured out, he followed the path until it veered from where he expected. He was no longer on a path to Julia's home, and without that, he had no idea where they were headed.

He kept his nose low and moved forward. He slowed down as he followed the path that first Sophia, and then Eleri and Christina, had followed. He had to pause and make sure he was reading everything right.

At last, he stopped, pulling up short.

Shit.

Sophia Lambrecht went to the right and Eleri and Christina went left.

Which way should he go?

105

"Shit, Christina." Eleri had her phone out in front of her, tracking herself on the GPS … for all that was worth.

"We lost the trail." Christina filled in with a sigh.

This was too important to lose the trail, but Eleri noticed for the first time that the red mark on Christina's head bandage had grown larger. "You're bleeding."

Christina shrugged, as if to say, *it happens*. But it wasn't supposed to.

They needed Donovan. They needed to know where the fuck Sylvia Lambrecht was going.

"We've completely lost her. Where did we even branch off?" Eleri had used her spell to light the footsteps, but in the daylight, it was difficult to see the results. They'd often gone ten or fifteen feet before finding the next one. Unless Sophia Lambrecht had long-jump capabilities, it was merely a failure of her magic. It didn't matter what the cause was, though. They were lost.

"Let me look at your head." At least that was something she could do, but Christina tried to brush her off. "Please, let me look."

The bandage was elasticized sticky tape and it was easy enough for Eleri to pull it up. What she was doing, out in the Everglades, was not sanitary, but she pulled out the gauze with the red spot on it, folded it in half, and stuck it back under, hoping to provide more padding right where it was needed. She next peeled the tape a little and rewound it tighter. "Hope I don't give you a headache."

She had given her partner a larger and dumber-looking bump. Christina shrugged again and Eleri could only believe that was likely Christina's everyday attitude, but she needed to be sure. They couldn't afford to miss signs of a more serious head wound simply because there was too much going on.

"We need to go back." She turned around and tried to backtrack using the GPS. Were it not for the phone, she would have absolutely no idea where in hell they were or which direction to head. Even so, the phone soon told her that she wasn't even capable of retracing their own steps very well, as the path split on more than one occasion.

How far behind were they? Her nerves crinkled, raw on the ends. They were missing an abduction in progress, and she just knew this was supposed to be their chance to catch Sophia or maybe Sylvia in the act.

She had no idea where she'd veered off the original path. So Eleri recast the spell looking for footprints and found one. "Shit, we've backtracked too far, Christina."

But Christina had already turned around and was making headway, her eyes focused on the ground. Maybe Eleri should let her partner do that and keep her own eyes up.

It was then that she heard it—from up ahead came one sharp bark.

Son of a bitch, she thought happily.

"Donovan!" She tried not to yell it too loud, knowing that he would hear it. Sure enough, another bark came quickly.

Eleri didn't even have to motion. Christina took off running even before she did. Eleri was left bringing up the rear.

Donovan had found the path when they couldn't. Luckily, he had the speed to come back and find them. Giving one soft bark, he turned and ran ahead, making sure they now knew exactly where to go.

He was just out of sight when he barked three times in rapid succession. Definitely something was going on. Had he seen it or heard it?

Eleri and Christina raced to catch up.

She first saw Donovan standing on what little trail existed. Still, he watched something in front of him. Eleri kept running. She shouldn't be able to be seen, so she didn't worry, but she and Christina pulled to a sudden stop behind her partner.

Sophia Lambrecht stood quietly facing away from them before turning to look backwards, and Eleri was grateful that Donovan was the only one who could plausibly be seen. He'd already handily stepped off the trail.

It was clear that Lambrecht had seen nothing of importance as she turned and scanned her surroundings. She'd looped around, taking a path hidden in the Everglades but peeling out at just the right point to arrive behind a business. She stood carefully wedged behind a sturdy trunk, watching the back of a building. Cars parked between them and the brick, occasionally crunching the gravel, and even Eleri could smell the beer and whiskey from inside. Or maybe she was smelling the empties in the dumpster. She couldn't tell.

Every now and then, a car would pull into the lot or someone would come out the back door.

This was what had saved them. She knew if Sophia's victim had been here when she'd first arrived, they never would have found her. Luckily, their killer had to wait, and it had allowed them to catch up. Well, that and Donovan.

For a while, they, too, stood motionless, wondering who the woman in tactical gear was waiting on. At least it allowed Eleri to catch her breath. But then the back door opened and Sophia Lambrecht stepped out into the open.

"Hey!" She waved and offered a friendly smile. "How are you doing?"

"Dr. Lambrecht?" The name was slurred. Axel Randal was trashed at midday and he was going to be easy pickings.

Donovan was already stepping forward, as was Christina. Though they moved slowly, Eleri put her hand out, open palm flat, motioning them to hold back and wait.

Sophia said something else, but the best Eleri could make out was likely something like, "I know what you did to your step-daughter."

Axel's reaction made Eleri understand that, whatever Sophia's words, it had been a threat. A snarl formed on his already sullen expression.

He pulled back and swung. But Sophia deftly maneuvered and he missed her entirely. She was quick, suddenly up on the balls of her feet and swinging back like a trained soldier. She punched him hard in the lower gut and they all flinched as he doubled over.

But somehow, Axel came up again. Lightning fast, his fist was ready and he should have caught her under the chin, but instead—with her quick evasion—he only managed to nail her in the eye.

Christina was ready to pull forward, but Eleri still held them all back. They wanted to catch Sophia fully in the act. Sure enough, in another moment, Sophia was behind her next victim, executing an excellent triangle chokehold and watching and waiting patiently as he finally passed out and slid heavily down her body into the gravel.

Looking up furtively, Sophia didn't see that she was, in fact, being carefully watched. She quickly pulled something from a pants pocket, jabbed it toward her mouth, and then toward his chest. Only after the move was executed did Eleri figure out she'd pulled the cap off a syringe with her teeth and injected him.

Then, in another improper medical move, she recapped it and stuck the needle back in her pocket. She was carefully controlling all of the evidence. Nothing was left behind here on the gravel. No blood. No syringe. No stick mark in the usual place for the ME to find. There was nothing to tie back to her.

Grabbing Axel under his arms, she slightly lifted and dragged her victim backwards out of the parking lot. She dropped him at the edge, quickly coming back and covering the lines in the gravel.

A soft, clicking sound next to her made Eleri turn her head. She motioned to Christina about the sound, but Christina was taking pictures of the whole thing. *Brilliant.*

Then they watched as Sophia reached into another of her many pockets and pulled out a harness, the one Eleri had seen. Dirty and stained, possibly with the blood of the others, it would be excellent at pinning the crimes on her.

Carefully pushing one of Axel's arms through each hole, Sophia tightened the straps quickly before wrapping her arm through and heading away.

She disappeared into the Everglades, dragging her quarry behind her.

106

This was it, Eleri thought as the three of them turned and began to follow Sophia Lambrecht. Or Sylvia, or however she wanted to think of herself.

Eleri had no idea if they had a confirmed case of DID. What she did have was the woman carrying Axel Randal away after having knocked him out.

The tarp she had so carefully saved from the southeast cabin had been close to useless. While they'd been tracking Sylvia and also trying to catch up on sleep, she and Christina had lifted what fingerprints they could. There had been blood on the tarp. Initial field samples showed that it was human and was from multiple sources, exactly as expected.

But the cabin was burned. Literally, this time. And not being able to lift more than a partial print meant they could only prove who'd been killed there, not who'd done the killing.

Had Jesse Nash not sent the text with the information about rumors flying around town, Eleri would have been in favor of arresting Lambrecht and dealing with finding the evidence later. But now they had the woman dead to rights. They just had to follow her.

However, as Eleri walked through the woods, her chest tightened. The stark feeling of being followed had disappeared once they'd spoken to the Miranda wolf by the car the other night. None of Christina's facial recognition software had picked him up, not from the excellent image they'd picked up when he'd visited the new room and looked directly into the camera.

They hadn't wanted to run him through FBI sources. Right now, for whatever reason, Eleri would have felt better with another wolf with them—even if it was their unknown stalker. She distrusted him, but didn't feel he was a danger to them, and she needed his skills.

Donovan was running forward, maybe catching up, maybe getting within sight or scent and turning around and coming back to alert Christina and Eleri. As soon as they acknowledged him, he would turn and run the other direction. He had to be traveling almost three times as far as the rest of them, but he was keeping them on track.

The day was sunny and hot and, though the Glades provided cover, they trapped the humidity. Eleri still had her gun raised, clasped in both hands, but she released one to wipe sweat from her forehead.

Maybe she shouldn't have hidden herself. A mistake, Eleri thought now. Originally, the idea had been to have Sylvia Lambrecht not know that she'd been seen. But they now had clear evidence of her abducting one of the very people she had been baited for.

As Eleri turned to Christina, the low dark feeling in her chest—the one that said something was very wrong—started to take over.

"Christina," she said. "Can you uncover us?"

But the words had barely left her mouth, the harsh whisper still hanging in the air between them, as she heard one sharp bark followed quickly by Donovan's wild cry of pain.

107

Donovan felt the white hot pain in his side. It almost felt like it cauterized as it cut a path through him.

He managed to go about three more steps before he fell, his legs no longer working. It wasn't until he hit the ground with a thud that he realized what had happened.

Bullet.

He'd been hit.

He lifted his eyes—almost the only part of him he could still control—to see Sylvia Lambrecht standing in front of him, gun aimed, ready for a finishing shot. And he couldn't get away. A low rumbling came to him through the earth and he wondered if it was her angry heartbeat.

She'd clearly had enough of the dog following her, and this Lambrecht had no issue with taking out those who were in her way.

He'd been too close behind her, had followed her for too long, or just pissed her off by existing. It didn't matter; he'd been shot and he knew what it meant that he was already starting to feel cold.

Eleri and Christina would catch up at any moment. Fighting for the strength to lift his head—she'd either kill him or she wouldn't, and there was nothing he could do about it—he scanned the area. It surprised him how heavy he suddenly was. Consciously, he realized he must be worse than he thought. She must have hit something vital.

This is bad.

Sylvia Lambrecht disappeared into the woods, the sound of a closing door accompanying the move. She dragged Axel Randal away and they faded between the trees. Donovan had watched the deer near his home and admired their uncanny ability to step into the foliage and lose themselves completely and immediately. Sylvia Lambrecht seemed to have done the exact same thing.

His eyes were pulling closed, the ground wet beneath him, but warm. Was it his own blood?

Shit, he thought, now was not the time to be a hindrance to his team. The other part of his brain kept going, ignoring the wound and the damage. The door sound likely belonged to a cabin. Eleri had been right—there was a third kill spot.

The rumble he'd been hearing grew louder and so did the hint he heard at the back of his brain.

"Donovan! Donovan!" Eleri still called it out in a normal tone, knowing that he would hear it. If he could have, he would have smiled at the thought and though he lifted his head to bark to her in return—to let her know that he was here and fine—when he opened his mouth, no sound came.

108

Eleri's brain raced. *Why wasn't Donovan answering?*

In a few short steps, she had her answer. Every muscle seized as it tried to fight off what she saw with her eyes and knew to be true.

The whimper had been Donovan, and it was as bad as she had feared. No. It was worse.

The bullet had torn through him and she could see the open wound. He lifted his head as though to say something to her, but he couldn't.

Everything hit her at once. They couldn't save Axel Randal. They had to save Donovan.

They were going to lose Sophia Lambrecht, because surely she'd rushed this kill on her way out of town. This was too sloppy, too obvious. It wouldn't work for her to return home and pretend her way through her normal, daily life again.

The woman was going to disappear.

None of that mattered now to Eleri.

She wasn't sure she could save Donovan, but she couldn't live with herself if she didn't do everything she could. Sliding her arms under him, she tried to pick him up and run, but she couldn't lift him.

When was the last time she'd tried to carry her partner? It would be one thing to sling human arms over her shoulders and drag him out. It was another to do that when he had a bullet wound, clearly torn through his side, blood gushing freely. And another thing still when he wasn't even human right now.

Her tactical vest hindered her and she couldn't get to what she needed so she quickly peeled the Velcro, the sound loud enough to alert everyone within miles of exactly where she was. Maybe that was good.

With her vest finally off, she tugged at her shirt next, taking it off and stuffing it into the wound, applying as much pressure as she humanly could. Christina was beside her, hands also working, though Eleri didn't quite know when or how Christina had arrived. Clearly the woman had been running right next to her the whole time, but Eleri's brain was clogged with fear, filtering things in and out, trying to make sense of what she could see and what she couldn't, who she could save and who she didn't care about.

The world shifted and blurred in front of her. Eleri jolted for a moment as though an earthquake was the last thing they needed before she realized it was her own tears stealing her vision. That was an interference she couldn't afford. She blinked them back and pushed harder on the wound, enough to make Donovan offer what would have been a harsh yelp on a good day. Today it was an airy whine.

"Together." Christina looked Eleri in the eye and when Eleri clearly didn't understand, she repeated it. "We can carry him together."

But how far in were they? They were parked at the office… could they make it back? And where could they possibly take someone like Donovan once they got him out of the Everglades?

"First things first," Christina said as Eleri realized she must have spilled the whole jumble of her thoughts right out of her mouth. "Tie the shirt around him for pressure."

Somehow, Christina was the only one who still had a working brain. Eleri did as told, still scrambling for all the pieces.

"You there, me here." Christina pointed and slid her hands under Donovan as well before instructing, "Lift."

The sound that came from Donovan's throat was neither human nor animal. Both women flinched as the red that already stained the bandage bloomed larger. The movement had done him no favors, but not moving him was certainly a death sentence.

Again Eleri wondered, where would they take him? A veterinarian? Would the veterinarian note that his anatomy was odd? Would a vet put as much effort into saving this large, odd dog whose breed he couldn't identify as a hospital would into saving an FBI agent? But Donovan didn't look like the kind of patient who would be admitted to a hospital now.

She had no idea where local vets might even be …

They ran, feet pounding, every movement hard, each jolt costing Donovan more blood. Her arms and legs ached as she tried to devise a way to run blood from her own system into his as an on-the-fly transfusion. Never mind that she had no idea if they were even a blood type match.

As they neared the SUV, she realized she was cold and sweaty, her muscles used up and shaking. Christina looked none the better, but she was still the only one fully functioning.

"Into the back," Christina said, somehow managing with superhuman strength to lift Donovan away from Eleri. Eleri tripped and fumbled with the keys, her fingers no longer working at the time when they were most important. As Eleri hauled the back open, she laid hands on her partner once more. She couldn't feel him breathing.

When was the last time she'd felt Donovan move? When had she last felt the pressure on her hands shift? Or heard him whine?

Was he even still alive?

She was about to close the trunk and run to the front of the car, but Christina's hand stayed her. "Give me the keys. I'm driving. You climb back here with him. Keep. Him. Alive."

Christina practically threw Eleri into the trunk next to Donovan. She automatically reached into the thick, slick fur and curled her fingers. It should have been a comfort to hold onto him, but instead she was instantly covered with blood. It was everywhere. Her makeshift bandage had stopped nothing.

Christina slammed her way into the front seat, starting the car and throwing it into gear.

"Where are we even going?" Eleri asked as Christina stopped mid-turn in the parking lot and began punching at her phone.

Next to her in the back, Donovan offered one long sighing breath and quit. The car didn't pull out. They didn't have a specific direction to head. And Donovan didn't move.

With her first clear thought since she'd seen him, Eleri lifted her hands covered with her partner's blood and aimed them upward toward the roof of the SUV. There wasn't even enough space to lift her arms over her head, so she wouldn't be able to cast properly. But she still had to try.

She could have cast a spell to save her partner, but had no idea if that would work. Instead, she called out to the only person she thought could help.

109

Eleri and Christina crashed through the Everglades. She'd shoved food in her face, barely washed her partner's blood off of her hands, and come directly back here.

They'd both agreed it was the only thing they could do after leaving Donovan.

He's alive, Eleri reminded herself. He's alive. Or at least, he was when she'd left him.

Would she ever see him again? Would she even know what happened?

Leaving him had been uncomfortable, but she'd been shoved aside and told that no one would touch or help her partner if she stayed. So if they stayed, he would die. She and Christina had reluctantly left him in the hands she had chosen.

Catching Sylvia Lambrecht wasn't just her job now. It was revenge. Sylvia Lambrecht had shot Donovan and Eleri wasn't going to let the woman get away.

"Cast the spell," Christina urged harshly.

When Eleri tried, she could feel that her blood sugar was precipitously low. They'd been trying to eat but, honestly, she didn't think there was any way to feed or fuel the deficit she'd suffered. Her spell almost crackled and fizzled at her fingertips. She cast it by sheer force of will, determined to do this one thing.

Together, they watched as the footprints glowed in front of them, this time with a fierce illumination. *Son of a bitch*. If she could have just made that happen a handful of hours ago, maybe everything would have been okay. But it wasn't.

She was here.

They took off again, pounding their way through the Everglades with little concern for the noise they made. Christina had covered them both this time, and Eleri hadn't even bothered carrying the sachet. If they got separated and became visible, so be it. She would simply fire at the woman.

They passed the still-bloody spot where Donovan had fallen and Eleri purposefully aimed her gaze in front of her. If she looked, she would fall to her knees and not go any further. By training her eyes forward, though, she found the cabin and ran toward it, Donovan's possible demise pushed away to another time.

At the cabin, they both skidded to a stop, opening the door and peering inside. The sight and scent of fresh blood assailed them. An orgy of evidence greeted them. There had been no attempt to clean it up or hide anything that would implicate her. This was Sophia Lambrecht's swan song. She knew she wouldn't come back from this.

They left the cabin door swinging open. Eleri didn't care. She simply ran farther, faster through the woods, leaving the cabin behind, too. The footprints they followed were pressed into the dirt, the occasional drag mark alongside them assuring her she was following the right track.

This time, Eleri saw what she didn't see before: The spell had cast on more than just the footprints. Blood was also illuminated along the way. Bright, almost pink, like the footprints, it was not the shade of luminol but had a similar effect.

They were moving so fast in their pursuit, Eleri almost tripped over the body of Axel Randal.

Like the others, it had been left bent and discarded. Now as Eleri looked, she saw what she'd learned so long ago: the body always told the story of the killer. In some cases, the bodies were posed, hands crossed reverently, or organs removed, or new marks displayed. But here the bodies had been dumped, left behind like the trash Sophia Lambrecht declared them to be.

But Eleri didn't stop for long. The footprints continued away from the body. There was nothing they could do for Mr. Randal now, and she wasn't sure he deserved their time anyway. However, Sophia Lambrecht needed to be apprehended.

The two agents followed, running for a few miles until they realized they were making a loop. Still pounding their way through the Everglades, the flats of Eleri's feet hurt. Her ankles had twisted on rocks more times than she could count, but as long as she was still going, she couldn't afford to care.

She was going so fast that she almost smacked into a wall. The Glades had spit them out in the back of Sylvia Lambrecht's office, right where they'd started. From the point they'd had to drag Donovan back to get to the SUV. This time, of course, they'd parked at the bar, so they were nowhere near their car.

It seemed that Sophia Lambrecht had come back to the office. So they stalked the building, heading around slowly toward the front to find that her car was still in its spot.

Eleri didn't have Donovan's sense of smell and she fought the concern of whether he still had anything. Her anger flared again, the constant fuel she was running on.

With a glance to Christina, she saw the same confusion in her partner's face. Could Sylvia Lambrecht be here just sitting in her office? With a shrug to each other, they pulled their weapons and barged in the front door.

It swung wide easily, already unlocked.

Inside, they saw the lobby was deserted. The two women cut a straight path to the office door. They didn't even knock. Christina reached out to grab it and barge her way into the office, but it didn't give. Eleri's brain suddenly registered the red note that hung in the middle of the door. The sign was flipped to say "In Session."

Is she fucking serious? Eleri thought—or was she not even there?

With a harsh breath, she brushed Christina's hand out of the way. As Eleri reached for the doorknob, the tumblers clicked beneath her touch and the door swung open to reveal a surprised Sylvia Lambrecht and a patient.

The doctor sat on one overstuffed chair, her dress in place, her legs crossed, a surprised expression on her face. One of the local schoolchildren was on the couch, looking up in distress at the agents and their aimed guns.

Sylvia clearly had no idea why they were here. "Can I help you, agents?"

110

Eleri lifted her gun, wishing she could sniff the air but knowing what her eyes told her. This was Sylvia.

"You—" She nodded only with her head to the kid. "Get out of here."

He looked like he was about to barf and he moved so fast that he scrambled up and over the arm of the chair, tripping and stumbling as he hit the ground. Eleri hated that. He didn't deserve this and probably he knew this woman only as his therapist, his very good therapist. He would miss her.

But even as the kid carefully pushed his way between the two agents, scrambling out the front door behind them, Eleri saw the shift in Sylvia's face and repeated her words. "FBI. You're under the under arrest for the murder of Axel Randal."

The confused expression disappeared, and the sudden and complete change was startling. The face was now angry. The hands now splayed on her own thighs as she pushed upward.

"You have no right."

Eleri almost barked out her own laugh. "I have every right. I'm the FBI."

The words came out almost as though she were the whole organization.

Christina kept herself together better than Eleri did. Every other second, Eleri's brain flipped to worrying about Donovan before coming back to the present. She grounded herself here in the office by commanding the doctor's compliance.

"Place your hands behind your back."

Christina pulled out handcuffs, looking to run this in an orderly fashion.

Sylvia, or maybe Sophia, Lambrecht—Eleri didn't even know—now took several steps toward them. The moves were lethal in their looks, definitely those of a trained soldier. Eleri kept her finger on the trigger, ready to pull it at a moment's notice.

The woman's hands were out by her side, as though she were surrendering herself peacefully, but the tension in her entire body told Eleri it wouldn't happen that way.

Sure enough, as Christina stepped forward, and Sylvia turned as if to present her hands behind her back, her hands disappeared.

Christina, being smart, took instantaneous steps backward, getting herself immediately out of the way of whatever action Sylvia/Sophia was going to throw at her.

Though Sylvia created a whirling ball of motion that no one could get their hands on, it wasn't disorganized. And when she stopped, Eleri could see why she'd gone into the flurry of swinging arms and kicking legs. It was cover.

She now faced them with a gun in her steady hand, aimed directly at Christina … as if knowing that would stop Eleri more effectively than pointing it at her.

Eleri tried to talk her down, even though she just wanted to shoot. But a game of "Who's faster?" could be deadly. "You can't win this. Surrender."

Lambrecht shook her head *No* with a careful, slow motion. "The only way for me to win is if you don't take me in at all. We won't survive prison."

We. Interesting.

"Sylvia won't?" Eleri tried again, wondering if she should act as though they were truly separate people. But it had been thoroughly the wrong thing to say.

Lambrecht's head tipped slightly, her expression turned sardonic as if to say *You know that's not who I am.*

"Sophia," Eleri corrected herself. "We can protect you."

The laugh that erupted from the woman's throat was evil, awful, bitter, and scared. Again, the wrong thing to say.

“Put the gun down,” Eleri commanded again, but in that moment she understood that, for Sophia Lambrecht, death was preferable. And Lambrecht made the decision.

This gun wasn't silenced. Everything in the room felt the shock wave as Sophia Lambrecht pulled the trigger and shot Christina.

111

"Holy shit!" Christina yelled at the top of her lungs as she staggered backward.

Sophia Lambrecht's eyes went wide as she saw what had happened.

Slowly, she loosened her grip and aimed her gun to the sky.

Eleri, despite the stinging feeling in her palm, hadn't even realized what she was doing. But she hazarded a quick glance to see there was no hole in her hand.

It had to be spellwork. It wasn't as a show of strength, but her own standard reaction, that she opened her fist and let the bullet clatter to the floor, spent and misshapen, probably carrying the imprint of her palm lines.

That was going to hurt later, she thought. But it sure as fuck was better than the bullet going through the center of Christina's chest.

Taking a deep breath to steady herself, Eleri said, for one last time. "You're under arrest."

It seemed her words activated Sophia once again to what was happening. The bullet she'd shot that hadn't found its mark was only the first step. This time, she turned the gun to Eleri.

But Eleri was too quick and too unwilling to play one more round. She dropped to one knee, aimed upwards, and pulled her trigger three times in rapid succession.

She hadn't wanted to do it, but she had to. Fuck Sophia

Lambrecht. Fuck her for shooting Donovan, and fuck her for trying to shoot Christina.

The woman's face looked stunned as she stumbled backwards. She'd wanted a death by cop, and she'd gotten it. Her gun clattered to the floor as Christina, having gotten herself together, stepped forward, her own weapon still aimed, and she kicked Sophia's out of the way.

A harsh red bloomed on the woman's chest and her breath gurgled as she tried to inhale. She slowly slid down the side of the desk she'd stumbled into as her legs collapsed out from under her. She looked to Eleri and the words that came out of her mouth were a surprise.

"Thank you."

But as she finally slipped into a seated position, her eyes looked up again. This time she was scared. Her hands clutched at her chest.

She tried to cry out, "What happened? What is this?" but the words gurgled and Eleri watched with little remorse as it was Sylvia Lambrecht who died in front of her.

112

Eleri spent her time writing up their reports, explaining to Sheriff Tucker about the evidence against Sylvia Lambrecht, and that Donovan was unavailable for comment.

How could she tell the outside world that he had been shot? And that she'd then let someone take him away for surgery, apparently in a veterinary office, not knowing when he would come back.

She worried about her decision. She cast spell after spell, asking for an answer, but was given none.

She and Christina reassured each other they had made the right call. A hospital wouldn't know what to do with Donovan's odd anatomy even if he were in human form. They might write up papers on him. He might survive the surgery, but he wouldn't survive that kind of exposure and neither would other wolves like him.

But it hadn't even been an option. He was in no shape to change into his human form in time to get to the hospital, and the hospital certainly wouldn't have taken him the way that he was. She could have taken him to a veterinarian, but she'd had no idea where one was or if they would save him.

There was no way Eleri could have said, "He's an FBI agent and you will save his life." So she'd knelt over her partner as he was dying right in front of her, raised her hands in the cramped back of the SUV, and focused on the one face she knew that understood the problem.

The Miranda wolf had been there within ten minutes. He'd moved Donovan to his own car and said only, "I've got this."

Eleri didn't trust that asshole any further than she could throw him, but he was the only option they had.

Now they didn't even know if Donovan had lived or died. If they'd saved him but had forced him into Miranda Industries.

She'd told Walter that Donovan was missing and how. She'd written it into the reports so SAC Westerfield understood and could pull every string he had to get his agent back. She'd debriefed Sherriff Tucker and evaded answering his questions about where her partner was.

But, so far, nothing had moved.

"How long can I stay and wait?" Her expression must have been as bleak as it felt, given Christina's response.

"I can stay forever."

Eleri had shoved this feeling down. The waiting, the not knowing. She was ten again, and her world had fallen apart again. Her partner was missing ... again. Would she dream of Donovan the way she had of Emmaline?

Would she fail him the way she had failed her sister? For Emmaline had lived ten years after her abduction, but Eleri hadn't found her for almost twenty.

"I can stay forever," Christina said it again, as though chanting a mantra to herself. Eleri could, too.

Turning, she glanced through the suite as though Donovan would come out the door of the now-unused bedroom. As she rotated, she spotted a white envelope that had been slid under the door. Eleri picked it up easily, expecting it to be hotel information about checkout or a bill.

But that had been stupid. She wasn't paying attention, so she touched it with her bare fingers, opening the flap and pulling out the thick letterhead before seeing what it was.

She almost dropped it. This page—also on Miranda letterhead—had only a series of numbers across the middle.

"Christina!" She almost choked it out. "It has to be about Donovan!"

But what was it?

Christina looked up.

Shaking the paper angrily, Eleri demanded, "What even is this?"

She was more than mad at herself for not having been more careful, but there was nothing she could do about that now. Christina motioned for her to bring it closer.

They didn't even try to dust for prints. The two of them examined it thoroughly but quickly.

"Not coordinates like last time."

She tossed out ideas about the string of numbers. "Off-shore bank account?"

"Password?" Christina asked, but answered herself, "to what, though?"

They went through several other options, before Christina softly said, "It looks like a case number."

"An FBI case file?" Eleri asked.

"Look at where the dashes are, it matches." She nodded at the page Eleri was still clutching like the lifeline it was.

With a quick glance to each other, Eleri and Christina plopped down on the couch in a synchronous movement. Christina was already clicking away on her laptop as Eleri turned her attention to the screen.

"Holy shit. It *is* a case file number." She peered at it as they quickly read through the case notes, each of them silent except for Eleri to tell Christina to scroll.

A team of agents had taken down a drug runner and turned him. He wasn't prosecuted.

"The case isn't closed ... or it was purposefully left open," Eleri mused, a frown on her face. "And what does this even have to do with anything?"

But it must have something to do with Donovan. The Miranda wolf had been here... he'd risked their cameras and their wrath to deliver it.

"Check the filing agents?" Christina was calling up the names before she even finished suggesting it.

There were two agents on the case and Christina clicked through to the first name. Eleri didn't recognize him, and when she looked to Christina, the other woman shook her head and shrugged, too. But the second...

"Holy shit." It was the Miranda wolf.

"He was an FBI agent?" Christina murmured it.

"This case is five years old."

It took them a moment of all looking at each other silently, probably each playing scenarios out in their head. Eleri almost whispered her theory. "They turned the guy they captured. So they used him to put the agent who caught him in undercover."

Sure enough, a search of the agent brought up nothing after that case. No new cases, no closed cases, no record of employment or dismissal.

"He's working a case against Miranda from the inside!"

"Has he been inside Miranda for that long?"

Eleri felt the bloom of relief in her chest that—*thank God*—the person she'd turned Donovan over to was an FBI agent.

But she was thinking even as she was relieved, *it wasn't enough.*

So this was an agent? But where was Donovan?

Had he not contacted her because he couldn't? Because he was dead?

She didn't feel that he was, but she'd gotten nothing when she reached out… *nothing*.

"Eleri look." Christina, realizing Eleri was lost in a tangle of worry, tapped her on the arm. She'd pulled his ID card up on the screen. "Look at this."

The lines that defined the top and bottom of the information each had a tiny diamond at the ends.

Eleri stared. "He's NightShade."

ABOUT THE AUTHOR

AJ holds an MS in Human Forensic Identification as well as another in Neuroscience/Human Physiology. AJ's works have garnered Audie nominations, options for tv and film, as well as over twenty Best Suspense/Best Fiction of the Year awards.

A.J.'s world is strange place where patterns jump out and catch the eye, little is missed, and most of it can be recalled with a deep breath. In this world, the smell of Florida takes three weeks to fully leave the senses and the air in Dallas is so thick that the planes "sink" to the runways rather than actually landing.

For A.J., reality is always a little bit off from the norm and something usually lurks right under the surface. As a storyteller, A.J. loves irony, the unexpected, and a puzzle where all the pieces fit and make sense. Originally a scientist and a teacher, the writer says research is always a key player in the stories. AJ's motto is "It could happen. It wouldn't. But it could."

A.J. has lived in Florida and Los Angeles among a handful of other places. Recent whims have brought the dark writer to Tennessee, where home is a deceptively normal-looking neighborhood just outside Nashville.

For more information:
www.ReadAJS.com
AJ@ReadAJS.com

www.ingramcontent.com/pod-product-compliance
Lightning Source LLC
Chambersburg PA
CBHW020253030726
47499CB00001B/187

* 9 7 8 1 9 4 8 0 5 9 9 2 3 *